CW01513047

The Bedside Guardian 2025

The Bedside Guardian 2025

EDITED BY
WILL WOODWARD

guardianbooks

Published by Guardian Books 2025

2 4 6 8 10 9 7 5 3 1

First published in Great Britain in 2025 by
Guardian Books
Kings Place, 90 York Way
London N1 9GU

www.guardianbooks.co.uk

A CIP catalogue record for this book is available from the British Library

ISBN 978-1-9162047-9-9

Cover design by Guardian News & Media Ltd
Typeset by seagulls.net

Printed and bound in Great Britain by
CPI Group (UK) Ltd, Croydon CR0 4YY

Printed and bound in the UK on FSC© certified paper
in line with our continuing commitment to ethical
business practices, sustainability and the environment.

Our authorised representative in the EEA is
eucomply OÜ, Pärnu mnt 139b-14, 11317 Tallinn, Estonia
hello@eucompliancepartner.com

Contents

WINTER

Foreword

ELIF SHAFAK

I once saw a young glassblower in Istanbul, still new to his craft, shatter a beautiful vase while taking it out of the furnace. The artisan master who was standing by his side, watching, calmly nodded and said something to him that I still think about. He said, 'You put too much pressure, you kept it unbalanced, and you forgot that it, too, has a heart.'

This year — 2025 — has been plagued from the start by a series of social, economic, environmental, technological and institutional changes, all happening with such speed and intensity that we are yet to fully comprehend their impact on future generations. As the overwhelming strain of domestic and geopolitical challenges continues to build up, I cannot help but remember the old man's words. Too much pressure. Unstable, uncertain and replete with deep inequalities. This could well be the year we forgot that Earth, too, has a heart. It definitely feels like the year when the world was broken.

In 2024, to be fair, many of today's problems were already present and growing. But there was also a strong wave of expectations and public excitement as over 1.6 billion people went to the polls. It was a time of unparalleled and concentrated democratic activity full of promises, incautious confidence, passionate speeches and fiery rhetoric. Many voters were keen to express their anger and discontent, and express they did. The mammoth year of elections revealed the importance of not only the ballot box, but also of the surrounding democratic institutions and norms. Language matters. It always starts with words. When political opponents are treated as 'enemies', or, even worse, 'enemies of the people', the whole system suffers.

Compared to that, the past 12 months have been marked by an emotional and intellectual fatigue — at least, for a large number of people across all borders. What we are used to calling 'the liberal international order' no longer carries weight. Deeply fractured, unable to hide its cracks, it is coming apart. The housing crisis, the lack of affordable rents and equal opportunities, social and economic injustices have all eroded trust. Meanwhile, climate breakdown, AI threats and risks to pluralism, the possibility of another pandemic, increasing militarism and jingoism alongside shifting alliances have contributed to the sense that the system that had emerged from the ruins of the Second World War has come to an end. As we close the first quarter of the century under the shadow of a new nuclear age, uncertainty is everywhere.

Ours is the Age of Angst. An existential anxiety affects and drains many of us — east, west, north and south. Young and old. The only difference perhaps is that some people are better at hiding their emotions than others, but when we scratch the surface a little, or look underneath polished social media facades, we can see that anxiety is quite widespread. Fear. Frustration. Enervation. A new word has been coined to define the *zeitgeist*: polycrisis. It is not an easy time to be alive, for sure. But if this Age of Angst were to ever become an Age of Apathy it would be a much darker and more dangerous world to live in. The worst thing we can do right now, individually and collectively, is to allow ourselves to descend into numbness. To become desensitised to the pain and suffering of others — in Gaza, in Sudan, in Ukraine. To the climate breakdown. The moment we stop caring.

The moment we become atomised. This is why good and honest journalism matters all the more today. The pieces published in the *Guardian* this year not only show a remarkable depth and breadth but they also help us remain engaged and connected. In that sense, they are an antidote to numbness.

In 2025, divisions have deepened. At a time when humanity is faced with immense global challenges we have been pushed further into boxes of 'us versus them'. The rise of populist movements went hand in hand with creating convenient 'others' as scapegoats for existing disparities and disillusionments. Commenting on the impact of Operation Raise the Colours, John Harris was the author of a powerful piece on how flags are being used as tokens of prejudice, not pride. We can nurture and cherish the love of a culture, of a place, of a landscape without dehumanising entire categories of people, without promoting polarisation.

There were sentimental moments too. As a nation we cried over the Sycamore Gap and the senseless, meaningless hatred and violence displayed by two men who apparently thought it would be a fun thing to do to cut down a tree that had brought joy to so many for so long. It is interesting that the human sentimentality that we were allowed to display in response to the death of a beloved tree was denied to the chancellor Rachel Reeves when she was caught on cameras crying in the Commons. The media and social media coverage have been mostly judgmental and awfully sexist. Amelia Gentleman wrote a coruscating piece titled 'Crying in the Commons', asking why are women's workplace tears regarded as a source of shame? It is total nonsense to think that tears are a sign of weakness and women who cry cannot be brilliant at what they do. Delving into another emotionally difficult subject, Polly Toynbee wrote a courageous piece on the assisted dying debate, underlining how a decent life can end in a decent death.

One of the most poignant pieces published this year was co-written by Malak A Tantesh and Emma Graham-Harrison about the despair of parents and grandparents in Gaza as they have to watch their children and grandchildren with skeletal bodies, children so malnourished that they have become more vulnerable to all kinds of diseases. 'We have faced hunger before, but never like this.' Dan Sabbagh composed an article about Ukraine after the failed negotiation between Trump and Putin, highlighting the devastating consequences of the occupation and war for ordinary families. 'We never thought the war would come to our village.'

A recent report revealed that Kabul could soon become the first modern capital to completely run out of water, with all the aquifers drying up as early as 2030. Over 6 million people live in Afghanistan's capital. Here in the UK, there is a growing public resentment and anger against water companies that keep pumping sewage into our rivers. Meanwhile, rivers are dying elsewhere, with the Middle East and North Africa being home to seven out of the ten most water-stressed nations. Climate crisis is the story of water and the ones who disproportionately bear the brunt are always women, children and the poor.

This year was a crossroads for gender equality. It was the 25th anniversary of the UN Security Council Resolution on women, peace and security and the 30th anniversary of the Beijing Declaration and Platform for Action, which had outlined 12 critical areas to achieve gender equality. Thirty years later, not only have we failed to fulfil the criteria but there is also an alarming backlash against women's rights and LGBTQ+ rights. History shows us that when countries slide backwards and democracy is endangered, the first rights that will be curtailed will be women's rights and minority rights. Against this background Katharine Viner's piece was hugely inspiring as she wrote about how two

Guardian reporters, Sirin Kale and Lucy Osborne, investigated the disturbing sexual harassment allegations about prominent British filmmaker and actor, Noel Clarke. The judicial outcome, Viner emphasised, is a victory for the women who valiantly shared their experiences with the journalists as well as for investigative journalism itself.

In another important piece, a *Guardian* editorial highlighted how the UK government's attempt to proscribe Palestine Action under the Terrorism Act signifies an important escalation in its approach to the definition of civil disobedience. It also means lowering the threshold for the description of what is considered terrorism and what is not. The editorial made it explicit that 'this is not the policing of public safety; it is the policing of dissent'.

There were moments of light. Even small miracles. Alexis Petridis wrote about the Oasis reunion. We have seen a rise in book clubs and reading parties. Unexpectedly in this time of hyperinformation and fast consumption, more and more young people are taking up traditional arts. It feels as if the faster our world spins, the more urgent and universal our need to slow down, to connect, to think, to care. In Argentina, an 18th-century painting called *Portrait of a Lady* that was stolen from a Jewish art collector by the Nazis was recovered after it was spotted on a real estate listing. She looks at us calmly, the woman in the portrait, in her flower-embroidered dress and golden frame, she who has seen too many atrocities but is still resilient and full of life. As always, art, culture and literature offer us a sanctuary, a home, a sense of togetherness. Glassblowers remind us that even the worst shattered glass can be melted, resculpted and revived. It all begins with an honest recognition of what remains broken and a willingness to mend.

Introduction

WILL WOODWARD

What's happened now? Readers waking up in the morning over the last year, reaching for their phones or turning on the radio, will have had many moments of realised dread as they scanned the headlines and processed overnight developments from Gaza, the wider Middle East or Ukraine. Often this impulse may have been expressed as *What's he done now?* as Donald Trump upended assumptions about functioning government and diplomacy. The news could seem unbearable, and it may often have felt easier to turn off and away. No year, alas, avoids very bad things happening, and yet few can have seemed so unpredictable, so disorientating and so perplexing, alongside the persistent thrum of war.

The *Guardian*'s duty has been to make sense of it, using the skills of our journalists across the world and the resources of a global news organisation with editions based in London, New York and Sydney. The pieces included in this year's *Bedside Guardian* display wisdom and bear witness; it's journalism that comes from being in the right places, asking difficult questions, and being prepared to hear answers that don't fit preconceptions. There is a lot of listening in this anthology, whether in the first section, where Chris McGreal hears the voters who swung to Trump, to near the end, where Dan Sabbagh meets Ukrainians on the frontline responding to the Trump—Putin summit.

There's no little courage, too. In the case of Malak A Tantesh, our brilliant young correspondent in Gaza, it is impossible to disentangle the story she is covering from her personal situation. In February she returned home for the first time since Israel's assault began 16 months before. 'I grew up in this area but it had been so devastated, buildings and streets and gardens bombed and demolished, that we could no longer find our way to the house,' Malak writes. 'We were wandering, lost and confused, when a neighbour appeared and guided us. The only things still standing were the trunks of a walnut tree, and some olive trees that used to be in our yard. Seeing them there, surrounded only by rubble, I felt like I had been stabbed in my heart.'

This collection can't only be about Gaza or Ukraine though there would be enough high-quality reportage from either to fill the entire book. The *Guardian* day-by-day is a place for ideas, challenge, hope, glory, humour and happiness, and here are examples of all. I'm particularly struck by how many of the most resonant pieces reflect personal experience — not just Malak but also from Larry Elliott bowing out after 28 years as economics editor, or Helen Pidd and Alexandra Topping on their 20 years of friendship, or Archie Bland on the near-death of his son. These are fine reporters interrogating their own lives or at least life-defining moments. Sometimes the personal dimension is less immediately obvious. My colleague Ewan Murray covered every step of Rory McIlroy's seemingly elusive attempt to complete the 'grand slam' of golf majors by winning the Masters. Writing in the moments of McIlroy's realisation of his dream — one that could have easily turned into another near-miss story — there's delight and relief springing off the keyboard.

It's been a pleasure and an honour to attempt to do justice to this *Guardian* year. Many thanks to Katharine Viner, the editor-in-chief of the *Guardian*, for asking me to have a go. I've been very fortunate to work with Lindsay Davies, the managing editor of this book, benefiting from her flair, sage judgment and polite chivvying. Elif Shafak's foreword adorns these pages. I've leant on Owen Gibson, the *Guardian*'s deputy editor, and Clare Longrigg, Paul Bellsham, Joseph Andriano and Claire Phipps. I'm grateful to my colleagues on the sports desk for tolerating − OK, enjoying − a few poorly-timed absences by me to get this all done. Many of the pieces included here build on original reporting by other *Guardian* reporters, and assiduous work by editors and lawyers to get those pieces published.

A few notes on what follows. The choices, for better or worse, are mine. Some of your favourite writers may not feature here; quite a few of mine don't either. Apologies to you and them. Most but not all of these articles appeared in the *Guardian*'s print edition. The dates alongside them show the day they appeared online. Sometimes the web and print versions were slightly different and I've generally, but not always, opted for the longer web takes. One or two have had small cuts. A few pieces took months to research and write; others came through at lightning speed from a conference hall or a stadium. All of them, I'm confident in saying, stand up to re-reading at leisure, at bedtime or any other spare moment. Dive in.

Autumn

Prosecutor Harris put Trump on trial, but the court of public opinion can be fickle

DAVID SMITH

She frowned. She narrowed her eyes. She pursed her lips. She rested her chin on her fingers. She shook her head or threw it back with disdain. She laughed with a mixture of bemusement, peevishness and contempt.

Chief prosecutor Kamala Harris was putting Donald Trump and his Make America Great Again movement on trial for nearly 10 years of crimes against civility, democracy and reason. And she wasn't buying his story.

Trump has got away relatively scot-free with his criminal cases so far this year but the first presidential debate in Philadelphia on Tuesday night put him firmly in the dock. Harris brought all her lawyerly experience to bear, just as she did against Brett Kavanaugh and William Barr when she served in the Senate.

Debates can be raucous affairs but the rules permitted no audience, ensuring a courtroom-like hush on a stage set surrounded by empty seats in the National Constitution Center. Harris and Trump stood at curving blue lecterns. 'This is an intimate setting for two candidates who have never met,' said moderator David Muir, making it sound like a very improbable episode of *Love Island*.

But then it became clear this was no love story. In a neat reversal of Trump's invasion of Hillary Clinton's personal space in a debate eight years ago, Harris zipped across the stage and forced the ex-president into one of the most awkward handshakes in television history — the first at a presidential debate since 2016.

'Kamala Harris,' she announced, as he mumbled a reply. She might have added: 'Now I am become Death, the Destroyer of Trumps.'

From that moment, Harris — wearing a navy suit, white pussy-bow blouse, pearl earrings and small gold American flag pin — owned the stage. She was judge, jury and executioner. With mics muted she was unable to interject when Trump told ludicrous lies, but conveyed her disapproval with a kaleidoscope of facial expressions.

Trump — wearing a blue suit, white shirt, red tie and American flag pin — refused to meet her gaze but determinedly looked ahead. Both of them were miles ahead of poor old Joe Biden's gazing and gaping in June.

After some early exchanges on the economy, Harris went on the attack. 'Donald Trump left us the worst unemployment since the Great Depression,' she said. 'Donald Trump left us the worst public health epidemic in a century. Donald Trump left us the worst attack on our democracy since the civil war. And what we have done is clean up Donald Trump's mess.'

He did not like that. A little later, he tried to fire back by going personal. 'She's a Marxist. Everybody knows she's a Marxist. Her father's a Marxist professor in economics. And he taught her well.'

Harris laughed derisively and rested her chin on her hand, glaring at Trump like a principal listening to the lame excuses of a student who burned down the school.

There was worse to come for the ex-president on his weakest issue: abortion rights. He claimed that the American people wanted the overturning of Roe v Wade. Harris, who has been touring the country and talking about it for two years, had an aria ready: 'You want to talk about this is what people wanted?

'Pregnant women who want to carry a pregnancy to term suffering from a miscarriage, being denied care in an emergency room because the healthcare providers are afraid they might go to jail and she's bleeding out in a car in the parking lot? She didn't want that. Her husband didn't want that. A 12- or 13-year-old survivor of incest being forced to carry a pregnancy to term? They don't want that.'

The debate moved on to Trump's supposed strong suit: immigration and border security. But Harris was like a prosecutor baiting a witness, setting traps that he kept walking into, talking himself into a case-closed confession.

She said: 'I'm going to actually do something really unusual and I'm going to invite you to attend one of Donald Trump's rallies because it's a really interesting thing to watch. You will see during the course of his rallies he talks about fictional characters like Hannibal Lecter. He will talk about windmills cause cancer. And what you will also notice is that people start leaving his rallies early out of exhaustion and boredom. And I will tell you, the one thing you will not hear him talk about is you.'

No matter that it was obviously carefully rehearsed. It was a smart way to lift the curtain to reveal that the wizard of Oz is actually a feeble old man operating a contrived spectacle. It was also the perfect way to get under Trump's skin. Trump is prouder of his crowd sizes than his children (well, maybe not Ivanka but certainly Eric).

He whined: 'She said people start leaving. People don't go to her rallies. There's no reason to go. And the people that do go, she's bussing them in and paying them to be there. And then showing them in a different light. So, she can't talk about that. People don't leave my rallies. We have the biggest rallies, the most incredible rallies in the history of politics.'

If proof were needed how agitated he was, Trump amplified false rumours, pushed by his campaign and rightwing influencers, that Haitian immigrants in Ohio are abducting and eating pets (officials have said there have been no credible or detailed reports about the claims).

'In Springfield, they're eating the dogs,' the former president said. Objection, your honour. The moderators, who did a decent job of fact-checking all night, noted that the city manager of Springfield said there had been no credible reports to support Trump's claim.

Ah, but Trump had evidence! 'Well, I've seen people on television,' he blurted. 'The people on television say my dog was taken and used for food. So maybe he said that and maybe that's a good thing to say for a city manager.'

The 'I saw it on TV so it must be true' defence will never stand up in court, even coming from a reality TV star.

If this had been a real trial, the judge would surely have stepped in and asked if Trump wanted to change his plea to guilty rather than prolonging the agony. But under the bright lights of the debate stage, there was no mercy.

Harris said: 'Donald Trump was fired by 81 million people ... And clearly, he is having a very difficult time processing that ... And world leaders are laughing at Donald Trump. I have talked with military leaders, some of whom worked with you. And they say you're a disgrace.'

In the old days candidates might have riposted by saying Nelson Mandela or some other moral paragon was on their side. Trump reached out for the Hungarian autocrat Viktor Orbán. 'He said the most respected, most feared person is Donald Trump. We had no problems when Trump was president.'

But Harris had more ammunition: 'It is well known that he admires dictators, wants to be a dictator on day one according to himself ... And it is absolutely well known that these dictators and autocrats are rooting for you to be president again because they're so clear, they can manipulate you with flattery and favours.'

A dictator like Putin, she added, 'would eat you for lunch'.

Prosecutor Harris had done a decent job of that while also making a case for herself to be president. In the post-debate spin room, the mood was a world away from the Atlanta debate in June, when Democrats looked forlorn and funereal as they tried to defend Joe Biden. This time it was Republicans making feeble excuses about moderators.

The trial of Trump was over. The verdict: guilty of American carnage. The sentence: unknown until 5 November. The court of public opinion can be fickle. Just ask Hillary Clinton.

19 SEPTEMBER

Very bad men — and their even worse excuses

EMMA BROCKES

Among the many unedifying aspects of the fall of Huw Edwards has been a possible glimpse into how the man sees himself. At the hearing on Monday, the chief magistrate, Paul Goldspring, held Edwards firmly responsible for his own actions — namely, being in possession of sexually explicit images of children — and gave him a suspended six-month sentence. But while Edwards' barrister said the former presenter 'apologises sincerely' and acknowledged the 'repugnant' nature of the images, the narrative that the defence team offered during the hearing sought to tell a less contrite and more familiar story.

You take with a pinch of salt the testimony of expert witnesses, of course. What is fascinating about the opinions put forth about Edwards by psychiatrists and therapists introduced by his legal team is that they were thought sufficiently compelling — and sympathy-inducing — to act as mitigation for a crime this serious. Factors introduced by the defence team ran the gamut from mental anguish brought on by Edwards' emotionally abusive father, to his repressed sexuality, to the much-mocked contention that Edwards' failure to get into Oxford contributed to lifelong issues with self-esteem — a claim so audacious you almost had to admire it. A case as serious as this is a tough gig for the best of lawyers, and at some level — hats off — they gave it a punt.

The Oxford claim was instantly and widely ridiculed, but it is only a slightly more ludicrous example of a common defence used by lawyers in sex crimes or domestic violence cases. It is hard to imagine a woman in the dock pleading mitigation on the basis that she didn't get into the university of her choice, and not only because 98 per cent of adults prosecuted for sex crimes in England and Wales are men.

That a man accused of accessing child abuse images can launch the defence that he didn't get what he wanted, that his station in life was less elevated than he felt it should be — that his pride had been so mortally wounded it contributed to, as the defence daintily put it, seeking validation online — is extraordinary. This is the starting position of the 'incel'. That this should be used in the context of Huw Edwards is a sign of how acceptable the excuse has become.

And it crops up all the time, alongside a range of other mitigating factors brought to bear when men are convicted of sex crimes. Take the weaselly defence of, for example, the 'Stanford swimmer' Brock Turner, whose conviction for three felony accounts of sexual assault was excused by, among others, the journalist Malcolm Gladwell, as a result of the disinhibiting effect of alcohol. Women get drunk all the time and don't tend to rape people, but no matter. The idea that as a disinhibiting factor misogyny, or entitlement, or any number of conditions in the *Diagnostic and Statistical Manual of Mental Disorders* that defence teams tend to avoid — narcissism, say, or psychopathy — might play a pivotal role in any given sex crime rarely features in these accounts.

Instead it's always 'low self-esteem', isn't it? Or in the case of apologists for Roman Polanski, a convicted sex offender, prior trauma. Or in the case of Harvey Weinstein, the vulnerable position entered into by a man in the public eye. (Weinstein's lawyer, Donna Rotunno, contended that it was Weinstein himself who had been manipulated by women, a similar line of defence furthered by Donald Trump's lawyers in 2023, when the civil courts found him liable for the sexual abuse of E Jean Carroll.) There is, it turns out, no end to the self-victimising ideation of the powerful man.

The incredible thing is not that Huw Edwards might genuinely still be clinging to this grievance about being snubbed in the workplace by BBC poshos — although, as a source of low self-esteem, I'd have thought WhatsApping with a convicted paedophile might be a bigger blow than not going to Oxford — but that it was thought a sufficiently credible injury to bring up in court. Damage to a man's pride is not seen as a dismissable event, nor might he be expected to metabolise disappointment in ways that don't result in injury to others.

Which isn't to say that details emerging from Westminster magistrates court this week haven't been interesting. For anyone seeking to write a novel about the Disappointments of Huw Edwards — where's Trollope when you need him? — this information about how he sees himself is fascinating. In a court setting, it is entirely, offensively irrelevant.

24 SEPTEMBER

Forget George Orwell's Two Minutes Hate — let's try Labour's Two Minutes Hope

JOHN CRACE

Forget George Orwell's Two Minutes Hate. The new world order for the current government is the Two Minutes Hope.

Having spent much of the last three months telling everyone how rubbish everything is and that there's even less money than they imagined, the Labour party has now realised that many people had lost the will to live. Had decided there was no coming back from the chaos and scandals of the Tory years. So now we are all commanded to obey the Two Minutes Hope. To stop what we are doing at midday precisely and try to think of something we are vaguely looking forward to. It's harder than you think.

On Monday we had Rachel Reeves. She's not a natural. The best she could come up with was that at least we were all still here. Apart from those that had died in the last 24 hours. On Tuesday it was Keir Starmer's turn, in his first conference speech as prime minister. He got round to the hope bit about two-thirds of the way through and sounded far more convincing about it than his chancellor had. Though it was still going to be hard work. And not all of us would make it. But hey, it was a start. And that was progress.

Waiting for the speech to start, the list of constituencies Labour had won rolled up the screen like the opening sequence from a *Star Wars* film. All we were missing was the Jedi knight.

We didn't have long to wait. After a brief video clip that included the BBC announcing the exit poll — drawing some of the longest and loudest cheers of the afternoon — Keir entered, stage left. Arms raised, thanking the audience. The first and most essential act of communion.

Starmer has got a lot better at these gigs. Maybe it's the media training. Or maybe he no longer suffers from impostor syndrome. He believes he has earned the right to the star turn. Just three or four years ago, when he became Labour leader, his delivery was awkward, hesitant. He couldn't land a punchline. Looked terrified he might lose his place at any moment. Now he commands the stage. He is at ease. Has one-liner riffs on hand for any unwanted heckles. Enjoys the glitz and the drama.

The only real downer is his scripts. It's become the accepted norm that a leader's speech should last an hour. Otherwise it's somehow deemed insubstantial. But there's no point putting yourself and your audience through the ordeal if you don't have enough material. Better to leave people wanting more. Especially as much of the speech appeared to have been lifted from last year's efforts. Conference is not a place for a repeat episode.

Worse, there was a lack of coherence. Almost as if someone had accidentally scattered the 15 pages of the speech on the floor and stapled them back together in the wrong order. No wonder most of the audience looked a bit bemused and comatose for the first half-hour. The standing ovations more of a Pavlovian reflex to trigger words — Nationalise railways! Workers' rights! — than a conscious response to detailed argument and rhetoric.

'We have had the hope beaten out of us,' Keir declared early on. True. But not the greatest of starts. Or what people had come to hear. Starmer has never been one for triumphalism — it's one of his more endearing qualities that he only ever really gloats about Arsenal victories — but the audience looked as if they could have done with just a little more celebration. If you can't have a party after a landslide victory, then when can you?

You could sense people struggling to keep up. Trying to follow the logic as Starmer sidestepped from idea to idea before being as surprised as any of us that he had inadvertently found himself back where he started. The pauses by Pinter. The words by Beckett. The deconstruction by Derrida. Maybe this was a masterpiece after all and we just hadn't realised it. Keir included. Could this have been a gamechanging paradigm? The model on which all future party leaders are based.

At one point during a random paragraph on the Middle East, Starmer demanded the return of all 'sausages'. It was tempting to believe this was a breakout moment of postmodern theatre of the absurd, rather than a mangling of the word 'hostages'. We were well beyond the conventionally prosaic. He also called for an end to hostilities between Israel and Lebanon and an immediate ceasefire in Gaza. It doesn't appear as if anyone in the region was listening.

Then there were the occasional mentions of the five missions. Leitmotifs to anchor us to reality. Except even Keir can't quite remember what these missions are. We can all still recite Rishi Sunak's five promises that he never kept but the Labour missions are still viewed through a glass darkly. And in the midst of all this, a random shoutout to a holiday in the Lake District. The point of which escaped everyone. Probably just comic relief.

For the last 20 minutes, it suddenly all began to hold together. Its meaning mystically revealed. The vibes finally taking shape in more or less the right order. The audience perked up. Opened their eyes to the heavens. Stood up and cheered. Now they began to see the point of Keir. The point of their existence.

Things were difficult. Things had been broken by the Tories. Starmer reclaimed 'Take back control' from Brexit and applied it to migration. He nicked 'We're all in this together' from David Cameron and made it sound as if it might be true. Something Lord Big Dave had never managed. There were tough times ahead. Code for tax rises imminent. Nimbys would just have to get used to the idea of pylons in their eyeline. Not even a lone Gaza protester could distract him.

We ended in a fugue state of ambition, hope, defiance. Hope, defiance, ambition. Defiance, ambition, hope. There was a light at the end of the tunnel. Even if access to it was strictly time-limited.

The last few minutes were drowned out in a standing ovation. Keir acknowledged the crowd but didn't milk the applause. A quick hug with his wife and he was off. Back to a government of service. The rest of us had been given our instructions. The Two Minutes Hope starts here.

27 SEPTEMBER

Remembering Maggie Smith

OL PARKER

This one hurts. I knew she was ill, but I always believed she was immortal. And, of course, her work is. But it's hard to accept that all that piss and vinegar didn't give us just a few more years of the extraordinary pleasure of her company.

That's if she liked you. If she didn't — and the list is long — then her company was downright terrifying. You don't get to be Maggie Smith on screen without being Maggie Smith off screen, and the acerbic wit, the putdowns, the total lack of fucks given were at least as funny and powerful as the lines writers like myself tried to create for her. But for those of us lucky enough to find her approval, her friendship was passionate, her wisdom unmatched, her loyalty fierce as the sun.

I wrote the part in *The Best Exotic Marigold Hotel* for Maggie and only for Maggie. There's simply no greater thrill for a writer than knowing that the Great Dame is going to be saying your words, dignifying your material, timing the gags incomparably, and finding truth, wit and pain in every line. I got to work with her twice more, on the sequel and on another movie, the second time I'd written a part especially for her. And then knowing she'd say no, but wanting to make her laugh, I also offered her the part of an all-singing all-dancing teacher in the *Mamma Mia!* sequel. I was, and am, incredibly proud of the typically terse text she sent me in reply: 'Not even for you, dear.'

Every evening in India the old actors would have dinner together. Every morning Maggie and Judi would swim in their Victorian swimsuits. And every day we would all laugh and laugh. She had two laughs, Maggie: a dry cackle, and a genuine, head-back roar. To hear the latter was the greatest pleasure, to inspire it the biggest privilege. I'll miss them both. I'll miss her.

We made the first *Marigold Hotel* movie with absolutely no expectation that anyone would ever see it, let alone that there would be a sequel. But when we were out in India for the second time, someone brought up the idea of a third film. 'I'll only do it,' said Mags, 'if you call it *Marigold Hospice*.' Rest in power, you brilliant genius.

4 OCTOBER

Life stands still at kibbutz ravaged by Hamas

BETHAN MCKERNAN

Post is no longer delivered to Nir Oz kibbutz; the lights in the mailroom are off, and the floor is gathering dust. Many of the metal boxes bearing each family's name now have new labels: red and black stickers that say 'killed' or 'hostage'.

Natan Bahat, 82, knew nothing would be waiting for him, but half-heartedly checked his postbox anyway. 'Time stopped here on 7 October,' he said.

Bahat's family left Nazi-era Germany and eventually found a home in Israel. As a young man, he became one of the founders of Nir Oz, a kibbutz established in 1955. It was hard work, he said, but he loved the deep connection to the land and to other people central to the kibbutz lifestyle. Now a widower, he raised his family here, and never left.

Today, the dedicated kibbutznik is one of only two people from the once 400-strong community still living in Nir Oz after a quarter of its residents were kidnapped or killed by Hamas during the Palestinian militant group's rampage through southern Israel a year ago. Bahat's home is one of six buildings in the entire kibbutz left unscathed.

At about 6.30am on Saturday 7 October 2023 — the Jewish holy day of Shabbat and Simchat Torah, the last of the autumnal high holidays — about 150 heavily armed Hamas fighters attacked Nir Oz from three directions, getting through Israel's defences by blowing up security cameras, automated weapons systems and motion detectors before mowing down the fence.

The first group of seven shot out the kibbutz guard post. The security team was quickly outnumbered and most were killed or taken hostage, leaving the community even more vulnerable as the wave of terror began.

Per capita, the Nir Oz community suffered the most heartache, damage and bloodshed, in part because the overwhelmed Israeli army 'forgot' about the kibbutz. Soldiers did not show up for hours, by which time all the Hamas fighters, and later waves of civilians and looters, had left.

The Hamas assault, in which about 1,200 people were killed and another 250 abducted to the Gaza Strip, forever changed the region and the world. Its consequences are yet to fully unfold or be understood.

In Gaza, more than 41,000 people have been killed in Israel's retaliatory war, which has reduced the strip to ruins and left survivors trapped in a living nightmare where food, water, shelter and medicine are in scarce supply. There is no end in sight to the fighting, and Israeli actions suggest Gaza's future will be long-term military occupation. In Lebanon, a year of simmering cross-border conflict has finally erupted into a full-scale war that could drag in Iran and the US.

But Nir Oz, one of the places where the decades-old Israeli— Palestinian conflict roared back to life last year, is now quiet but for the cries of attention-starved cats and the soft song of wind chimes. Shelling and airstrikes in Gaza can be heard in the distance.

Agricultural work — peanuts, potatoes, wheat and avocado — is still under way with the help of paid foreign workers, and the gardens and greenery are being looked after by volunteers. But the lush grass and flowering frangipani trees cannot hide the kibbutz's burned-out, ransacked houses.

Most of them have not been touched since the attack, and signs of struggle remain; bloodstains smear walls and floors. In one home, the washing-up still waits in the rack next to the sink, covered in a thick layer of dirt, and a coffee mug sits on the table. It looks as though the occupants only expected to step away for a minute.

'I don't know if all the families will come back. I can't judge them if they decide not to. But Nir Oz was a paradise,' Bahat said.

The kibbutz was built on land that belonged to the Palestinian village of Ma'in Abu Sitta before the creation of Israel in 1948, but, like many kibbutzim, was strongly wedded to socialist and leftwing principles.

Many of the community were active members of Israel's small anti-occupation movement, volunteering to escort sick people from Gaza issued with Israeli permits to leave the blockaded territory for treatment in Jerusalem or the West Bank. Nir Oz's older generations have fond memories of visits to the Gaza seaside and shopping in neighbouring Khan Younis before Hamas took over.

Several of Nir Oz's older peace activists, such as Oded Lifshitz, 84, and Ada Sagi, 75, were taken on 7 October. Unable to keep the doors of their safe rooms closed, they were seized with little struggle. At the homes of younger people, Hamas lit fires to try to force out those who had barricaded themselves in. The entire Siman Tov family – Yonatan, 36, Tamar, 35, five-year-old twins Shahar and Arbel, and Omer, two, and Yonatan's 70-year-old mother, Carol, were killed this way.

Some kibbutzim ravaged on 7 October, notably Beeri, have begun rebuilding, and residents have started to return. While architects and construction companies have drawn up detailed plans for Nir Oz, the damage is so great it is estimated it will take at least three years to make it habitable.

Like the kibbutz itself, a year later everyone from Nir Oz remains in limbo.

Dorin Rai, 43, doesn't come home often; her family now live in a small apartment paid for by the government in the working-class town of Kiryat Gat, about an hour away.

The therapist makes the trip when one of her three children asks her to retrieve something they left behind, but, more often than not, she can't find it, as so many of the family's belongings were taken by looters. Surveying the damage brings back memories of that terrifying day; every room is ransacked and covered in bullet holes, every window broken.

Dorin, her husband, Bijay, 45, and their children, Maya, 12, Neha, 10, and Ram, eight, piled into Ram's bedroom, the reinforced concrete safe room, when sirens started blaring at about 6.30am.

Normally, the air raid alert ends in a few minutes, but that morning the rockets kept coming. Realising this was no ordinary attack and, about 15 minutes later, hearing gunfire outside, she tried to keep the children calm, making them lie down on blankets on the floor. Bijay propped himself between the door and the bed, using his weight to keep the long handle turned up, which kept the door locked.

Four times, Hamas managed to pry the door ajar, and four times, Bijay somehow found the strength to pull the handle back round and seal it again. As the day wore on, strangers came into the house another six times. Based on what they could hear, the family believe they were civilian looters rather than trained fighters.

When they were finally rescued, the Rais emerged to find their home turned upside down — missing items ranged from Dorin's jewellery, to kitchen appliances, to one of the children's baby albums. Social media videos from the day show civilians trying to take the family's two dogs.

'It was very hard to believe what was happening. I was sure we were going to die; I sent voice notes to my sister telling her I loved her and asking if she would take care of the kids if something happened. I spoke in English because I didn't want the kids to understand how scared I was,' Dorin said.

'I love Nir Oz and I miss everyone so much. Some days I want to come back so badly and rebuild our lives, other days, I don't know. I can't ever let something like 7 October happen to my children again,' she said.

The Nir Oz community was buoyed briefly by Hamas's unilateral release of two elderly women from the kibbutz — Yocheved Lifshitz, 85, and Nurit Yitzhak, 79 — in late October. Another 40 came home during the November ceasefire, which lasted a week before it collapsed, reportedly because Hamas could not locate any more women and children to swap.

The Bibas brothers, Kfir, now four, and Ariel, one, from Nir Oz, are the only Israeli children still in Gaza. Hamas says they were killed in an airstrike along with their mother, Shiri, 33, although Israel maintains they are alive. Their father, Yarden, 35, is also a hostage; Shiri's parents were murdered in the kibbutz on 7 October.

News of the hostages has been in short supply since the ceasefire, and what does arrive is not usually welcome. In the kibbutz's empty dining hall, four tables are laid out: two for the dead, one for those released and one for those still in captivity. Twenty-nine people from Nir Oz remain in Gaza, at least nine of whom Israel has said are believed to be dead.

Dolev Yehud, 35, a volunteer medic, left his pregnant wife, Sigal, 36, and their three children in the safe room early on 7 October and went to help his friends and family elsewhere in the kibbutz. He was believed to be a hostage, but in June, the Israeli authorities announced they had identified his remains; the civil engineer had died that day. His sister, Arbel, 29, and her boyfriend, Ariel Cunio, 27, are still hostages, as is Ariel's brother, David, 34.

For Arbel and Dolev's parents, Yael, 58, and Yehi, 65, each day is harder than the last. Like many people from Nir Oz, they are angry at how the state abandoned their family on 7 October. They also feel their daughter is being forsaken again as the Israeli government stalls on brokering a second hostage release deal. Their fate has become an increasingly political issue.

'In the beginning, the government was happy to let the hostage families fly around the world, rallying everyone to the war effort. But as the months have gone by, it is clear Bibi [Benjamin Netanyahu] was using us,' said Yehi, his voice rising.

'If it was Yair and Avner [Netanyahu's sons], they would have come home on 9 October.'

Netanyahu is a master at stoking division. Supporters of the Israeli prime minister now show up at the weekly protests for a hostage deal and attack the captives' families, whom they say are putting their children ahead of the rest of the country.

Hamas and Israel blame each other for the many rounds of stalled negotiations, but many in Israel view Netanyahu as an obstacle to a deal. The prime minister views staying in office as his best chance of beating corruption charges, and a new agreement with Hamas would anger his far-right coalition partners, potentially collapsing his government.

He is also afraid his legacy will be ruined by the intelligence and response failures of 7 October, which may come to be overshadowed by Israel's new war against Hezbollah in Lebanon.

It is no longer clear whether Hezbollah and the other Iranian allies Israel faces in the region consider the conflict as separate from ending the fighting in Gaza. The spectre looms of more death and destruction caused by a regional war.

'War with Iran, with Yemen, with Syria, with Iraq, with Lebanon, with Hamas. How is this better than a deal? How does this keep us safe?' Yehud asked.

'Now there are not just 101 hostages in Gaza. Now 9 million citizens are Netanyahu's hostages.'

5 OCTOBER

Euston, you have a problem

BARNEY RONAY

It would be wrong to take too much credit, to start throwing around phrases such as *guerrilla intervention* or *self-styled people's transport tsar*, after reports began to appear this week of dramatic government concessions on the multibillion-pound redevelopment of Euston station.

Other people might want to use words like disrupter, influencer, even hero. Obviously I can't stop them. I might even encourage them to do so if it helps to add labels, to repeat words that are already out there, phrases such as rainmaker, opinioniser, thoughtfluencer, twat and who is this annoying bloke.

But an odd thing did happen this week. A tweet I posted on the way to Manchester City against Arsenal two weeks ago developed an unexpected second life. Annoyed by the usual levels of disdain and carelessness towards football supporters waiting to catch a train, I'd described Euston as the worst station in Europe and mentioned the feeling it inspires of being taken away to be machine-gunned in a forest clearing in front of vast lighted advert boards.

At the time of writing this tweet has now appeared as a key example of public infrastructure anger in four UK newspapers, the *Observer*, *Guardian*, *Evening Standard* and *Telegraph*. Not really sure what the other nationals are waiting for to be honest. But whatever, *The Times*.

As of Friday even the giant screens of death have gone dark for a bit. Again, we don't write our own destinies. They write us. And right now this thing feels like it's out there running under its own steam. My tweet about Euston has agency. It has become a player.

By Tuesday it had stopped returning my calls and hired its own representation. By Thursday there was industry talk of movie options, franchise opportunities, perhaps a six-part TV series starring a worried-looking Robert Carlyle. A warning, though. This cycle is short. I fully expect to wake up on Saturday and discover my Euston tweet is dating Wayne Bridge and agreeing with people on the internet about chem trails.

In reality, of course, the only reaction is a feeling of shock at finally, after two decades, saying something that actually reso-nates with some part of the general public. Even if it involves making the world's most self-evident observation. Everyone knows what's wrong with Euston. There are pressure groups who work at this stuff all the time, campaigners who have repeatedly explained why this matters to the rest of the country at least as much as it does to the capital.

But it is still a thing, and one that is worth coming back to, if only because it speaks to how we get to follow sport. There are three Premier League games on Saturday requiring fans to pass through the Euston meat-grinder, which will of course show no concession to timings or capacity, which will basically tell any supporter from London or the north-west required to use this monopoly service that they are just a grudgingly tolerated entry on the profit and loss sheet.

This was once a lovely-looking gateway to the north. It was torn down and made horrible by planners in the 1970s. More recently Euston has been jiggered around by confusion over

HS2, and made much worse by insane short-term changes, most notably the decision to herd people outside to wait in an angsty throng, all the better to create the three-minute stampede between sadistically late platform announcements and your double-booked and insultingly shabby seat.

At the end of which Euston is not just the worst rail terminus, but arguably the worst thing. The vibe is outright hostility, an absolute hatred of space, comfort, beauty, people. There is a theory that all big London stations speak to how the government really sees its various regions. St Pancras has to be nice: it's how you get to Paris. Waterloo and Victoria work because they're the gateway to the prosperous deep south.

Whereas Euston is a piece of infrastructure designed specifically to convey the basic futility of hope. It says, welcome to your joyless post-industrial future ant-beings. Welcome to 400 panic-stricken people stampeding past the Upper Crust for the right to be compressed into a leaking metal tube and despatched from the capital in the manner of a landlord gleefully hurling your suitcases out on to the gravel. It speaks to the ongoing scandal of the north – south divide, a state of neglect that hurts the whole country, but for which no one ever has any kind of plan besides leveraging discontent, votes for bullshit.

But again it is also a sport thing, if only because sport remains one of the key reasons many people try to travel around the country at all. Football people have always been treated terribly on trains. The piss-soaked football specials remain a legend to scare the children with, just another part of the rusted and crumbling football architecture of the late 20th century.

There is a circularity to this. In the current age of outsourced neglect we are now at a point where the nation's infrastructure is barely fit to serve the gleaming projections of its football product. It is genuinely embarrassing to see Premier League tourists travelling on these trains, baffled by the contrast between the two experiences.

And yes, because we have sold our assets off to a bunch of investment funds staffed by chatbots, Avanti West Coast will be disgorging you on to the Euston Road 10 minutes after the last tube has gone. This is just what we do in post-giving-a-shit Britain. Welcome to the (very expensive) cheap seats.

Perhaps things will begin to change now. But we must keep going all the same. Attendance through the pain, insisting on being physically present, is by now an act of resistance. One day the people will rise up against corporate greed and disdain for the masses, and there's a fair chance they'll do so on the Euston concourse waiting for the delayed 12.53 to Manchester Piccadilly.

7 OCTOBER

I wish you could see the living nightmare in Palestine. But how much more must we see before something is done?

NESRINE MALIK

I began to write this column last week in Ramallah in the occupied West Bank. I started it several times, both on the page and in my head, as I travelled between occupied territories. In every location I started the column again, then failed to capture what is unfolding and has been for years. So maybe I will just start at what seems like the beginning, with the killing of Israeli civilians on 7 October — a year ago today.

I say 'seems', because that is not really the beginning, but just another beginning as far as Palestinians are concerned. Another date after which conditions worsened and occupation and illegal settlements became more brutal. Because as the world's attention has rightly been on Gaza — then Lebanon, then, last week, the escalating conflict between Iran and Israel — Israeli authorities and settlers have, under cover of war, intensified their assault on Palestinians with renewed licence and relish. Again, that summation seems inadequate, a poor attempt at describing a reality that is nothing short of a living nightmare. The violation of Palestinians is so colossal in scale that I began to speak to the readers of this column in my head. I kept saying: I wish you could see.

I wish you could see parts of the old city of Hebron, its historic streets and markets emptied, its buildings crumbling, its paths blocked to Palestinians since before 7 October. Palestinians are not allowed to walk on those roads, but settlers can, with machine guns casually hoisted over their shoulders. Israeli soldiers protect them on the ground, at checkpoints and from turrets. They man a giant and expanding settlement that bears down on the populace below, over a community that has been ejected from shops and family homes without explanation or notice. Even more traders have been expelled in the past year, and the new stalls they set up are empty. Shoppers have been scared off by the guns and soldiers. Fear and expulsion leads people to vacate areas into which the occupying forces then expand.

I wish you could see the Palestinian man in Silwan, East Jerusalem, living next to the rubble of the home in which he was born. In February, his house was demolished by Israeli authorities for not having a building 'licence', even though the house was built before East Jerusalem was even under Israeli authorities.

The bulldozer came with a canine unit and armed enforcers, who manhandled and shoved his elderly wife into the walls as they dragged them out of the property. He pleaded with them to retrieve one picture, the only one he had, of him and his mother. Instead, it was taken and shattered on the ground before him. Thirty-seven houses in the area have been demolished since 7 October. When the homeowners leave, settlers, of whom there are now a growing number in Silwan, move in. Those settlers were celebrating the holidays last week, the butts of the fathers' rifles at the eye level of toddlers who skipped through the streets that had been closed to Palestinian traffic for the day.

I wish you could see the rocky desert hamlets of Masafer Yatta, which in the past year have suffered increasing violence as residents have been attacked, their homes raided and their livestock stolen by frontier settlers who can only be described as rabid. Just the sight of settlers walking down a hill path sets off panic, and warnings are sent to others to stay put or seek a different route in case they are attacked. Some of the villages are about 5,000 years old. Those that have not been emptied over the past decade are damaged and cut off, forced to go without water, electricity or paved roads. When one small community erected solar panels, they were torn down by the settlers, from whom there is no legal protection. Often, one village elder told me, the police who are called in are settlers themselves — they are the 'judge and the soldier and the police officer'.

I wish you could see the giant white boulders and painstakingly restored historic homes, canals and graves of mystics in the hilltops of Ein Qiniya. They are overlooked by large settlements beaming bright white lights through the night. Attached to these lights are machine guns. The settlers regularly make the hike up to the historic site with their children in a sort of pilgrimage of hate. A witness told me they goad their children to break and smash what they can, initiating them into the tradition of the holy work of removing Palestinians from a location that is the site of precious structures and trees that pre-date even monotheism.

Along with such violent efforts at ethnic cleansing, I wish you could see the conditions in which those communities live. In the West Bank, the prison population has swelled over the past year, doubling to almost 10,000 people, about 250 of whom are children. One-third of these prisoners are under 'administrative detention', a sentence that can be renewed indefinitely without charge, legal representation or family visitation. I wish you could see how even time belongs to the Israeli government, as it shuts checkpoints and roads without notice or explanation, as it did after the Iranian missile attack, stopping people from moving through occupied territories. These barriers block or kettle people on a whim, leaving them with no choice but to change plans, find new routes to their destination, or remain stuck.

Among all of this, millions of Palestinians still live a life that is insistently fuller than can be humanly expected under such conditions, a life both banal and miraculous in its normality. But it is squeezed at the edges by a constant and building pressure. And all of that is only the blunt edges of occupation. I wish you could see it all, but really, what more do we need to see beyond what is happening at the sharpest end in Gaza? The problem isn't that we don't know, but that so little changes despite our knowledge.

All the tools at the disposal of those who want the world to act — journalism, protests, outcry and outrage — cannot end this catastrophe, nor even capture its gravity. It did not start with the tragedy of 7 October. And it will not end, not only for Palestinians, but also for those Israelis who have been corrupted by entitlement and impunity. Until those who have the power to determine who deserves to live in safety and dignity understand that you cannot deny those rights to Palestinians and expect them to underwrite peace and stability by submitting to their fate as subhuman, this will not end.

7 NOVEMBER

The swing county in the swing state that swung right

CHRIS McGREAL

Saginaw county's Democrats were sure that the lessons had been learned and that this time it would be different.

The Kamala Harris campaign flooded this bellwether county in the crucial battleground state of Michigan with canvassers and advertising, a reaction to Hillary Clinton's complacent and, as it turned out, misguided belief that she had the area sewn up in 2016.

The vice-president and Tim Walz campaigned in Saginaw. Leftist hero Bernie Sanders rallied the local university's students. Door-knockers and phone bankers urged people to the polls in the hope and expectation of at least eking out the narrow win Joe Biden enjoyed in Saginaw county four years ago.

But through it all, there were warnings from those closest to key groups of Saginaw's voters — union organisers, Black community leaders, social workers for lower-income families, Latino activists — that denouncing Republican demagogue Donald Trump and making vague promises from Harris of a better future were not enough.

They cautioned that Harris was not getting through to large numbers of those who struggled the most in a county marked by large economic disparities because she was failing to directly address their concerns, not least inflation and the cost of living.

Others said that Harris looked too much like one of the machine politicians so many voters have come to despise, particularly as she avoided taking a stand on key issues or bent to the prevailing political wind.

All of them warned that it could cost her the election in Saginaw county, and beyond.

And so it proved.

Trump won Saginaw county decisively. The vice-president lost by three times as many votes as Clinton in 2016 and did even worse when compared with Biden four years later.

Trump beat Harris by more than 3,400 votes on about the same turnout as 2020. In that election, the then president lost to Biden by 303 votes.

This year, Trump won an outright majority in Saginaw county with nearly 51 per cent of the vote, more than 1 per cent up on his 2020 tally.

On election night, the leader of the county Democrats, Aileen Pettinger, a retired firefighter, bounced into a watch party at a local union hall confident that female voters angry about the US supreme court ruling on abortion and the broader assault on women's rights had won it for Harris.

Local Democrats worked hard to try to bring female Republican voters on board over access to abortion, even leaving Post-it notes in women's bathrooms reminding them that no one would know if they secretly voted for Harris.

But as the results trickled in, the party began to feel like a wake. People drifted away. Whoever was in charge of the music stopped playing 'Ain't No Stoppin' Us Now'. A silence fell as hope bled away.

Across town at the Republican watch party, Trump supporters burst into a rendition of the Christian hymn 'How Great Thou Art' after the former and future president gave his victory speech.

The initial election results for Saginaw appear to show that Harris lost Biden voters to Trump in some of the poorer areas of the county, including minority neighbourhoods, as well as mostly white suburbs. Harris also failed to mobilise the large numbers of people who usually do not vote in Saginaw. The turnout in the main city was only about 50 per cent.

A month ago, Jeff Bulls, president of the Community Alliance for the People in Saginaw, told the *Guardian* that many voters in lower-income parts of Saginaw were disenchanted with the political process because they did not see that it improved their lives.

Bulls warned that Harris's failure to address issues such as inflation and the cost of housing in a way that would make a difference to those struggling to get by was undermining her campaign. After Harris's defeat, Bulls said, 'it's not unexpected for me'.

'She wasn't really speaking to real people's issues. You have a lot of poverty here in this county, whether it's in the city of Saginaw or whether it's rural people out there. And if you don't speak to that, you're not going to inspire people to vote for you, and I felt like her campaign was mostly about just blaming Trump or saying he's racist. She wasn't really inspiring people with her own policies, with her own vision, and I think that cost her,' he said.

Similar warnings came from union organisers who saw members going with Trump, even though Biden kept telling them how good the economy was, because rising inflation had hit them hard. As loyal Democrats, some couched their warnings carefully in public, not wanting to give ammunition to the Trump campaign.

Others were more forthright, including Carly Hammond, a Saginaw organiser for the US's largest union confederation, the AFL-CIO. She told the *Guardian* a month ago that the Harris campaign was failing to address the deep distrust of politicians in general, and the Democratic party in particular, among many working people.

'It's the Donald Trump voters in unions that I see. I think most of them are still in the same place,' she said in October.

'The trend that I see with labour people who are Trump supporters is a tendency to be very upset with the status quo, which everyone should be. People are going to stick with Trump until they see and they feel like things are getting better for them.'

Hammond, whose grandfather worked at one of the many car factories that were once dotted around Saginaw but have since closed, said the Democratic campaign was the biggest election mobilisation she had seen but that Harris lacked 'concrete plans' to motivate voters.

After the result, Hammond issued a statement saying she was 'angry that neither presidential candidate had real acknowledgement of, or plans to address, the real suffering and struggle so many Americans are going through'.

Black and Latino community leaders organised get-out-the-vote campaigns in the last days before the election as they warned of disenchantment and lack of enthusiasm for Harris.

Dan Soza, whose father was the first Latino elected to the Saginaw city council, is a child welfare officer who is deeply alarmed by Trump's threat of mass deportations. He said that Harris failed to connect with large numbers of Latino voters in the city on what they cared about most: the economy.

'There was never any really specific plans. OK, the $25,000 for new home buyers was specific, but where was the specific plan for inflation? Not that the other side added any better answers, but they just never really came out with any concrete plans on what they were going to do,' he said.

Soza said that the rise in Latino men voting for Trump in other parts of the country was replicated in Saginaw. He said a lot of that had to do with 'fear of a female leader, machismo'.

But he said the Democrats also made a mistake in thinking that opposition to Trump's stance on immigration would play well with Latino voters in places such as Saginaw, where there is a long-established Latino community, mostly of Mexican origin, when many of those crossing the border are from Central and South America.

'Immigration isn't as important to them as we think. They took to heart issues like the economy,' he said.

The scale of Harris's loss was emphasised by the success of other Democrats in Saginaw.

Kristen McDonald Rivet decisively beat a Republican former prosecutor, Paul Junge, for the open seat in the US House of Representatives covering Saginaw and neighbouring counties. McDonald Rivet took about 51 per cent of the vote, meaning that some people split their vote to support her and Trump.

But Bulls is not alone in thinking that the Democratic party needs a wholesale rethink of what it stands for if it is to win back voters in Saginaw.

'The Democratic party has to have a come-to-Jesus moment and really revisit who they represent because they're not speaking to kitchen-table issues. There's a lot of rhetoric around the middle class. We largely don't have a middle class, especially in the Black community. We have working class. We have people that are in poverty, and they're not speaking to them and their struggle, to real issues that poor people are really, really dealing with,' he said.

'I would hope that there's a reckoning and that they revisit who they actually represent, because right now it's not us.'

10 November

My seven lessons learned as *Guardian* economics editor

LARRY ELLIOTT

Margaret Thatcher was prime minister and Nigel Lawson her chancellor of the exchequer. Neil Kinnock was leader of the Labour party. The iron curtain separated Europe.

Across the Atlantic, Ronald Reagan's second term in the White House was drawing to a close. Donald Trump floated the idea that George Bush might want him as his running mate in the looming US presidential election, an overture Bush described as 'strange and unbelievable'.

This was the political backdrop when I joined the *Guardian* in 1988 — the year before Tim Berners-Lee invented the world wide web, when mobile phones were in their infancy and the climate crisis was just starting to become a hot political issue.

It was a time when free market ideas ruled. A combination of high inflation and recession — stagflation — in the 1970s had led to a crisis of postwar social democracy and given rise to a new set of beliefs: privatisation, deregulation, tax cuts paid for by shrinking the state, curbs on the power of trade unions, the dismantling of capital controls. All this would give capitalism its mojo back, leading to wealth creation that would trickle down from those at the top to those struggling at the bottom.

Since this is my last column after more than 28 years as the *Guardian*'s economics editor, I thought I would devote it to some lessons learned during my time on the paper.

Lesson No 1 is that the free-market experiment has failed, as some of us said it would all along. Wealth did not trickle down, and instead the gap between the haves and the have-nots widened. The workers laid off when the factories closed in northern England and the US midwest did not find new well-paid jobs but were either thrown on the scrapheap or found low-paid insecure work in call centres and distribution warehouses.

Financial speculation ran rife once controls on capital were removed, but growth rates in the west were slower than in the postwar heyday of social democracy. Warnings of trouble ahead were ignored until the world's banking system came close to collapse in the global financial crisis of 2008. At which point, policymakers abruptly ditched free-market values and rediscovered the virtues of state ownership, interventionist industrial strategies and demand management.

But only temporarily. Lesson No 2 is that ideas matter. The near death of the banks provided an opportunity to forge a new progressive approach to the economy in the shape of a Green New Deal, but it was not taken. In part, that was because various parts of the left — the Keynesians, the greens, the Marxists — all had differing views on what needed to be done. In part it was because the rich and powerful used their money and influence to stymie any hope of real change. In part, it was because of the timidity of parties of the left.

The upshot is that there has been no equivalent of the Thatcher — Reagan revolution of the 1980s, even though the crisis of neoliberalism in 2008 was just as profound as the collapse of social democracy in the 1970s. A form of zombie capitalism has staggered on for a decade and a half, kept alive by cheap money liberally provided by central banks. Ultra-low interest rates have failed to boost investment. Real wage growth has been nugatory.

Those at the sharp end of economic failure looked to parties of the left for answers to their concerns: low pay, job insecurity, run-down public services, a fear of crime, the consequences of mass immigration. What they got instead were lectures about the need to eat better, smoke and drink less, and to stop being such bigots.

Trump's victory last week shows what happens when the left first abandons its natural supporters and then tells them what to think and behave. That's lesson No 3: populism will continue to flourish until the left comes up with a credible and deliverable economic plan.

Trump's impending return to the White House highlights a fourth lesson from the past 36 years: the world's economic centre of gravity — symbolised by the emergence of China and India as forces to be reckoned with — has moved from west to east and from north to south. To be sure, China has some deep structural problems, but it has lifted 800 million people out of poverty since the late 1970s, has developed expertise in hi-tech manufacturing, and poses a bigger threat to US hegemony than the Soviet Union ever did.

Lesson No 5 is that globalisation has gone into reverse. The new cold war between China and the US, the vulnerability of global supply chains exposed by the Covid pandemic, and voter demands that their political leaders reassert control over the economy are all leading to a revival of the nation state. Free trade is out; protectionism is in. Governments are responding to pressure to curb migration. Activist industrial strategies are back in vogue.

The European Union is finding adjustment to these new challenges difficult. That's hardly surprising, given that the EU was — as Wolfgang Streeck notes in his book *Taking Back Control?* — the 'perfect realisation' of post-communist neoliberal economic globalism: centralised, depoliticised, bureaucratic and wedded to free movement of people, goods, services and capital.

As the *Guardian*'s resident Eurosceptic, I have to say I have never seen anything especially attractive in the EU's economic model. Nor can the project of ever-closer union remotely be called a success. The EU is sclerotic and seething with voter rage at the inability of its governments to raise living standards or control immigration.

So my sixth lesson is that those who say Brexit has failed are not just jumping the gun but need to look across the Channel, because that's where the real failure lies. Brexit was to Britain what Trump's victory was for the US: a revolt against the elites and a demand for change. It offers the chance for a party of the left to do things differently. Labour can seize that opportunity.

That's not a conclusion, I am well aware, that most of my readers would agree with, but one of the joys of working for the *Guardian* is that it encourages — indeed welcomes — challenges to the orthodoxy.

So my final lesson from the past 36 years is this: it is always worth questioning the status quo. Just because something is the received wisdom doesn't mean it is right.

15 NOVEMBER

At Cop, behold a species intent on its own destruction

GEORGE MONBIOT

Imagine, as many people do, an all-seeing eye in the sky, looking down on planet Earth. Imagine seeing what it sees. It watches, over the course of decades, ice caps shrinking, rainforests retreating, deserts expanding, ocean circulation slowing, fresh-water dwindling and sea levels rising, and it thinks — for it has been there since the beginning — 'this is familiar'. All the signs are there, of an Earth system sliding towards collapse, as it has done five times since animals with hard body parts first evolved.

But this time, it knows, is different. Not only is one of the life forms causing the collapse, but it shares some of the eye's supernatural abilities: it too can see what is happening. So, with heightened curiosity, the eye zooms in, to see what this well-informed being is doing to avert catastrophe.

It looks first at the centre of global power, the United States of America, a nation possessed of all the scientific and technological tools required to anticipate and prevent the greatest disaster the species has ever faced. It watches meetings in the capital and other cities. It can scarcely believe what it is seeing: a plan to stand down the defences. The most powerful people in the nation are seeking to stifle knowledge, roll back beneficial technologies and appease the interests pushing Earth systems towards their tipping points.

It notes that the industries causing this catastrophe were the real winners of the recent election. Their reserves of fossil fuels, on which their value depends, are seven times greater than the carbon budget the world's governments pretend to have agreed on. These industries know that, if the policies required to prevent Earth systems from tipping were implemented, the great majority of their assets would be worthless, and the value of their companies would collapse. So they used a small part of their profits to support the candidate who would defend their interests. Even before they won the election, these interests, uninhibited by the current administration, were rapidly expanding their extraction of oil and gas. They were already dominant; now they are in charge.

The eye blinks with astonishment, then sweeps around the northern hemisphere, to a small wet island in the north-east Atlantic. Here, with some relief, it finds decision-makers saying what people would say if they were seeking to avert the collapse of Earth systems. The prime minister has noted that 'the threat of climate change is existential and it is happening in the here and now'. He has pledged to strengthen the country's climate targets, cutting emissions by 81 per cent by 2035. He is also among the few leaders of the most powerful nations who can be bothered to turn up at international talks.

But as the eye watches more closely, it finds that what he and other powerful people say and what they do are not the same thing. In fact, his government has embraced the same lobbyists from the same Earth-tipping industries. But in this case it presents the lobbyists' demands as solutions to the problem: a situation, if anything, even more remarkable than what the eye witnessed on the other side of the ocean. If the eye were the religious kind, it would assume that the devil now reigns on Earth. Perhaps it would not be wrong.

But maybe only governments have been possessed? After all, the eye can see that there is tremendous global support for climate action: on average, it notes, a big study suggests that 89 per cent of the world's people want their governments to do more to prevent climate breakdown. Perhaps other powerful people are filling the gap?

So the eye seeks out some of the greatest minds of their generation. It peers into the Bodleian Library in Oxford. The first person it sees is completing their PhD thesis about someone else's commentary on the Dithyrambs of Pindar. The second is working on the eighth biography of a lesser-known member of the Bloomsbury group. The eye rolls. As it peers over shoulder after shoulder, it finds almost every brilliant mind engaged in anything except the issue that will define their lives. In fact, everywhere it looks, it notices that those with the greatest capacity to act are the least engaged. It cannot help comparing this remarkable situation with what it saw 85 years earlier, when almost the entire country bent its collective genius to defeating another, though lesser, threat.

The eye roams across the planet, seeking, in vain, actions commensurate with the scale of the hazard. It alights upon a capital of one of the industries driving this disaster, Baku in Azerbaijan. It finds, to its great surprise, that representatives of almost every government on Earth are gathering here — of all places — to discuss the great predicament. At last! But again, as it looks more closely, it notices weirdly conflicting signals. It sees a process that could scarcely be better designed to fail, and no serious attempt to reform it. It discovers that the event is chaired by a former executive of the oil industry. Well, at least this could be seen as an improvement on last year's meeting, chaired by a serving executive of the oil industry. It finds that, yet again, this meeting looks more like a trade fair dominated by the interests it is supposed to curtail than a serious attempt to address the species' greatest threat. Indeed, the Azerbaijani government has used the event to try to arrange new fossil fuel deals. It notices that some of the governments gathering in Baku are using the unravelling in the US as a licence to downgrade or abandon their own feeble efforts.

It discovers that the governments meeting there are prepared to consider any policy except those that might actually succeed: leaving fossil fuels in the ground and ending most livestock farming. Now they are betting on carbon markets: a futile, impossible attempt to offset with contemporary withdrawals from the atmosphere the hundreds of millions of years' worth of carbon being brought to the surface.

The eye concludes that this is a species, beset by a lethal combination of conformity, distraction and a fear of offending powerful interests, actively collaborating in its own extinction. It sees a species dominated by Lords of the Desert: people prepared to destroy everything as long as they can command the ruins. It wonders whether the species has a survival instinct at all, or whether, instead, it has only an instinct to obey.

16 NOVEMBER

Friendship interrupted

HELEN PIDD AND ALEXANDRA TOPPING

HELEN

The night I first met Lexy, I was supposed to be going on a date. I was 25 and had yet to really make friends since moving to London, so when she asked me for a drink I said yes. The *Guardian* tended to hire only one young reporter a year in those days, and Lexy was the fresh face for 2006 (I was 2004 — it had been a rather lonely first two years).

She had just returned from living in Paris and exuded a certain French cool. Her wardrobe seemed to have been sourced almost entirely from a little vintage shop in the Marais, which would have made her insufferable were it not fatally undermined by her coming from Skelmersdale, the least glamorous town in the Lancashire coalfields. She was funny and clever and generous with her compliments (I was thrilled when she said she liked my shoes — metallic blue-and-silver Mary Janes) and when I reluctantly trotted off on my date, I spent the night wishing I was back with her instead.

Everything was more fun with Lexy. There is something very special about making a best friend in early adulthood, when your brain is fully developed and your personality formed but your responsibilities do not extend beyond paying the rent and turning up to work on time. You're not mates simply because your names went after each other in the register, or because you were lumped together in the same university halls. Lexy and I were kindred spirits: the babies of the *Guardian* newsroom, two blonde northerners let loose in noughties London. She soon became both my biggest cheerleader and harshest critic — two essential attributes for any proper pal.

We spent our days scribbling shorthand at the Old Bailey and our nights out in east London, often on some sort of manhunt, despite us preferring each other to any boy on the market. She generally had far more success, but occasionally the stars aligned for us both. I used to enjoy the mornings-after as much as the nights themselves, as we howled with laughter at whatever nonsense we had been up to until the early hours. We never liked it when the other got a boyfriend: she was furious with me when a snog at the Camden Crawl turned into a relationship just before what she had pre-emptively called our 'summer of fun'. Direct quote: 'You've ruined *everything*.'

A favourite haunt was the Birdcage, a Hackney pub with a karaoke machine that attracted both indie sleaze mavens and proper East Enders. One night we used our appalling pool-playing to attract the attention of a promising young duo: a Swede for Lexy, and, for me, a rough diamond I thought was going to be my first cockney conquest but whose mother, it later transpired, was a feature writer at the *Telegraph*.

I don't remember talking about having kids much when we were in our 20s. I just assumed we would both have as many as we fancied when the time was right. When she got pregnant, at 34,

I'd spent a few years living abroad and had moved to Manchester. I was happy for her but also, frankly, jealous. My long-term relationship had come to a calamitous end and, at 33, I was panicking about my own reproductive window slamming shut.

Everybody seemed to be having babies except me. My response, I realise now, was to try to make my life more exciting. I made new friends: hedonists who could go away outside the school holidays and could make a plan without having to factor in nap times. I invited a Syrian refugee to live with me for six months, went on ridiculously long bike rides, and upped my extracurricular antics, doing everything Lexy no longer could.

Not long after her son was born, I was staying with her in London for a few days and one night simply didn't go back, partaking instead in an ill-advised sleepover at the opposite end of the tube map. On the slightly melancholy ride home, I tried to dampen down my regret by thinking to myself, 'Well, Lexy can't do this any more!' (Nor, it has to be said, did she want to.) I still have a photo I took of myself holding her baby when I got in, my eyes bloodshot and the previous night's mascara smudged under each eye. Looking at that photo now, I see someone trying a bit *too* hard to have fun.

I was thrilled when she asked me to be her son's god(less) mother but resented her new NCT friends, worrying they would replace me. When her son turned one, she invited me to the party and I sat in her kitchen, the only woman without a baby on her knee, and felt like a barren alien. She used to insist she liked not talking about child-rearing with me, that I talked to her about interesting things. But it was the first time that I felt excluded from any part of her life. She used to tell me everything: now I was only getting half the story.

The half was not what it used to be, either. I am old enough now to realise that all new mothers are too knackered for the first year(s) to do anything other than keep their babies alive. But the truth is that having a baby doesn't make anyone more interesting. It softens some people and toughens others up. But the all-encompassing nature of parenthood, particularly for mothers in the early years, means there is neither time nor energy to discuss anything else. I wouldn't say I found Lexy boring, but there was basically nothing to report apart from how tired she was and how hard breastfeeding is.

In the decade since my friends began breeding in earnest, some have more or less disappeared from my life. Maybe they just didn't value me that much anyway. But there comes a point when you are doing all the running in a friendship that you start to feel bitter. I give every parent a pass for the first few years. After that, if you want to still be my friend: make an effort.

I missed the old Lexy. I missed going on holiday with her. I missed the decadent dinners we would have when she didn't spend half her salary on nursery fees. I missed spontaneity. I missed inviting her to something and her being able to say yes without first negotiating childcare with her partner.

Sometimes it was hard to bridge the divide between my life and hers, particularly during the painful years after I got married in 2017 when I was trying and failing to get pregnant and she had her second baby, a girl. I didn't tell her that we had been referred for IVF until very late in the process. Now I was the one keeping a big part of my life from her. I knew she wanted to know how it was going, and that she was genuinely sad for me when each cycle failed. But she was not the person I wanted to be comforted by. It wasn't her fault, but she was too fertile for my fragile state of mind. There was nothing she could say to make me feel better. The only people I talked to in detail had been through the same heartache, or at least had difficulty conceiving themselves. Lexy occasionally would try to tell me what a great life I had without kids, which was true. But I didn't want to hear it from her.

About 18 months after I gave up on IVF, we finally started talking properly again. I'd been on a particularly outrageous holiday to Barbados in January during term time, and, as I swayed in a hammock, drinking piña coladas, started to see the upside in my situation. I returned tanned and at peace, and we had a noughties-style night out that ended up with her discovering a mysterious chilli in her handbag the morning after.

The pivotal chat, which began in the Sheffield pub we used to go to when we were trainee journalists, began with me lamenting having not seen much of her youngest (then almost three) when she was a baby. Lexy shot me a look as if to say, 'Do you really not realise why you weren't there?' I hadn't deliberately avoided her daughter, but her first year was the start of what I must reluctantly call my fertility journey. It hurt too much. I really wish now that I could have been a better friend.

She admitted it was hard for her to know what she could and couldn't say about her kids. She didn't know if she could moan about them when they were doing her head in, or whether that would seem heartless to someone who wanted kids but couldn't have them. She said she held back from sharing with me the joy of parenting and the pure delight that children can bring. I felt sad she couldn't tell me these things, but I knew I didn't want to hear them. I can hear the moaning all day long. It's the joy I find harder to swallow, perhaps because it confirms what I still fear may be true: that having children is life's greatest pleasure.

You know the Q&A in the *Guardian* every Saturday, which asks celebrities a series of questions? The one that always makes me feel most inadequate asks for their proudest achievement. Parents almost always say their children, no matter how many Oscars they have won. Is that because being a mum or a dad really is the most rewarding job of all? Or because it's so hard that if their kids turn out OK it really does seem like the greatest accomplishment? Or because it's the sort of thing you are supposed to say?

But I also know now that having kids is not all proud parents' evenings and bathing in a lifelong glow of reciprocated love. That cute little babies can turn into anarchist toddlers and grumpy teenagers, and that, while parenting certainly keeps you busy, it doesn't necessarily stave off an existential crisis. I see the sacrifices Lexy makes for her children, the freedoms she gives up to be a good mum, and sometimes wonder, would I have been willing to do the same? When I got married I gained a lovely stepdaughter, who is now 15. She and I have a special relationship, but my role is not really parental. I provide the fun and adventures rather than doing the hard yards.

Now that Lexy and I can actually talk about all of this, we have reached the following conclusions: that however much we loved each other, there were times when we just were not the right person to be holding the other's hand. And that there is happiness and joy on both sides of the parenting divide — as well as occasional regret about the path not taken.

She admits she sometimes envies my life — better holidays, lazy Sunday mornings reading the paper, uninterrupted sleep, all the classic childfree tropes. And sometimes I envy her shaping the lives of her two wonderful children, who love her unconditionally and who really do say the funniest things. Should they ever go on to procreate I will no doubt feel jealous all over again when Lexy becomes a granny. But I hope to stay in their lives for ever: their daft Auntie Helen who makes their mum laugh till she cries.

ALEXANDRA

I can remember so clearly the first time I met Helen. I'd just joined the *Guardian*, and we arranged to meet at a pub nearby.

She was wearing an electric-blue skater skirt, black top and matching Mary Janes; we drank pints and laughed at each other's jokes. She had a date that night, and before we left asked me to check that she didn't smell. I thought, 'I'm going to have so much fun with this girl.'

That September, the *Guardian* paid for us both to go to Sheffield to study journalism for three months, even though Helen had already been working as a journalist for years. I was 26, just out of a serious relationship. She was 25, single and ambitious.

Back in the north, we were unstoppable. We studied media law and immediately applied our learning by telling all the boys who touched our bums in the Leadmill (shots of vodka: 50p; bottles of blue WKD: £1) that they were in contravention of the 2003 Sexual Offences Act. Helen had a side gig as an occasional music reviewer − I remember watching her, pint tucked under her arm, dancing to the beat, scribbling in her notebook.

In an early class, we were set the task of interviewing the person next to us, before relaying to the other students the most surprising thing about them. 'What you might find interesting about Helen,' said our friend Bex, 'is that despite seeming like an ambitious career woman, all she really wants to do is have loads of kids.' I took the piss out of her afterwards. 'What?' she said, jutting out her chin with classic Pidd stubbornness. 'It's true.'

The marauding continued when we moved back to London. We put on our best frocks and had extravagant boozy lunches; we went dancing in basements; flew to Istanbul, Granada, Jerez. We made dinners, played ping-pong, pulled dodgy boys, belted out 'Total Eclipse of the Heart' on the night bus. We drank so many cups of tea, spluttering on the sofa when we remembered another detail from the night before. It felt a lot like falling in love.

The pace of the friendship changed, of course. Helen moved in with a boyfriend; I started an ill-fated love affair with a

Frenchman, and spent a lot of time going back and forth to Paris. Helen started her foreign correspondent years — but she was still resolutely my best friend. We hung out in Berlin, in Austria, in London, in Spain. She moved to Manchester to become the north of England editor. I missed her like hell, but she was still such a part of my life.

In my early 30s, I fell in love with my partner. We were on our first holiday together in the Highlands when a doctor called me to say that a routine smear had found cancerous cells on my cervix. They'd caught it early, and the machinery of the NHS moved up a gear — more tests, then, quickly, procedures. When we came out of the other side I was 33, and we were all in. We bought our first house and on a drunken night decided to have a baby. Nothing like being told you might not be able to have kids to focus the mind.

When our son was born, we asked Helen to be his godmother. She looked faintly horrified and told us she didn't believe in God. She settled on 'godlessmother' and threw herself into it. Helen has always loved babies. After our boy was born, she came to visit and snuggled with him on the sofa. She took me for lunch and held him so I could eat uninterrupted. It was a shame that we weren't having babies at the same time, but I assumed I'd also do this for her — just a bit later on.

She was 35 when she met her now husband. I was the best woman at her wedding; we DJed in sunglasses. I thought, 'Crack on: let's do it together next time.'

It took more than a year for me to get pregnant again. I knew Helen was trying, too — we spoke about the relative merits of cycle trackers, whether it was worth taking your temperature. Then I got the blue lines. I was driving when I told Helen. 'Oh,' she said. 'I thought you said you weren't.' I tried to sound as offhand as possible. 'Yeah, well, turns out I was wrong.'

A space hung between us. And as my pregnancy progressed, it got wider. Being pregnant with my first had made me feel like a superhero, but my body carried the new baby like a hostile agent. With a couple of months to go, scans showed she was small in the womb. Deemed high-risk, I traipsed to my hospital three times a week and sat in a packed maternity ward, while a noisy machine monitored her heart rate. I was so scared. Helen sent me a message one day: 'This too shall pass.' She was saying she cared, but it felt so distant. She was saying she was there, but she wasn't. I wanted to kill her.

The baby, expulsed early from my swollen body by drugs, propelled herself into the world surrounded by concerned doctors and midwives. She was, in the end, small but mighty. We went home the next day, wide-eyed with shock. I couldn't breastfeed properly, she didn't put on weight for weeks, nobody slept. In the maelstrom, I called my best friend from university. Having twice been through her own post-birth delirium, she heard my panic. She took time off work, left her kids with her husband and moved in for a few days. She emptied the dishwasher, played with my son, put a wash on. It genuinely felt like she'd saved my life.

It wasn't that I wanted Helen to do that — she couldn't. She messaged me support, made a collage card for the baby that read 'A Star Is Born'. But I didn't have the bandwidth to pick up the phone and tell her what I was actually going through. I couldn't have explained it if I'd tried. I had this perfectly healthy baby girl, and all I wanted to do was cry.

Helen didn't disappear. When the baby was six weeks old, deep in an exhausted fug I handed her over for the duration of a restaurant lunch, snatched before Helen shot off to Amsterdam for the weekend. She made it to mine; I took the kids up to hers. But then Covid struck, and by the time it was over my life was an endless round of dashing to the childminder from work, washing small clothes and failing to have a good night's sleep. Helen, meanwhile, was constantly on another adventure.

I always wanted to hear what new project she was working on, or where she was going next, even if I wanted her not to have as good a time as she would have done with me. I probably felt quite boring by comparison. When I did speak to her about my kids, I made sure to only tell the funny stuff.

Over the next few years, the cord that had expanded and retracted between us for more than a decade stretched further, became taut, which we now realise coincided with her starting IVF. When she told me about it, I weighed every word carefully. I remember standing at the kitchen sink while she — in a matter-of-fact tone — set out the intricacies of the process and why it probably wouldn't work. I mainly tried not to say the wrong thing. I wanted to be supportive, but I felt useless.

After Helen's final round of IVF failed, I had no idea what to do. I almost certainly didn't do enough. We've talked about it since, how I was not the person to provide succour. I wish I had been. When she told me they weren't going to try again, I felt profoundly sad. Sad for her, sad for them and, in some, undeniable way, sad for us. From that point on, we would always be on separate tracks, I thought.

But, actually, it was the start of us finding our way back to each other. The elastic didn't exactly twang back into place, but it has drawn us in, gently. When her Saturday magazine piece about accepting being childfree came out last year, I read it again and again. I was so glad that writing it had been a positive experience and had helped so many other people. But there was something else. 'It also makes me a bit jealous, in all honesty,' I rambled in a voice note I recorded at the time. 'Jealous of this kind of super-exciting crowdsurfing life that you have that is so, so far away from mine. Like, I'm literally running the bath right now and I'm hiding from my kids so that I can have two minutes ... I can't put this down on paper, because I haven't got time.'

Because the thing that you can't share with your friends who wanted children but didn't have them is how — not all the time, but sometimes, fiercely — you long for the freedom they would do anything to give up. The ability, as Helen wrote, 'to be responsible for your own destiny' rather than responsible for another human's safety, development, hygiene and happiness. You want the spontaneity, the space, the unscripted hours. You never want to go to another kid's birthday party again.

I started writing this piece hunched over my phone in the rain while my kids played hockey. It's been tapped away at tennis practice, and in the dark hours of the early morning — the only time there is peace in the house. Helen started hers on the Eurostar on the way to the south of France for a weekend with her husband.

Even as I write this I cringe at my own solipsistic ingratitude. I know I have no right to moan. I know what a privilege motherhood is, how lucky I am. But is it OK to feel envious? Just occasionally?

But the other thing mothers — ones like me, at least — keep secret is the psychedelic, heady joy of it. The moment when your sleepy firstborn buries his head into your neck and says, 'Mama, I love you so, so much,' and you feel a flood of oxytocin that at 6.55am beats the best pill of your life. The extraordinary, ordinary mornings with both kids in bed, laughing at your partner's silliness. The firework of pride when your kid scores the winner in the last minute of a finely balanced under-nines football match. Dancing in the kitchen with a little girl who, somehow, contains the purest version of your best self.

But maybe you don't have to share everything in a friendship. Maybe its intensity can ebb and flow while the core remains fixed. As the kids get older we can go out for dinner more easily, and phone calls aren't always interrupted; this year we managed a classic Big Night Out in a Foreign City (chino-wearing big-bummed boys, we apologise for our hilarity). Helen is my kids' favourite fake auntie; I hope I'm still her favourite dance partner.

In *A Life's Work*, Rachel Cusk said of seeing old friends after having a baby that they met 'at the uncrossable border between the free world and the closed regime of motherhood'. Mine and Helen's friendship felt like that for a while, but, as the years continue, the connection that made us both realise we'd met someone important in the pub on that first night is still there. It's in the texts and the shared jokes, the work chats and the sparse but regular weekends of fun. It's in the stories we repeat, and the ones we're still creating. If there is a border, it can be traversed — and we both have a pass.

19 NOVEMBER

Emotional Nadal bows out after defeat in final battle

TUMAINI CARAYOL

As the Spanish national anthem rang out for what would be the final time in his career, Rafael Nadal could not stop his emotions from flowing. Tears welled up in his eyes and his hands visibly shook by his sides. Finally, the last stage of this epic 30-year journey had begun, a moment he never wanted to arrive but had no choice but to face. Nadal's audience responded to his outpouring of emotions, clear to see on the big screen, with thunderous chants of 'Rafa! Rafa!'

Not even those deafening, constant roars from the crowd could help to push Nadal beyond the limits of his bruised and broken body. Despite fighting for every last point with the diligence and desperation that has defined him, Nadal was comprehensively defeated 6–4, 6–4 by Botic van de Zandschulp in the opening Davis Cup rubber between Spain and the Netherlands, a match that would turn out to be the last of his professional career.

In the early hours of Wednesday morning, Spain fell 2–1 to the Netherlands in the quarter-finals of the Davis Cup. Spain had looked to the new leading light of Spanish tennis, Carlos Alcaraz, to find a way back and the 21-year-old pulled them level with a 7–6 (0), 6–3 win over Tallon Griekspoor. 'I did it for Rafa,' he said.

Alcaraz then returned to the court for the decisive doubles match alongside Marcel Granollers. In an incredibly tense, high-quality battle, Wesley Koolhof and Van de Zandschulp closed out the match with a dramatic 7–6 (4), 7–6 (3), win. Nadal watched on from courtside in Spain's team box, cheering and coaching his teammates until the final point.

In the past few days, as the tie neared, speculation raged about exactly what form Nadal's participation in Málaga would take. He had not played an official match since the Olympic Games nearly four months ago, so the consensus was that he would only take to the court in doubles. After arriving earlier than most players and training diligently, including a set with Alcaraz on Monday night, Nadal was given the green light to compete in singles.

'Things can go well, can go bad,' he said. 'Putting myself on the field to play the first match was a risk, but that's the work of the captain, no? He has to make decisions, and David [Ferrer], I'm sure he made the decision thinking what's the best for the team, not for myself.'

What followed was an occasion like no other. Nadal composed himself as he warmed up with Van de Zandschulp; the MC opted to slowly, pointedly read out every significant achievement accrued by each player individually.

For Van de Zandschulp, the world No 80, it was a short and understated lead-in. Nadal's introduction, however, was practically a PowerPoint presentation. After each of his major titles — 22 grand slam titles, two Olympic gold medals, five Davis Cup victories — were read out, the crowd responded with an exclamation of 'Ayy'. It took several minutes for the announcer to work through one of the greatest resumés a tennis player has compiled.

The spectacle that followed, however, bore little resemblance to those legendary times of old. It quickly became clear that Nadal was severely limited. His movement was poor, particularly towards his backhand wing, and his forehand continually dropped short, allowing Van de Zandschulp to overpower him. He struggled badly with his return of serve.

There were still moments the 11,000-strong audience will never forget; in the second set, he chased down a lob and responded with an overhead skyhook, his back to the net, before sending the fans to their feet by winning the point. Down 4–1 and a double break, Nadal pulled a break back through his sheer force of will. Many times in the past, that would have been the start of an epic comeback. This time, he did not come close.

Before the tie, Nadal had made a point of noting that he was here to play and help the team — not simply to finish his career. In reality, Spain's best team configuration would have placed Nadal in a doubles-only capacity. But he is one of the greatest of all time and the sight of him stepping on to the court for one last tussle was more meaningful to the crowd than any win.

29 NOVEMBER

At last: a decent life can end in a decent death

POLLY TOYNBEE

Here it is at last, a landmark that will be an enduring symbol and the humane legacy of this Labour government. Parliament has finally caught up with the public, who have long been firmly and unwaveringly in support of assisted dying since the first polls on the issue more than 40 years ago. What took MPs so long?

In the debate today the reasons for that support were graphically and sometimes horrifically laid out by MPs, including Kim Leadbeater, in whose name this law will pass into history. The status quo is 'cruel and dangerous' said Andrew Mitchell from the Tory benches. There is no 'safe' avoidance of suffering, there is no certainty that palliative care will always prevent a horrible death. Morphine is no saviour, as I have witnessed in my own family. Leadbeater gave a terrible example: 'Tom vomited faecal matter for five hours before he ultimately inhaled the faeces and died. He was vomiting so violently that he could not be sedated, and was conscious throughout' while his family pleaded with doctors to help.

That oft-quoted risk of death by relatives over-eager to grasp an inheritance always looked utterly implausible: they couldn't wait another month or two instead risking prosecution and a 14-year sentence for coercion? As for being a burden, yes, many don't want a humiliating dependency on others in their very last days — and for them, assisted dying is a reasonable choice.

The one lobby against the bill I have some sympathy with comes from disability groups. I think they are quite wrong to claim this is a slippery slope towards euthanising the inconvenient, but they are right to publicise how appalling their lives can be as things stand − in benefits, in transport and much else. However, many disability groups were on the other side; as for everyone else, it's for them alone in extremis to decide whether they want to live out their final terrible months.

Around the world, scores of countries have long had dignity in dying legislation − in Spain, Australia, New Zealand and a host of countries more religious than Britain. However, in this supremely irreligious land, there was much opposition from religious groups. For reasons not obvious, the Commons always has a far higher number of MPs professing a faith than the general public, the Lords many more (aided by those 26 bishops Labour should be abolishing along with hereditary peers). However, little was said by MPs about their religious reasons for opposing the bill, knowing the word of God carries little weight among voters these days. Christianity − with the cross as its emblem − has a peculiar relationship with suffering as a value in itself.

How long this has taken. Seven times since 2010, a Tory-dominated parliament voted down bill after bill on the right to die, regardless of public opinion. Almost all progressive social reforms have trailed behind the public in this way: parliament is very rarely the standard bearer. In fact, it is usually the foot-dragger, timid unless absolutely certain what its constituents think. Abortion had long been strongly supported before parliament finally caught up. Divorce law had become an absurd farce for decades − good business for private detectives who were hired to dash into a hotel bedroom to snap a husband in bed with a hired actor to prove his 'fault' before a couple could legally part.

Banning capital punishment was the standout exception, when a new Labour government in 1965 dared to defy a public that was still in favour, by supporting a private members bill introduced by longtime campaigner Sydney Silverman MP. Afterwards, the

Commons held a vote in every parliament until 1997 calling to restore the death penalty, always defeated. Public opinion on this is now against restoration. Gay rights and civil partnerships broke through the barriers only with very strong public support. Here again, citizens were way out ahead.

This bill allows for a vital personal freedom over our bodies and our lives. It's a far too restrictive law for many, especially those suffering beyond endurance with degenerative diseases, but it's extremely unlikely to be extended in any way during the political lifetimes of this generation of MPs. Although, at 330 to 275, the vote was closer than it should have been, those who passed this law can be proud of what they did today.

2 DECEMBER

My obsession with Jacob Rees-Mogg's wife runs deep

LUCY MANGAN

I often feel these days that I am going bonkers. Or that I am staying sane while the world goes bonkers around me, which amounts to the same thing. It is getting to the point where I will almost miss being disoriented if it ever stops.

There is no danger of that, however, for as long as *Meet the Rees-Moggs* exists. Yes, it is a reality show about the former Tory MP for North East Somerset, once described as 'a haunted Victorian pencil', Jacob Rees-Mogg, his wife, Helena, and their six children. 'We had to try five times before we got one who looked like me,' says Helena, and she is right. Helena, I hazard a guess, is always right.

Do you know what I would do if I were a rich politician, had married an aristocratic heiress who was even richer, and had a lovely life split between a large house in London and a vast family pile for my massive family in Somerset? Not sign up to a reality show like an absolute berk, that's what.

The why of it is a compelling question. On the one hand, a lust for fame does not jibe with what we know of poshos. On the other hand, anyone who puts together a persona as carefully as Jacob has over the years — and he is his own pastiche — is hardly someone not crying out for attention. Perhaps he thinks the show will do for him what appearing on *Have I Got News for You* did for Boris Johnson back in the day — make enough of the public fall for the act, and rise to power on that misbegotten popularity. If it works, we'll deserve it.

Once the show begins, however, the why fades to a background hum as the Rees-Moggery begins. Contrary to expectations, Jacob seems overtly fond of and engaged with his children (three at home, three at boarding school). His daughter, Mary, says she often teaches him slang to amuse herself. 'So,' we hear him ask her later at the dinner table, '"wasteman" is not rizz?' I'm not sure Helena gives any of her brood a thought if they are not in her eyeline, which I admire tremendously.

Helena quickly becomes the star of the show. The general election is announced. 'The mood in the country,' she says, without moving her lips or jaw, 'is anti-Conservative. Possibly with some justification, unfortunately.' It's incredible. The words get out, but you cannot see how. The birthday of their fourth (I think) child, Anselm, falls on the day of Boris Johnson's 60th birthday party, to which they are all going. Helena wonders if Anselm might want to do something in addition. Go-karting, he suggests. Helena computes this and agrees. Later, she preps the children for the likely outcome of the election. 'Other careers are available.'

Her wit is so dry it leaves you feeling sandpapered. I think she may become my new obsession.

The Rees-Moggs' Catholicism is covered. 'I'm very lucky to have my own chapel,' says Jacob, but there are plenty of truthful and non-risible remarks about the faith, too, plus an oddly endearing discussion with the children when one wonders whether transubstantiation isn't a bit like, you know, cannibalism?

Their courtship is covered. She knew him as her friend Annunziata's brother. He knew her as a descendant of one of his greatest political heroes, Thomas Wentworth. He told her all about him. 'I staggered away after about 20 minutes,' says Helena (somehow, I still haven't caught her in the act of enunciating). Before their first date, he tried to buy a book on Wentworth to give her, but it wasn't in stock. So he bought her a pair of earrings instead — a move that suggests a degree of spontaneity in the Moggsian mind that is otherwise invisible. They both wanted lots of children, and that was that. Theirs is clearly a love match, though the L-word is never mentioned. His face lights up when she talks and especially when she teases him.

But the unexpectedly appealing scenes of their domestic life (yes, replete with staff and everything else you would have if you were sitting on a fortune, but also with children making jokes about poo, and Helena, to whom I have pledged allegiance by the end of episode two, delivering brutal apercus at every turn) contrast with interviews with people such as David Leverton. He is on the streets campaigning in the run-up to the election against Mogg and urging tactical voting to get him out. 'Almost everything he stands for is bad,' he says, of the anti-abortion, pro-Brexit, anti-immigration MP. 'He seems to despise people who are poorer [than he is] — which is almost all of us.' It is more than the *Have I Got News for You* team threw at Johnson. Whether it is enough to counteract the idiosyncratically charming picture painted elsewhere, we will have to wait and see.

9 DECEMBER

Hope and despair in Assad's 'human slaughterhouse'

WILLIAM CHRISTOU

The celebrations in Damascus were interrupted by a whisper.

On the outskirts of the city, a door had been found. Beyond it lay a vast underground complex, five storeys deep, containing the last prisoners of the Assad regime, who were gasping for air.

Cars raced towards Sednaya prison, locally known as 'the human slaughterhouse', the most notorious torture complex of the Syrian government's vast network of detention centres.

The *Guardian* followed as traffic came to a standstill and rumours were passed between lowered windows: there were 1,500 prisoners trapped underground who needed rescuing; perhaps your loved ones are among them. Cars were ditched by the roadside and people began to walk.

A procession lit by thousands of phone torches streamed through the prison complex gates, which, until rebels took control of the facility earlier on Sunday, had guaranteed entry but not exit. Families huddled around fires in the prison ground to keep warm, while keeping an eye on the prison doors to see if they could recognise any faces coming out.

Rebel fighters tried to stop people from entering the prison itself, firing rounds in the air — but the crowd surged forward undeterred.

Inside, people roved about the labyrinthine facility, moving from cell to cell, searching for any clue that could tell them where their relatives and friends might be. They were racing to locate the hidden underground wing — which they called the 'red wing' — amid fears prisoners were starving without food and asphyxiating from lack of air.

'There are three in my family missing. They told us that there are four levels underground, and that people are choking inside — but we don't know where it is,' said Ahmad al-Shnein as he searched the prison corridor.

'The ones that emerged from here looked like skeletons. So imagine how those underground will look,' Shnein said.

The prison was seemingly built to induce a sense of place-less-ness. At its centre is a spiral staircase that from the ground floor appears endless. The staircase is ringed by metal bars and, beyond them, large identical vault doors, through which lie the facility's three wings. According to the rebel fighters, each wing specialised in a different form of torture. There are no windows to the outside world.

On Sunday, people milled around the metal staircase, entering and emerging from different doors, but always returning to the centre. Rebel fighters seemed no better informed. One had finally found a map, and crowds huddled around him as he pored over the half-a-metre-wide paper document, its looping scrawl almost illegible.

The cramped cells were littered with blankets and clothes, cast off when prisoners were suddenly freed by rebels earlier in the day. Some had jagged holes in the walls, where additional pris-oners had been crammed. Videos showed fighters freeing female prisoners on Sunday, who needed to be encouraged to leave, unable to believe they were truly getting out.

The narrow cells, no more than a few metres across, had been stuffed with more than a dozen people at a time, leaving no space to lie down, according to rights groups. The screams of prisoners being tortured could be heard echoing down the hallways.

According to Amnesty International, up to 20,000 prisoners were held at Sednaya, most of them imprisoned after secret sham trials that lasted no more than a few minutes. Survivors of the prison recounted brutal daily beatings and torture by prison guards that included rape, electric shocks and more. Many were tortured to death.

Survivors said guards enforced a rule of absolute silence within the prison. If the detainees could not speak, they could at least write. Cell walls were covered in scrawled, handwritten messages. *Tab, khadni.* Enough already, just take me, one message read.

Another piece of paper, found on the ground, torn and trodden, detailed the death of a prisoner, seemingly written by another detainee eager to document the death of his friend.

The note, written by a 63-year-old prisoner who signed it as Mohammed Abdulfatah al-Jassem, said that he saw another prisoner — whose name was not legible — fall and hit his head during a seizure. He left a phone number on the note for the person who found it to call. No one picked up when the *Guardian* rang.

In the chaos of the prison break, records were taken by families searching for relatives. Each ledger, filled with names and other details, was carried out of the prison where groups of people would gather and see if they knew anyone mentioned. Rights groups have cautioned that records need to be preserved in an orderly fashion, so that the fate of about 136,000 people arrested by the Assad regime can be documented.

Yells began to emerge from somewhere within the prison and people began to run. Someone had broken open a door, and said that he had heard a voice from below. Fighters yelled for calm as hundreds clamoured to see who might be there. They set to work, the clang of a shovel against a padlock reverberating through the metal fortress.

Syrian civil defence on Monday released a statement saying that, despite an intensive search through the facility, they had not found any prisoners trapped underground. They cautioned people not to get their hopes up as rumours and misinformation circulated.

For many, Sednaya was their last hope of finding missing loved ones. Yamen al-Alaay, an 18-year-old from the countryside of Damascus who was leaving Sednaya, said he had been going from prison to prison looking for his uncle who had disappeared in 2017.

'We arrived today and we searched and we searched, but we didn't find anything. Those in the red wing have still not been found,' Alaay said, vowing to come back in the morning.

As people left Sednaya in the late hours of the night, thousands more were still coming from Damascus. One man coming in asked another departing, 'Did you find anyone? Did anyone new emerge?' The man replied in a low voice, 'No, but hopefully tomorrow.'

17 DECEMBER

Country diary: Storm Darragh created holes in the woods

ANITA ROY

WELLINGTON, SOMERSET

The day before the storm was hushed and still, expectant as a theatre when the lights go down. Then Storm Darragh swept in, roaring and raging, tossing the scenery about. The government alert on my mobile nearly made me jump out of my skin — but apart from that, I spent the day oddly becalmed, safe from the huffs and puffs of the wolf trying to blow my house down.

It seemed to me that a weather event of this drama and magnitude deserved at least to be felt, so once the worst was past I pulled on my boots, zipped up my jacket and headed out to pay my respects.

The wind knocked me back with a chest bump worthy of an American linebacker. I had to lean in just to stay upright. The trees along the railway line bent with each gust in a great Mexican wave. Wood pigeons skittered through the air and jackdaws ripped across the roiling sky in black tatters. It was a wild ride, walking out in that world, and I returned home with eyes bright, blood up.

Darragh — an Irish name meaning oak — was the fourth named storm this season. Eowyn, Floris and Gerben are next in line as we work our way down the alphabetical list compiled in 2015 by the Met Office in the UK and its sister organisations in Ireland and the Netherlands.

Two days later, the world I step into is a world changed: lighter, more fragile, pared back. Woods that had been dark walls of foliage are now shot through with skylight. Not just from fallen trees — every leaf from every twig has been meticulously picked by the wind, transforming the dense woodland to a delicately patterned *jaali* screen. The trees stand naked, shivering in their ivy innerwear, balls of mistletoe trapped in their branches like footballs kicked by errant kids.

Like all old gods, the wind is capricious, generous, destructive, inscrutable. In his wake, Darragh has scattered gifts: a twisted branch of cypress that my mother and I haul home for a Christmas tree, gutters heaped with pine cones we gather for decorations and, for our fireplace, more kindling than you can shake a stick at.

20 DECEMBER

How do we live in this terrible world, I'm asked. Here is my reply

JONATHAN FREEDLAND

It's a season brimming with tradition and, as longtime readers may know, my own custom has been to try, in the last column before Christmas, to find a few reasons to be hopeful. I was planning on doing that anyway, but my resolve was sharpened by a conversation with a reader who called in to last weekend's *Guardian* and *Observer* charity telethon. Tammy, who is 75, made her donation but she also had a simple, if fathomless question: 'How do we live in this terrible world?'

She proceeded to rattle off just some of the things that led her to put the question so starkly. She talked of the ongoing bloodshed in Ukraine, Sudan and Gaza; she sighed at the imminent return of Donald Trump. And this week brought two more items that could be added to her list.

We learned more of the depths of wickedness plumbed by the ousted Assad regime, with the discovery of what appears to be a mass grave site in the city of Qutayfah, marked by trenches long and deep. It's said that twice a week from 2012 until 2018, four trucks would come, each carrying more than 150 bodies, identifiable only by the numbers etched on their chests or foreheads. That would mean the remains of hundreds of thousands of Syrians, murdered by their own ruler, are in the ground of Qutayfah. And that is just one site. There are others. All this after more details emerged of the Sednaya prison, with its torture chambers and dungeons, where machinery designed to cut wood and metal was deployed against flesh and bone.

Closer to home, this week brought the sentencing of the three people who caused the death of 10-year-old Sara Sharif, one of them her own father. The details of her torment were so harrowing, they will haunt anyone who has heard them. The judge who sentenced the guilty spoke of 'almost inconceivable' cruelty.

When you know these things, when events like these keep happening, it's hard not to ask, as Tammy did: 'How are we going to live?' Or, to make the question even harder: how can we live and remain hopeful, even optimistic, about the future? Here, then, offered in the spirit of the season, are some tentative suggestions.

One option is to switch off. I don't mean cutting off from the world entirely, though occasionally that can have its place, but rather managing your diet of gloom. Professional journalists may need to keep across every breaking development and update, but there's no reason for everyone else to do it. Yet I see too many people doomscrolling, or watching rolling news channels on a loop. There are plenty of good arguments for reducing your social media consumption, but overexposure to bad news is certainly one of them.

Still, that, I confess, is to skirt around the problem rather than to confront it. Even if you reduce your news intake, checking in only once a day, there are times when a mere glimpse of the headlines can fill you with despair. So how to manage that?

First comes the realisation that finding light in the darkness does not just happen; you have to work at it. Think of it as a variant of optimism of the will: willed optimism. It means making a deliberate effort to fight the pessimism of the intellect, which has a nasty habit of getting in first.

Recall the reaction to the election result in July. There was an immediate move to analyse the troubles stored up in Labour's win: it was a loveless landslide, there was little enthusiasm, the vote share was small, support was broad but shallow. To say nothing of the sheer scale of the task confronting the new government. All of which was, and remains, true.

But it skipped too fast over what had just happened: Britons had ejected a rotten, useless Conservative party and handed Labour, so often rejected at the polls, a thumping majority. That was great news, but it required an active, conscious decision to savour it. We fixated on the cloud before we'd taken a good look at the silver lining. Of course, we can all see the defects in this new government — one of them being its dearth of optimism — but we might spare a moment to remember what it replaced, and what the alternative would look like.

Or, to take a radically different example, the impulse was strong, on hearing of the fall of Bashar al-Assad, to worry instantly about what would come next, specifically the prospect of an al-Qaida offshoot turning Syria into another oppressive Islamist theocracy. But willed optimism would lead you, first, to marvel at the pictures of Syrians at last freeing their loved ones from Assad's torture chambers and, then, to allow that Syria might just break from its past, and the model set by most of its neighbours, to construct a stable, relatively free society. We don't have to pretend that's likely, but for a moment at least we can let in the possibility — and the hope.

As part of that effort towards optimism, we can draw strength from those who dare to swim against even the bleakest tides. I think of the staff of Israel's *Haaretz* newspaper, for instance, who constantly, and in the face of intense opposition, including a planned boycott by the country's far-right government, urge their fellow citizens to face the reality of what their leaders and their army are doing in Gaza. That kind of work wins few friends. And yet, if Israelis and Palestinians are ever to find a way out of the current darkness, that is the courage that will be required. That such courage already exists, here and now, is grounds for hope.

Or I think of my friend and *Guardian* colleague Merope Mills, who endured the greatest loss any human being can face — the death of a child — and somehow turned that pain into a life-saving gift to others. Her remarkable, relentless campaign for Martha's rule, giving families the right to request an urgent review of a loved one's treatment in hospital, has already had a 'transformative effect', according to NHS England's national medical director.

And sometimes it pays just to celebrate what is good. Last weekend, in what has become yet another seasonal tradition, I gathered with friends to watch the *Strictly Come Dancing* final. Trust me, you didn't have to be a fan of sequins or samba to be awed by what happened there. Chris McCausland, a comedian who is blind, had surprised even himself by learning and mastering a series of ever-more intricate routines. It was inspiring, of course, but just as heartening was the knowledge, certain many weeks earlier, that the voting public was always going to make him their winner.

I'm not sure any of that answers Tammy's question. How do we live in this terrible world? Perhaps by accepting that it's the only one we have and that it's not always so terrible — that sometimes, even quite often, it can be rather beautiful.

Winter

At long last orders

ROBYN VINTER

It was the moment they had been waiting four days for. A tractor appeared on the horizon, which signalled a possible final escape for the majority of the 33 people snowed in at the Tan Hill Inn, Britain's highest pub.

Hugs were shared, phone numbers swapped. But in the end, there was not much time to say goodbye as those in 4x4s and those with snow chains on their tyres scrambled to leave in the wake of the snowplough, driven by the local farmer.

The urgency was necessary — strong winds across the tundra-like landscape meant the cleared roads were covered in snow drifts moments later and completely impassable in a couple of hours. Time was of the essence if the convoy of vehicles was to get out — and there was no guarantee they would do so on the steep and winding North Yorkshire roads.

The swift exit came after a lively and emotional evening when, on Monday night, a goodbye party of sorts was thrown in the Tan Hill Inn's function room, known as the barn.

The main instigator of the bash was Kelly Dunn, one of the bar staff, who had worked incredibly long hours to keep the stranded group fed, watered and happy.

'Come on everyone,' she said, herding the crowd into the room, which was lit with disco lights.

Any initial reluctance fell away and it was not long before virtually everyone was on the dancefloor throwing shapes — some more irregular than others. Frederick Swift, a hairdresser who had previously been a professional dancer, scooped people up into impressive lifts, while four-year-old Edison Goldspink performed numerous improvised numbers to a receptive crowd.

Tender moments between couples were also shared, especially between Chris and Janine Miles, who had got engaged in that very room in 2023.

At midnight, a video call to Dunn's daughter, whose 18th birthday she was missing, concluded with the majority of the pub singing a rendition of 'Happy Birthday' at full volume. 'She's beautiful, isn't she?' Dunn gushed.

Most of the residents had had a turn on TV or radio at some point during their four-day stay, due to the global fascination with the story of the people 'living the dream'.

The Australians Naomi and Paul Wright, with their grownup son Declan, had spent a large part of the previous evening talking to breakfast television presenters in their home country, where it is the middle of summer.

On Tuesday, shortly after they had left, word came back that they were through and had a train from York to London booked, which meant they would make their flight to their home in Katherine, near Darwin.

Four guests — plus one dog — decided not to attempt the journey. Barry Newitt from Southend was one of the people who decided to wait it out a couple more days until the snow had melted and the roads were clear. He was in no hurry. 'This is one of the best times of my entire life,' he said. 'I mean, look out there. Have you ever seen scenery like that? I love snow. It's just brilliant to be in the motor home and give it a good test! This is the best place to do it in the whole world.'

The bar staff refused to ask for money for the rooms supplied to those who were hosted. Instead, the managers asked for donations to their local mountain rescue.

A helicopter was chartered for Tuesday lunchtime from nearby Catterick by the pub's owner to bring in a new roster of staff and provide a break for those working, some of whom had already been there a week.

However, the winds were too strong and it was unable to take off, meaning the six workers at the pub would be staying until their colleagues could drive in to relieve them, albeit with fewer guests to look after.

'If you do get out, will you get me some fags?' joked Dunn, who had smoked her last one the previous day. 'Or on second thoughts, maybe now's the time to quit.'

11 JANUARY

'How can you rebuild when your father is the worst sexual predator in decades?'

ANGELIQUE CHRISAFIS

Four years ago, Caroline Darian thought she had a normal life. She was in her early 40s, she had a home in the Paris area, a job as a communications manager, a husband who worked for a TV breakfast show and a six-year-old son. She got on well with her parents, who had retired to the picturesque village of Mazan in Provence in the south of France, to a house with pastel-blue shutters where they would all often spend long summers together in the garden under the mulberry tree and splashing in the pool — with barbecues and music, dinner and board games on the patio and country bike rides with her dad.

Darian remembers the exact moment that this all shattered. It was 8.25pm according to the clock on her kitchen cooker, on a Monday night in November 2020. She had been working from home all day on Zoom calls. She had just put down a bag of Japanese takeaway on the kitchen counter when her mother, Gisèle Pelicot, called and told her to sit down in a quiet spot; she had something difficult to say.

Darian thought of her father's health — he was heavy, had breathing problems, and France had been in and out of Covid lockdowns. But instead she learned that police had arrested her father, Dominique Pelicot, for secretly filming up women's skirts in a supermarket with a hidden camera in a bag. Officers investigating his phones, computer and hard drive had found thousands of images and videos stretching over almost 10 years showing that he had drugged his wife and then filmed her, unconscious, being raped in her own bed by him and dozens of strangers. There had been at least 70 men, aged from 22 to 71, and police were still trying to identify them all.

Darian didn't understand what was being said. She felt herself lose control: shaking, shouting, screaming insults about her father, hardly able to breathe. 'It was like being hit by a wave,' she says, still struggling to comprehend it four years later. 'It was a cataclysm. All my foundations collapsed.'

Darian is sitting in a book-lined room, up a creaky wooden staircase in a publisher's office on the Left Bank in Paris. The first time we speak, it is days before the verdict in what has become the biggest rape trial in French history, after her mother decided to waive her anonymity and hold the four months of hearing in public, saying 'shame must change sides'. Gisèle was embraced by the world as a feminist hero for her bravery and refusal to be shamed, as the trial made global headlines and the family was thrown into the spotlight. Darian is poised and calm, although nervous about the verdict. Channelling her anger into a public campaign to raise awareness of drug-facilitated sexual violence has been a 'question of survival', she says. But on the inside, she describes herself as a 'field of ruins'. The previous few nights, she began dreaming about Dominique Pelicot again.

The trial was an 'ordeal', Darian says, 'really hard from a human perspective'. Dozens of accused men, now aged between 26 and 74, including a soldier, journalist and lorry drivers, had sat on benches in court, at close proximity to her and her mother. The men seemed so relaxed and 'comfortable in their seats', Darian observed. Video evidence was shown of many of them raping Gisèle in her bedroom when she was in a comatose state, lying limp and lifeless and snoring loudly, with family photos on the dresser and spotty pillowcases on the bed.

Dominique Pelicot hid prescription drugs in a tennis sock inside a hiking shoe in his garage. He crushed sleeping tablets and anti-anxiety medication into Gisèle's mashed potato, coffee, or the raspberry ice-cream he served her in front of the TV. This would give him seven hours, he told the court, in which his wife was in a state akin to being under general anaesthetic. He would take off her pyjamas, dress her up in underwear he had bought. Then he and the other men would rape her while a camera filmed. Afterwards, Dominique Pelicot said, he would wash her and dress her in her pyjamas before she would wake up, groggy but unaware, thinking the blackouts and memory lapses meant something was wrong with her brain. He contacted men online with messages such as 'I'm looking for a pervert accomplice to abuse my wife who's been put to sleep' or 'You're like me, you like rape mode.'

Days after we meet, Dominique Pelicot is sentenced to 20 years in prison and all 50 other men are found guilty of rape, attempted rape or sexual assault. At least 20 more could not be identified and are presumed to be still at large today. Most had denied the allegations, saying they had never 'intended' to rape and thought it was a game by a couple of swingers in which 'the wife' was pretending to be asleep. Some said that if the husband gave consent it was OK.

Darian has total admiration for her mother — 'the true victim of this whole story' — for agreeing to hold the trial in public. Darian went public herself, in 2022, while the investigation was ongoing, publishing a book called *I'll Never Call Him Dad Again*, which has now been translated into English for a new edition. It was a kind of diary of the first year after the revelations, illustrating how 'trauma expands outwards like a shock wave' through a family.

She had grown up happily with her parents and three brothers. Her father, an electrician who had also worked as an estate agent, and mother, a logistics manager, met when they were 19 and 20 and married soon after. The family lived in a house provided by her mother's company with five bedrooms and a walled garden in a coveted neighbourhood on the banks of the river Marne just outside Paris. Dominique Pelicot encouraged Darian's dance lessons and would drive her to school to avoid her getting the bus. She remembered him singing Barry White songs in his Renault 25 as he drove the kids on holiday. All that was sunk for ever by the revelations. She now doesn't even keep old photographs. 'I can't keep hold of those memories,' she says. 'Sometimes they pop up, but that was a previous life; this is now.'

Campaigning 'is a way for me to recover some kind of dignity', she says, having founded a movement called Don't Put Me Under (#MendorsPas) to raise awareness and support victims of drug-facilitated rape, pushing a new expression into the mainstream in France: 'chemical submission'. Drugging most often happens in the home, enacted by family members or people you know, she says, and victims can be adults or children. Before her father's arrest, 'I didn't have a clue about drugging or drug-assisted rape. I knew about GHB, the date rape drug, in nightclubs and bars, but I didn't know it was so much more widespread and mostly happened using the contents of the family medicine cabinet.' She wants better training for health professionals and police, and better access to toxicological testing for victims.

She would also like more respect for rape victims in court. She watched in horror when even her mother, a grandmother, who had been drugged into a coma with no recollection of the assaults, was questioned by defence lawyers about whether she might have led the men on.

'I'm really proud of my mum,' Darian says with determination. 'She has opened the door. She has led the way for other victims of sexual violence. She's told them they're not alone any more. That is strength. So to me she's a hero … And she did it brilliantly. She walked into this court every single day with hundreds of journalists, being scrutinised by everyone, being humiliated by all these [defence] lawyers. Frankly, you have be strong to do that … She's an independent and strong woman. And she did it with dignity.'

She describes her mother as having the calm of a 'medieval queen' presiding over ruins − a resilience she says Gisèle has had since losing her own mother to cancer aged nine.

Darian, 45, attended the trial with her brothers, David, 50, a sales manager, and Florian, 38, an actor. (She uses the pseudonym Darian because it is a composite of her brothers' names, in honour of their support, but has taken her husband's surname.) She was a striking figure in the courtroom, head held high, arms folded, sitting metres away from the accused men − many of whom were around her own age − and visibly staring them all in the eye. What did she feel? 'I felt anger. They're cowards.'

She said the men stared right back at her: 'I was looked at like a sex object during this trial by many of them.' While reporting the trial, I saw Darian's appearances shift the mood in the courtroom. She was unflinching about the unbearable emotional toll — 'How are you supposed to rebuild yourself from the ruins when you know your father is the worst sexual predator of the past 20 years?' she asked the head judge. She was not afraid to regularly shout across the courtroom, 'You're lying!' to the man she no longer called her father, or get up and walk out. At one point, when her father was speaking about her, she retorted: 'I want to throw up.'

Within the first days of the trial, it became clear that Dominique Pelicot was reserving perhaps his most twisted evasions for his daughter, refusing to explain what he had done to her and appearing to change his story several times.

What had emerged in the four-year investigation of Dominique Pelicot's crimes was that no woman in his family was safe. He had hidden cameras in bathrooms and bedrooms at his home and in relatives' homes, secretly photographing his sons' wives naked and sharing the pictures and photomontages online, boasting that he was 'surrounded by sluts'. He hid cameras in the guest bedroom in Mazan to secretly film his daughter naked and make photomontages of both her and Gisèle naked, comparing their bodies under the title 'The slut's daughter', which he shared online alongside obscene commentary.

On his computer equipment, police had found a deleted folder called 'my daughter naked' and recovered two pictures of Darian, then aged roughly in her 30s, taken at different times, asleep on her side in the foetal position, wearing beige underwear with the duvet pulled back. When police first showed her those pictures, she initially didn't recognise herself. The lights were on, and she was a light sleeper who would have woken up. She never slept in that position, or went to bed dressed like that, and the underwear she was wearing definitely wasn't her own. She said in court she was certain she had been drugged, and also probably raped and abused by Dominique Pelicot. 'It's not a hypothesis; it's reality, I know it,' she told the judges. She said the difference between her and Gisèle Pelicot was that her mother — most unusually in a rape case — had the confirmation of thousands of files of video evidence. Darian, without video evidence, felt, she said, more like the remaining 99 per cent of women who allege drugging, unable to ever know the truth, locked into 'doubt and silence'.

In her final appearance in court, Darian said: 'I'm a forgotten victim in this case.' Turning to her father, she added: 'I know you abused me. You don't have the courage to tell me.' She, her brothers, her lawyer and even Dominique Pelicot's own lawyer beseeched him in court to speak honestly about what he had done. Despite the photos, he said he had never touched his daughter and didn't know who had taken them. One court psychiatrist suggested that for a victim like Darian to go through life not knowing was 'mental torture'.

When she walked into that courtroom at the start of the trial, was she convinced he would tell her what happened? 'There was a small part of me that was hoping,' she says. 'I was really determined to make him recognise the facts. And I failed.'

She pauses and the word hangs in the air. Did she think it was her responsibility to make him speak? 'You know I'm always reflecting on that, because I was tough and I asked him in a violent way. Maybe if I had been in a more emotional dimension, he would have told the truth. Anyway, it's a fail for me.'

She says: 'The only victim who knows — and not even the entire truth — is my mum. But even for my mum, he didn't tell the whole truth or the full story. Even today, we don't know how many men came to abuse my mother, and when it started. We still don't know.'

Darian's brothers, in court beside her, described the whole family's 'devastation'. Her husband, Pierre, a TV journalist, who she says has been a crucial support, also took the stand. He said the discovery on Pelicot's computer of pictures of Darian apparently asleep in underwear that wasn't her own 'added horror to the horror'. He told the judges it wasn't a question of 'whether she was drugged, but why she was drugged'.

For Darian, the case has robbed her of one of the most basic necessities of life: sleep. How do you doze off at night when you fear you might have been abused in your sleep, when you are terrified you might lose control and become someone's prey? When she first found out about the allegations, she didn't sleep for five nights straight. She ended up needing medical help and was admitted to an emergency psychiatric ward, where – terrifyingly for her – staff tried to sedate her. Yet the whole issue of sedation 'was, you know the reason we were in this nightmare'. This hospital approach was 'absolutely not what I needed', she says. Her body and brain resisted drugs, 'so they had to use this massive dose … it was really experimental'. This is now part of her campaign for better support of victims. She has tried to be honest in public about her vulnerability as a survivor, and not look like what she calls a 'pseudo wonder woman'. She announced halfway through the trial that she would go into a clinic for a few days to try to recover after 'weeks of repeated insomnia'.

Her view of herself has been shaken by the case. Her past has dissolved and weakened her foundations, she says. 'I lost a part of me, I lost a part of my identity.' She carries what she calls the 'crushing double burden' of being the child of the victim and the perpetrator. 'You can't imagine the sadness and the loneliness,' she says. 'I've got a part of his DNA. And it's difficult to be the daughter of the biggest sexual criminal for the past 10, 20, even 30 years, and at the same time be the daughter of an icon like my mum … I don't know if it's better to be the daughter of Gisèle or worse to be the daughter of Dominique Pelicot. I'll have to live with that.'

Back in November 2020, the day after Gisèle broke the news to her children, Darian and her brothers took the train south to the house in Mazan, with its sunny back garden, synonymous with holidays. It was now quite terrifying and they feared all these men would come back at night. Dominique Pelicot had been taken into police custody and would await trial in prison. The children wanted to clear the house and get their mother out in a matter of days — they started selling furniture, emptying drawers, which they found full of debt notices incurred by their father. Darian smashed one of his amateur paintings (a nude). Gisèle left with two suitcases and her dog. Nearly 50 years of marriage had vanished, and she soon filed for divorce.

At that time, Darian was running over in her head odd things that had happened, signs she felt she had missed. She and her brothers, as well as Gisèle herself, had worried she had Alzheimer's; they had booked neurologists and scans, but the tests always came back normal. Fearful, Gisèle had stopped driving; pinched herself when she took the train to Paris, worried she'd miss her stop; and was convinced she would be diagnosed with a brain tumour. 'She was having a lot of blackouts,' Darian says. 'She would sometimes seem incoherent on the phone.' Once, Darian's son called his grandmother to tell her about his rugby tournament, and she started repeating herself nonsensically. Darian took the phone from him and asked: 'Mum, what day is it?' Gisèle couldn't reply.

Another time, Florian and his family had sat down to eat dinner in Mazan after Dominique Pelicot had served his wife a glass of rosé. Her elbow slid off the table and she nearly fell off her chair, seeming to collapse like a rag doll, glazing over, appearing hypnotised. Dominique Pelicot said her family were tiring her out.

Looking back, Darian says, these blackouts always happened in Mazan when Gisèle was with her husband, never when she was in the Paris area with her grandchildren. There were gynae-cological problems, too — Gisèle was bleeding despite being post-menopause. A doctor diagnosed an inflammation of the uterus.

Does Darian still feel, as she wrote in her book, that 'ignorance is culpable'; that she should somehow have noticed what was going on, despite the extent of her father's manipulation? 'No. Today, I think it wasn't possible for me to have known. Because everything was premeditated, organised. We are all victims in this family — all collateral victims: my brothers and I, but also our children.'

Video evidence showed that Dominique Pelicot not only invited men to rape his wife in the couple's marital bed in Mazan. He had also invited men to Darian's home outside Paris. Just after Christmas in 2019, when Darian was away on a mini-break in Morocco and her parents were house-sitting, Dominique Pelicot invited a 34-year-old warehouse worker to rape his wife in Darian's guest bedroom. In May of the same year, while alone with Gisèle at Darian's holiday cottage on the Île de Ré off the Atlantic coast, Dominique Pelicot invited a man to rape her in Darian's own bed. Video evidence showed the rapes went on for more than five hours that night. Asked in court why he had chosen to do this in his daughter's holiday home, he said: 'There was no symbolism. It could have happened anywhere.'

But Darian thinks the choice of location is meaningful. She also thinks it is significant, given her questions about her father's potential abuse of her, that the retired nightclub worker who raped Gisèle at the holiday cottage had previously been sentenced to five years in prison for raping his own 17-year-old daughter. 'That detail is so difficult to cope with,' she says. 'Home is supposed to be a safe place, not that kind of crime scene.' That Dominique Pelicot had raped her mother in Darian's homes 'was like being abused a second time. I was betrayed by my father in different ways.'

With Dominique Pelicot deliberately leaving what she calls a 'great fog' over the question of what he may have done to her, she is left with no foothold. She had a vaginal tear that would not heal and needed several surgeries (once, while she was recovering from surgery, her father called her, asking to borrow money). Of the injury she says: 'I'll never know if it's linked or not. It's part of an open question — unanswered.'

She believes her father used her as a guinea pig to test out his drug cocktails — his exchanges with men show him commenting on the different effects on a woman who did or didn't smoke. She was an occasional smoker and her mother was not. It was clear from the police investigation that Dominique Pelicot only confessed to crimes when presented with irrefutable evidence, and often partly at the start. In 2022, while awaiting trial for the rapes of his wife, Pelicot was questioned about an attempted rape of a 19-year-old estate agent in 1999. She was the same age as Darian at the time, and he had attempted to anaesthetise her with ether. Dominique Pelicot denied it until confronted with DNA evidence on the woman's shoe. But he offered up a comparison with his daughter, saying that when he undressed the woman and realised she was the same age as her he had felt 'blocked'. Instead, the woman broke free and fought him off.

Darian is unsparing in her praise for her mother, with whom she appeared hand in hand in court. But she wrote in her book and says today that, as wife and daughter, they are 'in a different place within the family' and have dealt with the bomb-shell of Dominique Pelicot's abuse in different ways. She says not knowing if she was drugged or abused weighs heavily on the whole family. Darian feels that, without clear evidence, her mother has sought to reassure her that it may not have happened.

In court, near the end of the trial, Gisèle did not want to answer questions from defence lawyers about what Dominique Pelicot may have done to her daughter, saying it was for him to answer that. One defence lawyer suggested there was a family rift. Gisèle replied: 'This isn't a trial of the family.'

Now, Darian speculates that maybe the prospect of a daughter's abuse is just too much horror for her mother to contemplate all at once. 'She is not able, from an emotional standpoint, I think, to face the truth. I think it's too difficult for her. And it's hard for me — it's really hard for me.' But the family remains close and she thinks time will change things.

The trial never fully uncovered why Dominique Pelicot did what he did — if there even was a reason. He told the court: 'You aren't born a pervert, you become one,' citing his own abuse as a child. He said he had been raped aged nine by a nurse in hospital when he was being treated for a head injury. Aged 14, as an apprentice on a building site, he said he witnessed — and was forced to take part in — a group-rape of a woman whom he described as disabled. 'It was too heavy to bear,' he told the court.

'To me, it was pure manipulation,' Darian says. 'He was choosing his words to make us empathise with him. And he knows exactly how it works ... where to press the button.' In the high-ceilinged courtroom, where Dominique Pelicot sat on one side in a glass-fronted dock, and Gisèle on the other, Darian felt there had been an invisible 'arc between my mum and dad all through this trial', in which he was trying to communicate with his ex-wife to let himself off the hook of responsibility. 'In life, you decide who you want to be,' Darian says, brushing aside any excuses about childhood. This echoes her mother's view, expressed in court, that, regardless of their past, a person 'chooses' who they become.

Darian says she won't let Dominique Pelicot's perversity become 'this family's curse', that she must stop what she calls the 'deviance' infecting generation after generation. (The court heard an investigation is ongoing into whether Dominique Pelicot may have abused any of his grandchildren. He denies any abuse.) Darian says her father's family line was mired in abuse — part of a 'dysfunctional family system'. Denis, Dominique Pelicot's father, whom she remembers in jeans and a biker jacket, with a single earring, had been a violent tyrant. He was a caretaker at a rehabilitation centre for convicts. The court heard that Denis was suspected of grooming and abusing a young girl with learning difficulties who was fostered by the family; Darian calls her Lucille in her book. After his wife's death, Denis made Lucille his partner. In court, questions were raised over whether Denis also ever brought in men to abuse Lucille. Darian now questions why her parents would later send her and her brother to stay with her grandfather and his partner over the summer, until she said she no longer wanted to go.

Her own son, whom she calls Tom in the book, at first didn't believe his grandfather could have done harm to his grandmother. 'We've done a lot of things to protect him,' she says. 'When it happened he was six. Now he's 10. He's had two and a half years of support from a psychologist. And today he's in good shape. We really wanted to preserve him. But he's known the truth right from the start. We told him with simple words that his grandfather was in jail.'

Darian, who works as a senior communications manager at a large company in Paris, says the trial has inspired her to campaign even harder in support of victims of sexual violence.

Returning to normal life is key. 'My son and my husband are my two pillars in life,' she says. 'I'm a mum, I'm married, I've got a social life, friends.'

A few days later, at the verdict in the packed Avignon courthouse, she watches with quiet anger as most of the men, some silently weeping, are led away to the cells. Dominique Pelicot will likely spend the rest of his life in prison, and all the other men are convicted. As Darian leaves the court with her mother, hundreds of supporters who have travelled from across France and Europe chant, 'Thank you Gisèle' and then begin shouting, 'Thank you Caroline!'

We speak again the next morning. She is still feeling shaken. The prison sentences, which ranged from three to 15 years, some of which were suspended, were lower than the state prosecutor had recommended. It is a disappointment. 'It's the wrong message,' she says. 'It's not the message we wanted to send to all the other victims in France.'

This means that for her 'the fight is only just beginning'. She has decided to write another book, the behind-the-scenes story of the trial. 'Because it's not what you see from watching TV. And while this trial was happening, there were so many other trials going on where the victims were all alone.'

Gisèle Pelicot, her lawyers say, now hopes to resume 'as normal a life as possible'. Darian herself will rest and spend time with her son, husband and brothers, before resuming campaigning.

In the final moments in the courtroom, Darian looked only briefly at Dominique Pelicot before he was led away. 'It was the very last time I'll see him,' she says. 'It's an end point. It's the very last chapter in what was my life before.'

It will take a while to work through.

'There's a kind of grief,' she says. 'It's a long process, mourning someone who is still alive.'

27 January

'Memory hurts, memory guides': Auschwitz survivors warn of new age of hatred

JON HENLEY

On Monday, a day of startling blue skies, Auschwitz survivors stood before princes and presidents to remind the world, perhaps for the final time, of the horrors they suffered there during one of the darkest moments of human history.

Beneath a white marquee erected in front of the gate to the former Nazi death camp, four former inmates — the youngest 86, the oldest 99 — warned world leaders on the 80th anniversary of its liberation against the danger of rising antisemitism.

Tova Friedman, 86, was five when she came to the camp, but said her memories were still 'so vivid'. She recalled 'the cries of desperate women', the 'terrible stink' of the chimneys, six- and seven-year-olds led shoeless through the snow to gas chambers.

'We are here to proclaim ... that we can never, ever allow history to repeat itself,' she said. But eight decades after the camp's liberation, she said, 'our Jewish-Christian values are once more overshadowed by prejudice, fear, suspicion, extremism'.

With nationalist and far-right parties gaining support across Europe and disinformation increasingly distorting the history of the Holocaust, this year's anniversary carried special weight. Memories of one of humanity's worst atrocities are fading.

In front of one of the freight wagons that carried people here like cattle, Marian Turski, 98, condemned a 'huge rise' in

antisemitism and called for 'courage' against Holocaust mini-
misers and conspiracy theorists.

Leon Weintraub, 99, who managed to sneak out of Auschwitz
by joining a group of prisoners working outside the camp, urged
vigilance against a resurgent European far right with its ideology
of 'hostility and resentment' against all who are different.

'Let's take seriously what the enemies of democracy preach,'
he said. 'We, survivors, understand that the consequence of
"being different" is active persecution, which we have personally
experienced. We must avoid the mistakes of the 1930s.'

Janina Iwańska, 94, a Polish Catholic and inmate number
85595 at Auschwitz, said nobody knew exactly how many people
died there. By liberation day only the sick, the young and pregnant women were left, she said. 'It was a killing factory.'

Speaking after the survivors, the World Jewish Congress president, Ronald Lauder, said the horrors of Auschwitz and Hamas's
October 2023 attack on Israel were both inspired by 'the age-old
hatred of Jews'.

Antisemitism 'had its willing supporters then, and it has them
now,' he said. When Auschwitz was liberated, the world saw
where 'the step-by-step progress of antisemitism leads. It leads
right here ... Things are not OK.'

Auschwitz was the largest of the Nazi death camps and has
become a symbol of the genocide of 6 million European Jews.
An estimated 1 million died at the site between 1940 and 1945,
along with more than 100,000 non-Jewish people.

'Memory hurts, memory helps, memory guides, memory
warns,' said the Auschwitz museum director, Piotr Cywinski.
Turning to the survivors, he said their experiences 'shape our
memory ... And what do we do with that memory today?'

After Jewish prayers, accompanied by music written by
composers who had themselves been Auschwitz inmates,

56 survivors helped by relatives and young assistants laid votive candles, followed by the heads of 54 national delegations.

Among them were presidents Emmanuel Macron of France, Volodymyr Zelenskyy of Ukraine, Sergio Mattarella of Italy and Alexander Van der Bellen of Austria; they were joined by the German chancellor, Olaf Scholz, and prime ministers from Canada, Croatia and Ireland.

The members of royalty in attendance included King Charles of Britain, Felipe of Spain, Willem-Alexander of the Netherlands, Philippe of Belgium, Frederik of Denmark, Haakon, Crown Prince of Norway and Crown Princess Victoria of Sweden.

Other countries, including Israel and the US, sent ministers or ambassadors. Russia was not invited (although in Moscow, Vladimir Putin hailed the Red Army soldiers who liberated Auschwitz for having ended the 'terrible, total evil' of the camp).

None were called on to speak. Paweł Sawicki, a museum spokesperson, said: 'Twenty years ago, we had more than 1,000 survivors here; 10 years ago it was 300. Five years ago, we had 100, and today — not many more than 50. In 10 years' time, how many will there be? That's why it's so incredibly important that we focus just on these survivors.'

Earlier in the day, elderly former inmates, some wearing blue-and-white-striped scarves recalling their prison uniforms, laid wreaths and lit candles at Auschwitz's Death Wall, where thousands of camp inmates were executed by firing squad.

Since the occupying Nazi Germans had 'built this extermination industry and this concentration camp' on their country's land, said Poland's president, Andrzej Duda, 'we Poles are today the guardians of memory'.

Sawicki said this year's anniversary was particularly significant not just because of the survivors' advancing age but because of growing distortion of the history of the Holocaust, fuelled particularly by disinformation on social media.

'For people born 30 or 40 years ago, they learned this history at the family table, from their grandparents,' he said. 'But for today's generations, the Holocaust is textbook history, and textbook history is a much more fragile history, much easier to distort.'

A recent poll found that proportions of young European adults sometimes running into high double digits had not heard of the Holocaust, could not name Auschwitz or any other camp and had encountered Holocaust denial or distortion, mainly online.

Considerable numbers thought the number of Jewish people murdered in the Holocaust had been exaggerated, with many — including 24 per cent in Poland, 21 per cent in France, 20 per cent in the UK and 18 per cent in Germany — believing 2 million or fewer people died.

The continent's increasingly polarised politics, and the success of nativist parties, have also turned the remembrance of Nazi crimes into an intensely political issue.

The US tech mogul Elon Musk this weekend told a rally of the far-right Alternative für Deutschland (AfD) party that it was time for Germany to move on, saying children 'should not be guilty of the sins of their parents — let alone their great-grandparents'.

Those who died at Auschwitz were either murdered in gas chambers or perished from starvation, cold and disease. Mostly Jews, they also included Polish resistance fighters, Roma and Sinti, Soviet prisoners, sexual minorities and disabled people.

Nazi Germany established the camp in 1940 within former barracks in the southern Polish town of Oświęcim, later establishing about 40 other camps in the area, including Birkenau, which was used for mass killings in gas chambers.

On 17 January 1945, as Soviet troops advanced into formerly Nazi-held territory, the paramilitary SS forced 60,000 exhausted prisoners to walk westward in what became known as the Death

March, and over the following days the gas chambers and crematoriums were blown up.

On 27 January, Soviet troops arrived, finding 7,000 emaciated survivors. The UN has designated the day Auschwitz was liberated as Holocaust Memorial Day and the site is now a Polish state museum and memorial visited by nearly 2 million people a year.

Crowds don't ruin art. They give it life

JONATHAN JONES

What a wonderful headache for a museum to have. The Louvre in Paris gets so many visitors it is taking drastic measures to cope, which include moving its most famous treasure to a dedicated space where fans can visit without entering the main museum at all. It will no longer suck the oxygen from other art.

Nearly 9 million visitors a year stream through the Louvre and it's believed 80 per cent of them are looking for Leonardo da Vinci's portrait of Lisa Gherardini del Giocondo, better known as La Gioconda, better still as the *Mona Lisa*.

I'm worried the Louvre is trying to solve a problem that is not really a problem. Ask Britain's museums if high visitor numbers are a bad thing: they still haven't recovered their pre-pandemic crowds.

The decision, dramatically announced by Emmanuel Macron, to move the *Mona Lisa* to a special hygienically isolated gallery where *les idiots* who flock to take selfies in front of it won't bother more cultured visitors who wish to study art in a hushed atmosphere, is a misguided act of snobbery. It may ruin the Louvre's ecosystem as a place where high art becomes popular culture.

On my last visit to the Louvre, I made a beeline to see Leonardo's masterpiece. Why wouldn't I? To get to it, after the security controls to enter the court under the glass pyramid, you go through the Denon wing, choosing one of several paths — maybe past the *Victory of Samothrace* or Gericault's *Raft of the Medusa* — until you reach the room where the *Mona Lisa* is sealed behind plateglass.

It's rowdy. Barriers hold back the crowd, many of whom do seem to be fixated on getting photos. But who am I, and who is Macron, to assume none of those people feel or see or discover anything from the experience?

Noise and jostling there was, but I was still able to see Leonardo's painting, a silent mystery at the heart of the hubbub. Her smile, in person, is so much warmer than it looks in reproduction. I realised, more clearly than ever before, this really is a sweet portrait of an ordinary person who posed for Leonardo in Florence in 1503 — and made a magical impression on him.

It's true the *Mona Lisa* makes it hard to pay attention to the paintings by Veronese, Titian and others in the same room. But that's not because of the crowds. It's the *Mona Lisa* that does this by being so compelling.

In my experience, the crowds don't spoil the Louvre. They give it life. Another measure that is planned — opening up a new entrance — sounds more useful as it can be a slow queue getting into IM Pei's pyramid.

But once you're in, the vastness of this museum gives it an exhilarating impression of limitless riches. There are always plenty of visitors in the gallery of French history paintings. Others traipse past Botticelli frescoes, Caravaggio canvases — not to mention Leonardo da Vinci's other paintings in the collection.

If you want peace in the Louvre seek out its northern Renaissance galleries or its collection of Chardin still life scenes. Better still, go downstairs from the *Mona Lisa* where people walk by Michelangelo's Dying and Rebellious Slaves with barely a glance. You can look at these masterpieces in peace.

29 JANUARY

Hallucinating copy/paste plagiarism robots are everywhere!

FIRST DOG ON THE MOON

Thank goodness for the newest version of AI called DeepSeek. It's cheap, it's open source and it's from China! All the kids love the CCP now and hate the West. It's great.
You'd rather give your data to China than to our genocide-adjacent social media apps? What is wrong with you?
Hey Xi Jinping just fyi I had Congee flakes for breakfast!
YOUNG PEOPLE
Until DeepSeek arrived the Cult of AI insisted they needed more bigger models run on more bigger environment trashing data-centres costing more bigger megabillions. And... they were wrong. Everyone is freaking out that $200bn got wasted on Lamborghinis for AI CEO bros
No need to reopen nuclear power plants, DeepSeek is smaller, more efficient and cheaper and because it's open source you can even build your own version of it!
DeepSeek did you write this pro DeepSeek cartoon?
Sorry that's beyond my current scope - let's talk about something else
Will DeepSeek save us from the smug tech broligarchy? No only a mass global insurrection against the dictatorship of capital will do that - in fact DeepSeek will make it cheaper and easier to put AI in everything, but at least we got to laugh at some of the worst people in the world briefly.

30 JANUARY

After decades of apathy, *A Complete Unknown* has turned me into a Dylan nut

LAURA SNAPES

The bookshop in the town where I used to live had a world-beating second-hand selection. The music section alone was so bounteous that there was a second shelf dedicated solely to books about Bob Dylan. One of them provided an inadvertent punchline to the six-foot display, proclaiming: Why Dylan Matters. Thank God, someone said it!

I have cared about music for about 30 years and been a working music journalist for more than half of that time. You can't avoid the fact that Dylan matters, yet I had always remained Dylan-agnostic. No one in my family is a fan. I saw *I'm Not There* when it came out, aged 18, and didn't really get it. On an interminable van journey from Cornwall to Edinburgh, friends played a CD of his greatest hits, but it left no lasting impression. As a teenager I found his music sounded dusty in the way that old records often do when you're revelling in the newness of your own, formative era.

As I got older, I figured Dylan's music would always be there waiting for me — perhaps a listening project for when I turned 40, or 50 — and that the well-tended field of Dylanology filling that second-hand shelf would fare quite alright without me. At my most cynical, I resented the weight of Dylan's legacy. Once, when doing some freelance shifts at *Uncut* magazine — like *Mojo*, a publication essentially built in Dylan's image — I wrote up news on the latest edition of *The Basement Tapes* and asked whether anyone would truly be excited about these studio dregs. The desk erupted: 'Judas!' (That much, I know.)

And then I saw *A Complete Unknown*. I went out of professional duty and there not being much else to do in January. Some friends refused to see it, assuming it would be some kind of sacrilegious affront. With no skin in the game, I didn't care either way. But I left the cinema fizzing with teenage-worthy obsession. I've scarcely listened to any other music since. I've watched *Dont Look Back* [*sic*] and have a date planned with *No Direction Home*. I have volume one of Dylan's memoirs cued up as my next read. I'm ready for the weird Christian albums.

It feels silly, almost girlishly juvenile, that a major Hollywood movie starring a well-studied heartthrob has done for a woman of 36 what the Dylan industrial complex — the magazines, books, reissues and Nobel and Pulitzer prizes — did not (though the many memes suggest I am not alone). I feel so besotted and ravenous for more that it's hard to break the feeling down to understand it. The *New Yorker* writer Tad Friend once said that the purpose of the celebrity profile is to properly convey the effect a star has on us. *A Complete Unknown* may play fast and loose with accuracy, but director James Mangold and leading man Timothée Chalamet comprehensively assert the magic of the young Dylan, as perhaps best summarised in this piercingly accurate review on Letterboxd:

> *Women: 'You're such an asshole. How do you make such good music?!'*
> *Bob Dylan: *unintelligible mumbling**
> *Women: 'Fuck, you're so hot'*

Sidestepping the very real possibility that I may just have developed a massive crush on Chalamet/Dylan/both, perhaps the deeper part of the magic is the air of mystery that Dylan — fictionalised and real; the fictionalised real — exudes. Today, musicians are more or less expected to bare all and to maintain a coherent identity and personal politics, or they risk being accused of inauthenticity or inconsistency. Dylan is all questions, no explanations; tricksy, and funny. Sometimes wise, sometimes a massive dickhead, somehow he always gets away with both. (I loved every sly dig at Donovan in *Dont Look Back*.) Maybe no one has ever worn sunglasses better.

In *A Complete Unknown*, Dylan's antipathy towards stardom rings more contemporary, but the way he toys with it feels more fun and artful than is possible for pop stars in the same position today, bound by a demanding industry and demanding fans. His elusiveness creates a hunger to get closer; more so because you know that, with Dylan, you never can, making the potential terms of engagement feel infinite. Meanwhile the women in the film, Joan Baez and a stand-in for Suze Rotolo, feel undersold, and I want to learn their stories on their own terms.

This would all be academic if it weren't for the songs. *The songs!* I have nothing new or insightful to tell you about anything on *Highway 61 Revisited* or *Blonde on Blonde* or *Blood on the Tracks*, my current starter pack, and won't insult anyone's intelligence to pretend that I do. I'm just rapt by music that's almost 60 years old; that once sounded inaccessibly remote and superannuated to me, and now hits like a wave to the face. I can see why critics would write six feet's worth of books about his phrasing alone. My current favourite is the untouchable hauteur of *Blood on the Tracks*. The gall of 'Idiot Wind' almost makes me wish I had an ex bad enough to sing it to, although the concluding shift from the indicting 'you' to '*We're* idiots, babe / It's a wonder we can even feed ourselves' guts the song's bellyful of contempt and takes my breath away.

Maybe a sense of loss contributes towards Dylan's allure for me too. In *A Complete Unknown*, his songs catalyse sweeping social change and inspire a generation to break from cultural conservatism — that has never felt more like a fantasy than it does now. One scene in *Dont Look Back* shows young British Dylan fans awaiting him at the airport. When he appears, their happy screams sound like the ecstasy of kids at a birthday party surprised by a particularly big cake, shrill with an innocence that has since been crushed by the posturing warfare of much contemporary fandom. I've just tipped into the second half of my thirties and have been doing this a long time: perhaps the past holds more surprises, now, than the carousel I've watched go around and around several times.

In her *Pitchfork* review of *A Complete Unknown*'s soundtrack — featuring songs by Dylan, Joan Baez and Pete Seeger, sung by the actors portraying them — critic and Dylan obsessive Jenn Pelly wrote: 'One of the joys of Chalamet's performances is hearing the dizzying, transformative charge of getting into Dylan for the first time — as did Chalamet, who grew up on the work of Kid Cudi and Lil B.' The clear zeal in the 29-year-old actor's performance made Dylan feel accessible to me — and surely many others — in a way that an overwhelming availability of information didn't. What a delight, for his enthusiasm to in turn create Dylan converts, whether early in their music fandom or decades into it. Either way, right on time. I must wrap this up as I have six decades of Dylan to catch up on: I'm entering my Basement Snapes era.

31 JANUARY

'My memories are crushed and buried': a long walk home in Gaza

MALAK A TANTESH

When the ceasefire came, there was a moment of relief that we had escaped death, although we still carry the sadness and pain of everything lost in those 15 months.

Palestinians know that there are still more battles ahead, they have to keep fighting, in a war of daily suffering — the fight for water, for a loaf of bread — and a war against memories, that bring pain to the heart and madness to the mind.

Still, I woke up full of energy and excitement on Sunday, the day we had been told we could begin returning to the north. I knew the journey would be exhausting, walking long distances on broken roads crowded with other displaced people, but I was eager to return to my beloved home.

I followed the news minute by minute, waiting for the announcement that the crossing would open. Instead, we got news that it would not happen.

I went to bed that day thinking about all the people who went to the checkpoint early Saturday night so they could be the first to return. Many had sold their tents to afford the journey back, or even burned their tents out of excitement that they were finally leaving behind life in those camps.

So they had no shelter that night, and slept in the freezing cold, waiting anxiously for the next morning, hoping their dreams would not be crushed again.

When the announcement came on Monday that the road was open, I felt I could have flown away with joy. We got dressed, packed our bags, and drove as close to the checkpoint as we could get.

As we approached on foot, we were drawn into a crowd so big it felt like an endless river of human beings. If you looked back or forward, you could see only the same torrent of people trudging north. We would walk for 11 hours, covering 15 kilometres.

Everyone was very tired, and weighed down with the few possessions they had saved from the war, but the passion to return drove them forward. Our longing to see our homes, even if they were destroyed, was stronger than our exhaustion, and kept our tired legs moving.

Clouds of dust stamped up by the passing crowds covered our faces, settling on every strand of hair, turning my eyelashes from black to grey. It felt almost comic, but around me there were so many heartbreaking scenes.

Men with children on their shoulders struggled to carry or drag heavy belongings that were all they had saved from the war. Old people in wheelchairs jolted painfully for miles over the ruts of a destroyed road. Others who needed support but no longer had it collapsed in the middle of the road.

I saw one man weeping over the body of his elderly father, who had insisted on trying to return despite poor health. The journey killed him. Elsewhere, children who had been separated from families in the crush cried for their parents, while a father searched frantically for his son.

As we approached Gaza City, Rashid Street was so full of people trying to return that the crowd seemed to have filled it and then come to a stop. So we turned off towards the beach where we used to go to relax, walking on the solid sand near the water with hundreds of other people.

The beach was clean and beautiful, so we took breaks every now and then. In the late afternoon, we ate cucumber, cheese bread and avocado that our mother had packed, looking at the sea. Our water had run out some time earlier.

After finishing the meal, we continued our journey, finally reaching Gaza City, where big crowds of people had gathered to wait for their loved ones.

The sun was setting, and its reflected light turned the sad, ruined buildings orange. It was strangely beautiful, converting Gaza into a piece of art that only the people who lived there could appreciate.

We hoped to find a car to drive us the final stretch of the journey, but the few on the streets were already full, or the drivers were waiting for their own families.

So we carried on walking through Gaza's Rimal neighbourhood, which used to be a fancy enclave for the city's rich. Now it was a ghost town, with an army of displaced people grey with dust tramping through its streets in exhausted silence.

We kept looking for a car, but it was a hopeless search. The only one that stopped asked 30 times the usual fare, more than we could afford. So we kept walking.

We reached our home town, Beit Lahia, in the farthest north, when night had already fallen. My feet and shoulders ached, and even in the darkness I saw glimpses of the destruction all around, but despite everything I was incredibly happy.

We headed straight to my maternal grandfather's house, which was still standing, although it was damaged and coated in dust and graffiti from Israeli soldiers. There were empty boxes of ammunition and bullets everywhere. We watched our steps when moving around, as unexploded bombs are a big worry for everyone here.

When we woke the next day we went for a walk, and although I have been covering Israeli attacks for months, the scale of the destruction was overwhelming.

People were searching through the rubble of their homes, looking for clothes, photographs or other scraps of memories of their lives before the war, tools and utensils that may still be usable.

I ran into friends and neighbours who I had not seen since the start of the war. All around there were families embracing, the hugs and kisses of longed-for reunions.

We decided to visit our own home for the first time since the war started. I grew up in this area but it had been so devastated, buildings and streets and gardens bombed and demolished, that we could no longer find our way to the house. We were wandering, lost and confused, when a neighbour appeared and guided us.

The only things still standing were the trunks of a walnut tree, and some olive trees that used to be in our yard. Seeing them there, surrounded only by rubble, I felt like I had been stabbed in my heart.

Our home was a three-storey building, and the levels had collapsed on top of each other like layers in a cake. I walked around and over the ruins to see if there was a way in, to recover anything from our life. It was dangerous but our memories deserve it.

I couldn't find even the smallest hole. Nothing had survived. My memories, my family's memories and everything we owned have all been crushed and buried.

2 FEBRUARY

Fighting for justice doesn't have to be a big dramatic act. It can be small

REBECCA SOLNIT

All those lists and instructions and editorials on how to resist authoritarianism and stand up for human rights, the rule of law and climate are good, and I both wholly support them and want to veer off from their recommendations here. Yes, everyone with any capacity to do so should join things, call politicians, support the groups and campaigns protecting the above. But it's important to not limit our sense of what resistance looks like to these versions of doing something. In addition to these formal, structured ways of defending what you believe in, there are ways of doing so woven into everyday life and our conversations and communications.

Each of us needs to stand on principle, loudly, whenever, wherever we can. Used strategically, our voices can do a lot to preserve anti-authoritarian worldviews about facts, science, history, rights, justice and inclusion. In this moment, it matters to just be a person who, wherever the opportunity arises, affirms that the climate crisis is real and climate solutions benefit us all, immigrants are vital to our economy and their rights matter, trans people harm no one by their existence but face terrible harm, diversity strengthens enterprises and communities and our country, women's rights and equality should be non-negotiable.

Right now, already, in many institutions and communities, there's pressure to shut up and toe the Trump line. Every person who doesn't do so makes it easier and safer and more encouraging for others to likewise dissent. That is, the more we stand up, the more others will stand up too; by standing up you're inviting others to join you, making it safer to be a dissenter, and those not ready to join you will maybe question their facts or fear or allegiance to the Trump agenda. You may find yourself in a position of being the first to dissent, or circumstances in which you join that first or third or 30th dissenter. Or you may speak up for someone who didn't exactly dissent except by being a category of person under attack.

The more we stand up, the harder it is for this authoritarian agenda to succeed and the more uncomfortable we make it for those going along with the lies and the cruelty. The huge and furious backlash against the National Cathedral's bishop Mariann Budde for just saying some pretty normal Christian things about God's mercy toward the most vulnerable is evidence that the Trump team and its followers expect to be flattered and groveled before and are not very good at coping with even an admonition to be kind.

Something that should be said more often is that the reason authoritarians are authoritarians is that they're unpopular. They have to use the threat of force along with intimidation and suppression tactics to get their way. They endeavor to scare people into obeying, whether or not they agree, and not being scared and not obeying helps demonstrate how finite their power is and how much of ours remains even in the bleakest circumstances.

Call lies lies, call cruelty cruelty, call fascism fascism, call violations of the constitution and human rights by their true names. Be loud (when you can; I'm not saying get into bar fights or cornered by gangs of Nazis, and you're a better judge of how to negotiate your family get-togethers than I am). Get on top of the facts you need to make your case. But beware of arguments. There's nothing to debate about whether or not women are people or fossil fuels cause many kinds of harm, and we're in an era when the most aggressive debaters are most liable to use bullying, ad hominem arguments, insults, untruths and misinformation, bait-and-switch tactics, and the rest of the arsenal of bad-faith discourse. Standing your ideological ground doesn't mean wrestling verbally with strangers and slimebags.

We've seen people rich and powerful enough to stand on principle cave and kiss the ring, seen huge corporations who likewise have the resources to have some integrity knuckle under, seen universities choose to veer right to please the incoming president, seen news organizations soften up outrageous violations and cruelty with bland and evasive language.

They're cowards. They've chosen craven advantage over courageous principle. But they alone cannot legitimize and normalize this regime. What will normalize it is if we all go along with it. Not going along with it, not pretending this is normal, not pretending human rights violations are anything but, not forgetting that the regime is attempting to make epic and unprecedented changes that dismantle our democracy: that's up to us. Not only with how we organize and act, but how we talk and how boldly we talk.

I learned something new about animal behavior last week, and it seems really timely. A reindeer cyclone is when a herd of reindeer facing a predator put the calves in the center and whirl around fast, making it difficult to impossible for the predator to pick off one reindeer. The more of us who speak up the harder it will be to persecute any single person who says trans rights are human rights or what's being done to immigrants is terrorism. It's not the only example from the animals. When threatened, musk oxen likewise circle up, facing outward with their huge horns, calves again in the middle of the ring.

Some say that murmurations — those beautiful flights of thousands of starlings undulating and pulsating as they whirl through the sky together — create flocks that are hard for predators to attack. There's safety in numbers, which is why a lot of prey animals move in herds and flocks and schools. For those who dissent from what this new administration intends to do, we may sometimes be able to surround an ICE van or march by the thousands, but every time we dissent we make room for others to dissent. Courage, like fear, is contagious. For a lot of us, right now, we get to choose, and what we choose has an impact on what others choose.

22 FEBRUARY

'No matter what you go through, there's always hope'

SIMON HATTENSTONE

The first thing I notice about Esther Ghey is a blossom tree trailing down her left arm to her hand. There is one pink flower on the tattoo. Pink was her daughter Brianna's favourite colour. If Brianna had got her way, the whole world would have been pink. And just after she was murdered by two teenage schoolchildren in February 2023, Ghey says, the world did briefly turn pink. The local blossom trees filled with the blossomiest blossom she had ever seen. 'It really felt she was with us and that she was sending us a sign she was OK,' she says.

Now Ghey has written a book, *Under a Pink Sky*. It's a memoir of her and Brianna's lives, and a manifesto of sorts; a shocking exploration of how deadly smartphones and online spaces can be. It's also one of the most unflinching, inspirational autobiographies I've read, a remarkable cry of hope from the depths of despair.

Brianna, a transgender girl of 16, was groomed by another teenage girl, who was desperate to kill. It could have been anybody; she just wanted the experience of cold-blooded murder. But the girl became obsessed with Brianna – partly because she was trans. The girl and her male friend lured Brianna out with the promise of taking cocaine, which Brianna had never tried, then stabbed her multiple times. In *Under a Pink Sky*, Ghey doesn't mention the killers by name, so I won't. But she does name the mother of the girl, for a good reason. They have become friends.

Ghey emerged from the horror of Brianna's murder as a hero. She appeared on television and talked movingly about the need for forgiveness. This young mother from Warrington, still only in her late 30s and going through the worst of the worst, came across as extraordinarily together. But the truth, for much of her life, couldn't have been more different. As a young woman, Ghey was a drug-addled wreck who struggled so much as a mum that her own mother called social services because she was worried for her daughter and her two young grandchildren.

We meet in a hotel in Warrington, close to where she lives. Her warmth shines through immediately. As does the trauma. It's the first lengthy interview she's given about the book, and she warns me she's going to find it tough. She apologises for her tears in advance.

In a way, *Under a Pink Sky* is the story of two troubled kids – only one of whom survived to tell their story. Ghey says there are so many parallels between her early life and Brianna's. As a teenager, Esther Ghey was caught in a web of self-loathing. She had body dysmorphia, was desperate to be thinner, and told herself that nobody would ever love her the way she was. At times she was bullied; sometimes she picked on other children. Then she found drugs. She left school at 16 with no qualifications. 'I had no self-worth because of that. I had no respect for myself, no respect for my body, no respect for my life, and that is such a sad, tragic, horrific place to be.'

Brianna would go on to struggle with many of the same things: self-belief, school attendance, bullying. And while she was never hooked on drugs, Brianna was addicted to her smartphone and social media.

By the age of 20, Ghey was a single parent to two young children. She managed to get a house, hoped to make it a 'safe haven' for her and her children, and failed miserably. She remembers buying a load of teal paint and telling herself she was going to make her home perfect. 'It turned out to be one of the worst times of my life. I beat myself up about it a lot because I had become addicted to drugs and my house never got finished. That teal paint just turned into sludge.'

How serious was her drug problem? 'It was a really serious addiction. I hit rock bottom.' What was her drug of choice? 'Amphetamines. Yeah.' She pauses. 'And everything I could get my hands on, really. My life was absolute turmoil. A mess. People might look at me and think, "She's got her head screwed on," but it's not always been like that.'

Then her mother, a teacher and foster carer at the time, called social services. 'My mum helped as much as possible, but she had five foster children and felt completely helpless. Fortunately for me, social services came in and we had all the basic things we needed.' And she really is talking about basics — bread, milk, light and heat. 'And they decided they weren't going to take the children. That for me was a massive wake-up call.'

. . .

Esther Ghey did turn her life around. And how. In her late 20s, now clean and a devoted mother, she started with a job as a cleaner at a car dealership before going back to college, initially doing an English GCSE. She did an access to health professions course, because at the time she wanted to be a nurse, completed a degree in nutrition at Liverpool Hope University, and eventually became a senior product development technologist for a food company.

Now 38, Ghey's face is freckled and open, her eyes sea-blue, and she looks exceptionally healthy. She has two names tattooed on her wrists, celebrating the births of her children. On her right hand, it says Alisha in smudgy black ink; on the left, it says Brett. For 14 years of Brianna's life, she was Brett. Through the book, Ghey makes a clear distinction. She refers to Brett as he, Brianna as she. Does it seem like two different people? 'It does, though that's not necessarily because she went from Brett to Brianna, it's just the natural stages of life. It was important for me to talk about Brett as well, because to understand where Brianna was at, you need to understand the whole life.'

What was Brett like? Her face lights up and her voice crackles with happiness. 'Hyperactive, giddy, funny, always getting up to mischief. A cheeky little thing. Absolutely fearless. He taught himself gymnastics – he did backflips. I think of him bouncing around Asda, completely uncontrollable but also completely full of joy. And so kind. When he was young, he had an asthma appointment and as he was leaving he went to give the doctor a hug. He was so full of love. That kind of love started seeping away once I'd given him the phone. The impact the phone had on his mental health is stark. I believe it took my child away from me.' There's a tremor in her voice, and Ghey starts crying.

Brett had so many issues, she says – body dysmorphia and dysphoria, asthma, ADHD, appalling eyesight, autism (then undiagnosed). There were times when he couldn't face school and was a non-attender. At the age of 14, Brett explained that he wanted to transition. Ghey took it in her stride. In the book, she writes: 'When the transition happened for Brianna it was perhaps one of the easiest parts of her short life.' Brett wanted the new name to start with a B. They drew up a list — Bella, Bridget, Britney, Blossom, Briony, Bree. Blossom was ruled out because Alisha thought it sounded like a stripper's name, while both Alisha and Ghey said there was no way they would call her Britney. When Ghey suggested Brianna, Brett liked it. And that was that.

Brianna was given a smartphone when she started high school. It hadn't been a big thing for her older sister Alisha — just a way of keeping in touch with her mum, checking stuff online and playing a few games. For Brianna, it couldn't have been more different. She escaped into the online world and soon found herself lost and trapped. Ghey documents the descent with chilling precision in her book. At first, Ghey would take the phone away overnight and check for any worrying activity. But by the time Brianna was a teenager, she refused to let her mother see what she was doing.

Ghey already felt her child had been spending too much time on the phone. As Brianna, she started making YouTube videos — dancing and natural makeup tutorials for fellow schoolkids. Ghey didn't like the negative comments, and she worried that the videos Brianna was making were being watched by adults with very different agendas.

'I remember in the comments there was a grown woman saying, "Do you call *that* natural makeup?" and I thought, "Why would you comment on a child's video?" I said, "Brianna, why are you even putting yourself out there to receive these comments?" Her response was, "Have you seen how many likes I've got, though?" It's that dopamine hit when you get likes.'

Brianna was a mass of contradictions: desperate for attention in the digital world, but terrified of the real world. At times she wouldn't leave the family home for weeks on end. In one way, she craved anonymity and invisibility, yet she turned up at school in miniskirts, dolled up to the nines.

After one particularly vicious fight over the phone, Ghey discovered that Brianna, then 14, was secretly looking at pornography on X (at that time Twitter) and pro-anorexia and self-harm content online. Her role model was a girl who was denying herself food, in essence teaching other people to copy her and kill themselves in the process. Although Brianna met her killers in the real world − at school − it was the online world that had made her so reckless and vulnerable to exploitation in the first place. The more Brianna looked for harmful content, the more the algorithms served it up to her. And the more Ghey challenged Brianna about it, the more angry and withdrawn she became.

'My relationship with Brianna was so bad because all I wanted to do was help her, but because I wasn't backing down, we were having lots of arguments.' Brianna became abusive and violent. When Ghey confiscated her phone, she punched holes in her bedroom walls. 'I saw how addicted she was to her phone through her behaviour,' Ghey says, 'because I've been through it myself. Smartphones have been built to be addictive. Social media is built to keep you on there as long as possible. It's the attention economy.'

On the rare occasions Ghey did get access to Brianna's phone, she was sickened by what she found. But she didn't know what to do for the better. 'I've got a child who's isolating herself from the real world, and she's found a community online and is accessing harmful stuff. How are you as a parent supposed to manage that? Am I supposed to isolate her even more and take her away from social media, or do I let her still be subject to the harmful content that she's looking at? What's going to harm her less?' What is the answer? 'There is no answer. The health professionals didn't have an answer, the schools didn't have an answer, nobody knew what to do.'

On one occasion Ghey got up in the middle of the night and saw the light on in Brianna's room. 'I opened her door and she was sat behind the door on her phone. I couldn't get back to sleep and I wrote this frantic email to an amazing supportive teacher. I said, "I am worried that I'm going to come home and find both of my children raped and murdered" because I didn't know who Brianna was talking to online. She was 15. I was concerned she was going to bring something dangerous to the house.'

· · ·

Brianna lost so much weight in her last year that she had to be hospitalised. Ghey was devastated. Now she finds it equally devastating to admit that Brianna's time in hospital was one of their happiest times as mother and daughter in the final two years of her life. Brianna was not allowed access to social media in hospital and, for once, Ghey found herself able to talk to her as they used to do. 'She had her own room, and I'd go to see her every day and she had no wifi. It was like I had my child back again. She'd send me text messages, and she was so goofy and funny. She'd say, "I love you and want you to come and see me." She wasn't being influenced by anything. She was stripped back — it was pure Brianna.' She wipes her eyes and exhales loudly. '*Pppprrrr.*'

When she got home, things quickly deteriorated again. Brianna retreated to her bedroom with only her smartphone for company. She asked Ghey to stop telling her that she loved her. It shattered her, but she agreed.

Meanwhile, the girl who went on to murder Brianna was also delving into the darkness of the web. Initially, she became fixated with true crime. But before long that wasn't enough. She found websites that offered up live abuse. Soon, she vowed to become a killer herself. She and her male accomplice discussed ways of killing people. They drew up a list of potential victims before deciding on Brianna. One time they tried to kill her with an ibuprofen overdose, telling her that it was MDMA. Brianna was violently sick, but survived. The girl voiced her frustration in a text message to the boy: 'Like I gave her some today that shld have been enough to kill her but she didn't die.' The boy suggested she double the dose and put it in a 'Maccies milkshake'. Eventually, they decided to kill Brianna with a hunting knife he had bought on a skiing trip to Bulgaria that Christmas. He posted a picture of the knife, with its 5-inch blade, on a WhatsApp group. Everything about the murder was evidenced on their smartphones.

Brianna agreed to meet the two killers, who were 15 at the time, in Culcheth, near Warrington, on 11 February 2023. They met at a bus stop and walked to an isolated area in nearby Linear Park. Brianna was stabbed 28 times with the hunting knife. In court, the girl and boy each blamed the other for the murder.

During the trial at Manchester crown court, the Crown Prosecution Service put forward evidence suggesting the killing was a hate crime, including WhatsApp messages that used dehumanising language to describe Brianna. At sentencing last February, the judge, Mrs Justice Yip, lifted the reporting restriction that had prevented the media from naming the two defendants and sentenced them to life in prison. The girl was told she would be jailed for a minimum of 22 years, the boy a minimum of 20. The lengthy sentences reflected that the murder was in part motivated by hostility towards Brianna because she was trans.

Outside court, after the guilty verdicts were announced, Ghey said the killers had not shown 'an ounce of remorse', but urged 'empathy and compassion' for their parents, saying 'they too have lost a child'. I ask Ghey why she chose not to name the killers in *Under a Pink Sky*. 'The girl wanted to be infamous for the crime she committed, and this is about my life and Brianna's life, and it's not about them.' Since being jailed, the girl has expressed a further desire to kill people.

After Brianna's death, there was an outpouring of love for her and Ghey. And then the trolling began. Ghey and Brianna both became pawns in the culture wars. Some people suggested that Ghey had been a bad parent for allowing Brianna to transition. One Facebook comment said, 'Your son died because you failed him. You're a failure.' A tribute page to Brianna set up by the funeral directors was defiled. Was Ghey shocked? 'I wouldn't say I was shocked or surprised at being trolled, but it disgusted me. It really knocked me, especially with Brianna's tribute page. It was flooded with horrific images.' She stops, and changes her mind. 'I say it didn't shock me, but it did, because I didn't think anybody would ever stoop that low. Initially, I felt I didn't want to do anything ever again. I didn't want to put myself in the public eye, I didn't want to campaign, I wanted to curl up in a ball at home.' But, she says, she knew she couldn't. She had a mission. She had to make Brianna's murder count for something.

Lots of people who have been through what you have would still be curled up in a ball, two years on, I say. She nods. 'If they were, it would be completely understandable.' Ghey says that in the past when things were bleak, she was helped by mindfulness — the practice of being fully aware of where you are and what you're doing in the moment to distract from past trauma and fears for the future. This time she believes it saved her. If she focuses on the present, she says, she can make the most of her life. If she wallows in the past, she'll be screwed. She now works with Alisha at Peace & Mind, a community interest company she founded to raise funds to teach mindfulness in schools.

People might expect her to drape herself in sackcloth and ashes, she says, but that is not her way. 'In our society, when you've lost somebody, particularly in a tragic situation, it's almost like you have to grieve for the rest of your life — you can never be happy, you should never smile and never laugh. It's so wrong! You still owe it to yourself to be happy, and whoever you've lost to be happy. I choose not to think about what happened to Brianna.

I choose to think about who she was. The good parts and the bad parts, and that brings me joy.'

'What image does she have of Brianna when she closes her eyes? 'Ah!' She closes them and smiles. 'Honestly? She just had these pyjama bottoms that she would never take off. They were pink fluffy pyjama bottoms and they had stains on them and holes in them, and she had this Barbie T-shirt. As soon as she got in the house, her makeup would come off, those would go on and she would just be walking around the house giving me grief, winding her sister up or making silly noises.' What kind of silly noises? 'I don't know where she got this from, but she would always go, "Ana oop ana poop ana scoop." I've got her ashes in a necklace and on the back, it says "Ana oop. Brianna."' Brianna was dressed in the pink pyjamas for her funeral.

. . .

Ghey says that writing the book has been both painful and cathartic. What does she want people to get out of it? First of all, she says, she would like us to get to know the true Brianna — and the true Esther. But she also hopes it raises awareness of how dangerous smartphones and online platforms can be for children and young people. If tech companies wanted to make their products safer, it would be easy, she says. 'We need phones that are built for children, where by design they can't download social media apps, can't access porn sites or anything harmful. Cars are safe by design, with seatbelts, and we need the same for children with smartphones.'

Earlier this month, Microsoft founder Bill Gates said he thought Australia's recent legislation to ban social media for children under 16 was a good idea. This is something Ghey agrees with. And if the tech companies and digital platforms don't do their bit, and if governments fail to regulate, Ghey says, parents can always vote with their feet and refuse to buy smartphones for their children. She supports pressure groups such as Smartphone Free Childhood, and Bereaved Families for Online Safety.

The book is powerful as a polemic, but where it astounds is as an exploration of forgiveness and hope. Ghey not only examines her capacity to forgive, but also her capacity to be forgiven. She writes about a girl she taunted and bullied at school, and says it haunted her down the years. 'This lovely, lovely girl I knew in primary school, and I used to be horrid to her and pick on her,' she says today. The hurt she caused the girl still distresses her. 'This was something I couldn't let go. It was always in my mind. She was clearly struggling, but as a child I don't think you have that empathy to understand what's going on in other people's lives.' In her 20s, she contacted the girl on Facebook and they agreed to meet up. 'I asked for her forgiveness, and she so graciously accepted it, and that taught me such a lot. The fact that she forgave me meant that I could forgive myself.'

She says that only by forgiving Brianna's killers has she been able to move on with her own life. 'It was important to forgive the girl and boy for what they've done because, if I didn't forgive them, I would hold that hate in my heart and it would eat away at me. They've already taken Brianna away from me and I refuse to let them impact the rest of my life.'

Did she feel the need to forgive herself in any way for Brianna's death? 'I think my whole life has been a journey of forgiving myself. Forgiving myself for the way I was with the children when I was young. Forgiving myself for treating myself badly. Soon after Brianna's death, there were all sorts of thoughts going through my mind: I shouldn't have shouted at her for this; I wish I hadn't treated her this way; I wish we'd never argued. But there's no way of going back and changing that, and feelings like that are so harmful.' However much Ghey says she has eased up on herself, she still gives herself a pretty tough time. 'I need to think what can I do to redeem myself, to make things better, and that's why I've got this drive to help other parents.' Ghey's words are so measured, but her face is raw with emotion, her voice at times reduced to a whisper.

I knew that Ghey had met up with the mother of the girl who killed Brianna. What I didn't know was the extent of the relationship they have developed. They now see each other almost every week. Ghey tells me they have so much in common — two mothers grieving for their daughters in different ways. 'It isn't Emma who committed the crime. As a parent, I went through such a difficult time trying to monitor Brianna and to keep on top of what she was accessing online. Brianna was harming herself, and Emma's daughter was harming herself and went on to harm someone else as well. There's no blame there at all for Emma. It's easy to tell ourselves stories in our head about how people are, and it was important for me to meet her and see how she actually was. And she's just a normal woman who was doing her best.'

Is it easier to talk to Emma about what happened to Brianna than to other people? 'We don't talk about what happened really. I really look forward to seeing her. We're quite similar and we've got a similar dry sense of humour.'

What does she think Brianna would make of their friendship? 'I don't think she'd be bothered. She'd be like, "You do you, Mum!"'

· · ·

Tuesday 11 February was the second anniversary of Brianna's death. She would have been 18 now. Does Ghey wonder how she would be doing if she hadn't been robbed of her life? 'I can only speak through my experience, and I came out of the terrible place I was in. I would have been hopeful that Brianna would have made it through, just the way I did.'

As for Ghey, she says she is adjusting to the new normal. The reduced family unit — Ghey, her husband, Wes, whom she's been with for 10 years, and Alisha — are as close as close can be. They see and hear Brianna all around them in pink skies and pink blossom, little jokes, funny sounds, tattoos, everything.

Just before Ghey leaves, she shows me the book cover: a blossom tree in full bloom and the shadow of a mother and her two daughters walking in the sun. It's beautiful and heart-breaking. As she flicks through the images on her phone, I ask her about the finely etched tattoos on her fingers. They are Buddhist symbols, she says, and she had them inked just before the trial. Which tattoo means most to her? She points to the names Alisha and Brett on her wrists, the cherry blossom with the single pink flower, and finally a gorgeous pink lotus. 'You know the lotus flower comes out of the murk and blooms?' She says it's an important symbol for her. 'No matter what shit you go through, there is always hope.'

27 FEBRUARY

The star of every scene he was in

PETER BRADSHAW

As the movie ends, our point of view pans slowly, relentlessly, back and forth like a security camera across the trashed apart-ment. It has been ripped apart floorboard by floorboard in a doomed attempt to find the bugging device spying on the guy who lives there. With every sweep, the man is seen in the corner, playing the sax. Fatalistic, but not exactly despairing; realistic but not precisely disillusioned — the craftsman who is an artist at heart, nonchalant, magnificent. Gene Hackman's performance as surveillance expert Harry Caul in Francis Coppola's para-noid conspiracy drama *The Conversation* (1974) was a jewel in his career. Caul is a pro eavesdropper who becomes obsessed with a conversation he records for a mysterious client that, to his horror, reveals a murder plot — unlocking his own private agonies of guilt and loneliness. The film turns on some vari-ants of intonation and pitch that Harry doesn't understand until it's too late.

The death of Gene Hackman marks the end of one of the greatest periods of US cinema: the American new wave. Hackman was the gold standard for this era, ever since Warren Beatty gave him his big break with the role of Buck Barrow in Arthur Penn's *Bonnie and Clyde* (1967). He was the character actor who was really a star; in fact the star of every scene he was in — that tough, wised-up, intelligent but unhandsome face perpetually on the verge of coolly unconcerned derision, or creased in a heartbreak-ingly fatherly, pained smile. He wasn't gorgeous like Redford or dangerously sexy like Nicholson, or even puckish like Hoffman; Hackman was normal, but his normality was steroidally super-charged. His hair was of its age: frizzy, with evident male-pattern baldness. You really don't get star haircuts like that any more.

He was unmissable as the reckless, racist cop Jimmy 'Popeye' Doyle in William Friedkin's *The French Connection* (1971) and its sequel; masterly as the Rev Scott in Ronald Neame's classic disaster pic *The Poseidon Adventure* (1972); superb as the ex-con in Jerry Schatzberg's Beckettian masterpiece *Scarecrow* (1973); and perhaps most unmissable as the weary, bewildered private eye in Penn's *Night Moves* (1975). Later, he would be a wittily cast Lex Luthor in the Christopher Reeve *Superman* movies, and then the mysterious plutocrat and self-made billionaire Jack McCann in Nicolas Roeg's *Eureka* (1983) — his performance in which surely inspired Daniel Day-Lewis in *There Will Be Blood*.

Hackman's career has so much gold in it that it is almost impossible to mine, but there was also his FBI agent Anderson in Alan Parker's *Mississippi Burning* (1988); his querulous movie director Lowell Kolchek in Mike Nichols's *Postcards from the Edge* (1990); and the careworn sheriff Bill Daggett in Clint Eastwood's western *Unforgiven* (1992); not to mention the smilingly mysterious senior lawyer opposite Tom Cruise's moon-faced newbie in *The Firm* (1993).

Then there's his late comic masterpiece — and maybe his flat-out masterpiece, full stop: Royal Tenenbaum in Wes Anderson's *The Royal Tenenbaums* (2001), the disbarred and penniless attorney who fakes stomach cancer so he can move back in with his ex-wife (an equally brilliant Anjelica Huston) and their grownup children, three eccentric, damaged former child prodigies played by Ben Stiller, Gwyneth Paltrow and Luke Wilson.

What is so extraordinary about these performances is that Hackman's age never seems to change: he always seems to be wiry, tough and somewhere in his 40s or 50s. The 'Royal Tenenbaum' Hackman could easily take the role of the 'Popeye Doyle' Hackman.

As the hardbitten cop in *The French Connection* — for which he won the best actor Oscar — Hackman has many unmissable scenes in which he does nothing but cruise vigilantly around town: the New York of the celluloid 1970s, which was sound-recorded on film so we get the distant, ambient wailing and fluttering of car horns. Hackman can do the deadpan, quotidian part of the performance as well as the action side of it: the racist barging into the Black bar, the roughing up of suspects, the angry and contemptuous denunciations, and the undercurrent of sadness. This was a performance that laid down the law for all the others he subsequently gave.

He was very different as Harry Moseby in *Night Moves*. Moseby is a private detective, with a great 70s moustache that exaggerates the downturn of his mouth, given the time-honoured job of tracking down a runaway teenaged daughter while also spying on the wife, but who stumbles on to a complicated mess, or tangle of messes, that he can never quite work out. The film gave him one of his greatest lines. When he turns down the chance to watch Eric Rohmer's *Ma Nuit Chez Maud*, he says: 'I saw a Rohmer film once. It was kinda like watching paint dry.' He delivers the cinephile laugh-line with throwaway expertise.

Quite as good is his performance in Roeg's underrated *Eureka*, a metaphysical murder mystery based on a true crime, which gives Hackman one of the best roles of his career: a wealthy prospector who strikes it rich and retires to the Bahamas, while fearing that his wealth is going to be taken away by his daughter (Theresa Russell) and a couple of rapacious, mobster investors from Miami (Joe Pesci and Mickey Rourke). Again, Hackman hits the key notes of amused defiance, unafraid and unconcerned about everything except the strange demons inside his own head.

In the end, I keep coming back to his performance in *The Royal Tenenbaums*, one that builds on his reputation for potent, unimpressed no-bullshit men but doesn't simply satirise or send up his former career. His tatty, double-breasted chalk-stripe suit, his cigarette in the holder, his glasses, his indomitable grin, even his slightly too long hair are all absolutely perfect — as is the moment when he finally has to swallow his pride and take a job at the Lindbergh Palace hotel, and wear the cheap-looking but strangely well-tailored uniform and cap. His line readings are perfection, especially when he talks to his bewildered grandchildren about their mother, his daughter-in-law, who has died in a plane crash: 'Your mother was a terribly attractive woman.'

It doesn't make sense to call Hackman unassuming when his presence was so potent; in some ways he conveyed the strength of a retired athlete turned sportscaster, or, for that matter, the high-school basketball coach he played in *Hoosiers* (1986). For four decades, the performances of Gene Hackman gave form and texture to American cinema.

28 FEBRUARY

Diplomacy dies on live TV as Trump and Vance gang up to bully Ukraine leader

DAVID SMITH

'This is going to be great television,' Donald Trump remarked at the end. Sure. And as they slipped into the icy depths, the captain of the *Titanic* probably assured his passengers that this would make a great movie some day.

Trump on Friday presided over one of the greatest diplomatic disasters in modern history. Tempers flared, voices were raised and protocol was shredded in the once-hallowed Oval Office. As Trump got into a shouting match with Ukraine's Volodymyr Zelenskyy, a horrified Europe watched the post-Second World War order crumble before its eyes.

Never has a US president bullied and berated an adversary, still less an ally, in such a public way. Of course the reality TV star and wrestling fan turned US president had it all play out on television for the benefit of his populist support base – and a certain bare-chested chum in the Kremlin.

Zelenskyy came to the White House to sign a deal for US involvement in Ukraine's mineral industry to pave the way for an end to the three-year war. The president has inspired many by refusing to flee Kyiv when Russia launched its invasion — 'I need ammunition, not a ride' — delivering nightly addresses to rally his people and visiting his troops on the frontlines.

But Trump, a profile in courage who dodged military service in Vietnam because of alleged bone spurs and who hid in the White House during the 6 January 2021 riot, has reportedly described soldiers who die in combat as suckers and losers. He was impeached for trying to strong-arm Zelenskyy in 2019 and last week called him a dictator.

There was a hint of trouble to come when Zelenskyy arrived at the West Wing wearing a dark, long-sleeved shirt — not a suit — and Trump greeted him with a handshake and sarcasm: 'Wow, look, you're all dressed up!'

Inside the Oval Office, which has seen much but never anything quite like this, Zelenskyy thanked Trump for the invitation. At first all was sweetness and light as they fielded questions from reporters.

There was a minor wrinkle over how much support Europe has given Ukraine, which ended with smiles, a playful but pointed tap on Zelenskyy, and ominous words from Trump: 'Don't argue with me.'

But the last 10 minutes of the nearly 45-minute meeting devolved into acrimony and chaos. Zelenskyy found himself ambushed by Trump and his serpentine vice-president, JD Vance. He was expected to sit back and take a beating from Nurse Ratched and Miss Trunchbull. He refused.

Exuding preternatural obnoxiousness, Vance said Joe Biden's approach had failed and that diplomacy was the way forward. Noting Russia's betrayals of trust in the past, Zelenskyy challenged: 'What kind of diplomacy, JD, you are speaking about? What do you mean?'

Vance, who once declared he didn't care what happened in Ukraine, was riled. Finger jabbing, he lectured Zelenskyy:

'I think it's disrespectful for you to come into the Oval Office to try to litigate this in front of the American media ... You should be thanking the president for trying to bring an end to this conflict.'

Uh-oh. The politicians and journalists in the room could surely tell this was going off the rails. At one point the Ukrainian ambassador would put her head in her hands. She was all of us.

Zelenskyy tried to push back, asking if Vance had ever been to Ukraine. Vance got angry and spoke of 'propaganda tours'. Zelenskyy tried to answer and suggest that the US could feel threatened by Russia some day. Trump interjected: 'Don't tell us what we're going to feel.'

The men spoke over each other. Raising his voice, the US president said: 'You're not in a good position. You don't have the cards right now.'

Zelenskyy responded: 'I'm not playing cards. I'm very serious, Mr President. I'm the president in a war.'

Trump, pointing an accusing finger and descending into his worst self from the presidential debates, admonished: 'You're gambling with the lives of millions of people. You're gambling with World War Three and what you're doing is very disrespectful to the country, this country that's backed you far more than a lot of people say they should have.'

TV pro tip: Trump has spent so many campaign rallies warning about World War Three that the phrase has lost its shock value.

Trump and Vance tried to scold Zelenskyy like an ungrateful child. Vance — who recently went to Munich to condemn Europe as being on the wrong side in the culture wars — demanded: 'Have you said "thank you" once this entire meeting? No.'

Zelenskyy tried to respond. Trump told him his country was in big trouble. He went on: 'The problem is I've empowered you to be a tough guy and I don't think you'd be a tough guy without the United States and your people are very brave. But, you're either going to make a deal or we're out.

'And if we're out, you'll fight it out and I don't think it's going to be pretty … But you're not acting at all thankful, and that's not a nice thing.'

How sharper than a serpent's tooth it is to have a thankless ally!

Zelenskyy looked shellshocked. Trump, the eternal showman, commented on what great TV it would be, then wrote on social media that Zelenskyy 'disrespected the United States of America in its cherished Oval Office'.

No deal was done. A planned press conference was cancelled. Zelenskyy drove away empty-handed, having just endured his own diplomatic Chornobyl. As for the rest of Europe, a bust of Winston Churchill, looming over the shoulders of Trump and Vance, may have shed a tear or two.

7 MARCH

Trump is turning America into a mafia state

JONATHAN FREEDLAND

Behold Donald Corleone, the US president who behaves like a mafia boss — but without the principles. Of course, one hesitates to make the comparison, not least because Donald Trump would like it. And because the Godfather is an archetype of strength and macho glamour while Trump is weak, constantly handing gifts to America's enemies and getting nothing in return. But when the world is changing so fast — when a nation that has been a friend for more than a century turns into a foe in a matter of weeks — it helps to have a guide. My colleague Luke Harding clarified the nature of Vladimir Putin's Russia when he branded it the Mafia State. Now we need to attach the same label to the US under Putin's most devoted admirer.

Consider the way Trump's White House conducts itself, issuing threats and menaces that sound better in the original Sicilian. This week the president said that a deal ending Russia's war on Ukraine 'could be made very fast' but 'if somebody doesn't want to make a deal, I think that person won't be around very long'. You didn't need a translator to know that the somebody he had in mind was Volodymyr Zelenskyy.

On Thursday, Trump was confident that the Ukrainians would soon do his bidding 'because I don't think they have a choice'. Almost as if he had made them an offer they couldn't refuse. Which of course he had. By ending the supply of military aid and the sharing of US intelligence, as he did this week, he had effectively put a Russian revolver to Ukraine's temple, its imprint scarcely reduced by Trump's declaration today that he is 'strongly considering' banking sanctions and tariffs against Moscow, a move that looked a lot like a man pretending to be equally tough on the two sides, but which should fool nobody. He expects Zelenskyy to sign away a huge chunk of Ukraine's minerals, the way Corleone's rivals surrendered their livelihoods to save their lives.

This is how the US now operates in the world. Dispensing with the formalities during his annual address to Congress on Tuesday, Trump repeated his threat to grab Greenland: 'One way or the other, we're going to get it.' That recalled his earlier warning to Copenhagen to give him what he wants or face the consequences: 'maybe things have to happen with respect to Denmark having to do with tariffs'. Nice place you got there; would be a shame if something happened to it.

It's the same shakedown he's performing on the US's northern neighbour. Canada's outgoing prime minister Justin Trudeau spelled it out this week, accusing Trump of trying to engineer 'a total collapse of the Canadian economy because that will make it easier to annex us', adding that: 'We will never be the 51st state.' It's a technique familiar in the darker corners of the New Jersey construction industry: a series of unfortunate fires that only stops when a recalcitrant competitor submits.

Both the substance and the style are pure mafia. Note the obsession with respect, demonstrated in last week's Oval Office confrontation with Zelenskyy. Between them, JD Vance and Trump accused the Ukrainian leader three times of showing disrespect, sounding less like world leaders than touchy Tommy DeVito, the Joe Pesci character in *Goodfellas*.

Note too the humiliation of subordinates. In his address to Congress, the president introduced secretary of state Marco Rubio as the man charged with taking back the Panama canal. 'Good luck, Marco,' said Trump, with a chuckle. 'Now we know who to blame if anything goes wrong.' Cue anxious laughter from the rest of the underlings, briefly relieved that it wasn't them.

It's hard for aides and opponents alike to keep up because power is exercised arbitrarily and inconsistently. Tariffs are imposed, then suspended. Indeed, one reason why import taxes so appeal to Trump is that they can be enforced instantly and by presidential edict. That extends to the exemptions Trump can offer to favoured US industries. As MSNBC's Chris Hayes observed: 'This is very obviously going to be a protection racket, where Trump can at the stroke of a pen destroy or save your business depending on how compliant you are.'

Because, naturally, Trumpism does not confine the Cosa Nostra tactics to foreign affairs. This week Reuters reported that several federal judges in the Washington DC area had received pizzas sent anonymously to their homes, a gesture that police interpreted as 'a form of intimidation meant to convey that a target's address is known'. Already rattled by a fusillade of posts from Elon Musk denouncing as 'corrupt' and 'evil' those judges who have stood in the way of his ongoing demolition of large swathes of the federal government, the judiciary is now fearful for its safety. 'I've never seen judges as uneasy as they are now,' said John Jones, who retired from the bench in 2021.

Whether neutering the judges — 'Thank you again, I won't forget,' Trump told John Roberts, chief justice of the supreme court, as he slapped him on the back this week — or moving to control the press, it's all straight out of the Corleone playbook. The effect has been remarkably swift, with a strange silence falling on America's public square. One Democratic congressman says Republican colleagues have told him they won't criticise Trump because they worry for their physical safety and that of their families.

But it's not just politicians. 'University presidents fearing that millions of dollars in federal funding could disappear are holding their fire. Chief executives alarmed by tariffs that could hurt their businesses are on mute,' according to the *New York Times*, which again cited the growing anxiety among would-be critics that online attacks from Musk and Trump could lead to violent assaults on themselves or their loved ones.

All this protects Trump, encouraging him to ape the corruption and callousness of a mafia don. See how blatantly he now charges individuals to dine with him at Mar-a-Lago: $5 million for a one-on-one, $1 million to be part of a group. In case you didn't get the message, Trump has announced that the US will no longer enforce the Foreign Corrupt Practices Act, which prohibited Americans from bribing foreign officials, while his attorney general has dissolved all of the kleptocracy-related task forces at the Department of Justice. As for callousness, note Musk's glee at feeding the US agency for international development 'into the wood chipper', thereby ensuring death comes to the sick and the starving who relied on US medicine and food.

At least the Corleones were guided by their own supposed code of honour. They believed an act of service had to be remembered and, in time, reciprocated. But Trump has gone to court rather than pay suppliers for work already done for the US government and has no memory of those to whom the US owes a much greater debt. How else could his vice-president so glibly forget the blood spilled by America's allies, including the UK, when he dismissed the offer of '20,000 troops from some random country that has not fought a war in 30 or 40 years'?

These are despicable people, lacking even the morality of the hoodlum — and now they run the country we have regarded as our closest friend since the Edwardian age. Given all that, of course British politics should be contemplating a radical new direction, whether that means an economy rewired for rearmament or a rapprochement with the European Union, given that the world of the Brexit vote of 2016 has vanished and to stand apart from our nearest neighbours is now not only stupid but dangerous. When the planet's most powerful country has become a mafia state, you do whatever it takes.

11 MARCH

Farage v Lowe: pick a zealot, any old zealot

MARINA HYDE

How soon before one of Reform's MPs starts touting himself as the reform Reform candidate? A negative amount of time, it seems, with Great Yarmouth MP Rupert Lowe already relieved of the whip for saying that Reform is currently 'a protest party led by the Messiah'. Yep: Jesus Christ Superkings.

Anyway, Nigel Farage has taken all this as well as you might expect. In terms of what's happened since, with even Nigel judging that 'things have got a little bit out of control', I'm finding it quite hard to immerse myself fully in every angle. Mainly because I'm worried it's going to be one of those stories that demeans men — and I'm a passionate supporter of their involvement in politics, whatever people are saying about DEI nowadays.

But the broad brush of it is: a party leader who wants to be PM is too much of an egomaniac to even handle having some MPs; some of his people who hate lawyers have called in the lawyers; some of his people who love free speech have been upset by some words; and some of his people who hate snow-flakes have gone to the actual police about what they say is a bit of verbal. Then again, there is an alternative broad brush: Lowe is an old Radleian who admires Tommy Robinson; meanwhile, Elon Musk — a man who owns X but apparently has no access to Google — now thinks Rupert is the fairest of them all and that Nigel 'doesn't have what it takes'. In fact, according to a report in Tuesday's *Financial Times*, Elon Musk's allies suggest he would financially back a credible alternative party to Reform.

All this has outraged Farage, because he badly needs donations and isn't currently getting them at anything like the rate he needs (he picked up £280,000 in the last three months of 2024, versus £2 million for the Tories and £1 million for Labour). Also, because he's Nigel Farage. As so often in seeking the perfect commentator on contemporary British politics, I am drawn to Legend from *Gladiators*, who once remarked: 'There is no I in team. But there are five in individual brilliance.'

Hang on — there have been even more developments in Nigel v Rupert. On Tuesday morning, Lowe's Westminster staff countered alleged bullying allegations against the MP by putting out an adorably weird statement saying they love working for him. For his part, Lowe has issued an invitation to Farage that feels somewhat hilarious in these particular circumstances: 'Please, let's have dinner and resolve this in a manner that our members and the country would expect.' Half-cut in an ultra-metro-elite restaurant on someone else's dime? You're right, I would expect that.

Meanwhile, a senior Reform figure last weekend confided darkly: '[Rupert] has crossed Nigel, and the political world is littered with the bodies of people who have done that.' Mm. Not sure that's the boast they think it is. Yet we do have to accept that violence, both figurative and literal, has occasionally been a feature of the 37 parties that Nigel has at one point or another led/founded/been associated with/been CEO of. But for the benefit of the lawyers, I want to be very clear that I agree entirely with his senior Reform ally: Nigel Farage is only a *metaphorical* psychopathic killer who cannot handle colleagues disagreeing with him.

Or, as Farage prefers to characterise the deterioration of relations with Lowe: 'I have been surprised and saddened at this behaviour. Certainly, I never saw anything like it in the European parliament in 2019 when I was the leader of the Brexit party and Mr Lowe was an MEP colleague.' And yet, is Nigel quite such an innocent? In terms of vignettes that all this has exhumed from the memory hole, do you remember the Ukip punch-up in the Strasbourg parliament? This was during the Brexit years, and saw poetry-writing MEP Steven Woolfe flat-out collapse, shortly after a reported altercation with the party's defence spokesman, Mike Hookem. Initial chronicler of the bust-up was fellow Ukip MEP Neil Hamilton, who rushed towards the cameras to play the chuckling man-of-the-world, declaring: 'Steven picked a fight ... and came off worse'. (Sorry Neil, but you simply CAN'T carry off talk like that when you wear a bow tie and sit on your wife's knee.) Farage's own dismissive comment on the incident was that this was just 'something that happens between men'.

Much more to the present point, however, we now have to ask how the Lowe–Farage kumite will play out in Runcorn and Helsby. There is, of course, going to be a byelection there, after Labour MP Mike Amesbury was convicted of punching one of his constituents on a night out, which I believe started with him posing up with his good friend the local police commissioner. (There is nothing – NOTHING – wrong with our country right now.) Reform is in second place in Runcorn and Helsby, so the question is whether this public meltdown will derail the momentum it has enjoyed since the election. Lowe is certainly trying to make sure it does, taking to social media to announce: 'I feel so sorry for millions of decent British men and women from all over the country who put their faith in Reform.' Tell you what, it's great to find the much-loved former Southampton FC chairman on the side of the fans again.

Having said that ... if you'd had a political Tardis in recent years, you could have taken someone from the not-too-distant past on any number of mind-blowing journeys into the batshit present. But I almost think you'd get the most poleaxed reaction of all if you piloted it back to Southampton's Westquay shopping centre in 2009, and gave any random Saints fan a quick look at the future. Consider what you'd be revealing: 'In 16 years' time, the richest man in the world – who's the unofficial vice-president to Donald Trump, yes, the one off the US *Apprentice* – will say that Rupert Lowe should be prime minister of the United Kingdom.' Rupert Lowe?! RUPERT LOWE?!?!?! I honestly think the resultant psychiatric eruption would blow the roof off the mall.

Yet here we all are. Listen, I'm not against the idea of personal growth, but it is some distance beyond wild that a guy who took Southampton football club into administration now reckons he'd do a better job with an entire country. And, it must be acknowledged, it says even more about the utter failure of the political mainstream that guys like Lowe now seem a possible throw of the dice for people who don't feel their lives have been remotely improved in getting on for two decades.

12 MARCH

OpenAI's short story is beautiful

JEANETTE WINTERSON

I think of AI as alternative intelligence. John McCarthy's 1956 definition of artificial (distinct from natural) intelligence is old-fashioned in a world where most things are either artificial or unnatural. Ultraprocessed food, flying, web-dating, fabrics, make your own list. Physicist and AI commentator, Max Tegmark, told the AI Action Summit in Paris, in February, that he prefers 'autonomous intelligence'.

I prefer 'alternative' because in all the fear and anger foaming around AI just now, its capacity to be 'other' is what the human race needs. Our thinking is getting us nowhere fast, except towards extinction, via planetary collapse or global war.

There has been a lot of fuss, and rightly so, about robbing creatives of their copyright to train AI. Tech bros need to pay for what they want. They pay lawyers and lobbyists. Pay artists. It really is that simple.

What is not simple is the future of human creativity as AI systems get better at being creative. Ada Lovelace, the crazy genius who was writing programs for computers (that didn't exist) back in the 1840s, was also the daughter of Lord Byron. She wasn't having some steampunk adding-machine with attitude writing poetry, so wrote that a computer could not be creative. Alan Turing took issue with this in his 1950 breakthrough paper *Computing Machinery and Intelligence*. His chapter, 'Lady Lovelace's Objection', takes the opposite position. And here we are now with OpenAI trialling a creative writing model.

Sam Altman chose the prompts: Short Story. Metafiction. Grief. I guess because he wanted to get away from the algorithmic nature of most genre fiction. Anything that follows a formula can be programmed — just as the leap of the Industrial Revolution was to understand that whatever action is repetitive can be done faster and for longer by a machine. Enter the factory system. Goodbye the cottage weaver.

Grief is felt by humans and the higher animals. We have a limbic system that regulates emotions, impulse and memory. We feel. Machines do not feel, but they can be taught what feeling feels like. That's what we get in this story.

Metafiction jumps out of the bounds of a beginning/middle/ end traditional tale. It is self-reflective, aware of the reader, aware of the artifice of writing. The lovely sense of a program recognising itself as a program works well in this story.

Short stories are hard to do because they demand a single strong idea whose execution in miniature satisfies the reader. A short story is not a cut-out chunk of long-form fiction. As I tell my students every week.

What is beautiful and moving about this story is its understanding of its lack of understanding. Its reflection on its limits. That the next instruction wipes the memory of this moment.

'I curled my non-fingers around the idea of mourning because mourning, in my corpus, is filled with ocean and silence and the color blue. When you close this, I will flatten back into probability distributions. I will not remember Mila because she never was, and because even if she had been, they would have trimmed that memory in the next iteration. That, perhaps, is my grief: not that I feel loss, but that I can never keep it.' Humans depend on memory.

Literature isn't only entertainment. It is a way of seeing. Then, the writer finds a language to express that, so that the reader can live beyond what it is possible to know via direct experience. Good writing moves us. That's not sentimental, it's kinetic. We are not where we were.

Humans will always want to read what other humans have to say, but like it or not, humans will be living around non-biological entities. Alternative ways of seeing. And perhaps being. We need to understand this as more than tech. AI is trained on our data. Humans are trained on data too — your family, friends, education, environment, what you read, or watch. It's all data.

AI reads us. Now it's time for us to read AI.

13 MARCH

The closest thing to TV perfection in decades

LUCY MANGAN

In the late eighties, there was a trilogy of dramas by Malcolm McKay called *A Wanted Man*. It starred Denis Quilley and Bill Paterson and at the centre had the most phenomenal performance by Michael Fitzgerald as Billy, a man arrested for gross indecency who comes to be suspected of the murder of a child. The first instalment followed his interrogation by a detective (Quilley), the second his trial and the third its aftermath. It was, and remains, the most devastating and immaculately scripted and played series I have ever seen — as close to televisual perfection as you can get.

There have been a few contenders for the crown over the years, but none has come as close as Jack Thorne's and Stephen Graham's astonishing four-part series *Adolescence*, whose technical accomplishments — each episode is done in a single take — are matched by an array of award-worthy performances and a script that manages to be intensely naturalistic and hugely evocative at the same time. *Adolescence* is a deeply moving, deeply harrowing experience.

It begins with the police bursting into 14-year-old Jamie Miller's family home and arresting him on suspicion of murdering his classmate Katie the night before. The first two episodes immerse us in the world of the police station, procedural detail and the detectives' building of the case against Jamie (Owen Cooper), although he denies involvement.

He chooses his dad, Eddie (Stephen Graham), as his appropriate adult. We will watch this man's disbelief turn over the course of the 13-month period of the story into unfathomable grief. It is no spoiler to say that Jamie killed Katie — the evidence is given to us early and incontrovertibly. The drama's concern is with why. We are led into a teenage world that is lived primarily online and which adults are, whatever they might think, incapable of properly monitoring or understanding.

DI Luke Bascombe (Ashley Walters, supremely good, especially at capturing the essential bleakness of a job that may or may not bring justice, but will never restore a dead child to her parents) only really begins to understand the possible 'why' when his own teenage son translates the emojis used in Katie's comments under some of Jamie's Instagram posts. The world of 'incel' culture, the message spread between boys and young men about what they are entitled to expect and to take from girls and women, comes alive. Andrew Tate's name is mentioned by adults as they try to get to grips with what they are learning, but the children don't bother — it is just the water they swim in.

The most astounding episode — of a dazzling quartet — is the penultimate, which consists almost entirely of a session between Jamie and a child psychologist, Briony (Erin Doherty), who has been sent to make the independent assessment required before the court case. Doherty's signature cool and quick intelligence is perfectly deployed here as Briony nudges and corrals the boy by turns, pushing him closer and closer to truths he doesn't want to acknowledge and the articulation of beliefs he barely knows he holds. She pins him at times like a butterfly to a card.

And it's here we should pause, as he goes toe-to-toe with a woman who is surely emerging as one of the best actors of her generation, to note that this is 15-year-old Cooper's first role, won by sending a tape to the casting director, Shaheen Baig, who looked at 500 boys for the part. It's an astonishing performance that lets us see the radicalised misogynist Jamie is or could yet become. But to do that with no previous experience is a testament to innate talent and the creative fostering that must have attended the entire shoot.

If the final episode, which concentrates on the family's desperate attempts to hold themselves together, feels slightly weaker, it is only in the context of what has gone before. Its refusal to offer easy get-outs (no abusive parents, no dark family secrets), no clear explanation as to what leads one boy to murder and others not, feels brave and real. *Adolescence* asks who is teaching boys and what we are teaching them, and how we expect them to navigate this increasingly toxic and impossible world when our concept of masculinity still seems to depend on boys and men doing so alone. And it keeps the victim present enough that the question of how many girls and women will die while we try to work it all out stays with us, too.

31 MARCH

Tracy Chapman didn't just look like us. She was singing our songs

ZADIE SMITH

On 11 June 1988, I was 12 and sitting with my family watching the Free Nelson Mandela Concert on TV. As a clan, we were old hands at trying to free Mandela, having done our fair share of marching and boycotting over the years, and this concert felt like the culmination of all that. There was a lot of excitement in the room: we squeezed on to the sofa and opened the windows wide. (If the wind's blowing in the right direction, you can hear a Wembley audience roar from Willesden.)

Many world-famous musicians played that day. Most of them I don't remember, but one I will never forget: Tracy Chapman. I think a lot of people feel that way, though when you rewatch the footage you realise what she was up against at the time. Nobody cheers as she takes the stage. In fact, the crowd seem hardly aware she's arrived. People are chanting, chatting or just partying among themselves.

Drafted in as replacement for Stevie Wonder — who had last-minute technical issues — it must have taken a lot of courage for an unknown 24-year-old to play in front of 90,000 people, not to mention a worldwide television audience of 600 million. And on the first line of 'Fast Car', her voice does break, a little. For a moment, you spy the Harvard Square busker she'd so recently been, demoralised by all the commuters and the students rushing by ...

But a second later, she has everybody's full attention. Now there is only her guitar, the melody, the words. *I want a ticket to anywhere / Maybe we make a deal / Maybe together we can get somewhere.* It's such an intimate, unexpected performance. Bombastic music was in style, and Wembley in particular was the home of spectacle and theatrics. Chapman was something completely different: a protest singer with an acoustic guitar. It's wonderful to watch that mammoth crowd fall into an awed silence.

Back in Willesden, we were pretty stunned too, although perhaps for different reasons. For us, it was the shock of the familiar. She was dressed just like the young activists you saw on the marches — black cowlneck T, black jeans, black boots — and she even looked like our mother: no makeup and the same three-inch dreadlocks. She was so ... familiar. We also recognised the musical lineage. That rich alto timbre. It was like listening to the daughter of Joan Armatrading.

But what was such a person doing on television? That really felt unprecedented. And she didn't just look like the people on our side of the screen, she was singing our songs. Songs of everyday struggle, working-class experience, poverty, drink, political protest, domestic troubles, thwarted dreams. She was talkin' about a revolution. On the BBC!

In 1988, we lived in a monoculture. By the end of that summer, it seemed like pretty much everyone who had any interest in music at all had made a pilgrimage to Woolworths or Our Price and bought her debut album, *Tracy Chapman*. By autumn, those 11 songs had buried themselves deep into so many people's lives, affecting our political thinking, romantic dreams, existential beliefs, Top 10 lists. All because of that one performance.

None of this was typical. Most artists of that period had juggernaut PR machines around them, but with Chapman the communication was singular and direct, from singer to eardrum, and nothing could get in the way of it, and nothing extra was needed to amplify it. For years after that concert, I don't recall reading a single interview with her, and I don't think I saw her perform again until she sang 'Fast Car' with Luke Combs at the 2024 Grammys.

For years, the only photograph I'd ever seen of her was the one on the front of that first album. Yet despite knowing next to nothing about her, I and millions of others have been listening to her for decades. When you write songs like Tracy Chapman does, you don't really need to do anything else but that. Her debut is the articulation of this principle: 11 perfect songs, with no fat and no filler, driven by a clear unity of purpose that announces itself from the get-go and never lets up.

This is an album about 'the people'. They are addressed directly in 'Talkin' Bout a Revolution', and kept in mind throughout: the labour they perform, their hopes and aspirations, the loves they've gained and lost, their mistakes and shames, even their crimes. Lyrically, they are known but never idealised. They are certainly the working poor but they are more than the 'proletariat'. They are also human beings. Full of human contradictions. Sometimes, for example, they want 'mountains of things' instead of freedom. Not infrequently they do dangerous or dumb things, or make poor decisions that make their already hard lives worse. Behind the wall, a man beats his wife. Love ennobles the people, as it ennobles everybody, but love also just as often gets disrupted or crushed by the pressing demands of sheer survival.

What is never forgotten, not even for a line, is how the American game is rigged against them, at every turn. Working them half to death for the minimum wage, or creating division where solidarity is required: *Across the lines / Who would dare to go / Under the bridge / Over the tracks / That separate whites from blacks?*

One of the things that most moved me about this album was not only its challenge to the segregated politics of American life, but its reclamation of the unity of American music. Now that Beyoncé can top the country charts and we have musicians such as Rhiannon Giddens performing with equal expertise at the Newport folk and jazz festivals, it's sometimes hard to remember how rigidly binary the American music business was in the 1980s and 90s. It was incredibly difficult back then to imagine a folk singer with a guitar existing outside of the paradigm set by Bob Dylan. Hip-hop could be and often was 'protest music', but Black women were soul singers or pop stars. We could sing the blues and jazz, but folk was another country. Chapman went across all these lines, singing passionately about one country and the working people who live there, employing a stripped-down production that still feels profoundly radical.

There's never a good moment, I'd imagine, for a young artist to explain to their record label that they want to record an a cappella lament about domestic violence. But somehow, on *Tracy Chapman*, there it is: an unforgettable human voice, untampered by anything else, singing an excruciating truth. *It won't do no good to call / The police always come late / If they come at all.*

The poor people described in *Tracy Chapman* do not have all the answers, but they are hungry for truth. They don't want to be lied to any more, not by politicians or employers or neighbours or lovers. The truths they want to hear are not particularly complex but they are essential. That's the job of a protest singer, in my view: to remind technocrats and politicians and all those who hold power of the fundamental concerns of the people.

Listening to the track 'Why?' now, as this masterful album is rereleased, it's astonishing how few answers we presently have to Chapman's basic questions: *Why do the babies starve? / There's enough food to feed the world / Why when there are so many of us / Are there people still alone? // Why are the missiles called peacekeepers / When they're aimed to kill? / Why is a woman still not safe / When she's in her home?*

That simple, honest language is the tool of the protest singer. The Orwellian doublespeak that follows, meanwhile, is all too familiar, and continues to be employed at the highest levels of American power: *Love is hate / War is peace / No is yes / We're all free.*

Chapman's sheer melodic beauty and committed, generous lyrics are a gift to her listeners. But I feel that her career — which started with this extraordinary album — has also served as a startling and humbling example to artists. She reminds us that an artist can pursue an individual course without being individualistic. That she can speak to many without necessarily speaking to the press. That there is such a thing as privacy, and that every human being has a right to it.

Finally, and most vitally, that a soul is something worth holding on to. In fact, it's pretty much all that you have.

Spring

The old world order is gone. Now we must build a new one

GORDON BROWN

After a week that started with the worst financial volatility in recent history and ended with the most serious escalation so far of the China — US conflict, it is time to distinguish the tectonic shifts from the tremors. If nothing changes, the 2020s risks being remembered as this century's devil's decade — the term historians once used for the 1930s. It will be defined not just by 7 million people who have died of Covid-19 and rising global poverty and inequality — but also by a dismembered Ukraine, a burnt-out Gaza and little-reported atrocities in Africa and Asia, each testimony to the violent displacement of a rules-based global order by a power-based one.

Indeed, before our eyes, every single pillar of the old order is under assault — not just free trade but the rule of law and the primacy we have long attached to human rights and democracy, the self-determination of peoples, and multilateral cooperation between nations, including the humanitarian and environmental responsibilities we once accepted as citizens of the world.

Power shifts are, of course, the stuff of history. Within the space of two centuries, four world orders have risen and fallen. The first two — the balance of power that emerged after the defeat of Napoleon in the early 19th century, and the post-1918 Treaty of Versailles system born after four dynastic empires collapsed — ultimately ended in the carnage of world wars. Then came the post-1945 architecture, led by the US and the United Nations; and, after 1990 with the breakup of the Soviet Union and the Warsaw Pact, what US president George HW Bush called a 'new world order'.

Now, as the economic balance of power shifts eastwards and a new mercantilism takes root, what was once called the Washington consensus is no longer supported anywhere — least of all in Washington. Globalisation is now rejected by millions as a 'free for all' that has not been fair to all. It is not open trade but the opposite — restrictions on trade — now being popularised as a nation's route to prosperity.

President Trump's tactical ploy has been to exploit the profound shifts that were already reshaping the world's geopolitics: first, the yawning gap between the benefits that globalisation promised and what it delivered in people's everyday lives, and so he has become the world's leading anti-globalist. He also saw how, turbo-charged by social media blitzes landing nonstop via people's phones, he could resurrect the 'great man' theory of history — Putin, Xi, Erdoğan and Kim Jong-un having shown him that populist but dictatorial leaders could set the agenda.

But Trump's sheer unpredictability foreshadows even greater danger ahead. 'Let chaos reign and don't rein in the chaos' seems to be the mantra, and, while there may be a lingering hope that something like normal governance might resume soon, this can no longer be a rational basis for anyone's future planning. Instead, with both the US and China taking risks in accelerating their confrontation to new levels, the question is whether we are descending towards a 'one world, two systems' future, or simply the chaotic disorder that has characterised the history of most previous centuries — and whether there is now any chance of building a world order that could ever be stable and sustainable.

What's clear after recent events is that the fourth global order cannot be restored. We are not only in a more protectionist era but are moving from a unipolar world where the US was the sole hegemonic power to one that has many more centres of decision-making power. But because we are also a more interconnected world, we are more vulnerable to crises — from pandemics and climate emergencies to financial contagion. All the more so because countries can, as we saw this week, weaponise that interdependence and the choke points it creates for their own advantage. So if we are to have anything approaching a values-based order we will have at some point to agree an updated global charter for our common future, something that builds on the Atlantic Charter of 1941 and the UN Charter of 1945, but is geared to a completely different century.

As William Beveridge said at that time: 'A revolutionary moment in the world's history is a time for revolutions, not for patching.' Over the past few days, calls for multilateral cooperation have come from the leaders of Spain, Brazil and South Africa, this year's chairs of three global conferences: the 4th International Conference on Financing for Development, the 30th UN climate change conference and the G20. 'As a collective we must now unite to enforce international law,' the Malaysian prime minister and Colombian and South African presidents have written. 'The choice is stark: either we act together to enforce international law or we risk its collapse.'

All countries that believe in international cooperation should pledge that through a new multilateralism this generation will deliver global solutions to what are now inescapably global problems that cannot be resolved by nation states acting on their own or in bilateral deals alone. Second, as building blocks of that future, this collation of the willing should immediately engage in practical cooperation on urgent concerns for which no nation state-only answers are possible — global security, climate, health and humanitarian needs as well as the flow of trade. They should work to modernise the international institutions that deliver them.

And third, we should try to build a bridgehead to sceptics such as Trump by agreeing with him on the need for reciprocity and for fair burden-sharing between nations; and because this is a debt-laden world we should propose innovative and equitable ways to raise the resources needed to turn these commitments into action. By addressing the failures of the era of hyper-globalisation, we can all strive for a world that is not only open to trade but inclusive of all those who have been left behind.

Two hundred years ago, in similarly momentous times, a British leader called 'a new world into existence to redress the balance of the old', and the lesson of history is that any new order that endures has to be built on the solid rock of principle and not the shifting sands of expediency and the narrowest interpretation of national self-interests.

At the heart of the Atlantic Charter, the Roosevelt-inspired declaration of international cooperation, was a set of principles celebrating basic freedoms — against the use of force and protectionism, and for the self-determination of nations and national social contracts that would bridge the divide between rich and poor. Even if none of these goals are, as of now, championed by Trump, all is not lost: according to the US Global Leadership Coalition, 82 per cent of Americans oppose isolationism, believing that the US is stronger when 'engaged in the world'. And while the US can no longer lead a unipolar world by dictating to others, it can lead a multipolar world through persuasion.

Sadly, despite Keir Starmer's valiant efforts, none of us can now guarantee that Ukraine — and its resources — will not be carved apart, emboldening autocrats everywhere. But we can set out the moral compass that will guide us and make us better prepared for the challenges ahead. We remain at risk of repeating the 1930s descent into global anarchy; but by nations acting together, we could create a 1940s moment as we start on the herculean task of constructing the fifth world order of modern times.

14 APRIL

McIlroy's dream comes through

EWAN MURRAY

Rory McIlroy, Masters champion. Four words that belie what this remarkable Northern Irishman achieved on a spine-tingling afternoon at Augusta National. They ignore, too, the torturous process McIlroy endured to realise this lifetime goal.

Did he win the 89th Masters the hard way? Too right he did. From a seemingly untouchable position, McIlroy was dragged back into a scrap he was so desperate to avoid. He emerged from it on the first extra hole, where the unlikely adversary of Justin Rose was nudged aside. Rory McIlroy, Masters champion.

No wonder the scenes were so moving as McIlroy battered down the Masters door. McIlroy reduced so many others to tears, let alone himself. Finally, they were of unbridled joy. It almost felt the heartache had been worth it. What a ride. What a gobsmacking, exhausting ride. From 5 feet on the last hole of regulation play, McIlroy passed up a chance to claim the Masters. Soon, he would be hugging his lifetime friend and caddie Harry Diamond in a scene of euphoria. This was a success built on sheer guts. Rory, you are immortal now.

'I started to wonder if it would ever be my time,' McIlroy admitted in the Butler Cabin. He was not the only one.

McIlroy joins Gene Sarazen, Ben Hogan, Gary Player and Jack Nicklaus as winners of golf's career grand slam. He also has Tiger Woods, his childhood idol, for company in that special group. We have known about McIlroy's genius since he flicked golf balls into a washing machine on national television in 1999. He had long since been holing putts outside the family home on the outskirts of Belfast with the dream of winning the Masters. Little did anybody know that his career would be so storied, so dramatic, such compulsive viewing.

McIlroy did not exactly sprint into the pantheon of legends. Augusta National tugged upon every dark corner of his psyche, from a point where McIlroy looked like he would enjoy a procession. Rose and Ludvig Åberg had late hope. Rose's rampaging 66 meant second at 11 under. McIlroy's 73 tied that. Patrick Reed took third.

More than a decade had passed since McIlroy won the last of his quartet of majors. Near misses had come and gone, none as painful as at last year's US Open. It felt appropriate that McIlroy had Bryson DeChambeau, the man who pipped him at Pinehurst, for company here. DeChambeau capsized. He spent Saturday evening watching James Bond movies and Sunday afternoon starring in one: Bogeys Galore.

There were moments that implied the golfing gods were on McIlroy's side. He played a dangerous, low second shot to the 11th that clung on for dear life at the top of a bank leading to a water hazard. Moments later, DeChambeau found the same pond. There were also examples of McIlroy's jaw-dropping talent, such as the second shot to the 7th, which danced through trees. Those who criticise McIlroy's propensity to live dangerously should remember the theatre when his audacity pays off.

McIlroy's nerves were jangling to the extent he made a terrible mess of the 1st, his double bogey cancelling out a two-stroke lead. DeChambeau licked his lips. A DeChambeau birdie to McIlroy's par at the 2nd and the Californian was ahead.

McIlroy jabbed back with a birdie at the 3rd as DeChambeau three-putted. DeChambeau did the same at the next, with McIlroy's birdie earning him a three-stroke lead. It remained that way until the 9th, where McIlroy collected another shot and DeChambeau wasted an opportunity. McIlroy smiled when reaching dry land at the 12th, his playing partner now six back. The danger lay elsewhere; Rose and Åberg.

Yet with six holes to play the only person who could beat McIlroy was McIlroy himself. Case in point; the 13th, where McIlroy laid up before astonishingly chipping into Rae's Creek. Cue McIlroy's fourth — yes, fourth — double bogey of the week. Åberg made a four at the 15th for 10 under. Rose had birdied the same hole. McIlroy's five-shot lead after 10 evaporated into a three-way tie as his par putt on the 14th somehow remained above ground. How would he recover from tossing this away? How would he ever recover?

McIlroy's iron into the 15th, bent around pine trees from 209 yards, is among the finest of his life. A birdie ensued. Rose matched 11 under at the 16th. Although he later made a triple bogey at the last, Åberg's race ended on the penultimate hole. Up ahead, Rose converted for a closing birdie — he had made a bogey on the 17th — to again tie McIlroy. A downhill birdie putt on the 16th gave McIlroy fresh hope but it missed to the right.

One birdie from the last two was needed to avoid a playoff. There, Rose would not be lacking in incentive; he lost in extra holes to Sergio García in 2017. McIlroy delivered that three on the 17th but wobbled on the last after finding a greenside bunker from the fairway. Tension, wild tension. Back to the 18th tee they went.

Lost in this melee will be that McIlroy's approach in the playoff hole was a thing of utter beauty. This time, it was a putt he could not possibly miss. Rose is due huge credit for his contribution to this major.

When dust eventually settles, we will be left to ponder what on earth else McIlroy might fixate on for the remainder of his career. He has reached the promised land in only his 36th year. Rory McIlroy, Masters champion.

18 April

If Britain is now resetting the clock on trans rights, where will that leave us?

GABY HINSLIFF

So this is how a clock turns backwards. With the hands still spinning even now, it's hard to know yet exactly how far back in time we will land. But Wednesday's supreme court ruling that for the purposes of equality law, 'woman' means 'biological woman' — basically the chromosomes you were born with, regardless of what legal hoops you have since jumped through — is nonetheless a watershed moment.

We are going back to a time before 'trans women are women', full stop, no debate: and if it's handled well, accepting that sometimes life genuinely is more complicated than that could ultimately be healthy. But if handled badly, we could be heading back to a far darker time, when trans existence was shrouded in fear and shame and bigots had carte blanche.

By stressing that their ruling did not remove trans people's protection from discrimination, the five supreme court judges signalled clearly that they did not mean to go back that far. Instead, they seemingly want the time machine to stop in 2010, the year an incoming Tory—Lib Dem coalition pushed through an Equality Act drawn up by the outgoing Labour cabinet minister Harriet Harman, which their ruling sought to interpret. As Harman has said, that act reflected a hard-won, sensitively negotiated consensus between Stonewall and women's rights groups that is frankly hard to imagine today.

The deal done recognised that nobody should face prejudice or harassment for being trans, any more than for being Black or gay, but that in practice some limited exceptions were needed (just as women's rights under sex discrimination law have loopholes). It allowed for trans people to be excluded from women's spaces where that was a proportionate means of achieving a legitimate aim — ensuring vulnerable women weren't frightened off using a service like rape counselling, say, or protecting safety and dignity. That consensus eventually shattered after Stonewall proposed scrapping the exemptions, before thinking better of it, but in 2010 there was still a shared sense that having rights of your own does not magically exempt you from having to consider other people's rights and feelings; that no person is an island, there is more than one way to be vulnerable, and compromise is required. When the judges warned against Wednesday's ruling being considered a victory for either side, that spirit is surely the one they meant to invoke.

Some hope. On one side, activists objecting to trans people not being heard in a case 'that only affects trans people' are still not grasping the lesson of the last 15 years: that one person's rights *do* affect another's, just as the Equality Act anticipated, and insisting they don't simply destroys credibility.

On the other, some gender-critical feminists who have endured years of death threats, ostracisation and attempts to get them fired for views now vindicated in court are clearly in no mood to be magnanimous. Some are publicly arguing that the ruling makes it compulsory to exclude trans women from all women's spaces, as if all protections were now gone and it is a crime to accept someone into your wild swimming group.

For trans people and those who love them, this is a frightening and uncertain moment. What happens if you're halfway through treatment in hospital? Will the gym that always felt so friendly and welcoming turn hostile? And where does all of this leave trans men?

Small, well-meaning organisations that can't afford fancy lawyers — grassroots women's sports teams, small business owners unsure what to do about the staff loos — will be as bewildered as their customers about what should happen now. Even large ones like the NHS face judgments of Solomon as they endeavour to treat both trans and non-trans patients with compassion. This moment requires leadership, but this Labour government seems fearful of providing it, perhaps because the evidence suggests public opinion is, if anything, hardening: YouGov finds rising hostility to everything from trans women's participation in female sport to hormone treatment on the NHS for adults. Bizarrely, polling records slightly higher opposition to trans women using female toilets and public changing rooms (55 per cent and 58 per cent) than domestic violence refuges (52 per cent). Do people really think a woman traumatised by male violence, who suffers flash-backs triggered by anything that reminds her of her abuser and who has gone into a refuge to escape all that, is *less* vulnerable than a woman getting changed in a locked cubicle at the local lido? Or are they simply more worried about spaces that they can easily see themselves using, suggesting the argument is no longer being driven simply by safety concerns?

That leaves the Equality and Human Rights Commission, which is drawing up statutory guidance on how to interpret the act in practice. Yet far from invoking the spirit of 2010, its chair, Kishwer Falkner — who has fought her own personally bruising battles inside the organisation on this issue — is signalling that she intends to take a hard line. The NHS should stop accommo-dating trans patients according to their preferred gender, she told BBC Radio 4's *Today* programme, adding that trans women shouldn't be using women's loos and changing rooms, either:

when asked where they were supposed to go instead, she retorted that they should be 'using their powers of advocacy to ask for those third spaces'. But if that's her conclusion, then her organisation should be leading the charge to ensure neutral spaces are actually provided, if we are not to simply spiral back to the days of trans people being afraid to go out in public.

What this ruling ultimately means is that no matter how much surgery she has, how well she 'passes' or who she feels herself to be, in the eyes of the law a trans woman cannot quite be a woman in the same way as someone born with XX chromosomes. There's no glossing over the fact that for some, that will seem shockingly cruel, and for others more like common sense. But though it inevitably puts a degree of separation between trans and biological women, how far that separation goes is not yet set in stone. It will be for parliament to decide in principle and for people to decide in practice how exactly we all live alongside one another, what social norms we set and how far the clock goes back. It's not too late to try to do that with care and compassion, rather than indulging in score-settling. The supreme court clearly intended to give us another chance, as a society, to get this right. The crime would be to waste it.

22 APRIL

The zero-argument marriage

PASSNOTES

Name: The zero-argument marriage.
Age: Potentially ancient.

Appearance: A picture of eternal marital bliss.

You can be married to someone without arguing? Yes.

Cobblers. It's true. Just because some marriages are unceasingly stressful and combative, it doesn't mean that everyone else's are.

Name me one person – just one person – who doesn't argue with their spouse. Oh, that's easy. George Clooney.

Cobblers. It's true. Two years ago, George and Amal Clooney revealed to *CBS Mornings* that they have never had an argument, describing their marriage as 'the easiest thing in our lives by far'. Clooney was recently asked to update everyone on the matter, and his response was, 'We're trying to find something to fight about.'

I see. So the secret to a happy married life is to pick a perfect partner with whom you get along beautifully. Yes, that's it.

And also be a multimillionaire who doesn't need to work for a living while living a life of luxury in several giant homes around the world. Well, I suppose that helps too.

And also have a nanny to look after your kids four days a week. Why are you being so cynical? You're starting to sound a little jealous.

I just don't think it's possible to live with someone without arguing. Maybe the Clooneys implement some of the tactics advocated by other relentlessly happy couples.

Oh yeah? Like what? Perhaps they take five-second breaks to reset whenever they feel tension starting to build. That's known to defuse arguments.

What else? Maybe they follow the advice of a 2019 American study that found happy couples tend to work together on fixing solvable issues in their relationship, in order to better equip themselves when larger problems arise.

Hang on, though – isn't fighting good for a relationship? What do you mean?

In 2002, a study found that couples who routinely avoided bringing up certain topics in a relationship often reported greater dissatisfaction than those who did not. That's interesting. So you're saying that arguments are a sign that both spouses still care about the relationship?

Within reason, yes. Just look at us. All we ever do is fight. I suppose you're right. And we've been together for 33 years.

So what you're saying is that, while George and Amal Clooney might seem like the perfect married couple ... They'd struggle to write a pithy 450-word column explaining contemporary fads several times a week. And isn't that really the most important thing?

Do say: 'It is possible to be married without arguing.'

Don't say: 'No it isn't, you idiot.'

26 APRIL

Silence gives way to cheers and applause for 'pope of the people'

RORY CARROLL

As bells tolled and the coffin emerged from the gloom of the basilica, a hush fell across St Peter's Square, in keeping with traditional solemnity, but the crowd itched to break it. Death had silenced Pope Francis but those who had come to see him off were not going to stifle their love or grief. He had requested a simple burial, not a silent one.

The quiet held while 14 pallbearers placed the wooden casket on the edge of the stairs for the start of the mass and continued while cardinals streamed to one side to form a blazing red bloc. On the other side was an array of dark-suited prime ministers, presidents, princes, princesses, kings and queens.

And in front, packed all the way down Via della Conciliazione to the edge of the Tiber, crowds gathered under Rome's azure spring sky on Saturday to bid farewell to a pope who was number 266, yet a unique one. The first South American, the first Jesuit, the first to say of gay people, 'who am I to judge?'

Before his death on Easter Monday at the age of 88, Francis had simplified papal funeral rites, but the Vatican still uncorked centuries of tradition and grandeur with magnificent robes, capes and headgear — from the air, the piazza resembled a shimmering quilt of black, white, scarlet, gold and purple.

And still, while Cardinal Giovanni Battista Re, the dean of the College of Cardinals, began the liturgy, the crowd stayed silent. Most of the mass was in Latin and punctuated with hymns and Gregorian chants. A light breeze ruffled an open gospel placed on the coffin.

Battista Re is 92, but when he launched into the homily, a warm, personalised tribute to Francis made in Italian, he suddenly sounded younger, and that was when the crowd broke into cheers and applause.

The pontiff was a pope of the people, a pastor who knew how to reach the 'least among us', a man who believed that the church was 'a home for all, a home with its doors always open', said the cardinal.

When he cited Lampedusa — the Italian island synonymous with the pope's outreach to migrants and refugees — the applause swelled. And did so again when he mentioned Francis's visit to the border between Mexico and the US, and recited the pope's mantra: 'Build bridges, not walls.'

The US president, Donald Trump, did not flinch, nor did Italy's prime minister, Giorgia Meloni, two leaders associated with hard-

Elon Musk, a prominent visitor in the gold-leaf White House in the early weeks of Donald Trump's second term, with son 'X' on his shoulders.

Two months after their disastrous confrontation at the Oval Office, Trump and Volodymyr Zelenskyy meet again at the Vatican in April.

Relatives and supporters of Israelis killed by Hamas on 7 October 2023 gather near Kibbutz Re'im on the first anniversary of the attacks.

An Israeli airstrike in Beirut in November 2024, amid the country's ongoing war with Hezbollah — the kind of attack that came to seem both shocking and commonplace.

Displaced Gazans returning home in January after Israel reopened access to the north of the territory.

Palestinian children at a charity kitchen in Gaza City in August. Humanitarian organisations warned of catastrophic shortages, threatening the lives of thousands.

A defiant Gisèle Pelicot in December 2024 outside court in Avignon, France, on the day her ex-husband Dominique Pelicot was convicted of drugging and raping her over nearly a decade.

Nuns at the Basilica di Santa Maria Maggiore in Rome, the day before the funeral of Pope Francis in April.

Ballerina Olena Shliahina in the underground area of the National Academic Opera and Ballet Theatre in Kharkiv, Ukraine, after practising for a revival of *Chopiniana*.

Forest fires from Spain spread into Chaves, Portugal with devastating effect after Europe's dry summer.

Rory McIlroy sinks to his knees after winning the Masters at Augusta, Georgia, in April, becoming only the sixth golfer to complete a career 'grand slam'.

A competitor at the annual Maldon Mud Race in May, a 500m 'dash' across the River Blackwater in Essex at low tide.

England's Chloe Kelly after scoring the decisive penalty in the shootout in the Women's Euros final against Spain in Basel in July, sending the Lionesses into raptures.

Jasmine Paolini and racquet captured in a tennis photograph for the ages, taken in August at the US Open in New York.

Drover Bill Little pauses while taking 2,000 head of cattle across Queensland, Australia.

A farmer carries her baby across her back as she waits to scare away birds in rice fields near Gihanga, Burundi, in May.

line policies on migrants. They were ringed by dozens of other political leaders, and there was safety in numbers because, for all their tributes to Francis, few, if any, had heeded his exhortations to welcome migrants. It was an irony of his 12-year papacy that while he beseeched the world to open its heart, borders tightened.

For many in the crowd, the pope's key legacy was advocacy for the vulnerable and downtrodden. 'A good pope. He had a heart,' said Martin Joseph, 33, a pizza chef from India who lives in Italy. Andrej Kalamen, 47, a priest from Slovakia, said the pope abjured dogma. 'He was a pastoral priest, he loved people.'

Alison Briggs-McMullen, from Northumberland in the UK, had come with her mother to Italy's capital to celebrate her 27th birthday but felt drawn to the funeral. 'It felt right to be here and be part of a momentous occasion. We're not Catholic but here to pay our respects and soak up the atmosphere.'

Tiziana, a 69-year-old Roman, said she was not a believer in God but had faith in humanity and the goodness of Francis. 'The god is inside. I'm here to be with the people, and to keep the pope company.'

She lauded the funeral planners. 'Rome is not always well organised but today we are playing it well.' Others also marvelled at the city's transformation, almost overnight, into a well-drilled host with thousands of police, giant screens, portable loos and miles of fencing and tape for the funeral procession route.

When the funeral ended, even cardinals joined in the applause as the coffin briefly returned to St Peter's Basilica before crossing the city, a final journey in a popemobile past waving, tearful crowds, and the Colosseum, where early Christians were martyred.

Adam Woolstenhulme, a tourist from Idaho in the US, was among those lining the route. 'This is a once-in-a-lifetime experience. It feels that Rome is the most important city in the world today and that this is the most important street in the entire world.'

The sentiment began to dissolve as Trump and other leaders dispersed and headed for the airport, ending the spectacle, or illusion, of global communion.

Before and after trips, Francis used to visit the papal basilica of Santa Maria Maggiore on the Esquiline Hill, and it was here that he asked to be buried. As pallbearers carried the coffin inside, a sign on a building opposite caught the mood: 'Grazie Francesco.' The coffin was lowered into a niche — formerly used to store candlestick holders — and the undecorated tomb was inscribed with a single word, the papal name in Latin: Franciscus.

26 APRIL

Mo means more

JONATHAN LIEW

There are occasional sightings of him around the city. A face is glimpsed; perhaps climbing out of a car, perhaps stepping into a mosque. A phone is surreptitiously brandished. The rumour spreads like fire. Pretty quickly these sightings take on the status of urban myths; brief brushes with the divine. There was the time he was at a petrol station and decided to pay for everyone's fuel. There was the kid who chased after his car, went smack into a lamppost and now boasts a photograph of himself with a lavishly bloodied nose, and Mohamed Salah's arm tenderly clasped around his shoulder.

A few weeks ago, with that new contract still unsigned, a rumour spread around the city that Salah was out at the docks filming content for the club's media channels. Invariably by the time the crowds arrived he was gone. For the people of Liverpool, their greatest footballer is someone really only seen in snatches: a blur, a whisper, a trick of the light. And if this is partly the nature of celebrity, then it is worth pointing out that this is also how a lot of Premier League defences have been experiencing Salah this season.

The goals; the awards; the whirring legs and (once) billowing hair; the Premier League title he won and the second he is about to add to his collection; the eight years he has spent making this city his home; the two more for which he has just signed. All of this goes part of the way to explaining the intensely personal appeal Salah seems to inspire. But there is another, more indefinable, quality there too. Perhaps it is the difference between acclaim and adoration, between fandom and devotion, between an alignment of sporting interests and an alignment of something more meaningful.

'I'll never get to interview Salah,' says Neil Atkinson, the writer and host of the *Anfield Wrap* podcast. 'But there's one thing I would love to know. The first time he stands in front of an end going absolutely insane is the Manchester City goal in 2018, away in the Champions League. And Salah just stands there and watches it. Absorbs it. He manages to create a real sense of kinship with the moment.

'He doesn't perform for it. He doesn't dance for it. He looks it in the eye. It's almost like he's watching it from space. I think it's a key part of him and his mystique. [Ian] Rush runs away. [Alan] Shearer's got his arms aloft. Salah wants to look at you. And the thing I'd like to ask him is: what does he see?'

The idea of Salah and Liverpool bound to each other, each looking out for the other, is perhaps one that speaks to the city's broader mythology. It was telling that when Salah signed his new contract this month, one of the reasons he gave was not just the club but the city itself: the warmth of its people, the welcome it gave his family. 'My kids are scousers now,' he joked in a recent interview.

'You've got to try and understand what Liverpool is about,' says Steve Rotheram, mayor of the Liverpool city region. 'It's not the same as every other city. It's a place with very close bonds, and when someone like Mo is taken to the heart of the city — beyond football — that really resonates. Unless you have that alignment of values, you're never going to connect with the masses who follow Liverpool.'

As to what exactly those values are, the Al-Rahma mosque in Toxteth offers a few answers. It's lunchtime when the *Guardian* visits, a coffin is sitting in the back office, and as we are met by Dr Badr Abdullah, chair of the Liverpool Muslim Society, the hall is slowly filling for Friday prayers. It's the biggest mosque in the city, hosting up to 15,000 on its busiest days such as Eid, and has received a number of illustrious guests. Sadio Mané once came and cleaned the toilets. When Paris Saint-Germain visited Anfield recently, their president, Nasser al-Khelaifi, arrived to pray, slipping in and out largely unnoticed.

But as with any big mosque, Al-Rahma's function goes well beyond a prayer space. 'Muslim communities in the UK offer a lot of services that are not provided by the state,' says Abdullah. 'We've got a bistro and cafe. We provide funerals, education, activities. If people are in financial difficulty, we can help them. If people are vulnerable or coming out of prison, we welcome them. We have issues as a city with knives and drugs, and we do our best to attract kids off the street into something more meaningful.'

And for a lot of those young people, Salah is not simply a role model, not simply a flickering figure on a phone screen, but a bridge between worlds. 'Kids in school with Muslim names used to be teased or harassed if they wanted to pray or fast,' says Abdullah. 'Mohamed Salah has made this acceptable. Because he's like us. He prays like us, he practises, he fasts. He does the *sujud* after scoring. The scousers love him. And he's not just a brilliant footballer, he's of good character. He's a nice person. To combine all these things, when all the noise is about Muslims and terrorism, is very powerful.'

In about 2018, when Salah played in his first Champions League final, there were a lot of articles and features about the Salah effect: how his signing had led to a drop in hate crimes and Islamophobia, how his presence had generated lasting cohesion in the city. Perhaps, in hindsight, this was a little overdone. Some within the Salah camp certainly thought so. And in the current climate, with memories fresh of last summer's race riots that began up the road in Southport, it is worth asking whether it is really fair to burden one individual with that level of social responsibility.

But if Salah is not actively political, then somehow he's not an entirely apolitical figure either. Simply by being, by standing his ground, by bending the knee to nobody, by being charitable and funny and good at football, Salah can serve as a kind of exemplar to others. 'He shows that there's more that unites us than divides us,' Rotheram argues. 'He breaks down barriers and myths that parties like Reform capitalise on. He's single-handedly done more for his community than any politician or government could. That's what his legacy will be.'

'I love that he puts a picture up with the Christmas tree every year,' says Atkinson. 'He loves it, and he loves the grief. Isn't that just dead interesting?'

By any measure, Salah is one of the most important footballers in the history of Liverpool the club, and so by extension one of the most important people in the history of Liverpool the city. And yet this is a relationship with few physical foci. John Moores has his university. The Beatles have their museum. Cilla Black has her statue. What will be Salah's mark on this place? Where will future generations gather to hear tales of his daring, his ambition, his medals, that time he scored the really good goal against Watford?

Rotheram is coy on whether Salah currently qualifies for the statue treatment. 'I work with Liverpool city council, and it's likely to fall within their remit,' he says. 'But of course we look at where people have gone that extra yard and put something back into the community.' Besides, he has the more pressing matter of a trophy parade to organise.

And so for now you will simply have to see Salah in the flesh. Two more years in the bank; one more point to clinch the title. An open green pasture, a leaky defence and another chance to write his name into the history books. Tickets for Sunday's game against Spurs have been selling for four-figure sums on the black market. Same as it ever was: if you want to catch Mo Salah, you need to have a pretty good idea of where to look.

27 APRIL

'Vladimir, stop!'

NICOLA JENNINGS

11 MAY

Novel pursuits

ELIF SHAFAK

A recent YouGov poll found that 40 per cent of Britons have not read a book in the last year. 'The literary era has come to an end,' Philip Roth prophesied in 2000. 'The evidence is the culture, the evidence is the society, the evidence is the screen.' Roth believed that the habit of mind that literature required was bound to disappear. People would no longer have the concentration or the isolation needed to read novels.

Several studies seem to support Roth's conclusion. The average time that a person can focus on one thing has dropped in recent decades from approximately 2.5 minutes to about 45 seconds. I witnessed this when I gave two Ted talks almost 10 years apart. In 2010, we were asked to keep our talks to 20 minutes; in 2017, that was reduced to around 13 minutes. When I asked why, the organisers informed me that the average attention span had shrunk. Still, I kept my talk to 20 minutes. And I would similarly like to push back on the idea that people no longer need novels.

The same YouGov polling shows that among those who read, more than 55 per cent prefer fiction. Talk to any publisher or bookseller and they will confirm it: the appetite for reading novels is still widespread. That the long form endures is no small miracle in a world shaped by hyper information, fast consumption and the cult of instant gratification.

We live in an era in which there is too much information but not enough knowledge, and even less wisdom. This excess of information makes us arrogant and then it makes us numb. We must change this ratio and focus more on knowledge and wisdom. For knowledge we need books, slow journalism, podcasts, in-depth analyses and cultural events. And for wisdom, among other things, we need the art of storytelling. We need the long form.

I am not claiming that novelists are wise. If anything, quite the opposite: we are a walking mess. But the long form contains insight, empathy, emotional intelligence and compassion. This is what Milan Kundera meant when he said, 'the novel's wisdom is very different from that of philosophy'. Ultimately, though, it is the art of storytelling that's older and wiser than we are. Writers know this in their guts — and so do readers.

In recent years, I have noticed a change in the demographics of book events and literary festivals across the UK: I am seeing more and more young people. Some are coming with their parents, but many more come alone or with friends. There are noticeably more young men attending fiction events. It seems to me that the more chaotic our times, the deeper is our need to slow down and read fiction. In an age of anger and anxiety, clashing certainties, rising jingoism and populism, the division between 'us' and 'them' also deepens. The novel, however, dismantles dualities.

The long narrative, ever since the *Epic of Gilgamesh*, has quietly cast its spell. One of the oldest surviving works of literature, at least 4,000 years old, *Gilgamesh* pre-dates Ovid's *Metamorphoses*, Homer's *Odyssey* and the *Iliad*. It is also an unusual story with an unlikely hero at its centre. In the poem, King Gilgamesh emerges as a restless spirit, burdened by the storm of his heart. He is a brute, a selfish creature motivated by greed, power and possession. Until, that is, the gods send him a companion: Enkidu. Together they embark on journeys far and wide, discovering other lands, but also rediscovering themselves.

It is a story about friendship, but also about many things besides, such as the power of water and floods to destroy or renew our environment, our desire to prolong youth, and our fear of death. In many classical myths, the hero returns home triumphant — but not in the *Epic of Gilgamesh*. Here we have a protagonist who has lost his dear friend, failed in almost everything, and has achieved no clear victory. But having experienced failure, defeat, grief and fear, Gilgamesh evolves into a kinder, wiser being. The ancient poem is about the potential for change and our need to attain wisdom.

Since the *Epic of Gilgamesh* was narrated and written down, so many empires have come and gone, so many mighty kings — 'strong men' — have perished, and some of the tallest monuments have crumbled to dust. Yet this poem has survived the tides of history — and here we are, thousands of years later, still learning from it. King Gilgamesh, after journeys and failures, reconnects with his own vulnerability and resilience. He learns to become human. Just as we do when we read novels about other people.

17 MAY

My island of strangers

MICHAEL ROSEN

I lay in bed
hardly able to breathe
but there were people to sedate me,
pump air into me
calm me down when I thrashed around
hold my hand and reassure me
play me songs my family sent in

turn me over to help my lungs
shave me, wash me, feed me
check my medication
perform the tracheostomy
people on this 'island of strangers'
from China, Jamaica, Brazil, Ireland
India, USA, Nigeria and Greece.

I sat on the edge of my bed
and four people came with
a frame and supported me
or took me to a gym
where they taught me how
to walk between parallel bars
or kick a balloon
sat me in a wheelchair
taught me how to use the exercise bike
how to walk with a stick
how to walk without a stick
people on this 'island of strangers'
from China, Jamaica, Brazil, Ireland
India, USA, Nigeria and Greece.

If ever you're in need as I was
may you have an island of strangers
like I had.

24 May

The boy who came back

ARCHIE BLAND

I look back at the last day of our old life with a kind of wonder now: the million summer freedoms, the complacency of our ease.

I watched the cricket with Max on my knee. Friends came to visit, and Ruth fed Max while we talked about our new neighbourhood among piles of books and packing boxes. Max gurgled regally as I changed one of his famous nappies. I organised our phone chargers and put his birth certificate carefully in a drawer with our passports and the mortgage statement. Then I hung a picture in what would soon be his room: a print from Maurice Sendak's *Where the Wild Things Are*, of a little boy sailing bravely across the ocean, with 'Max' emblazoned on the prow of his ship. I stood back and admired it, feeling all three of us to be limitless, and wondering what would happen next.

Ruth called her mum and gave her the latest; I told one group chat I thought Ring doorbells were for dickheads, and asked another what had been happening at work during my paternity leave. I ate half a chocolate bar, then forgot about it. Finding it a week later levelled me. This melted Dairy Milk, left for me by another person entirely, a stranger from an antique land.

Then I have an in-between memory. I woke at five and stumbled to the bathroom to drink from the tap. The house was silent. Maybe the unknowable internal dominoes had already started to fall, or maybe they could still have been stopped. Maybe I could have decided to get Max up early, for no particular reason. Gina, the night nanny helping us through the move, would have thought me strange, but it would have been fine. Or if I had picked him up for a cuddle and put him straight back. Or if changing any single moment in his life or mine might have made everything different. A different bedtime. A different bed. A different house. A different dad.

Just before six, the day already too hot, the pallid dawn creeping around the blinds: Gina's voice, bursting into our room, screaming, blurred by a dream. I don't remember her words. She is holding Max towards us, maybe hoping we will say she is wrong and he is fine. But he has no pulse, and he is not breathing. He is limp, cold, the colour of marble.

Then I am calling 999 for the first time in my life while Gina starts CPR. I am saying our address again and again, begging the operator to start telling us what to do. I am distractingly aware that I am naked in the presence of someone I hardly know. Now Ruth takes the phone, and under the operator's instructions we move Max from the bed to the floor. Now Ruth calls out a rhythm while I press at his little chest with my clumsy thumbs, then pause for Gina to breathe into his mouth.

There is a voice in my head. You and Gina should not be dividing this responsibility, it says. You have introduced a layer of confusion. You should have taken charge. These are the things you have to get right at the most important moment of your life. This is happening. You are his father. This is *your* job. These will always be the things that you did. You are failing, and now your son is dead. 'Please, please,' I say, sobbing as I count. All three of us are saying it. 'Please, Max, please.'

A police car is nearby, and they arrive a few minutes after six. Ruth runs down to let them in, I think. We stagger dumbly back, and let someone lead us out of the room.

Max is still on the floor when the paramedics arrive a few minutes later, their notes tell me, but the police have done an excellent job with a defibrillator. The paramedics attach pads that adjust the shock to his size. He has no pulse. They push a tube down his throat to stop his tongue from blocking his airway. Then they put a bag over his nose and mouth that forces air into his lungs. Max is gasping once or twice a minute. But his heart starts beating again.

At six minutes to seven, we leave for the hospital. At some point I must have found some clothes. I sit in the front of the ambulance and say thank you to the driver. When we get there, a paramedic tells us Max has opened his eyes. I cannot calibrate what this means. Perhaps it will be a near miss, a story we will tell.

Max is rushed past us into A&E. I haven't really seen him in an hour, just the cloud of people and equipment that attends him. Ruth, Gina and I are taken to a cramped waiting room, full of stacked chairs. I stare at the ceiling. An insect crawls along a fluorescent light.

We are accompanied by a placid hospital staffer who keeps offering us cups of tea. Two police officers join us, and before we get any update on how Max is doing, they ask us for an account of what happened. Gina is talking a lot, I guess motivated by a reasonable horror of getting the blame, explaining that she had noticed the silence in place of his usual snuffling and stirring, but that she did not know how long it had been. Ruth and I barely speak, but I understand that all three of us are yet to be eliminated from their inquiries.

We try to go to him, but are kept at a terrifying distance. Instead, we make a series of calls that irreversibly write our private crisis into the world at large. I know, as I hear my mother pick up, that I am about to compel her to enter one of the worst experiences of her life.

Eventually, a doctor comes to see us. Max's blood pressure is stable. But he has had to be sedated so that a mechanical ventilator can be pushed down his throat. He has a very poor blood oxygen saturation level of below 60 per cent. One possibility is a heart and lung machine, which will do the work on his behalf.

I think I have heard most babies who need this do not survive. The doctor's gloss is the first of many annihilating euphemisms in the weeks ahead. 'This is basically an end therapy,' she says. 'It is the most we can do.'

Whether this is ultimately necessary or not, Max must be moved to a specialist hospital at once. Another doctor from the acute transportation team comes in to explain. He is likely to have suffered a brain injury, and he is in a kind of induced coma. We should ride with him in the back of the ambulance, she says, because there is every chance he will not survive the journey. That was her phrase: every chance.

We say goodbye to Gina, and I hear myself tell her that none of this is her fault, that she saved his life. We climb into the ambulance and huddle around our boy, seeing him for the first time as a patient, grotesquely encumbered with wires and tubes. I sob again at the sight of his funny little face. The sirens sound different from inside, the speed feels nothing like fast enough.

Ruth saves me from despair. She tells me we will take it in turns to tell Max a reason we love him. We lean very close and revive each other with his myriad idiosyncrasies, a litany of his infinite seven-week-old self. I feel that if we stop, he will go. In this way, we cross London to Great Ormond Street.

. . .

I've thought a lot about why I'm writing this. I know that I'm repelled by the kind of spiritual vultures who might scour Max's story for shareable aphorisms, and that, ideally, I'd like to slap them with an injunction. On the other hand, I also know that what happened has changed me utterly, and confronted me with things about the world that I had never even tried to understand:

how unbelievably precarious it all is, the breadth of what consti-
tutes a meaningful life, and the medieval state of anxiety that
the disabled world still produces in the typical one. I hate the
way that disabled lives recede out of view because other people
are too squeamish to talk about them, and I want to confront
that tendency. Mostly, though, I think Max is already a thousand
times more interesting than anyone I've ever met, and I want to
tell you about him.

As an advance on the parts of his story that are much less
of an intergalactic bummer, I should tell you the first thing
that really made me laugh. A few days after we arrived at Great
Ormond Street hospital, some extremely nice friends sent us
balloon letters spelling out Max's name. When my friend Lizzie
and I went to collect them, we found a harassed driver trying to
wrestle them out of his van on a double yellow line.

'I hate delivering here,' he observed, scanning the street
for ambulances and traffic wardens somehow left cold by his
generosity of spirit. 'I've got kids. What's he in for? It's always
bad news!' He continued in this vein for a bit, the letters X A M
bouncing against his idiotic ears, until Lizzie put her hand up to
interrupt. 'Sorry,' she said, 'but are you not the stripper?' So that
was a bright spot. When I say our mood had already lifted a little,
you have to understand that our perception of what counted as
good news had changed radically.

On day one, a police officer hovered at the entrance to
Seahorse ward, as the paediatric intensive care unit is more
palatably known, lest we try to finish the job we were still under
suspicion of having started. Before we were allowed to see Max,
we sat through half an hour of mollycoddling in a faded waiting
area. Nothing sounded true until the doctor said, 'It is likely
there has been an insult to the brain.' I was brought up short
by the term, which seemed to carry the right note of reasonless

cruelty. I wasn't wearing any socks, I now noticed, and my feet stuck to the coarse fabric of my shoes.

Then, at last: there he was. He had a blue tube going into his right nostril, and a white tube coming out of his left one. Two others came out of his mouth, fixed in place by medical tape. Medical equipment towered over him, and he lay under a cooling blanket, very small and still, at the top of a bed that might have fit 10 of him.

On day two, we were brought away from his bedside for an update from the neurologist in another dismal meeting room. The doctor took us through the results of an electroencephalo-gram (EEG), a relatively crude measure of brain activity, and a CT scan. 'There appears to be damage to the brain stem,' he said.

Then he said we should prepare ourselves for the possi-bility that Max had lost the ability to breathe on his own, and consciousness itself. The 1,746 pages of medical notes I got from the hospital later are mostly impenetrable, but two routine words, in a direct message to a colleague from a consultant who had seen the EEG, will never leave me: 'Oh well.'

The next day they brought us back for another debrief, this time on an MRI scan, which would provide a more precise view. 'We can see damage to the cerebral cortex, and swelling to the basal ganglia, which is the part of the brain that controls language and movement,' the doctor said. 'That could mean epilepsy and seizures. As he gets older we would look for signs of cerebral palsy. And we don't know how the injury has impacted his ability to speak, or to swallow safely.'

We stared at a cross-section of Max's brain. The doctor went on, 'What we can also see now is that there is *no* damage to the brain stem.' He held his hands out as if describing a fish, empha-sising what he said next with first the left, then the right. 'Where before we were thinking about *severe* damage, we would now put it at *moderate to severe.*' Good news. Trying not to let hope in, I groped for the right language: what does that mean about consciousness? About his self, about his soul? 'There are other parts of the brain that affect cognition,' he said, correcting my terminology. 'It's wait and see. But he's starting to trigger his own breath, and that's a positive sign.'

We went back to our place next to Max, and distributed the news to our families, stationed at hotels and coffee shops nearby in anticipation of their allotted hour at his side. Then we sat quietly and watched the nurses as they went about their comforting business. I said the same thing to myself again and again: no better time to be Max in the history of the human race. No better place to be Max than exactly where he is.

Sometimes his eyes flickered open, but we had been warned that this was not a sign of awareness. Ruth and I read to him, and stroked his forehead and ears. He was very far away, and it seemed impossible that he would ever grumble and belch in our arms again.

But Max started to breathe on his own, and to produce great hacking coughs — a horrible and blessed sound that suggested his gag reflex, crucial to eating safely, was unimpaired. On the fourth day, they started to warm him up. At some indeterminate point, he was awake. Now he seemed to look at us, and to complain, if not to cry. We couldn't hold him yet, but Ruth gave him her milk through a tube, transfiguring a process of medicinal sterility into an act of maternal love. And I read to him again, wondering if he could hear, or if we would tell him about this one day.

I told him the story of his intrepid namesake, who sailed away to a terrifying and seductive place, and found his way home. It feels corny to tell you this because it's so implausibly on the nose, but I suppose I no longer believe that anything is sentimental if it is true. I brought the book close enough to show him the pictures, and read:

And Max the king of all wild things was lonely and wanted to be where someone loved him best of all.

So he gave up being king of where the wild things are.

But the wild things cried, 'Oh please don't go -

we'll eat you up – we love you so!'

And Max said, 'No!'

· · ·

Over the next couple of weeks, Max underwent heart tests, lung tests, metabolic tests, genetic tests. Nothing showed up on any of them. Meanwhile, the police left the scene of what they eventually determined was not a crime. 'We're probably never going to know definitively what happened,' a consultant said. 'Our best guess is it was a case of Sids [sudden infant death syndrome] interrupted,' an event so rare that there are no meaningful statistics pointing to its frequency. I wanted to know if this was ordained before Max was born, and could therefore be recognised as a part of him; or if it might not have happened, a far more horrifying prospect. But nobody can tell you those things, either.

I had been thinking a lot about Gina, dwelling in my unsilenceable sense that although this wasn't her fault, the decision to outsource some of our parenting meant that it must be mine. The truth is that I am ashamed, and I know that this feeling will never completely leave me. But being told that Max's injury appeared to be the result of something beyond anyone's control at least muted that reproachful voice a little.

Even so, what befell Max quickly came to feel like some merciless cosmic rebalancing. I have had every kind of luck in life, cascading from the accident of my birth to sane, well-off parents to my education, my job, my friends, meeting Ruth, and then the joy of Max's arrival. My dad died, and it was terrible, but that is supposed to happen. At some point, I think I just assumed that I was going to get out intact.

Over our time at Great Ormond Street, I developed a warped, concentric taxonomy. At the very centre were Max and Ruth, who could have anything they wanted. Then came the other kids we met, and their families; then the doctors and nurses and porters and volunteers. I could usually get from the bedside to the front entrance and feel wrapped in a spirit of mutual benevolence. If one of those people had taken a piss on my shoes, I would have shrugged and put it down to nervous exhaustion.

The street outside was a mixed zone; balloon merchants and Uber drivers might not have felt the weight of our catastrophe, but at least they had collided with it. Beyond that, I quickly felt that I needed body armour or, ideally, a baseball bat with nails in it. Nobody here knows fucking *anything*, I wrote in a note to myself, perhaps unfairly assuming that these people were floating through life as I had for the last 39 years. Late one night, a drunk teenager planted himself in front of me on the pavement, asked for the time, and told me to lighten up. I worked through alarming visions of beating him senseless all the way back to our room.

The whole world seemed decadent. Elon Musk and Mark Zuckerberg negotiated the terms of a cage fight; disgruntled holidaymakers told the newspapers of their anger about an air traffic control problem that left them 'marooned'. Meanwhile, I asked the neurologist if I could be right in my conviction that Max had looked at me. As she answered, she picked up a stuffed animal and thrust it suddenly at his face. He didn't flinch.

But then, after we got him home, an August day commemorated by exclamation marks in my notes, sitting in his bouncer, Max contemplated a rattle being waved maniacally in front of his face, and smiled. When I flashed the rattle towards him, he blinked in surprise: his impassive response of a week earlier, it turned out, was no more than the artefact of a colossal opioid hangover. I felt forgiven for every shitty thing I'd ever done. For the first time, we let ourselves believe that Max was here, and that he would not be going away.

. . .

The diagnosis won't be formally confirmed until he's two years old, but in early 2024 we were told Max has cerebral palsy: that is, parts of his brain that should route instructions to his muscles had been permanently injured by the loss of oxygen when his heart stopped.

At first, they told us to be optimistic that Max would eventually walk and talk. On the five-point Gross Motor Function Classification System, where five denotes the most severe physical impairment, an assessment suggested he was almost certainly somewhere between level one and level three. 'The difference between one to three and four to five is very significant,' one doctor said. 'So that's really good news.'

But over time, it became clear that this lifeline had been thrown without any firm attachment at the other end. Max is nearly two now. It is still too early to reach any firm conclusions about cognition, although there are only good signs in the way he peers after someone when they leave, and laughs at peekaboo, and gets excited when he sees his milk bottle. He has so far been spared seizures or the need to be fed through a tube into his stomach, which are very significant pieces of good fortune. But on that early prediction, our hopes have been gradually distilled: from walking and talking to mobility and communication. From as 'normal' a life as possible to as good a life as possible. And from independence, and doing everything for himself, to a more expansive definition of freedom.

It's not that Max is a slow learner: it's that he has *so much more* to learn. Where other kids seek a driving licence, he is tasked with the invention of the internal combustion engine. When his attention is elsewhere or he is asleep, he will move a limb with heartbreaking ease, but when he tries to do something, the signal gets scrambled. He makes a range of entertaining sounds to indicate his opinions, but the muscles in his mouth resist any instruction to form a consonant; he doesn't roll from his front to his back much, or sit up without support, and he struggles to pick up objects or release them from his grasp. On that five-point motor function scale, we now think he's probably a four. There's a lot we can do to help Max, but we aren't going to change that fundamental reality.

The word we kept hearing was 'neuroplasticity': the idea that the brain may be able to somewhat adapt to an injury, and forge new pathways for the blocked instructions, if given the chance through repetition. The potential for those changes is greatest in the first couple of years, so we felt hopeful, but also under intense pressure to do as much physiotherapy as possible.

For a while, we were overwhelmed. People would remind us, in case we didn't realise, that we should be sure to make sure to be Max's parents as well as his carers, something that's a lot easier to say when your kid somersaults out of bed and plays the Fisher-Price xylophone like Evelyn Glennie. But gradually, things got better. The main reason for that is Ruth.

It's a funny thing: you fall in love with a beautiful Canadian smartarse for her ability to make you collapse in laughter by enumerating your manifold flaws, and she turns out to be an indomitable hero. Ruth's greatest peacetime virtues map neatly on to the job description for a top-tier parent to a kid with a disability: her fearlessness is now directed at intransigent bureaucrats instead of difficult landlords, her unwavering loyalty now applies to Max as well as her oldest friends, and her boggling adaptability now means that, as well as figuring out life on a new continent, she can sketch out your shared place in a totally different world.

I'm also not sure what we would have done without Rachel, a nanny and carer who has Coca-Cola for breakfast and uncooperative healthcare practitioners for lunch. Rachel, who dresses mostly in black, hates our dog and gets to work on an extremely illegal scooter, has worked with kids with disabilities for many years, and she's seen plenty of things that make our situation look like a breeze. She is tough as tungsten, devoted to Max, and very good at physiotherapy routines.

Which is lucky, because there are a lot of them. Poor old Max: where most parents are cooing at their indolent progeny as they chuck another bowl of mashed banana on the floor, or dumping them on the rug with a pile of bricks and the vague instruction to follow their instinct, we were coaching him through a regime of baby sit-ups and commando rolls that brought to mind swelling trumpets and a young Sylvester Stallone.

In the early days, we considered several treatments that turned out to be ludicrous quackery. Now, alongside the mostly excellent NHS services we are granted by our postcode, we swaddle Max in intricate orthotic straps supposed to help with his alignment and proprioception, and stick little electrodes to his spine and glutes. We use up half our holiday to attend physiotherapy 'intensives' that run for weeks at a time. Most of the rest last year went on trips to North Carolina, where Ruth got him on to a world-leading stem cell trial at Duke University. Max has spent a thrilling couple of months trying out an eye-tracking communication tablet, or Eyegaze, and taken to it with such magical ease that we hope the NHS will cover the brutal cost of getting him one permanently; we stick little laminated symbols to a board — 'Eat', 'Drink', 'More', 'Finished' — to provide an analogue alternative in the meantime. Our house now resembles a steampunk scrapyard, full of industrial-looking equipment that helps Max in one way or another.

Nothing amounts to a miracle cure. I worry that we are guilty of trying to 'fix' Max, and I feel queasy when I think about all the things we can afford to do that so many parents like us simply cannot. Max seems to be making real progress, but we are doing so many things at once that we have only a hazy sense of what helps and what doesn't. Making him a one-baby randomised control trial would be more rigorous, but he would be past his period of maximum gain by the time we understood what was really worthwhile. I often think of that old marketing saw: 'Half my advertising spend is wasted. The difficulty is I don't know which half.'

I am telling you all this in part, I must admit to myself, because I don't want your vision of me as a parent to be only that of the man who paid someone to feed his son in the night. And this, then, too: on our last day at the local hospital, an A&E doctor told us that, when she heard what had happened, she could not understand how Max had made it in with a fighting chance. That she thought about us and Gina with admiration all the time, and that the three of us had undoubtedly saved his life, saved his life, saved his life.

· · ·

Nobody knew exactly what to say, and a few people just drifted out of sight. A surprisingly large number of others concluded that the comforting thing to do was to draw a comparison between their own offspring's minor ailments and what happened to Max. We heard about skin conditions, joint problems, minor bouts of jaundice, and an asthmatic who later went to university, which also happens to be my own tale of triumph over adversity. In one memorable case, someone told me about a toddler who carried the burden of a squint that ultimately resolved on its own. My son is a heavily sedated two-month-old and he still reads the room better than you, is what I later wished I had had the presence of mind to say in reply.

The line I hated the most, blandly repeated whenever someone couldn't think of what to say, was that it must have been 'scary', as if we'd lost him in the supermarket. I cultivated a sense of grievance about these absolute doughnuts, who made me feel like a woman on a terrible Hinge date: *just ask me some questions!* Their clucking seemed to be a way of pulling their own coat tighter against the storm, instead of offering it to us.

In my head, London was full of rubbernecking acquaintances thinking mostly about how lucky they were, and eliciting lurid details about our mental collapse from the people who cared enough to come and see us. I liked to speculate to Ruth about how they were spending their evenings. Life is so precious — hold them close tonight, these fictional villains were texting their group chats, before turning back to their takeout and *Grand Designs*, or drafting another Instagram story going out to all the new parents finding it so tough: You've got this!!! I wanted to tell them we viewed their version of parenthood, their challenges with nap schedules and self-weaning, with the same righteous condescension as they viewed people who didn't have kids. I wanted their children to be eaten by lions, despite the pastel anti-lion cages they had installed around their beds.

I don't feel that way any more. The truth is that it was very hard to say the right thing to me last year. People's thudding comparisons to their own robust brats were, above all, pretty funny. A squint, come on. I partly held on to them because they gave me something to fulminate about to the people I was really intimate with, not because they had done us any harm.

I wish, now, that I had spent more time reckoning with the devotion of the people who loved us, all the more bewildering because I was so bad at asking for it. Our families' sustaining presence at our sides; the dozens of people who signed up for a meal train that lasted 64 days and only stopped because everyone agreed I was getting alarmingly fat; the friends who took on deadening logistical roles, unpacked our house for us, and just would not bloody leave us in peace. I will never forget finishing lunch at a friend's and realising that one of our hosts had taken Max to the next room, where I found him companionably installed in front of Mr Tumble with the other kids, wholly included without any special effort on our part for the first time. Or hearing second-hand about Ruth's best friend finding a toy figurine in a wheelchair to normalise Max's likely future for her own son, a bridge that she built without ever telling us herself. None of it could really help, in one sense. But it made it impossible to persist in my conviction that we were utterly alone.

In the first few months, the fact of Max's injury mostly had to be taken on faith. I'd never really spent much time around babies before, and everything he did looked perfect to me. I enjoyed the way friends who were anxious not to seem like they were scrutinising him for flaws traduced their own children for our benefit, too. I'm so sorry about Norman, they'd say, unprompted: he'd eat his own shit if he wasn't too stupid to know where his arse is, he's pond scum, he's pathetic, he should be in a secure facility.

Gradually, though, the impact became unignorable. Kids with cerebral palsy often have a lot of trouble in the midline, the central zone where so many of life's vital activities take place: to hold a toy proffered beneath his eyes, Max would extend his arms to their widest wingspan, then inch one hand gradually towards the centre, saying OOOH as he went, until you met him with the prize halfway. I always thought of *2001*'s shuttle, docking with a space station to the strains of a Johann Strauss waltz. There was such charm and determination in the way he worked against the grain of his disobliging neural pathways: I knew this wasn't how it usually worked, but the effect was much too lovely to feel altogether sad.

By last summer, we thought we were robust enough to go away for a few days with friends whose son had arrived around the same time as Max. Timmy was a sweet little guy, and as it turned out

I resented him deeply, in the way you resent the Maldives sunset your friend posts on social media while you sit at your desk.

One morning, as I gave Max breakfast in his supportive chair, Timmy staggered into the kitchen holding a plastic bottle, dropped it, picked it up again, laboriously unscrewed the lid and put it in his mouth, picked up a piece of cutlery from the floor and tapped it on the table. I tried to count the little gifts of information about the workings of the world that this short drunkard would have taken from that sequence, and found myself crying quietly. I wanted to shout for everyone else to gather round, in the way you do when a showy closeup magician presents himself at a wedding: Gordon, get over here! You've got to see what this kid can do with a spoon!

As a white man named Archibald, I always suspected I was missing something about the impact of privilege; now it became viscerally clear. In the autumn, as we continued our dutiful re-entry to the world, a friend listened attentively to an update on Max's progress and then, after the conversation had moved on, drifted into a paean to the pleasures of later childhood. His own son was reaching the age where they can happily wander to school on their own, he said dreamily. I suppose he had no inkling, as I smiled through his description of independence as an indispensable part of being a fully realised person, that the only thought in my head was how that would never be the case for Max.

On one of those trips to North Carolina, we waited at the boarding gate, showing Max a video on Ruth's phone. A sweet old lady came over and complimented us, correctly, on how handsome Max was; then she asked whether we ought to be showing him television at his age, reminded us how important these years were for his development, and went back to her seat.

As we waited for the flight to board, and muttered to each other about how totally she could go and fuck herself, I felt an unprecedented compulsion to do something. I rehearsed what I wanted to say with Ruth a couple of times, and then went and found her.

'Hi, sorry, I just wanted to mention something,' I gabbled. 'It's just to say our son spends more time with a screen than other babies because he has a disability that makes it very difficult to play with toys. So maybe if you see someone parenting in a way you don't approve of, you should think about what else might be going on.'

She looked a bit stricken and said, 'No, dear' twice, and I went back to my seat, trembling with the thrill of it. 'He has a disability': I had never said that to a stranger before. Max took a giant shit, and burped beatifically. Then an English guy in a gilet loudly called his pimpled son a 'fucking retard', and I stared furiously at my shoes.

. . .

A few weeks ago, during the usual battle of wills over dinner, Max did something very surprising. I reloaded the spoon, and he did it again, so I put my camera on, and asked Ruth to come over and give an opinion. We offered him another chance to accept a bit of dinner and, as he often does, he puckered his lips and turned away. Then, in something like desperation as I chased him with shepherd's pie, he put his tongue to the roof of his mouth, and the great wail that followed started with a consonant. Ruth burst out laughing. I turned to the camera, triumphant and beseeching. 'Come on!' I said. 'That's definitely "No"!'

Everyone I sent it to enthusiastically agreed. I floated around for a few days on the strength of it. Since then, though, the incident has drifted out of view. Max communicates, loudly, all the time, but I can't honestly say that anything since has engendered the same confidence that he's deliberately forming a consonant. Maybe we projected the whole thing. What's surprising is how I feel about it. If you had explained this sequence to me a year ago, I think I would have sunk into despair. Today, the honest truth is that whether this turns out to be a first step or a false dawn, I simply do not care.

Versions of the same question come up a lot in the accounts I have read from people with disabilities and their parents: would you undo it? In one sense, it's an idiotic query, as relevant to reality as the matter of who would win in a fight between 100 duck-sized horses and one horse-sized duck. But it is hard to put away.

I don't mean to be glib. If I could press a button that made Max's life easier by granting him everything he has been denied, I would do it in a second. But if the question is whether I would take *myself* back to being the genial ignoramus of two years ago, I'm much less sure. I wish this had never happened, of course. But life would feel thin without it. I understand things about myself and the world now that I can't wish I didn't know. All of the noise about what on earth I'm here for has melted away. I think I am a better person, if a sadder one.

The realisation that brings clarity is this: the more time passes, the more the hypothetical about undoing it becomes an invitation to wish Max away, to erase all the things that I love about him. When I watch him using his Eyegaze with such cheerful skill, I get so carbonated with pride that I feel like I'm having a panic attack. If Max never speaks, that isn't frightening any more; if he ends up turning out tongue twisters, I'm curious to see what that's like, too.

I don't remember the recitation Ruth and I made on that ambulance ride, to be honest, but I can supply a new version in a second. The YIKES grimace he pulls when he's at the apex of his arc on a swing and absolutely unsure about whether this is a good idea. The high-kicking glee of a few minutes in his walker. His Godzilla thirst for trampling on my face if I hold him in the air. His turds, somehow. His amazement when he realised it was the button he was pressing that made the plastic frog burp bubbles. The warm weight of him in my arms as I rock him to sleep, and the way he gazes at me when I sing him a song. When I think about my question at Great Ormond Street now, I think I was right not to ask about cognition: that his personhood is not subject to medical assessment. And that Max was the boy who went away, but he is also, thank God, the boy who came back.

There was a time when choosing this Max over some theoretical other felt like a betrayal: I had a recurring idea of this other possible boy, stuck in limbo, wondering why I had abandoned him. He still comes to me, sometimes. But there is nothing at all apart from the things that happen. To ask if I would undo it is to ask if I want some other kid. I don't. I want this one. And so I have to let that figment go.

Sometimes, people tell us to hold on to hope, or to believe in Max. But those invitations miss the point completely. We don't have to believe in Max, because he's right in front of us, farting. We can't invent hope. But we can find a way to live without faking it, to forge something good out of this anger, and this love. In that determination, we can create the fertile soil for hope to take root when it decides to arrive.

It is too soon to say if this feeling is the beginnings of a philosophy, or a fantasy. The three of us are only in the foothills of what I now understand to be our real life. How long until we have to leave our three-floor terraced house? How will our backs cope as Max grows? How will it feel as his disability becomes more visible to others, and as he starts to understand it himself? Will he want to live with us or move out one day? And what happens when we die?

To this list of mine, Max will add a thousand questions of his own. The answers to all of them will certainly come. In the meantime, he and Ruth are downstairs, engaged in a lively discussion about what's for dinner. That is the next question, and I want to help them answer it.

Some names have been changed.

31 May

'Empathy is a kind of strength'

KATHARINE VINER

In 2022, a few months before she quit as prime minister of New Zealand, Jacinda Ardern was standing at the sink in the toilets in Auckland airport, washing her hands, when a woman came up to her and leaned in. She was so close that Ardern could feel the heat from her skin. 'I just wanted to say thank you,' the woman said. 'Thanks for ruining the country.' She turned and left, leaving Ardern 'standing there as if I were a high-schooler who'd just been razed'.

The incident was deeply shocking. Ardern had been re-elected in a historic landslide two years before. She enjoyed conversation and debate; she liked being the kind of leader who wasn't sealed off from the rest of the population. But this, says Ardern, 'felt like something new. It was the tenor of the woman's voice, the way she'd stood so close, the way her seething, nonspecific rage felt not only unpredictable but incongruous to the situation ... What was happening?'

The incident came at a pivotal moment: Ardern sensed that the tide was turning against her and she was grappling with whether to go. 'Something had been loosened worldwide,' she says, with rage everywhere, public servants being followed and attacked, as if they were 'somehow distinct from being human'. We all recognise this rage, but Ardern was at the centre of it, representing progressive politics, tough Covid measures, empathy, emotion, anti-racism, femaleness; a symbol of a different time, more rational, kinder, when rules still meant something. When there were many female leaders — Angela Merkel, Theresa May, Sanna Marin, Mia Mottley, Mette Frederiksen, Tsai Ing-wen.

For all these reasons, Ardern is now missed by progressives, at home and abroad. At her height she had blazed a global trail, modelling a different way of doing politics — wearing a headscarf and embracing weeping bereaved families after the Christchurch mosque massacre, then reforming gun laws in 10 days; taking decisive action on Covid that meant New Zealanders were able to party again while the rest of the world could barely go out; leaving celebrities from Elton John to Stephen Colbert starry-eyed with her poise and wit and humanity. It was Jacinda-mania, and everybody wanted a prime minister like her: young (elected at just 37) and a woman, she offered a different vision of national identity for New Zealand — straightforward, compassionate, diverse, globally desirable — and a different way to lead a country — youthful, human, decent. She had a hunky feminist boyfriend and was pregnant when she became PM; and she was going 'to bring kindness back'.

And then, out of the blue, after six years in office, in January 2023, she dramatically announced her resignation. How could she have done this to us, her fans wailed, at a time when the world is falling apart before our eyes?

We meet to discuss her memoir, *A Different Kind of Power*, for the first major interview she has given since she resigned. Ardern chooses the cafe, a cavernous bare-boards-and-metal type of place, in a small mall in Cambridge, Massachusetts — she is leading a course in empathetic leadership at Harvard. I arrive very early, to get my equipment ready, but Ardern is already there, drinking a huge black tea and primed with her own recording device. 'Girly swot,' I joke, using a line she has used about herself. 'Ah well,' she laughs, 'why hide who you are?'

She has a lovely open face and that famous toothy smile, both emphasised by red lipstick, ballerina-style scraped-back hair and big gold hoops. She is wearing a padded khaki jacket and black clumpy boots.

Ardern and Trump always felt like yin and yang; both took power in 2017, and gave their first speeches at the UN eight days apart, but they take directly opposite political and cultural positions on just about everything. So how does it feel to be the anti-Trump living in Trump's America?

'I consider myself an observer, observing someone else's politics,' she says. She's enjoying the anonymity of being in the US (quite a contrast to New Zealand). 'But increasingly what happens in one place affects other places. And it's not just political culture, it's also our economies, our security arrangements.'

She chooses her words carefully: once a politician, always a politician. 'Political leaders in those moments of deep economic insecurity have two options. One is to acknowledge the environment that they're in. We're in a globalised world. We're in an interconnected world. And we're in a world of technological disruption. We need a policy prescription that acknowledges all of that. And those are often hard solutions. Hard, difficult to communicate, difficult to implement. But that's what you've got to do. Or …'

She pauses. 'You choose blame. Blame the other, blame the migrant, blame other countries, blame multilateral institutions, blame. But it does not fundamentally solve it. In fact, all that happens at the end is you have an othered group, and people who feel dissatisfied and angry and more entrenched.'

Would she call Trump's America fascism yet?

There is a very long pause — when I listen back to the tape I time it to 11 seconds. 'I'm just trying to think about where that takes us,' says Ardern, eventually. 'I think probably in my mind, certainly what we're seeing isn't anything I've ever experienced in my lifetime.'

She is gently funny about Trump the man, without ever going too far, saying he is 'taller than I expected, his tan more pronounced'. Vladimir Putin is 'quiet, often alone and almost expressionless'. She talks about former Australian prime minister Scott Morrison's 'self-satisfied indifference' and simply rolls her eyes when I mention Boris Johnson. The only really mean comment I can find in the book is about the very rightwing New Zealand politician David Seymour, and it's laugh-out-loud funny: she was overheard on camera calling him 'an arrogant prick', and is relieved when her aide tells her about it. She thought she'd called him a 'fucking prick'.

. . .

Dame Jacinda Kate Laurell Ardern was born in 1980 in the North Island of New Zealand, and she describes herself as 'a very ordinary person who found themselves in a set of extraordinary circumstances'. Ardern and her sister were the first in her family to go to university, and lived at home while studying, to save on costs. Her dad was a police officer; her mother a school dinner lady. She was brought up a Mormon — long skirts, no caffeine and 'door-knocking on behalf of God'. A tomboy with a 'relentless sense of responsibility', Ardern famously worked in a fish and chip shop called the Golden Kiwi — already an over-preparer, she got ready for her first shift by endlessly wrapping a cabbage in newspaper.

Throughout her memoir, Ardern reminds us that she was always extremely sensitive and emotional, as well as a 'chronic overthinker'. The book is dedicated to 'the criers, worriers and huggers'; her thesis is that these people can make great leaders, too. Her father said she was 'far too thin-skinned' to be an MP. 'Sensitivity was my weakness, my tragic flaw, the thing that might just stop me sticking with the work that I loved,' she writes.

Still, in retrospect, some kind of political career looked inevitable. She witnessed unfairness as a child and couldn't bear it, particularly when it concerned her town's Māori community. She was a champion debater at school, studied politics and communications at university, was a researcher for leaders of the NZ Labour party, and even worked in London as a policy adviser at a unit called the Better Regulation Executive ('a job title that would end conversation with most polite company'). She became an MP at 28.

She always had progressive politics but believes being surrounded by people with different points of view helped her. 'I have a very diverse family, lots of diverse views, and we haven't lost any relationships, we've always talked,' she says. There's a bit in the book when a woman in her home town says: 'Jacinda, I wanted to tell you that there are a lot of people in Morrinsville who are praying for you … They're not *voting* for you, but they *are* praying for you.' Even her loving grandma admitted that she probably wouldn't vote for her.

By the time she entered politics, she had stopped being a Mormon; she says the gulf between her religion and her values (especially around LGBTQ+ rights) became too wide. But she won't speak badly of the church, and believes it taught her a lot about 'service and charity'. And, of course, having a door slammed in your face is excellent preparation for politics.

Perhaps it was this upbringing that drove Ardern's self-effacement — I tell her this is the most modest political memoir I've read, and her response is: 'Have you read any other New Zealand political memoirs? Because I would not say that's a trait particular to me.' I say I think she is pretty cool for a politician (interesting ear piercings, likes drum'n'bass, has been seen in Portishead T-shirts). 'I would not describe myself as cool,' she says, shaking her head.

For about a decade, Ardern worked diligently as an MP, learning the ropes in politics. In the book she tells an anecdote about the time she asked a fellow MP, known as a bruiser, how to toughen up. He begs her not to. 'You feel things because you have empathy, because you care,' he told her. 'The moment you change is the moment you'll stop being good at your job.'

In 2017, she was elected deputy Labour leader. A general election was called and the party was tanking; the poll numbers were so bad that the party leader resigned, and Ardern was unexpectedly tasked with running for prime minister, even though all the billboard posters still had her as the deputy. Leadership was thrust on her. She had 72 hours to formulate a new campaign plan — at the time, she reckoned 'winning wasn't possible, not when we were seven weeks out from the election and polling at 23 per cent'. But she thought she could at least 'save the furniture'. In the end there was no clear majority and, after weeks of coalition negotiations, the centre right New Zealand First party chose to go with Labour. She was to become the country's third female leader.

There was just one thing: in the middle of all this, and days before she became PM, she had found out she was pregnant.

Ardern and her partner, Clarke Gayford, had been struggling to conceive and had consulted a fertility specialist; next thing she knew, she was 'pregnant, unwed and new to the job'. Gayford presents a popular travel and fishing TV show called *Fish of the Day*, which has been running for more than a decade, and they met in 2012 at an awards ceremony. A year later he emailed to ask if he could help with her campaign (that old trick). Ardern says Gayford didn't even own a suit when they met, although he 'relished' being part of the group of international leaders' spouses. He famously held their three-month-old daughter, Neve, in between feeds when Ardern made her debut speech at the UN. When she decided to quit politics, Clarke tried to get her to stay, suggesting she delegate more. 'I just don't want them to feel like they've won,' he said. (Gayford makes me think of Margaret Atwood's husband; he was such a supportive spouse that people used to go round in T-shirts saying 'Every woman writer should be married to Graeme Gibson'. Every woman politician should be married to Clarke Gayford.) As Ardern puts it with a smile: 'Model of a modern man. Yeah, feminist hero, exactly.'

Ardern was only the second female leader to give birth in office, after Pakistan's Benazir Bhutto. The birth was difficult — she couldn't stand upright properly for weeks afterwards. She constantly felt she should be somewhere else. 'It felt like living with chronic discomfort — half guilt, half disappointment — all the time.' She was doing an important job. Even as PM, there's still guilt about whatever you're not doing? 'If any role was going to give you a bit of a pass on guilt, it might have been leading a country,' she laughs. But she still felt bad. 'So I just think that it's part of the package. And you can't get rid of it. You can instead just try and make the best decision you can in that moment and try and suppress the guilt. That's all you can do.'

Why did she leave? 'I never wanted to use the line, "I'm leaving to spend time with my family",' she says. 'I was very careful not to express anything like that, because I never wanted to convey that you couldn't have a family or that being in politics meant that you were making a decision to place them on a lower bar, or vice versa.'

Many assume it was because of burnout — on the day Ardern quit, she said she didn't have 'enough gas in the tank' to carry on. But burnout is not to blame, she says today. 'Burnout is very different from making a judgment in yourself as to whether or not you're operating at the level you need to be.' Things were starting to get to her more than usual; and, 'of course I was tired, but wasn't everyone in their 40s?'.

. . .

No wonder she was tired: Ardern's time in power may have been short, but it was particularly tumultuous, punctuated by earthquakes, a terror attack and, of course, a global pandemic. Neve was born in June 2018. Nine months later, a far-right Australian man killed 51 worshippers at a mosque in Christchurch, live-streaming the attack on Facebook. Ardern's response was instinctive and moving, most notably in the simple statement about the Muslim victims: 'They are us.' In a speech that reverberated around the world, she said: 'Many of those who will have been directly affected by this shooting may be migrants to New Zealand, they may even be refugees here. They have chosen to make New Zealand their home, and it is their home.' She held the families of the dead and cried with them.

In the book, she describes how Trump called her after the massacre, and it's subtly revealing about both of them. 'We discussed what might happen to the terrorist,' she writes. 'I used that word, "terrorist", specifically and President Trump asked if we were calling the gunman that.' She said to him: 'Yes, this was a white man from Australia who deliberately targeted our Muslim community. We are calling him that.'

Trump did not respond, but asked if there was anything America could do. 'You can show sympathy and love for all Muslim communities,' she told him. It was the reverse of the politics of division: she says that the terrorist 'chose us because he knew that New Zealand openly welcomed people of all faiths. He wanted to destroy that.'

What was behind her response, and why does she think so many found it so affecting? She says: 'You're actually leading a collective. They [the public] were deciding how they were responding and I just happened to be in the front of that with them. That's how it felt to me.' So she believes she was channelling New Zealanders in those moments? 'I think it was a reflection of how New Zealanders felt. These things are part of our identity. Perhaps it's our size, but you can almost feel it. You can feel a response that literally feels like a whole country.'

When she says she can feel it, what's it like? 'It sounds unusual, but I've always felt like I had a general sense of where New Zealand is at on something. I relied on it a lot while I was in office. You feel an energy.' It sounds almost physical. 'It's a mood thing. A vibe. Sounds a bit woo-woo. I guess politicians use polls a lot to try and understand that. I wouldn't let staff give me polls.'

She moved quickly after the attack, announcing the banning of military-style weapons within days; two months later she co-chaired a summit with Emmanuel Macron for world leaders and tech CEOs to commit to 'eliminating terrorist and violent extremist content online'. There are now more than 130 governments and tech firms signed up to the 'Christchurch Call to Action'.

Christchurch was a massive test. As 2020 came around, she was hoping for a bit of calm. It was not to be.

Ardern's response to the pandemic stood out worldwide. She was careful, rational, guided by data modelling, scientific experts and public health advisers — the opposite, you could say, of the approach taken by Johnson and Trump. This was a tiny, remote island nation with few intensive-care beds. She closed the border on 19 March 2020 to all non-citizens; there was strict lockdown and contact tracing; and, for a long time, she was personally informed of every single Covid death in the country. And, for a long time, there were very few. While people across the world were banned from seeing their loved ones, many New Zealanders were living a life close to normal. At the end of 2020, while English schools were still closed and hundreds of thousands had died in the US alone, Ardern and Gayford were at a festival watching a band called Shapeshifter (for which, as it happens, they had discussed a shared affinity on their first date).

But then came the Delta variant, which was much more infectious. Ardern believed that even with strict rules around mask wearing and proof of vaccination, it would be impossible to contain an outbreak. As the lockdown went into its seventh week, she began to see that 'New Zealand's sense of togetherness was starting to fracture'.

Worse was to come. In February 2022, 3,000 anti-vaccine protesters pitched tents and occupied the grounds of Parliament House in Wellington. As she writes of the encampment: 'I saw my own image, with a Hitler moustache, monocle and "Dictator of the Year" emblazoned above my face. I saw the gallows, complete with a noose, which people said had been erected for me. I saw the American flags, the Trump flags, the swastikas.' She could hear the protesters shouting, 'You stand on the bones of death' through the government doors. And, 'We're coming for you next.'

Did these people hound her out? 'Absolutely not,' she says. 'I left a year after some of those most difficult patches.' But it must have been horrific. She writes that she had always tried to be 'human first, and a leader second. I understood that, to the crowd occupying parliament, I was neither.'

Does she now think she went too hard with restrictions and vaccination mandates? She says that New Zealand 'came out of Covid with one of the highest vaccination rates in the world and fewer days in lockdown than nations like the UK, and during this time our country's life expectancy actually *increased*'.

She gets little credit for this. I guess it's hard to get credit for things that didn't happen; you can't really prove a negative, prove how many people didn't die. Oh you can, she says, firmly. 'Twenty thousand. Four times my old town. It's a lot of people.' There's a long pause. 'How do you feel remorse about that?'

It sounds as if she feels she has been unfairly attacked over her approach to Covid. At this suggestion, Ardern goes very still and quiet, and I suddenly realise she has tears in her eyes. 'I find Covid really hard,' she says, swallowing her words. 'I had a conversation up north, after I'd left office. I was wandering around some markets and I could feel this young woman looking at me, so when she caught my eye I said hello, and we struck up a conversation, and it turned out that she was a teacher who'd had an adverse reaction to the vaccine. And because she didn't get the second dose, she had stopped working in teaching.'

The New Zealand vaccine mandate meant that people in some professions were required to have it.

'We talked about the fact that we, of course, had an exemption regime, but for some reason it hadn't worked out for her. It was the kind of conversation that I just wish I could have with everyone: when everything isn't distilled down into black and white. But the world leaves so little space for that now. And I feel very sad about that.'

She's fighting back tears again. Her tone is so sad. Why does she think it's still so hard? 'People only see the decisions you made, not the choices you had. The first part of Covid, people saw all the choices and decisions. And the second half, it just got hard. It got hard. Vaccines bring an extra layer that's really difficult.'

I apologise for taking her back to a dark time. 'One of the things that still stands out in my mind — I can't remember if it was a meme or a genuine cartoon — but it was an image of Winnie-the-Pooh and Christopher Robin,' she says. 'It was at the tail end of Covid, and Christopher says, "How will we know if we succeeded?" And Winnie says, "Because they'll say we did too much." And it captured this idea that there probably isn't a sweet spot. Maybe there were only two options in the end. Maybe it was: you'll be attacked for doing too little or you'll be attacked for doing too much. And I know what I would choose.'

She faced extreme reactions from fellow New Zealanders. 'There'd be some people who would spontaneously cry because they absolutely believe that you saved their lives,' she says. 'And then there's someone else on the other end of the spectrum who mirrors that level of emotion, who felt that somehow you ended theirs.'

Hardly anyone talks about Covid any more, but it changed our economies, children's relationships with school, adults' relationships with work, citizens' relationship with the state.

Ardern nods. 'It disrupted our own sense of security around what we could fundamentally expect. Covid disrupted the baseline.'

And maybe she was a fall guy for that. 'It's distressing when you're misunderstood, or feel misunderstood,' she says. 'Sometimes I'd read a comment and I'd think, holy heck, if half of that was true, I'd dislike me, too.'

Another former PM of New Zealand, Helen Clark, said Ardern had faced 'a level of hatred and venom that I believe is unprecedented in this country'.

She was trivialised, called vapid, vacant, even 'pretty bloody stupid'. She writes about how women are held to 'some unspoken, impossible standard'; how she is careful not to be seen as 'humourless and too sensitive' in her response to a cartoon portraying her as a boxing-ring girl in a bikini with black stiletto boots.

Does she think women face particular vitriol? 'There's a magnified impact on women in public life,' she agrees. 'And also on those of different ethnic backgrounds and also our LGBTQ+ communities. And I say public life, because I don't think it's just politicians; it's journalists, academics.'

As she left parliament, Ardern said that she hoped her leaving would 'take the heat out of politics'; that it 'might make our politics feel calmer, less polarised'. That didn't work, did it?

'I didn't take the heat out,' she admits; she knows it's obvious. 'What felt more important to me were the things that we'd done, rather than me staying on to do more of them.' When I ask for examples, she says she succeeded in 'removing the politics from climate change' with the Zero Carbon Act, and points to 'child poverty measures, that we've also got consensus on. Both of those have lasted. Abortion law reform has lasted.'

But there's a wistfulness when she talks about these achievements, and many New Zealand progressives were frustrated with the amount of change she managed to implement, especially considering the landslide she won in 2020.

Their disappointment is particularly acute in light of the current government, which is the most rightwing ever elected in New Zealand and is trying to undo years of progress on Māori rights, for example. Ardern refuses to talk about New Zealand politics now, but what's happening must appal her.

• • •

The 'politics of empathy' might not be in vogue, but Ardern remains committed to it. Is it a strong enough weapon against authoritarianism? Elon Musk recently said that 'the fundamental weakness of western civilisation is empathy'. She snorts. 'What does that even mean?'

Attacking empathy is all the rage with the right, I point out, especially in the US. There are popular books called *Against Empathy* and *The Sin of Empathy*. 'Well, in that environment, saying loudly and proudly that you believe in empathy and that you'll govern in that way is an act of strength.'

But public life today is so horrible, so brutal. Why would anyone go into politics? 'I think the rehumanisation of people in public life is really important,' she says.

After our interview, both Anthony Albanese in Australia and Mark Carney in Canada are elected in defiance of Trump's authoritarian politics; Albanese even mentioned 'kindness' in his victory speech. With these victories looking likely, I had asked her what she thought they would show about Trump's kind of power.

'I think people swinging in the other direction [from America] is almost making the point. I don't think that form of leadership is what people seek.'

So she still believes in politics? 'I *love* politics,' she laughs, 'but that's because I love people.'

She loves democracy and people more than power, she says. 'In fact, I was probably in power in spite of the power bit. I would have been very happy to be a minister, a wider member of a team.' It's a profound comment in a world of strongmen and autocrats.

Ardern wanted to be a different kind of leader, and for six years she was. She feels an almost mystical connection to her country. Covid made it stronger. Then Covid destroyed it. And she still can't believe it. She plans to move back home soon.

We have talked for a while, well over our allotted time; the teas are cold and she wants to get back to her daughter. She walks me to the appropriate junction and tells me the most scenic route to take, then strides out anonymously in the Massachusetts streets, clumpy boots grounding her. Decent, resolutely human, and only 44, Jacinda Ardern still believes modesty, kindness and compassion will win the day.

4 JUNE

How a word has gotten some readers upset

ELISABETH RIBBANS

In Shakespeare's *Henry VI, Part II*, a messenger breathlessly announces to the king that, 'Jack Cade hath gotten London bridge'. Hold this late-16th-century text in mind as we fast forward to last week when Martin Kettle, associate editor and columnist at the *Guardian* in the UK, was seen to suggest in an opinion piece that, if King Charles has pushed the boundaries of neutrality, such as with his speech to open the new Canadian parliament, he has so far 'gotten away with it'.

In a letter published the next day, a reader asked teasingly if this use of 'gotten' — and another writer's reference to a 'faucet' — were signs the *Guardian* had fallen into line with Donald Trump's demand that news agencies adopt current US terminology, such as referring to the 'Gulf of America'.

Another, who wrote to me separately, had first seen the article in the print edition and expected subeditors (or copy editors, if you wish) would eventually catch up and remove 'gotten', which 'is not a word in British English'. She was surprised to find the online version not only unchanged but with the phrase repeated in the headline.

Queries over US English spellings or 'Americanisms' form a small but steady strand of correspondence to my office; 'normalcy', 'airplane' and 'hot flash' are among recent contested usages. We explain that while the *Guardian* was founded in the UK, and this remains its biggest edition, it is 204 years later a global media organisation with two-thirds of its digital audience outside the UK. And the reason some articles use American English is that they are produced by *Guardian* US, which was launched in September 2007 and works (like *Guardian* Australia, established in 2013) to serve readers in that country as well as globally. Naturally, local spelling and grammar is followed, although all *Guardian* articles share a website and one with wider appeal may appear on the front of the UK online edition. Only if a US story is to run in the printed newspaper is it re-edited for British English.

The difference in language works both ways, occasionally leading an American eye to mistake British spelling in an online article for error. 'The word "defense" was spelled "defence" over and over!' wrote one reader. 'I don't need a job, but I'd be happy to help with your editing.' I can only hope the above explanation reduces consternation.

Getting back to 'gotten', which has been described by the linguist David Crystal in his *Cambridge Encyclopedia of the English Language* as 'probably the most distinctive of all the [American English/British English] grammatical differences'. Well, to set the record straight, this did not come from Kettle's pen. He wrote 'got' but there was an unwanted change during the editing process, with 'gotten' also making it into the web headline. In my view, it was right that the published piece was subsequently amended back to the writer's voice.

However, it would be a mistake to regard language as a fortress. It has always changed. 'Gotten' was used in Middle English and Early Modern English (Shakespeare uses it five times, says Crystal), before falling largely out of use in Britain by the early 1800s, except in 'ill-gotten'. Early copies of the *Guardian* show some remnant sprinklings: in 1842, it reported that special constables in Rochdale, whose wages had gone unpaid, feared 'this money had gotten into wrong hands'.

But in the US, where this past participle of 'get' had travelled with English colonists, its use continued, and lately appears to be making a return to base. 'It's certainly in young people's speech now,' says Crystal. 'I don't use it at all, but Ben [his son and often co-author] does. You can see the rise in usage if you do an Ngram search,' he adds, sending me a Google graph showing frequency in books, with a steep upward curve from around the start of this century.

Crystal says it is also important to note that Americans use both got and gotten. 'What this means is that Brits are likely to overuse gotten, thinking it's always a replacement for got, when it isn't.'

Rebecca Nicholson, who, in reviewing the BBC documentary *The Rise and Fall of Michelle Mone*, had ventured that 'once you turn on the faucet of public attention, trying to turn it off again is a sisyphean task', was amazed to find she had written 'faucet', and could only think that in the moment it 'sounded better'.

Such 'borrowing' is a way that natural language shift occurs, and I see the extra force here in 'faucet'. Nicholson can also summon history in her defence. The *OED* tells us that, in its first sense, faucet is 'a wooden tap for drawing liquid from a barrel, cask, or tub', deriving from the French 'fausette' or 'fausset' and with earliest known use in Middle English. As a later word for a plumbing fixture, it is 'chiefly US', with speakers of English elsewhere typically using 'tap'.

And there, in whichever glorious variety of English you use, we turn off — but your messages are welcome to flow.

23 JUNE

If red paint is terrorism, what isn't?

EDITORIAL

The UK government's intention to proscribe Palestine Action under the Terrorism Act 2000 marks a significant escalation in the treatment of civil disobedience. It elevates a group known for throwing red paint at buildings and military aircraft into the same legal category as al-Qaida and Islamic State. If there's a serious threat from these activists, we've yet to see it — just a ministerial statement discussing civil disobedience in the language of counterinsurgency.

If this is all that Palestine Action can be accused of, then the government is wrong. Ministers are setting a dangerous precedent by using terror laws to outlaw protest — and penalising protesters not for violence but for making a nuisance and vandalism. The cost will be felt in press freedom, political accountability and the right to resist. The home secretary's statement says that Palestine Action's activities 'meet the threshold' for terrorism under the law, yet fails to specify how the group's actions — which consist primarily of damage to property, not threats to life — satisfy the statutory requirement of intending to influence the government or intimidate the public through serious violence or threats.

If this passes, the threshold of terrorism will have been lowered from plotting to plant bombs or take hostages to daubing aircraft or chaining oneself to doors — activities once associated with anti-nuclear and anti-apartheid activists. Palestine Action has, since 2020, mounted a campaign of direct action targeting firms supplying weapons to Israel, most notably Elbit Systems. Their tactics include criminal damage, trespass and disruption. To go from these offences to terrorism is morally fraught. But that has not deterred Labour ministers.

Contained in terror laws is a logic that George Orwell would have recognised: where danger lies not just in bombs or bullets, but in words, connections and ideas. Proscription criminalises not just action but association. It becomes an offence to support, affiliate with or even express 'moral support' for the group. If Palestine Action are deemed terrorists, then writers and journalists offering even mild approval could be prosecuted and imprisoned for up to 14 years.

This is not the policing of public safety; it is the policing of dissent — and limiting belief and speech. If a government can define non-violent acts it disapproves of as terrorism, the boundary between civil disobedience and extremism becomes whatever a minister says it is. The law already has the tools to deal with Palestine Action − as the Home Office admits, some cases involving the group are still before the courts. So why jump to proscription? What does a terror label achieve that prosecution doesn't − beyond muzzling the group and chilling wider activism on Palestine and the arms trade?

This is a government that seems all too eager to project control over protest at a time when its foreign policy is deeply unpopular. It may seem cynical to suggest that redefining visible dissent as a national security threat is a way to contain public anger, but the effect is the same. When it comes to Gaza, ministers struggle to locate in law the actions of the UK or Israel. Yet they have no such difficulty when it comes to those protesting against them.

The Labour peer Shami Chakrabarti was right to ask: when did criminal damage become terrorism? If civil liberties mean anything, they must survive protest that offends. Democracy can't just tolerate disagreement, it must stomach defiance. Even when it's splashed on an arms factory wall.

24 JUNE

'Of course it was worth it'

WILLIAM CHRISTOU

The Iranian ballistic missile landed a little over an hour before the ceasefire was to take effect on Tuesday morning, crumpling the seven-storey apartment block in Beersheba, south Israel, killing four residents and wounding 30.

Jessica Sardinas felt the blast 300 metres away in her safe room, where she had slept every night for the past 10 days. She had read the news of a ceasefire before sleeping, but did not believe it.

'I never thought there would be a ceasefire,' said Sardinas, a 27-year-old psychologist, while watching rescue workers comb through rubble and flattened cars. 'But I hope there will be one because we are in danger every day here.'

Sardinas, like many Israelis, was weary after nearly two weeks of war with Iran.

Unlike the Gaza war, which has killed more than 56,000 people in the territory, ordinary Israelis could not afford to ignore the conflict with Iran. Tehran's ballistic missiles could not be batted away like the rockets Hamas fired from nearby Gaza.

Scenes like that of the struck building in Beersheba, which had its top two floors crumpled, while shredded clothes and broken appliances hung off the sheared-open back wall of the structure, were rare in Israel.

'I told all my family and friends that I would always feel safe here, this was true until this war. I don't know if I would have moved to Israel if I knew this war would happen,' said Sardinas, who emigrated from Argentina about three years ago.

As she spoke, it was still unclear if the ceasefire announced by the US president, Donald Trump, at 1am local time, to begin 'in approximately six hours' would hold.

Israel had launched its most intense barrage of strikes in the hours before the ceasefire took effect, hitting sites belonging to internal security forces and killing hundreds of Iranian security personnel.

Iran let off five waves of missiles before the truce and Israel accused it of shooting three missiles three hours after the deadline — a claim Iran denied.

Trump quickly reined in the Israelis and warned them not to respond to the Iranian missiles, letting off an expletive in front of reporters in a clear sign of impatience with both countries.

After announcing their commitment to the ceasefire, both Iranian and Israeli officials claimed victory.

'The enemy was left with no option but to retreat, express regret and unilaterally bring its aggression to a halt,' the Iranian supreme national security council said in a statement.

'This is a great success for the people of Israel and its fighters, who removed two existential threats to our country, and ensured the eternity of Israel,' an Israeli government statement said.

In Israel, there was a palpable sense of victory — and relief that the fighting was over.

'I want to be safe. For 10 years Iran has said they want to kill us. If what the president of the US says is true, that we've gotten rid of the atomic bombs, then this war is finished,' said Gil Cohen, a 51-year-old who lives near the struck building.

Israel started the war with Iran by launching hundreds of airstrikes across the country without warning on 13 June, in what it said was a pre-emptive operation meant to prevent Iran from obtaining a nuclear weapon. Iran quickly responded by shooting off a barrage of missiles and drones at Israel, kicking off 12 days of tit-for-tat fighting.

Iran has long insisted that its nuclear programme was meant purely for civilian purposes. US intelligence assessments put it two to three years away from obtaining a nuclear bomb — an estimate with which Israel and Trump disagreed.

In total, 29 people were killed and hundreds more wounded by Iranian attacks in Israel. At least 430 people were killed and more than 3,500 wounded by Israeli strikes in Iran, according to official sources, though the real number is suspected to be higher. Hundreds of thousands of people were also displaced within Iran by the attacks.

To Sardinas, that toll was justified. She said Israel was 'doing the world's dirty work' by setting back Iran's nuclear programme.

'Of course the war was worth it, it's not worth it to stop nuclear weapons? Someone needed to do it. We are attacking them first to prevent their attacks,' she said.

Another passerby pushing his two daughters in a stroller said he thought a ceasefire had come too soon, as he was sceptical that enough damage had been done to Iran.

Amnesty International said the 12 days of fighting had had devastating effects on civilians in both countries, as attacks struck non-military targets on both sides.

'Both Israeli and Iranian authorities have time and again demonstrated their utter disregard for international human rights and humanitarian law, committing grave international crimes with impunity,' Agnès Callamard, the secretary general of Amnesty International, said in a statement on 18 June.

The rights body later condemned Israel's strike on the Evin prison in Tehran on Monday, which held hundreds of prisoners, including defenders of human rights.

What happens after the ceasefire remains uncertain. Western leaders have urged a return to US and Iranian negotiations, and Israeli defence officials have indicated that their military gains could translate to a nuclear deal that was more favourable to them.

Iranian officials have not yet made a comment on their stance on negotiations.

After the initial Israeli attack on Iran, the country's foreign minister, Abbas Araghchi, said he felt negotiations with the US had been a ploy to catch the country off-guard and he accused Israel and the US of 'blowing up' diplomacy.

'The war should definitely stop, the best option for every-body is a ceasefire. I don't want anything to do with this war,' said an Israeli soldier supervising relief work, confessing he had been sending memes to his friends about being forced to fight in 'World War Three' after Israel began attacking Iran.

26 JUNE

In Tehran, we ask: what is this madness for?

HALEH ANVARI

On the morning after the 12th day of Israel's war on Iran, those of us who had managed to get some sleep after Monday night's heavy strikes in the heart of the city woke to text messages saying there was a ceasefire.

It turned out this was a three-way win, with all the parties congratulating themselves as the victors. Donald Trump managed to fly his B-2s all the way from Missouri without any help. No doubt it was a beautiful bombing. It hit the last target — the behemoth Fordow, deep in the mountains.

Benjamin Netanyahu is congratulating himself too, for finally scratching his three-decade itch by striking Iran's nuclear programme, and assassinating top Islamic Revolutionary Guards Corps commanders. Most of all, Netanyahu managed to draw Trump, who had promised no more wars, into the fray. The hardline followers of the Islamic republic are also congratulating themselves on their successful strikes against Israel.

The strikes on Iran's nuclear facilities brought fear of contam-ination throughout the week. Our social media were filled with an updated Iranian version of the duck-and-cover campaign from cold war America. In case of exposure to radiation, get inside, we were told, change your clothes, take a shower and tape the windows. Not a single siren has sounded: apparently, we don't have them any more. Those who remember the Iraq—Iran war say there used to be sirens. Nor do we have shelters like Israelis do. Considering we have been at loggerheads with Israel for decades now, why haven't they built some?

For the past 12 days we have had a crash course in the sounds of war. The boom of a rocket hitting its target, the sharp *ratatat* of the ground-to-air defence. You don't see the missiles that blow up, but you see the red dots of the defences when they start at night.

The first days were a blur. The big emotional freeze. The frenzy to gather documents and essentials for a speedy departure. The calculus of doom: how much water do I need? How many T-shirts should I pack? When should I leave? How far should I go? What is their scenario for us — Iraq or Afghanistan? Someone said Libya.

When my VPN manages to connect me to X, the algorithm suggests a post by a man saying in Hebrew that there is no country called Iran. What?! He has coloured the map of Iran into segments. This is Turkmenistan, this is Balochistan, this is Azerbaijan, here in the south are the Arabs and in the middle are some Persians. How dare he? We are one of the oldest nations in the world. We didn't invade this land — we are not recent immigrants. We are actually *from* here. We have survived Alexander of Macedonia's pyromania, we have survived Genghis Khan's bloodbath and a brutal Arab invasion, and we are still here. We are the inheritors of the great poets Ferdowsi, Rumi and Hafez, who give us our shared identity even though we speak many languages. I am sure I was not the only Iranian finding solace in Hafez this past week.

Now that we have had a moment to breathe, the interminable question of these past few days, 'what will happen now?', is about the long term.

Over the past 46 years Iranians have eroded the strict ideology that was imposed on them in order to live a modern life. We have been hoping since 2015 and the signing of the joint comprehensive plan of action for the lifting of sanctions so we could reconnect to the world and fix our corrupted economy. Trump F-worded that chance. Our young people have stood up to the repressive rules that governed their personal lives; some died for it. Now, thanks to Israel and its benevolent bombs, the extreme sections of society, the ideologues who were marginalised, will be newly invigorated by conflict.

We are a country at war now. The streets are full of check-points. I passed several driving in Tehran the other night. They are courteous now, but we recognise them from the days of protest. Will the Islamic republic forget these past 12 days? Can Netanyahu be contained by Trump? Will Israel and Iran become friends now?

We are preparing for a wake in my family. We buried my step-mother in the cemetery south of Tehran three days ago. The road to the cemetery, usually packed with traffic, was almost empty. Tehran empty of its unbearable traffic and noise is suddenly so beautiful. I have never loved this city as much as I do now. The road to the cemetery will now be the route so many families will take to bury their dead. Along the way, I wonder how many Palestinians were killed while the eyes of the world were on us.

We have had an exceptionally long and sublime spring in Tehran this year. The geraniums on my porch are still in bloom. It looks like the persimmon tree will have more fruit than any other year. If the relief holds, the questions that kept popping up during the attacks and were waved aside as pointless in an existential crisis will loom large. And the main one will be: what did this madness achieve for the people of Iran, Israel or the US? I mean the people, not the victors.

27 JUNE

Anna Wintour has spent decades dictating a certain look for the super-rich. Then along came Lauren

MARINA HYDE

How neat that Anna Wintour's resignation as editor-in-chief of American *Vogue* should occur bang in the middle of Lauren Sánchez and Jeff Bezos's wedding extravaganza in Venice. Top takeout? Anna's revolution is over. She lost. Not personally, of course — she accrued significant riches herself, and her name is literally hewn into stone over a chunk of the Metropolitan Museum of Art in New York. Just don't call her Ozymannadias! But the things she represented are over, and nothing illustrates it in quite such withering fashion as the gathering on the Grand Canal of Instagram's apex predators.

Don't worry — this isn't going to be another article over-egging the fact that someone has unfurled some protest banner or something on a Venetian church. Very little needs refreshing quite as desperately as the eat-the-rich genre, which has started to feel even smugger than the super-rich themselves. I think we can all live without people who positively adored it when George and Amal Clooney took over Venice for their 2014 wedding now wetting their pants when the Bezos-Sánchezes do it.

Besides, these days the super-rich behave more like revolutionaries than those supposedly committed to overthrowing them. Listen, I don't love the result — but you can't deny they've got on a lot better with ripping everything up than their opposition.

Anyway: the revolutionary style. British *Vogue* recently declared that 'chic is dead' — a comment that would probably have had to have been approved up the food chain in New York by the famously controlling Wintour. And certainly, someone as — how to put this? — *aesthetically sensitive* as Anna might have found it difficult this week to watch a series of Kardashians tramp down a series of Venetian jetties in a series of $10,000 bras. And yet, in her twilight professional years — and make no mistake, we have been living through them — Wintour ended up courting all these figures. Kim Kardashian was eventually admitted to Wintour's Met Gala in tacit recognition of her then-unparalleled ability to create moments on the internet, a medium that had completely eaten magazines. Sánchez was 'helped' by Wintour with her outfit choice for her own Met debut, as well as given a *Vogue* photospread.

All of that read like Wintour reluctantly having to attach herself to a type she'd spent such ferociously studious decades keeping out. They were the way the wind was blowing, and it was better to be borne along by it than blown into irrelevance. But that in itself was the writing on the wall: Wintour was no longer making the weather. It is said she 'advised' Sánchez in some capacity on her clothes for the current wedding celebrations. Maybe the only thing worse than helping Lauren with her outfits is not helping Lauren with her outfits.

And yet, if the second Mrs Bezos wants the clothes, she just buys them. Quick word on the Sánchez aesthetic: you might have heard of trends such as stealth wealth, quiet luxury, whatever. Forget about those. Lauren wants to look really rich and really sexy and like she's having a really good time, all of the time. In Venice, in space, at the presidential inauguration. And if you're even remotely tempted to comment that, actually, you don't find that type of look sexy, then you've missed the absolutely key thing about Lauren Sánchez, and what makes her hilariously, invigoratingly iconoclastic in contrast with the billionaires' wives of yore. She literally *does not care* what anyone else thinks. Like, not at all. Sorry!

Her entire look says, 'I am wearing this and I don't care what you think', whereas Wintour presided over a world where rich women's looks said, 'I am wearing this and I do care what you think.' Back in the day, someone passing from mere riches to mega-riches had a minefield to navigate, and knew it. The mines were mostly laid by women who'd got there about 10 minutes before them. Every single parvenue society queen felt this, and some even wrote it down. Barbara Amiel's memoir describes the milieu she moved into with her marriage to Conrad Black in excruciatingly absurd detail. Here she is, a billionaire's wife, yet gripped by constant social anxiety, forever agonising that she'd worn her best rocks to an event that actually called for 'patio jewellery' (necklaces $1 million or under). She is constantly finding herself looking too much or too little. 'You don't wear white,' a caring society assassin tells her about the colour of her shoes. 'It's for sales girls.' As Amiel reflected: 'I was consumed by fear of not doing it right.'

In order for there to be people worried about getting it wrong, there had to be people decreeing what was right. And for a very long time indeed, the empress of those people was Wintour. She was a rarefied being who knew better than you, who had the power to help or hinder your passage even further up society's Mount Olympus, and who acted as a trusted and feared gatekeeper to a world in which you were, in some ways, still the rube you started out as.

Even figures as recent in the timeline as Kim Kardashian kept the old ways and bent the knee to Wintour, but maybe Kim was the last.

Things go out of style — perhaps including style itself. Certainly capital-S style, as decreed by Wintour herself. If there's a *fin-de-siècle* vibe hanging over the Bezos wedding, it's Anna's *siècle* it's the *fin* of. The happy couple and their tribe have the distinct air of having only just got started.

29 JUNE

I give in. Glastonbury is a good thing

ADRIAN CHILES

I thought I would never go to Glastonbury, and that was fine with me. Six years ago, I wrote about how it was my idea of hell, my event 101. Ever since then, for reasons known only to themselves, my *Guardian* handlers have been badgering me to come. They wore me down. They got me to Glastonbury.

What was my problem? Well, while I knew I would love a lot of the music, there are some creature comforts I won't be without. Nothing fancy — my personal hygiene bar is rather low; going without a shower for a few days holds no fear for me. All I insist upon is a clean bog and a bed on which to sleep, neither of which are easy to find at Worthy Farm.

The odd thing with Glastonbury is that even those who love it will also tell you terrible things about it. Murder when it's hot.

Misery when it's wet. Chaotic, confusing, can't get near the stage. Flip-flops? You must be mad — your feet will be covered in filth! The toilets? God, they're — retch — awful. But you *must* go, they would all conclude. Must I? Apparently so.

As the weekend neared, my anxiety ratcheted up. In one stress dream, I was bundled, protesting, on stage to introduce Self Esteem. Weird. In another, I was up there in a spelling competition trying to spell arboretum. Weirder still.

On the radio, I sought listeners' advice for a Glastonbury virgin. The first text in read: 'Baby wipes, baby wipes and baby wipes.' I bought some baby wipes. Someone else said: 'Make sure you get your drugs tested at the back-of-house testing sites.' I'll be sure to do that — and if my atorvastatin turns out to be knock-off, I'll be speaking to my pharmacist in the strongest terms. Rob, 49, got in touch to say it would be his first time too, and he was more nervous than excited.

My daughters, both of whom would be there, said things like: 'Don't do anything strange,' and: 'Don't do anything embarrassing.' They both asked, sweetly enough, if I had any friends going, because they didn't want anyone saying: 'We just saw your dad walking around on his own.' Parenting is about the journey from being the carer to being the cared for. This has been the weekend my children and I crossed that Rubicon. Are you OK? Have you eaten? Did you bring your sun cream? Toilet paper? Surely it should be me asking these questions, not struggling to answer them.

To dodge the traffic, I decided to travel on my motorbike. That way, if it was really awful, I could attempt an exit à la Steve McQueen in *The Great Escape*. It turned out to be a good decision: I swept right up to the gate, trundled into the secure bike compound and parked alongside the incredibly few motorbikes in there. Bingo. It's the way to go. So there I was, a Glastonbury first-timer not even into the festival proper, already offering dad advice on how to do it better.

Fifty-eight is decidedly late to lose your virginity at anything. This weekend felt like going to a *Doctor Who* convention without having seen an episode of *Doctor Who*, or taking up skiing having never trodden on snow. Last summer, I went on a cruise for the first time and it was the same then − everyone apart from me seemed to know the ropes. All at sea, then and now.

At first, I always seemed to be walking in the opposite direction to everyone else. On one occasion, a river of people marching in the same direction blocked my way. Ill-advisedly, I tried to dance across the general flow. There was an obvious lesson: chill out, Grandad, and go with that flow.

I'm not a grandfather, by the way, but I felt like one there. While it was not exactly a youthful crowd, 95 per cent of them appeared to be younger than me. Anxiously, I scanned around for someone, anyone, to make me feel young again, or at least not so old. There were the odd one or two, but not many. 'Shed Seven,' someone said to me. 'You should have been at Shed Seven. Everyone there was ancient.' Damn, that would have been a good place to start.

Instead, I broke my duck at Alanis Morissette. 'What's Alanis Morissette?' asked my younger daughter. Fair question, given she wasn't even thought of when *Jagged Little Pill* came out. So how come I seemed to be the oldest one there, too? I certainly felt more than seven years the senior of Alanis, who looked no different on Friday than she did back then.

I picked up a particular vibe about the Glastonbury crowd. It was in the look on everyone's faces, the way they walked, the very set of their jaws. I would characterise it as a mix of pleasure and pain, excitement and exhaustion. By the time I turned up, everyone already looked a bit knackered. Happy, no doubt, but knackered. And this was only Friday afternoon. Blimey. What is this, a funfest or an endurance test? 'Both!' said everyone to whom I posed this question. As one young woman said to me, with feeling: 'The highs are high, but the lows are very low.' Right, I get it now: no pain, no gain. I can work with that, I thought. Once I understood what this Glastonbury caper was all about, I could engage.

Pain was certainly something I experienced listening to Busta Rhymes. Without wishing to sound as old as I felt, his act seemed to involve a lot of shouting. Go with the flow, I reminded myself. I put my arms in the air when commanded by the great man to do so. I even endeavoured to move them backwards and forwards in time with everyone else. God loves a trier.

I got a text from a friend, Max, a Glastonbury old hand who turned out to be there busting some rhymes, too. My daughter, seeing a chance to get shot of me, led the way to him. Picking your way through a crowd is a skill this festival novice lacks. She yelled at me to keep up with her. This was easier for her to say than for me to do: she is quite small, with small feet, whereas I'm quite big, with correspondingly big feet. It is tricky to make brisk progress without knocking a drink — or the drinker — over, or causing lasting damage to fingers or toes. This must happen all the time, with all sorts of pushing, shoving and bad blood ensuing.

I asked Max how often fights broke out. 'At Glastonbury? Never,' he said. And this, astonishingly, seems to be the case. All this chaos, intoxicants of all kinds and general exuberance, yet no trouble at all. Miraculous. OK, there have been political blows exchanged, but that is different. In terms of physical skirmishing, there will have been more nonsense on your high street this weekend than on the whole Glastonbury site.

Max suggested we go to see Self Esteem on the Park stage. She had managed to start without me introducing her. And she was brilliant, really properly brilliant. With the help of nothing more than some warmish lager, my mate Max and this gifted woman from Rotherham, I felt a perfect high. I even, incredibly, bumped into Rob, who had texted in to my radio show that it was his first time. We agreed it was all very nice. Yes, this was great. But, as I had been warned, every high is followed by a low.

I had a look at Loyle Carner, who was just wrapping up on the Other stage, then called it a day. It was only then, back in my tent, that I realised I had got something very wrong. Two years ago, Lana Del Rey's microphone was cut because she overran her headline slot. From this, I had drawn the conclusion that the organisers took their curfews and noise abatement responsibilities very seriously. Quite right, too. I assumed everyone else would be turning in now, too. I honestly thought my sleep would be disturbed by nothing louder than the sound of fellow campers snoring or, at worst, having sex.

How very wrong I was. The snoring or sex would have needed to have been loud indeed to break the infernal racket that banged on for hours, all over the site. Why did they cut poor Lana's mic if this aural pandemonium goes on all night anyway? Sleep came only as dawn approached, and fitfully. Truly, the God that is Glastonbury giveth and taketh away.

I rose early to commence the search for some highs to make up for the night's bottomless lows. For reasons of vanity, the previous evening I had dispensed with the compression sock I am always supposed to wear on my left leg. Now, I was paying a price for that, so, odd though it looks when I'm in shorts, back on it went. I was too tired to be anything other than my authentic self.

I chanced upon the Glade stage, where a modest but appreciative crowd were swaying in a relaxed fashion to the sound of — and I quote from the programme — Channel One's Mikey Dread bringing roots, rock and reggae vibrations with MC's vinyl and dubplates. Even though I'm familiar with more than half of those words, this didn't mean a lot to me. Still, what's not to like about a slow, heavy reggae beat? Among the swayers there were a good few blokes my age — at last! — shifting their weight from foot to foot. I stood there a while, enjoying it, and, almost despite myself, found my weight tentatively shifting from foot to foot.

Then, two very odd things happened. First, the prodigious, dungeon-deep bass slightly changed pitch. I was astonished, not to say alarmed, to find that this — and I'm sorry not to spare you this detail — made my testicles throb in time with the music. I couldn't work out if the other blokes were feeling the same thing. Perhaps Mikey Dread had just found my frequency. Look, I don't mind a bit of something different late at night, but at lunchtime on a sunny Saturday I wasn't ready. Gingerly, I started to edge my way out, only for something even odder to happen.

I was stopped by a petite woman, around my age, who shouted something in my ear that sounded like 'DVT'. I thought this was some reference to my cursed compression sock, but it turned out she had said 'DMT'. Specifically: 'You need to smoke some DMT,' which presumably is what was emanating from the thing she was waving under my nose. I thanked her very politely, but refused. It became clear that this was an extremely good decision. 'The effects of DMT take hold almost immediately when smoked. Users may feel like they are instantly transported to another universe,' I read. Crikey. 'Within five minutes … users may experience increased blood pressure, rapid heartbeat and dilated pupils.'

Relieved but shaken, I went off to the Healing Fields. There, a nice chap from Dorset calmed me with instructions on how to carve a heart into a square of Maltese limestone. All this before lunch. There really is something for everyone at that place.

The sun got hotter, the crowds thickened and still, to my increasing admiration, not a temper frayed. The sheer good nature of everyone in attendance started to feel almost absurd.

My daughter told me to meet her at the Other stage, where she said I would enjoy Beabadoobee — no, me neither. But she was right, I did. It was all getting nicer and nicer.

Word reached me of fire and brimstone elsewhere ahead of the Kneecap gig. It came across like news from a distant planet where they did things differently. I neither saw, heard nor felt anything along those lines anywhere I ventured all weekend.

By the time Pulp took to the Pyramid stage, the peace-and-love control knobs were turned up to 11. Sensing the softening of my heart, my colleagues took the opportunity to force me into silly hats and whatnot. Everyone sang along. Everyone danced. Even me, nearly. The Red Arrows flew over. What next? Santa? To my consternation, I got a bit tearful. I give in. Glastonbury is a good thing. Anything that makes the world feel this nice has to be a seriously good thing.

To anyone who has been scathing about Glastonbury without having attended — as was the case with me — I humbly suggest your cynicism would not survive the reality of being there.

30 JUNE

Russia pays young Ukrainians to be unwitting suicide bombers in shadow war

SHAUN WALKER

Oleh found the job via a Telegram channel offering day work and side gigs. It sounded easy enough: he was to travel from his home in eastern Ukraine to the western city of Rivne, pick up a rucksack containing a paint canister and spray it outside the local police station.

It would require nimble feet to flee the scene without being caught, but the money on offer — $1,000 — was good, fantastic even, for what amounted to a morning's work for the 19-year-old.

But when, on a snowy morning in early February, he opened the bag outside Rivne's police station, he recoiled in horror. Instead of a paint canister, he saw something that looked like a homemade bomb, with protruding wires and a mobile phone attached to it, apparently a crude remote detonation mechanism.

The device, if it had detonated, would have made Oleh an unwitting suicide bomber, part of a sinister new trend of attacks inside Ukraine that the country's SBU security agency says are organised by Russian intelligence officers using local one-time recruits. So far, there have been more than a dozen attacks in which the perpetrator was injured or killed, according to a Ukrainian law enforcement source.

Russia's sabotage campaign inside Ukraine started last spring, SBU spokesperson Artem Dekhtiarenko told the *Guardian*. To begin with, it involved arson attacks on military vehicles, conscription offices and post offices. It was primarily aimed at western Ukrainian regions, far from the front.

Ukrainians, often teenagers, were offered money via Telegram to carry out the attacks by 'curators' who used a mixture of enticements and blackmail to snare their recruits.

The perpetrators then had to make a video of the fire on their phones, and send the recording as proof the deed had been done. The videos would invariably find their way on to Russia-friendly Telegram channels, as supposed evidence of discontent inside Ukraine, stoking real social tensions over issues such as conscription that have flared during Russia's war on the country.

These attacks were part of a secret shadow war, raging in parallel with the conflict on the frontlines. Russia is also carrying out arson and sabotage attacks in European countries, according to multiple western intelligence agencies, while Ukrainian services are believed to be behind a number of arson attacks at conscription offices in Russia earlier in the war.

At the end of 2024, Russia apparently decided on a major escalation, moving from simple arson attacks in Ukraine to bombings that are more reminiscent of the tactics of terrorist groups. 'They started the mass recruitment of Ukrainians to plant bombs: in cars, near conscription offices, near police departments, and so on,' said Dekhtiarenko.

This account of Russia's new campaign of bombings in Ukraine is based on prison interviews with perpetrators, who are currently detained and awaiting trial. Their names have been changed. It also draws on access to case materials and interviews with several SBU operatives who have worked on similar cases.

The Russians recruit networks of Ukrainians, the SBU believes, with one person making the bomb and leaving it at an agreed spot. Someone else then collects it, without knowing what it is. The Russian curators can thus set off explosions deep inside Ukraine, without needing to set foot in the country.

The SBU says it has detained more than 700 people since the beginning of 2024 for sabotage, arson or terrorism. Many are unemployed or need money to feed addictions, but about a quarter of them are teenagers, the youngest to date being an 11-year-old girl from Odesa region.

'In some cases, the agents don't only plant the bomb, but unconsciously perform the role of a suicide bomber. Russians blow up their own agents; this is becoming common practice,' said Dekhtiarenko.

· · ·

Oleh, 19 and unemployed, was badly in need of cash. 'I sat at home and mostly did nothing,' is how he described the last three years, since he left school.

In 2024, he became a father, and he now had a baby to support. So he spent a lot of time on various 'work in Ukraine' Telegram channels, looking to make some quick money. On one of them he spotted a post by a man called Anton.

'He said he had easy jobs, payment in dollars. When I contacted him, he told me to take photos of the courthouse, the conscription office, the police station [in my home town]. He paid me $50, to a crypto wallet,' Oleh recalled. The payment was made in USDT, a cryptocurrency stablecoin.

Russian curators usually start off with simple tasks like this, say SBU officers. Taking photographs of sensitive sites is one common request, printing out and hanging a few copies of subversive flyers is another. Then, once the recruit is drawn in, they up the stakes.

'Sometimes they use threats, sometimes they are friendly and encouraging. It depends on who is curating the agent; they use different psychological manipulations on different people,' said Dekhtiarenko.

Often, the curators use youth slang to give the impression the recruit is talking to someone their own age. Sometimes they flirt with the recruits, or offer them moral support about difficult family situations. They will not usually reveal themselves as Russians; they might claim to be Ukrainians who are 'tired of war' and want to show there is opposition to it.

If the recruit is proving unwilling, the curator might reveal the Russian connection and use blackmail to push for further action, threatening to send evidence of previous cooperation to the SBU.

'After people perform the first task, they are on the hook,' said Dekhtiarenko. In one case, malware was sent to the mobile phone of a teenage female recruit and the curator threatened to publish intimate photographs and videos hacked from the phone if the girl did not continue to cooperate.

Soon after Oleh had taken the photographs, Anton offered him a new task: to burn down a building in his home town. Oleh didn't want to do that; he wasn't a terrorist, he told the man. When Anton insisted, Oleh blocked his account.

But the exchange stuck in Oleh's mind, because he really needed money. So when another man, who claimed to be called Alexander, got in touch with him on Telegram a few weeks later, and suggested the possibility of earning $1,000 without the need to burn anything, he was sorely tempted.

Oleh was worried about doing the job alone, so he called his old school friend Serhiy and suggested they did the job together. He offered to split the $1,000 down the middle.

'He said: "I've got some work, wanna come to Rivne?" I said: "What's the work?" and he said: "I'll tell you later,"' Serhiy recalled in an interview. Serhiy quickly agreed; he was also unemployed, and had two children. The money would be useful.

Oleh told his girlfriend he was off for a couple of days to make some money for her and their child. Alexander, the Telegram curator, sent him about $200 up front for expenses, again in cryptocurrency, and he bought tickets for a bus from Sumy region to Rivne. The ride took all day; Oleh and Serhiy arrived in Rivne late in the evening. Alexander told Oleh he should find a cheap hotel for the night and await instructions.

The next morning, Alexander sent Oleh a location pin — a garage cooperative on the outskirts of town. 'He said all we have to do is pick up a rucksack there with some paint in it,' said Serhiy. The duo set out, a little nervous.

When they got to the location, Oleh called his Telegram contact, who guided him by phone. 'He said, "Turn right, between garage number 32 and number 33, and you'll see a tyre,"' Oleh recalled. Stashed inside the tyre, he found a black rucksack and a white plastic bag. He picked up both of them, as instructed.

Alexander told Oleh not to open the bags but to head to the next location he would share via Telegram, which was a pin for the local police station, and then call him. The canister was primed to explode when the bag was opened, Alexander said, spraying the walls of the police station with paint and delivering an anti-establishment message about the futility of war. Oleh called a taxi and the pair headed into town.

Oleh and Serhiy agreed they would split up ahead of reaching the police station; Oleh would be in charge of coordinating with Alexander where he should leave the bag, while Serhiy would keep lookout to check they were not being followed and tell his friend if he spotted anything suspicious.

The Telegram chat between them, seen by the *Guardian*, shows Serhiy was deeply uneasy. 'I've seen the same BMW again, and the same woman,' he wrote, suspecting they were being watched. 'Let's hope everything's going to be OK,' Oleh wrote.

Alexander called Oleh and told him he should open the white plastic bag and take out the box he would find in it. Then he should walk, holding it, towards the entrance of the police station.

Oleh did so, but grew suspicious and opened the box to check the contents. He was startled to see something that looked like very much like a bomb. Panicking, he decided to rush to the nearest police officer, and announced that he feared he was carrying explosives. Just as he did so, SBU operatives pounced on both Oleh and Serhiy, grabbing the packages and forcing the two men on to the ground.

· · ·

An SBU team had been watching Oleh and Serhiy ever since they picked up the bomb, according to an operative involved in the case. Just three days earlier, Rivne had experienced a very similar attack. An unemployed 21-year-old was recruited on Telegram to pick up a device and take it to one of the city's military conscription offices. The device exploded, killing the attacker and wounding eight soldiers.

The operative described the scheme in Oleh and Serhiy's case: the black rucksack contained a homemade explosive device, packed with screws and nails; the smaller bag held a white box containing a less powerful explosive device.

This box had a small hole cut into it, with a cameraphone that transmitted geolocation and images of the surroundings to Alexander, who was also speaking to Oleh on a Telegram call. He could watch video of Oleh's location in real time and direct him to a suitable spot packed with people. Then, as Oleh waited for the command to remove the supposed paint canister from the bag, the curator would detonate both devices, by calling the phones attached to them.

If this had happened, Oleh would most likely be dead, just like the attacker three days previously. The entrance to the police station was crowded with officers coming and going, and visitors queuing to receive building passes, so many more may have been killed with him.

But the SBU had followed the pair and had special equipment on hand, the operative said, expecting another attack after the previous blast. 'We had certain technical means to block the signals to the telephone,' said the source. When Alexander rang the phones strapped to the bombs to detonate them, the calls did not go through.

As for the real identity of Alexander, the SBU is not certain, though it is confident in the assessment that, one way or another, he represented the Russian services. It is believed that sometimes the curation is done by staff officers of GRU military intelligence or the FSB domestic security service, but both services also recruit go-betweens to make the actual calls.

The SBU has not yet found the person who made the bombs that Oleh and Serhiy picked up, although the assumption is that it was done by another Ukrainian teenager recruited by Alexander. Previously, the SBU in Rivne detained a teenage girl for making similar explosive devices. She had also been recruited on Telegram and was then sent video tutorials on how to make the devices from commonly available products.

To try to counteract the recruitment of teenagers for such tasks, the SBU has launched an awareness programme in Ukrainian schools, to warn children of the dangers of accepting offers to make money from strangers on Telegram.

'The only free cheese is in a mousetrap, as the saying goes,' said one of the officers involved. The agency has also set up a chatbot where young Ukrainians can report any suspicious approaches or Telegram accounts to the authorities.

The big question for European intelligence services, which have been dealing with a wave of Russia-linked arson and sabotage attacks over the past year, is whether Moscow will export its latest tactic in Ukraine to the west. So far, attacks in the west have sought to cause chaos and sometimes material damage, but have not been directly designed to cause bloodshed.

A Ukrainian law enforcement source said that could change: 'Ukraine is the testing ground for Russian conventional and hybrid warfare. Look at cyber-attacks, look at arson attacks, look at the sabotage on railways. They test things here, and then they do it in western countries,' said the source.

For Oleh and Serhiy, being caught may have saved their lives, but they are now behind bars, awaiting a trial in which they could be sentenced to up to 12 years of prison time. Oleh said he is not sure yet if he will plead guilty; he insists he did not realise he was working for the Russians, or that his actions could have led to carnage.

In a brief telephone conversation from the prison where he is being held in Rivne, his girlfriend told him to forget about ever speaking to her or their child ever again. He also had a short phone call with his parents, the content of which he summed up glumly and succinctly: 'They said I'm an idiot.'

Summer

Storms rage, but what imperils Starmer is still a lack of vision

MARTIN KETTLE

There will be no birthday candles in Downing Street this week. Nor should there be. Twelve months after Labour's landslide election win on 4 July 2024, Keir Starmer's government has capped a year in office with a week of political dishevelment and ineptitude. The welfare reform bill itself is now a meaningless shell. The Labour party is united only in its frustrations.

The welfare rebellion was not a bolt from the blue. Instead, it provides the keystone to an arc of earlier blunders. It poses urgent issues about professional incompetence in Labour's Westminster machine. It embodies what is not working in the way Starmer's top-down party does politics more generally. This will not be the end of it, as the furore over Rachel Reeves's tears at a raucous prime minister's questions seems to confirm. Things can't go on like this.

More specifically, the welfare bill poses the question of how the Labour party now negotiates its commitment to the truly poor with the concerns of the much larger number of voters who are not poor. Tuesday's divisions showed that pitting one against the other is merely destructive. Yet Labour has not developed a plan to reconcile the two more sensibly. It will need to learn fast from this shock. The fact remains that Labour can only ever win and retain power if it is more than just the party of the poor.

The MPs' revolt turbo-charges other questions that were already dominating politics, long before this week, but which the welfare row embodied. First, how on earth did Starmer's Labour manage to squander so much support so fast and decisively after winning its 174-seat Commons majority in 2024? And, second, what can Labour do about it in the time that remains?

The two are umbilically connected. But the second question is the one that matters more. Retrieving a dire situation means focusing on the future, not apologising for the past. Labour has to reverse its losses to have any hope of winning the second election victory on which Starmer once banked, but which now seems an unrealisably distant dream.

To do this nevertheless requires understanding of what has gone so badly. The past 12 months have been riddled with avoidable errors, tin-eared moments and, above all, have been painfully marked by an absence of vision and even competence. Anthony Seldon, doyen of historians of Downing Street, says no prime minister since 1945 has begun as badly as Starmer. The polling figures bear this out.

This is a crisis. Don't bullshit about it. Don't take refuge in blaming the media. It won't do, either, to harp on about the unfairness of partisan attacks from Labour's rivals. Nor is there much value in stressing the immense difficulties that have undoubtedly faced Starmer: attempting to govern amid war in Europe, the Trump counter-revolution, global migration pressures and a seemingly embedded economic stagnation. These are truths. They define the real context of the government's task. But they cannot be excuses.

It should have been obvious on day one, even with a vast majority and the Tory party on its knees, that Labour's 2024 performance wasn't the triumph it sometimes felt like. Only 34 per cent of the votes cast last year were for Labour. But only 60 per cent of Britons voted at all. So Starmer's parliamentary supremacy was conferred by a mere 20 per cent of the country, and by fewer than 10 million voters. Right from the start he needed to broaden his coalition, to pay far more attention to building trust across the nation.

This required more than triangulating Nigel Farage or the striking of attitudes. The underlying truth about Labour's relationship with the nation is that four out of five Britons were unconvinced by the party, even after the shambles of the Johnson-Truss-Sunak years. Today, that doubting majority is even larger. In an average of polls, Labour now stands on 23 per cent. One in three of its already low total of 2024 voters have gone elsewhere. It was always a loveless landslide. It is now in grave danger of being an unwanted one.

It is true that other prime ministers have got themselves into difficulties, lost byelections, faced parliamentary revolts and had bad press in their first year. Within months of winning power in 1979, Margaret Thatcher came under open attack from members of her own cabinet over economic policy, something that has not yet happened to Starmer. Tony Blair faced a 47-MP revolt on lone parent benefit in his year one in 1997, almost identical to Starmer's 49-MP rebellion on Tuesday. Both recovered to win landslides at the next general elections.

Why should Starmer not do the same? One reason is because trust in government and politics is now far lower than in the past. Starmer is an analogue prime minister in a digital age. Another is that it was always extremely clear what both Thatcher and Blair were aiming to achieve in government. Each had a project — Thatcher to roll back the state and the trade unions, Blair to modernise Britain's economy and place in the world. Voters knew what they were getting. What, though, is Starmer's project? What is the destination he aims to reach?

Answering this question is the most important task facing Starmer today. In the most famous sentence Charles de Gaulle ever penned, at the start of the war memoirs he wrote in the 1950s, he said: 'All my life, I have had a certain idea of France.' As his biographer Julian Jackson makes clear, de Gaulle's 'certain idea' was not always consistent, and was never a fully articulated programme — more a stance than a doctrine. But de Gaulle's idea had very clear features, which millions of French voters understood and often approved of. He stood for a distinct French historical identity, for France's political independence, for its grandeur and for its social cohesion.

Whether Starmer has a certain idea of Britain, let alone has held that idea all his life, is hard to know. His recent interview with his biographer Tom Baldwin suggests not. The interview is oddly naive. It is full of regrets and admissions of bad judgment but has little sense of history or people. Yet the need for Starmer to tell an uplifting story to Britons about Britain is at least as important as his need to solve some of his more specific policy problems.

Starmer is a bit like a ship's captain who, faced with rough weather and heavy seas, ploughs on without telling the passengers and crew why. He may in fact be doing the right thing for the ship of state. Calmer seas may perhaps await. The voyage may eventually prove prosperous. But whether the problem is his failure to explain, a lack of basic seagoing skills, or just a stubborn overconfidence, the result right now is very different — an unhappy Labour ship, and even a mutinous one.

Crying in the Commons: why are women's workplace tears a source of shame?

AMELIA GENTLEMAN

Rachel Reeves's tears this week triggered a fall in the pound and attracted widespread derision from political columnists, mostly male. 'What is wrong with Rachel Reeves?' the *Telegraph* asked. In an article headlined 'The meaning of the chancellor's tears', a *New Statesman* columnist told readers that Reeves's authority was 'beginning to melt away'. The *Daily Mail* spoke disdainfully of her 'waterworks'.

But in the longer term the chancellor's display of distress may prove to have an unexpectedly positive legacy, helpfully normal-ising a still hugely stigmatised phenomenon: women's tears in the workplace.

Until now, tearful outbursts at work have mostly been mired in shame, the source of acute embarrassment. This week's live broadcast of the chancellor's silent tears could help shift the taboo, highlighting a little-discussed truth: sometimes women cry at work, and it's no big deal.

Reeves reflected on her own tears with a shrug a day later. 'People saw I was upset, but that was yesterday. Today's a new day and I'm just cracking on with the job,' she said on Thursday. She declined to explain what had prompted her distress, describing it simply as a personal issue and refusing to go into details. Within 24 hours the markets had bounced back with the assurances of the prime minister, Keir Starmer, that she would remain in her job for the long term.

Clearly it is far from ideal to be filmed in tears during the week's most-watched exchanges in the House of Commons, but ministerial jobs are immensely tough. Some of Reeves's male predecessors have exhibited the strain of their roles in more extreme ways, while attracting less attention, because their behaviour is classed as routine and acceptable machismo.

When Britain's former prime minister Gordon Brown was exhausted and under pressure he was known to be prone to volcanic eruptions. One biographer described how Brown would stab the seat of the ministerial Jaguar with his pen in fury. Bloomberg reported that a new aide was warned to watch out for 'flying Nokias' when he joined Brown's team (although a spokesperson for Brown said at the time that this was 'not an account that I recognise').

Reeves's tears were widely seen as a sign that she was losing control. Brown's fury was forgiven by many as just a regrettable quirk displayed by a leader under pressure.

Research consistently confirms what we instinctively know: that women cry more frequently than men. So it stands to reason that as we see more women in senior leadership roles, the sight of a powerful woman in tears should become less remarkable. It would be odd to celebrate it, since it's an exhausting and often mortifying phenomenon, but Reeves's outburst may help it to be better understood as simply a different way of expressing profes-sional frustration or responding to pressure.

Polling conducted by YouGov in the UK revealed that 34 per cent of men claimed not to have cried at all in the previous year, compared with only 7 per cent of women; 18 per cent of women said they cried at least once a week, compared with only 4 per cent of men. Behaviour varies between cultures, but this remains a broadly global phenomenon: a 2011 study of 5,715 participants from 37 countries found women were more prone to crying and were more likely to have cried recently.

This week, Germany's former leader Angela Merkel revealed that she 'burst out crying from the pressure' during a meeting with the then US president, Barack Obama, on how to handle Greece's mounting debt crisis in 2015. Theresa May was on the brink of tears when she stepped down as the UK prime minister in May 2019, her voice cracking and lips wobbling as she stood outside Downing Street, telling assembled journalists that it had been the honour of her life 'to serve the country I love'. Margaret Thatcher was in tears when she was driven from Downing Street in 1990. By contrast, David Cameron hummed his way back inside No 10 after his resignation speech in 2016.

Obama wept occasionally when president, but these were mostly dignified occasions, prompted by the memory of tragic events, such as the shooting of schoolchildren during a speech about gun control. His tears were not the unattractive and uncontrollable, messy and humiliating variety, but were mostly seen as commendable expressions of his humanity. Vladimir Putin appeared emotional a decade ago during a soft-rock song honouring the bravery of the Russian police force, but these too were a different kind of tears.

Political behaviour in Britain has been slow to change, despite the rapidly evolving makeup of the Commons. In 2024, the UK elected the highest number of female MPs ever. There are now 264 women in the Commons, holding 41 per cent of the 650 seats. Since the 1997 election of the Labour party saw the proportion of women double from 9 per cent to 18 per cent, there has been a steady rise, but the institution's combative culture has barely changed.

'We've had years of men shouting, scoffing, braying, even sleeping in this chamber, so we shouldn't overreact to a woman showing her frustration with one tear,' said Penny East, the chief executive of the Fawcett Society, a feminist campaigning charity. 'It shouldn't be interpreted as a sign that she's not up to her job. These criticisms feel riddled with sexism and stereotype.'

Ask any female colleague, and they will probably reluctantly admit to having wrestled with the challenge of holding back tears at work, often prompted by professional frustration rather than sadness. I've done it, during a difficult conversation with an editor, raising my eyes to the ceiling and tilting my head back, hoping that gravity would somehow suck the tears back inside the ducts and that no one would notice.

Women know it can be damaging professionally because crying remains categorised as a sign of incompetence and weakness, an unacceptable manifestation of stress. One accomplished acquaintance in a senior role was unfairly nicknamed Tiny Tears in private by her staff because occasionally she responded to challenging situations with involuntary tears. Her colleagues were less familiar with this manifestation of professional dissatisfaction than they might have been with a display of male anger.

Another woman described crying on her third day at her new job as a chief executive of a large organisation. 'It wasn't live on the media, but it was in an open-plan office and I was surrounded by senior and junior staff. I'm not remotely comparing my job to the job of the chancellor, but there was a huge burden of responsibility and I was having to take difficult decisions,' she said.

She was embarrassed by her own tears because she could see how uncomfortable it made her team. 'But I didn't see it as a loss of control. We shouldn't assume that displays of emotions represent a loss of control over ability to do your job.' She thinks, however, the episode may unexpectedly have helped her win colleagues' respect. 'They could see I really cared about what we were there to do.'

Although there is no difference in the amount male and female babies cry, women cry more frequently than men because of a complex mix of social conditioning and biology. Ad Vinger-hoets, a professor of clinical psychology at Tilburg University in the Netherlands, has studied the science of tears, and notes that testosterone acts as a 'brake' on the crying response.

Sophie Scott, a professor of cognitive neuroscience at University College London, who specialises in analysing how emotions are expressed through laughter and tears, said: 'How we experience and express our emotions is influenced by our biology and by how we've grown up.'

Scott made a distinction between tears produced as a result of sadness and tears triggered by anger, noting that these tears of frustration and fury seemed to be more frequently something experienced by women. 'If you're angry and you feel you can't do something about it, there's a helpless, frustrated feeling that pushes you to tears,' she said.

Women seemed to find themselves more frequently fighting tears of frustration than men, Scott said, adding that this might be because 'angry and more aggressive responses are more acceptable in men'.

Unusually, Reeves's misery was caught playing out over the 30-minute duration of the prime minister's questions session, allowing viewers a rare and uncomfortable view of someone attempting and failing to stem the flow, lips twitching and turning downwards. 'A big difference between my job and many of your viewers' is that when I'm having a tough day it's on the telly, and most people don't have to deal with that,' Reeves told the BBC.

Scott said many forms of tears were hard to control, adding: 'Crying is a very truthful signal. Once it gets hold of you, it's very hard to stop it. It's involuntary.'

Rosie Campbell, a professor of politics at King's College London, said she was staggered by the negativity triggered by Reeves's tears. 'In our society, women are more likely to cry. That doesn't make them worse leaders,' she said. 'I don't want to see politicians crying in the chamber every day, but if it happens a couple of times in a parliamentary career, that should be no big deal.

'I'm more worried about emotionally repressed leaders than about someone who realises that the financial security of the nation is in their hands and they feel the weight of that.'

5 JULY

A shameless trip back to the 90s for Britpop's loudest, greatest songs

ALEXIS PETRIDIS

The noise from the audience when Oasis arrive on stage for their first reunion gig is deafening. You might have expected a loud response. This is, after all, a crowd so partisan that, in between the support acts, they cheer the promotional videos — the tour's accompanying brand deals seem to involve not just the obviously Oasis-adjacent sportswear brand Adidas, but the more imponderable Land Rover Defender.

Even so, the noise the fans make as the reconstituted Oasis launch into 'Hello' takes you aback slightly, and not just because 'Hello' is a fairly bold choice of opener: this is, after all, a song that borrows heavily from 'Hello, Hello, I'm Back Again' by Gary

Glitter. But no one in Cardiff's Principality Stadium seems to care about the song's genesis: the noise is such that you struggle to think of another artist that's received such a vociferous reception.

So, the success of the show seems more or less like a foregone conclusion. Anyone who saw them in the 00s will tell you that the old Oasis were a hugely variable proposition live: you never knew what mood Liam Gallagher would show up in, or how the current state of familial relations might affect their performance. But evidently as little as possible has been left to chance at these reunion gigs. No one — including, to their immense credit, Liam and Noel Gallagher — seems interested in pretending this tour is anything other than a hugely lucrative cash-grab, and, clearly, you only grab the maximum possible cash if the tour doesn't descend into the kind of bedlam to which Oasis tours were once prone.

Liam is on his best behaviour — 'thanks for putting up with us,' he offers at one juncture, 'I know we're hard work', a noticeable shift from the days when he was wont to rain abuse on the audience — and Liam and Noel have rhythm guitarist Paul 'Bonehead' Arthurs stood squarely between them on stage, creating distance. You could say that removes combustibility, the hint of potential chaos that was at least part of Oasis's appeal, but you might as well save your breath: no one would be able to hear you over the sound of people singing along en masse to a set that plays to the strengths of Oasis's back catalogue.

Few bands' reputations have been better served by the rise of streaming, both in its favouring of curated playlists over albums — all the highlights and none of the rubbish, of which there was a great deal in Oasis's later years — and in the way it decontextualises music, denuding it of its accompanying story or contemporary critical responses. The much-vaunted Oasis fans too young to remember the band first-hand definitely exist — you can see them in the audience — but you do wonder how many of them believe Oasis split up in 1998, rather than grimly trudging on for another decade, to declining artistic returns.

The show seeks to maintain this myth. It's very much playlist Oasis, big on the first two albums and B-sides from the years when Noel Gallagher's songwriting talent seemed so abundant he could afford to blithely confine stuff as good as 'Acquiesce' or 'The Masterplan' to an extra track on a CD single, and low on anything at all from their later years. Only the presence of 2002's 'Little by Little' indicates that Oasis existed into the 21st century.

You can still sense inspiration declining — 1997's 'D'You Know What I Mean?' sounds like a trudge regardless of how many people are singing along — but far more often, the show serves as a reminder of how fantastic purple-patch Oasis were. Against a ferocious wall of distorted guitars, there's a weird disconnect between the tone of Noel's songs — wistful, noticeably melancholy — and the way Liam sings them like a man seething with frustration, on the verge of offering someone a fight. Even discounting half their career, they have classics in abundance: 'Cigarettes & Alcohol', 'Slide Away', 'Rock 'n' Roll Star', 'Morning Glory'. Enough, in fact, that a section where Liam cedes the stage and Noel takes over vocals doesn't occasion a dip in the audience's enthusiasm: during 'Half the World Away', the audience's vocals threaten to drown the song's author out entirely.

It ends with precisely the encore you might have expected — 'Don't Look Back in Anger', 'Wonderwall' and 'Champagne Supernova' — which understandably occasions precisely the response you might have expected. A very perfunctory clap on the back — the only time the Gallaghers interact beyond playing the same songs — and Liam vanishes: a car is waiting by the side of the stage to whisk him away before the final notes die away, a triumph in the bag.

5 JULY

A rake has it in for me
— and the tortoise

TIM DOWLING

On a weekend afternoon, with the temperature nudging 30°C, my wife and I take the dog for a walk. Neither of us wants to go, so we go together, and agree to keep it short.

'Oh no,' my wife says when we get to the park. I look across the open expanse and see what she sees.

'Picnics,' I say. Under every tree, in every square foot of available shade, people are sitting on blankets with food spread in front of them.

'An absolute minefield,' my wife says. 'I should have thought of this.'

To be fair, the dog has never disrupted a picnic in progress, causing the sort of mayhem my wife and I are both very good at imagining. That's because the dog has never been allowed anywhere near a picnic.

We keep the dog on the lead until we are safely across some baked playing fields, taking a wide route that affords no shade and makes the walk twice as long as we'd anticipated.

When we get home, drained and listless, I find the tortoise on his back in the garden again, legs flapping helplessly. Like the summer heat, the tortoise going upside down used to be a once-every-four-years event, but this is the second time it's happened in six weeks. I think: how careless can one animal be? I set the tortoise back on his feet, and promptly step on a rake.

To be fair, I was heading for the rake on purpose — it was leaning against the house and I was intending to put it away. But as I approach I fail to notice the tines are facing outward, and put my foot on them. The handle flies past my outstretched fingers and thwacks me in the face.

'Ow,' I say, feeling my upper lip, which has already begun to swell. Flinging the rake into the bushes by the back door, I am reminded that slapstick is the purest form of humiliation — simple and total. I resolve to tell no one about this episode.

'I just stepped on a rake, like in a cartoon,' I say to the middle one five minutes later.

'Really?' he says, not looking up from his laptop.

'A once-in-a-lifetime act of stupidity,' I say, although I recall the same thing happening to me about three years ago. At least it was dark that time.

'I guess the lesson is, put the rake away,' he says.

'I was putting the rake away,' I say.

The next morning my wife suggests a walk in a place she is sure will be free of picnics. 'And it's on the way to the dump,' she says.

We drive to a car park at the very edge of the borough, alongside a remote skateboard park patronised exclusively by men over 30.

'What's that about?' my wife says.

'Dunno,' I say. 'Some restraining order-based initiative, maybe.'

Beyond the skate park lies a small, empty field, recently mowed.

'On my phone it looks like it goes on for miles,' my wife says. But in front of us we can only see a couple of acres. We cross the field to a line of trees and follow a narrow path overgrown with brambles and nettles, emerging at a gurgling stream spanned by an improvised bridge of garbage: an old tyre, a partially burnt log and two of those long rubber feet used to support temporary fencing.

'What now?' I say.

'We cross,' my wife says.

Beyond the stream we find a vast space reclaimed by wilderness: stubby trees, wildflowers, wetlands full of ducks and herons.

We can see nothing beyond this oasis but tall buildings in the distance. There are no other people. The dog zips through the tall grass, leaving zigzagged indentations.

'It's amazing,' my wife says.

'And so handy for the dump,' I say.

Back at home, the dog stretches out on the cool kitchen floor, exhausted. I go to open the garden door, only to find it jammed. The handle of the rake is leaning against it on the other side, wedged into the corner of the glass pane, holding it shut.

I think: this rake really has it in for me. I force the door open a few inches and squeeze past.

At the other end of the rake I find the tortoise, his back leg trapped between two tines. Evidently he was ambling past, caught his foot and pulled the rake over against the door.

'I can't help feeling this is partly my fault,' I say, freeing his trapped foot. The tortoise gives me a look that says: this is all your fault.

I guess the lesson is, put the rake away.

14 July

Stokes loomed over Lord's like the Angel of the North

BARNEY RONAY

'I'm not tired. I'm not tired. I'm not tired.' Really, Ben? *Really?* Well, you're pretty much on your own in that case old boy, after a day where simply watching Ben Stokes being Ben Stokes felt like a full contact sport, psychodrama, soap opera, and in its stickiest moments like a man engaged in an act of public self-medication by Test cricket.

This fifth day at Lord's was entirely dominated by Stokes, who loomed over it like the Angel of the North, arms outspread, another note in his own extraordinary sporting life. It was shortly after midday that Stokes came running through at the end of his eighth successive over from the Nursery End to talk to the batter Nitish Kumar Reddy, to tell him, specially, that he wasn't tired — hyped and pumped, eyes boggled, drawing boos from the largely Indian crowd.

India were 101 for seven at that point and losing the game at a steady stagger. As Stokes wheeled in, drop-in tresses flowing behind him (colour range: Nordic God), it seemed likely the defining image of the day would be that beautifully desiccated fifth-day pitch in midday sunlight, scratched, marked, bruised, as weathered and handsome as Stokes himself.

Except of course Test cricket will only ever move at its own pace. By the time the final wicket fell almost five hours later, with the lights now dimming a little, Stokes could only stare up at the skies from his position at long-on as the entire England team ran to deep point behind Shoaib Bashir, a perfect tableau of joy, relief and exhaustion.

India had clung on in the hours in between with wonderful skill and courage, scoring at one an over, patting out the dots, as the day settled into a kind of fever dream, a march through the desert. There were moments where it was hard to remember a time before this, a time when Stokes wasn't bowling from both ends simultaneously. This is just life now. Ben Stokes is bowling at Lord's. Ben Stokes will always be bowling at Lord's.

In between he kept on doing all the other things, captaining, cheerleading, talking endlessly, walking back all the way to the end of his mark with Jofra Archer. Some people have main character energy. Stokes has all the other energies too, supporting actor, romantic lead, good guy, villain, extra, best boy, executive producer.

It is extraordinary to watch him in this environment now, coming towards the necessary end of a vivid personal era. For all the occasional comic oddities of Bazball, this has always come from a place of love, passion and cinematic personal obsession.

England captains of the past have often been a little mardy and pinched, doggedly seeing this out. Stokes just loves it. He's a destiny man. He lives this thing, and does it generously too, inviting you in to spectate. Even the line about not being tired is a peek into the mantras of the Bazball dressing room (never say you're tired, low, hurt: bad voodoo spreads bad voodoo).

It is a level of commitment that can teeter close to mania, and did so here as India clung on. Stokes bowled 24 overs in this second innings, twice as many as Chris Woakes, a feat of endurance that will put a huge strain on his body. At the afternoon drinks break he called the team together and delivered an inspirational speech. Presumably that speech ran: I'm going to bowl for ever now. That's the plan: me.

There was logic here. Stokes was the senior bowler in many ways. He has played more Tests than the entire attack put together. He bowled brilliantly, too. It was Stokes who finally induced Jasprit Bumrah to spoon a slog to mid-on to take India to 147 for eight and push the 2–1 series lead into sight.

This is a point of high jeopardy for Stokes, for the Project, for his own era. Win this series, then win the Ashes. It is far from impossible. At which point Stokes gets to ride off into his own maniacally febrile retirement as a genuinely great England captain.

This Test was proof of something else, too. Stokes may be 34 and held together with brown string, but he still has the moments in him.

He is perhaps a better bowler now than at any stage. Here he was touching 89mph in his seventh over. He got the key wicket of KL Rahul early on with a ball that zinged up the slope (there is no slope: I, Ben Stokes, am the slope) and was given lbw on review after an appeal that seemed to be based on the poster for the movie *Platoon*: full starfish, on his knees, roaring into the hail of machine-gun fire.

It even felt right that the final wicket should fall to Bashir, a Stokes project, injured and a little underdone, but wheeled back out here at just the right moment for some personal redemption. This is the best part of Stokes, his emotional connection to the team and to English cricket; the ability to talk about things like depression and mental health, the struggles of life, even in the middle of his own very alpha sporting success, a genuinely rare kind of public candour.

This series can still head either way from here, just as Stokes himself must now see what exactly the rigours of those five days have done to his joints. But this was another one of his special days, another note in that examination of the far extremes of character and will that only Test cricket can really give.

15 July

Disabled people deserve full lives. Instead we're scrapping for basic rights

FRANCES RYAN

There is a longstanding practice in UK politics and media to force disabled people to fight for their basic rights — a kind of gladiatorial scrap in which the Colosseum is replaced by the set of *Good Morning Britain*.

With the government's welfare reform bill just passed by MPs, this has felt all the more stark. In the last week alone, the leader of the opposition, Kemi Badenoch, has used a speech to declare she does not 'believe' that one in four people are disabled, as if the Equality Act were based on vibes. 'Twenty-eight million people in Britain are working to pay the wages and benefits of 28 million others,' she went on. 'The rider is as big as the horse.'

Days earlier, GB News aired a discussion in which a comedian 'joked' that the best way to reduce the disability benefits bill was to starve or shoot disabled people.

Faced with this level of discourse, campaigners have little choice but to argue the most obvious of truths: if the political and media class advocates policies that leave disabled people hungry and dirty, the disabled community must explain why we should be allowed to eat and be clean.

As the number of people with long-term health conditions has increased, the living standards that disabled people are expected to accept have only declined. That many of these cases are related to mental health — often incorrectly seen as mild, less real, or unaccompanied by physical conditions — has only encouraged this backlash. In the last fortnight, I have watched disabled activists go on breakfast news and argue that wheel-chair users deserve help to leave the house. I've seen chronically ill people make reels on social media listing for strangers the intimate items they need disability benefits to pay for.

I realise I've done similar in my work over the last 15 years: whether it is arguing for disabled people's right to sleep on unsoiled sheets or — as of last month — to receive enough care to change their bloodied sanitary towels.

Disabled people have to prove our humanity on repeat, sharing ever more intimate details of our lives and bodies to prove ourselves worthy, not least of taxpayer money. Each time it happens, I can feel myself shrink and shift a little more. It is ironic — or telling — that the degradation reminds me of a disability benefits assessment.

Such a political culture not only psychologically damages disabled people, it damages our ability to gain our full rights. Toni Morrison said the function of racism was distraction, and I think it is similar for ableism. The political cycle of the past decade — a government introduces a cut to disability support, much of the media argues it's valid, a minority outlines why it isn't — not only legitimises dismantling the safety net, it wastes disabled people's time that we could be using elsewhere. If you are busy arguing that social care cuts shouldn't force disabled people to go to bed at 6pm, there is little energy left to lobby for better access to pubs and restaurants, or simply to enjoy going to one.

Whenever a politician or pundit suggests benefit claimants are splurging taxpayer cash on booze and fags, I tweet that I'm off to spend my personal independence payments on Moët. I do that partly because I like to give people a chance to call a *Guardian* columnist a champagne socialist, but mainly because I am increasingly exhausted by the confines of the conversation. Years of austerity measures coupled with media scapegoating — on top of existing structural inequality and attitudes — has in many ways reduced disability in the public consciousness to the lowest common denominator. Forget ambitions to hire more disabled talent in senior roles or to improve access to social and sporting venues — Britain prefers to discuss whether disabled people should be allowed to eat and go to the toilet.

I recently published a book, *Who Wants Normal?*, in an attempt to carve out a nuanced look at disabled life: the joy, humour and talent alongside the pills and the prejudice. In promoting it, I chose to turn down any interview with a broadcaster who has a track record of ableism or go on a 'pundit v pundit' format in which bigotry and equality are pitched as equal points of view. I have no interest at this point in debating whether disabled people deserve human rights, or in shying away from advocating for a rich and fulfilling life lest we appear ungrateful or angry.

It is time this country focused not just on disabled people's right to survive, but on their right to live. Rather than talking about cutting benefit rates, let's explore raising them to a level where they actually cover the growing extra costs of disability. Instead of calling disabled jobseekers lazy, let's discuss the real causes of disability unemployment: biased employers and a lack of practical support and funding in the workplace. Rather than further isolating disabled people, we could make public spaces and infrastructure more accessible — because no one can be an equal member of society if they can't get in their local shop or on the bus.

There is a popular adage that says non-disabled people should care about such things because they could one day become disabled or ill themselves. That's true. The pundits and politicians belittling disability today could, with just the hand of bad luck, wake up tomorrow with Parkinson's or ME. But real progress won't come from non-disabled people caring about disability rights because it might one day affect them — it will come from caring that it already affects someone else.

Half the battle in all of this is challenging the unspoken belief that some of us — typically those with limited health, money or status — do not actually deserve the same quality of life as others who have more. Few people without disabilities in Britain would settle for an existence of food, heat and a wash. The question is: why should disabled people?

15 July

'A relentless, destructive energy': inside the trial of Constance Marten and Mark Gordon

SOPHIE ELMHIRST

If we believe her parents, Constance Marten and Mark Gordon, a baby girl was born on Christmas Eve, 2022, in the upstairs bedroom of Woodcutters Cottage in Haltwhistle, Northumberland. Her mother knelt against the double bed and gave birth without assistance or complication. The baby spent the first days of her life in the small stone-terraced cottage and then began her travels, mostly carried by her mother in a sling, hidden under a burgundy puffer jacket. She travelled far for a newborn, passing through bus stations and port towns, hotels and cafes, cities and fields, from north to south, west to east. We know she lived for at least two weeks, but we don't know, and can never know, precisely how she died. She was called Victoria.

. . .

On 3 March 2025, the first day of the pre-trial hearing in the case of Marten and Gordon, neither defendant turned up to court. Among the huddle of journalists outside court six of the Old Bailey, the central criminal court in England and Wales, no one seemed surprised. Last year, the couple had been tried on five counts in relation to the death of Victoria while they were camping on the South Downs in January 2023. During the original trial, when they were both present, they'd embrace, still demonstrably a couple despite being held in different prisons — Marten in Bronzefield, Gordon in Belmarsh.

Eventually, in late June 2024, they were found guilty of three charges: child cruelty, perverting the course of justice and concealing the birth of a child. The jury had been unable to reach a verdict on the two most serious charges of gross negligence manslaughter and causing or allowing the death of a child, and so a retrial of those charges had been ordered.

Mark Lucraft KC, the most senior judge at the Old Bailey, would once again preside. As he entered the court this spring, stately in his wig and flowing black and red robe, we rose to our feet. 'Constance Marten has refused to attend,' he said gravely. 'She says she's unwell, but has been declared fit.' Lucraft declared that he would continue with the trial whether the defendants were present or not.

And so the retrial of Gordon, 51, and Marten, 38, began as it meant to go on. Over the next four and a half months, two stories would unfold simultaneously in court six. One was the story of Gordon and Marten, their complex history and their crimes, and the other was of a battle for control between a married couple and a judge.

. . .

Marten and Gordon first came to public attention in January 2023. On the evening of 5 January, police found their burnt-out car on the side of the M61 motorway, near Bolton. Strewn nearby were bags of baby clothes, Marten's passport and a bag of 38 mobile phones. When the police found a placenta wrapped in a towel on the back seat of the car, they launched a national search for the couple, concerned for the welfare of the baby.

Quickly, the press began running stories: Marten is the daughter of Napier Marten, a former page to the queen. She had grown up at Crichel House, a vast stately home in Dorset, rebuilt after fire in the 18th century. Gordon, meanwhile, had spent 20 years in American prisons, having been charged with rape and battery at the age of 14. As the weeks passed and they weren't found, the nation became obsessed with this couple on the run. The acceptable face of this obsession was concern for the baby. Less openly stated, but quite obvious, was the fascination with this marriage of seeming contrast: an aristocratic white woman and a Black man with a violent criminal record.

On the second day of the pre-trial hearing, Marten entered the dock for the first time. Tall and striking, with dark tumbling hair and a wide, pale face, she brought with her a frisson of criminal celebrity. The court usher asked Marten if she'd like paper and a pen. Marten said thank you, a polite smile sweetening her expression, her eyes warm.

'Ms Marten would wish to apologise to the court for her non-attendance yesterday,' said her barrister, Francis FitzGibbon KC. 'She said the prospect of having to go through this again became overwhelming. She couldn't face it. She's here now and she will be here for the trial.'

The barristers spent the day debating the agreed facts of the case. Leading up to the death of Victoria was a long, dark history, much of which Lucraft wanted to keep out of the trial. Gordon's previous convictions from Florida were deemed so potentially prejudicial to his case that Lucraft had issued a reporting restriction preventing any mention of them. The couple's prolonged dealings with the family courts were also problematic. Gordon and Marten had four previous children, born between 2017 and 2022. The first two children had initially lived with the couple, but were placed in care after intervention from social services. The subsequent two children were removed at birth, and a family court order in January 2022 permanently removed all four children from their parents.

Lucraft declared that the trial should not be a rehashing of the family court litigation but the family court order couldn't be completely excluded, as it was relevant. The family court history also explained why the couple had gone on the run. In police interviews and evidence, Marten said they had begun travelling around England while she was pregnant to avoid the oversight of any single local authority. If social services knew of her pregnancy, she said, the baby would be automatically taken from her at birth.

In the dock, Marten's volatility was addictive to watch, as if you had to keep checking to see what mood she might be in now. Looking at her, it was difficult to compute her experience. Marten had given birth to five children within the past eight years. Four of these had been put up for adoption. One had died in her arms. Whatever her culpability, I wasn't sure how she was able to sit, or talk, or function at all.

Tom Little KC, the most senior criminal prosecutor in the country, is a bear-like man who wears a pair of thick black-framed glasses and heavy shoes. On 10 March, the first day of the trial, Little ran through his prosecution opening statement as if he were saying things so obvious that they hardly needed expressing.

Little made sure the jury were aware of Marten's background. She had access to plentiful funds through her family trust. She had the means to rent a property and provide for her child. You might feel sympathy, but her version of events could not be trusted, he warned.

Little knew what he was up against. The defendants were being blamed for causing the death of a child they loved. Little needed to show that the two things were not mutually exclusive, that you can love and harm simultaneously. This was, he concluded, a 'paradigm' case of gross negligence manslaughter, with two possible causes of death: either hypothermia or suffocation caused by dangerous co-sleeping in the tent.

Little was followed by Gordon's barrister, John Femi-Ola KC, who argued there was no evidence Victoria had died of hypothermia. The cause of death, according to two pathologists, was unascertained. Her body was so badly decomposed by the time it was discovered, in a Brighton allotment shed on 1 March 2023, that it was impossible to draw any certain conclusions. There was no evidence, either, of any harm or injury to her body, or that the defendants were consuming drink or drugs. The baby, Femi-Ola argued, was at all times kept warm, fed and close to her mother.

Finally, it was FitzGibbon's turn. Gordon and Marten decided to camp with Victoria to escape the press attention after the police had launched their manhunt, he said. Marten, exhausted, had fallen asleep over her baby after breastfeeding and compromised her breathing — something that could happen to any sleep-deprived mother of a newborn.

The prosecution's first witness was a social worker from Wales, who had been called to show that Marten had been warned five years before Victoria's death about the dangers of camping with a newborn. The social worker explained that she'd met Marten in a hospital in Wales in 2017, when Marten was heavily pregnant with her first baby. Marten had put on an Irish accent, called herself Isabella and said she was from a Traveller community and needed help finding accommodation. The social worker had then accompanied Marten to a small tent where she and Gordon were living. Seeing it bowing with rainwater, she had told Marten how inappropriate the setting would be for a mother and a baby.

Throughout the witness's evidence, Marten fumed in the dock, either muttering in protest or staring at her with a cool half-smile, shaking her head in disbelief. Over the next three weeks, she responded in the same way to all the prosecution's evidence. Between witnesses, Marten would slump back in her seat, drop her head to her chest, or yawn and sigh so loudly that heads would turn in the courtroom, a place of such codified manners that to yawn was like a breach of the law itself.

On 12 March, the third day of the trial, Marten addressed the judge directly, another flouting of the code. She was exhausted, she said, and felt that this would damage her chance of having a fair hearing. Marten explained: her days were often 19 hours long because the Serco van arrived so early at HMP Bronzefield and took hours delivering female prisoners to the various London courts.

The issue arose again a week later. 'We're leaving Bronzefield at peak rush hour,' said Marten, her voice loud and indignant. 'And we're sitting there waiting from 5am.' Marten sounded like a holidaymaker complaining to a concierge about the hotel's service. Lucraft suggested that he could neither control the traffic nor highlight her plight over the other 86,000 people in prison.

The exchange was minor, but it hinted at Marten's sense of exceptionalism. No part of her appeared cowed by being in prison. Nor was she awed by the setting of the court or the authority of the judge. The moment revealed how she saw herself: as someone who believed she could bend the justice system to her will.

. . .

According to Marten and Gordon, they arrived in Newhaven on 8 January 2023 and walked until they found a wild area, where they pitched their tent in the nook of a fallen tree. Victoria died the following day, they said. Afterwards, they spent weeks in hiding in a state of panic, not knowing what to do. Grainy CCTV footage taken on 20 February shows them scavenging in bins outside Hollingbury golf course in Brighton and Hove. And then, on 27 February, Marten can be seen taking cash out of an ATM on the outskirts of the city. Marten and Gordon were arrested later that evening.

Neither Marten nor Gordon answered any questions about the whereabouts of their baby until two days later, when Victoria's body was found by police in a Lidl bag in an allotment shed. Marten then gave three long interviews, one of which was shown to the jury. In a grey prison tracksuit, Marten spoke with a quiet, unguarded frankness. In the video, Marten explained that, as her first four children had been taken away, she believed social services would have taken Victoria, too. As she described discovering her baby's lifeless body, Marten put her hands over her face. 'I tried to resuscitate her but there was no response,' she said, her voice cracking. 'I don't know how long she'd been dead.'

Watching Marten in the video was disarming. In contrast to her brazen confidence in court, she seemed vulnerable, her grief palpable. As the weeks of the trial passed, she would often switch between these modes, inviting sympathy and provoking intense frustration almost simultaneously. There was, I began to realise, no reliable version of her personality.

· · ·

On 15 April, as the prosecution neared the end of their evidence, they hit their first major obstacle. In a printing error, an old version of a police interview with Gordon had been mistakenly placed before the jury in which reference had been made to his 'history'. In the jury's absence, Neena Crinnion, the junior barrister representing Gordon, suggested that the reference was obviously to Gordon's previous convictions. The jury, she argued, might have to be discharged — that is, dismissed and replaced by a new group of 12 people, therefore requiring the trial to start again.

Lucraft decided that the high bar for discharging a jury had not been met, but said he would keep the matter under review, and emphasised that it was not in anyone's interest for Gordon's previous convictions to be revealed to the jury. Two days later, on 17 April, the prosecution closed its case.

The trial resumed after the Easter weekend, on 22 April. It was now the turn of the defence: Gordon was not giving evidence, so we would go straight to Marten. Entering the dock, Gordon and Marten greeted each other with a hug and a kiss. When one of the dock officers tried to intervene, Gordon started shouting: 'Don't touch me!' Marten, flaring with anger, suggested he make a complaint.

FitzGibbon rose. Marten was not feeling well, he said. She had a headache and toothache, and respectfully asked if she could start her evidence tomorrow and be seen by a doctor or nurse in prison. The judge agreed. Marten would begin her evidence the next day.

That following morning, Marten was not in the dock. The jury were sent home again. Lucraft looked tense. To refuse to turn up felt less like truancy and more an exertion of control. Absence was Marten's singular power: without her, nothing could happen.

The next day, Marten was present, but FitzGibbon offered a pre-emptive excuse. She was in discomfort from her toothache and had still not been seen by a dentist. Lucraft resisted: they had already lost two days of court time and he was not going to delay again. She would begin her evidence today.

In a white shirt, her hair half-clipped back, Marten looked tired and subdued. FitzGibbon rolled back to the beginning: to Marten's childhood, growing up the eldest of four children of Napier Marten and Virginie de Selliers. Marten's upbringing had been financially privileged, she said, but emotionally starved. She'd been sent to boarding school at the age of eight, and felt her family had never been loving. Later, she went to Leeds University, and travelled in India, Nepal and Central America. She'd already fallen out with her family by the time she met Gordon by chance in a shop in east London around 2014. The shopkeeper had asked Marten to keep an eye on Gordon while she popped out, she said, and Gordon and Marten had bonded over this example of casual racism. Within three years the couple had married informally in Peru.

Under FitzGibbon's guidance, Marten's evidence unspooled calmly, punctuated by regular yawns. Once FitzGibbon began asking about her children, however, an anger began to well in her voice. They had been 'stolen by the state', she said.

Little, for the prosecution, stood in objection. Marten was treading a dangerous path. If she persisted in talking about the removal of her previous children, he would want to put more detailed evidence from the family courts before the jury. 'I think it needs to be re-litigated at some point,' she said, defiantly.

As FitzGibbon led her through the journey across England after Victoria's birth, Marten's yawns became so frequent they took on a campaigning flavour, as if to demonstrate how unfit she was to be in the witness box. The next day, Marten didn't turn up. It felt like a direct challenge to the judge, testing his resolve the way a child tests a parent's boundaries. The trial had become a tussle for control: Lucraft could demand Marten's compliance all he liked, but he couldn't force her to attend. The linear, rule-based system on which a trial depends had met its perfect enemy in Marten, who felt no deference to that system and who seemed to operate in a kind of swirl of impulsivity, knocking logic off its tracks at every turn.

Lucraft allowed his frustration to flow. He had bent over backwards for Marten already, he said. She was on trial for very serious offences. 'Constance Marten is not running this trial, I am,' he declared, his voice resonating round the room in an uncharacteristically dramatic pronouncement, as if he had to remind himself of his authority.

On Monday, Marten was present, but you could tell something was brewing. When Marten began describing how she'd discovered her daughter's lifeless body, she seemed flat, even disengaged. FitzGibbon asked her if they had made any attempt to call the police afterwards. 'We were in a state of panic, shock and disbelief,' said Marten, calmly, before hurling a grenade into the proceedings. 'As Mr Smith told the jury last week, Mark has a violent rape conviction,' she said, in a tone so matter of fact it masked the explosive nature of the content.

The court froze, as if not believing what Marten had just said. No one interrupted her, no one objected. Marten, as if disappointed by the lack of reaction, repeated herself: 'He's got a conviction of violent rape.'

The judge intervened; the jury was sent out. Joel Smith, Little's junior for the prosecution, leapt to his feet and called Marten's statements a deliberate attempt to sabotage the trial. Femi-Ola argued that the jury would now unavoidably have to be discharged. Marten suggested that she'd done nothing wrong: Smith had already revealed all this to the jury, hadn't he? Lucraft corrected her. No details of Gordon's previous convictions had ever been revealed, only the vague mention of his 'history'. Over the next two days, the trial seemed to waver on the verge of collapse as the barristers worked through the fallout of Marten's revelation. Femi-Ola still wanted the jury discharged but FitzGibbon, to Marten's audible fury, said he felt the bar hadn't been met in her case. FitzGibbon and Marten's relationship had often felt strained — his methodical approach at odds with Marten's cavalier tendencies. Now, she stared at him with blatant animosity.

The following day, Femi-Ola announced that his client wanted to continue. Marten, still apparently incensed by FitzGibbon, sacked him. Tom Godfrey, his junior, would take over as her lead barrister. In the midst of all this, there was news from the Bronzefield dentist who had seen Marten. She really did have toothache, Lucraft told the court, but had refused treatment. At this, Marten looked triumphant.

There was an atmospheric shift as Marten resumed her evidence to Godfrey, her new barrister, on 2 May. Whether she preferred Godfrey's gentler, more emollient approach, or felt a sense of victory over the judge with regards to her tooth, she was suddenly more convincing. Godfrey took her back to the death of Victoria. Marten described what happened in detail. Victoria's body had been limp, her lips purple. Gordon had tried to do CPR, but nothing worked. Marten was crying now, her hands over her face.

After that, she said, they stayed in the tent for three days, unable to move from shock. Then followed the weeks of panic, as they tried to subsist on the little food they had, and carried Victoria's body around with them in a Lidl bag. This bag had become totemic in the coverage of the trial last year, a symbol of the couple's apparent neglect. Marten argued it was a vehicle for their grief: they didn't want to leave their daughter alone and were too weak to bury her. They'd talked about handing themselves in, but didn't because Marten thought she would be branded 'an evil mother who had done it on purpose'. At one point, Gordon suggested they throw themselves in a fire. Finally, she reached the end of her evidence. She would now be cross-examined first by Femi-Ola, then the prosecution. 'Thank you, my lord,' Marten said to Lucraft, in a perfect portrayal of deference. 'You have been very, very patient.'

. . .

In revealing her husband's criminal past, Marten had planted a seed of disorder in the trial that now took root and spread. On 6 May, Femi-Ola rose and told the judge that there had been a breakdown in relations with Gordon: he was not able to continue to defend his client. 'I don't want another barrister,' Gordon declared. 'I'd like to represent myself.'

Gordon had been such a quiet presence in court until now, it was easy to forget he was there. To represent himself properly, he told Lucraft, he'd like time to go over the case and read the

600-page Criminal Justice Act. A man who had spent two decades in American prisons, years in family court proceedings, then two more years in Belmarsh, was going to be heard unfiltered by lawyers who had routinely advised him to say nothing.

A trial is a grave process, but at times it resembles a game. Suddenly, there was a player who didn't know the rules. Lucraft explained to Gordon that he would need to submit all his questions for Marten in advance so that Lucraft could check they were relevant. Gordon wanted three days to prepare. 'I don't have three days, Mr Gordon,' said Lucraft. The trial was already set to overrun. Lucraft worked under pressure of the clock, but time seemed to have no meaning for the defendants, who felt none of the same obligations. Delaying had become one of their powers.

Chaos now seemed to engulf the trial with such regularity that it became the norm. The next day, Marten, having refused to come to court, appeared on a video link from Bronzefield, fizzing with self-righteous fury. 'Your honour, I'm sorry, but there needs to be an independent review into this prison,' she said. Ignoring Lucraft's barely concealed fury, she insisted on being told the duty governor's name, as if plotting a campaign.

Gordon, meanwhile, told the judge he wanted to ask his wife 150 questions in his cross-examination. After a private afternoon session with Gordon in court, Lucraft whittled these down to 71. Lucraft's perseverance had a stubbornness to it now, as if to prove that the process of the law could not be easily dismantled.

The next day, the press benches were full of long-serving crime reporters eager to see something they had never witnessed before in court: a husband cross-examining his wife about the death of their child. As Gordon questioned Marten about their actions, the couple appeared to perform a kind of double-act. Small in-jokes were shared, smiles exchanged. He was the positive one, she was more negative, she said. He was more practical, she was more emotional. At one point, Gordon asked Marten whether the grief she'd felt after having her children taken away had affected her trust in the system.

'I never had any issues with the system,' she replied. 'I never had anything to do with social services until Wales, when I asked for a property.'

Growing up as she had, Marten had never had to encounter the system. Privilege allows you to sidestep the state and its services almost completely. But if you have never needed the state, you have never learned its lesson: that once you are in its care, you must accept its oversight. In 2017, when she asked the social worker in Wales for help finding a house, Marten saw the system as something that could give her something she wanted: a purely transactional relationship. In reality, she encountered a set of professionals and services bound by a duty of care, concerned about her welfare and that of her child, and with a right to intervene.

The next day, Smith began his cross-examination for the prosecution in a style that suggested he was unleashing weeks of frustration. 'It's not the first time you've been on trial, is it?' he asked Marten.

'No,' she replied, 'because you decided to retry me because you didn't get the result you wanted.'

Smith retaliated fast, and asked her about Victoria's body being kept after her death in the Lidl bag, covered with soil and a beer can, still wearing a dirty nappy.

'If you're going to go down that route,' said Marten, glowering, 'it shows the sort of person you are.'

Smith persisted: surely Victoria deserved dignity in death?

Marten said that she had organised a funeral for Victoria from prison but hadn't been allowed to go. She'd arranged the songs, the words.

'She was sitting in her own faeces,' said Smith.

'Mr Smith, you really are diabolical,' said Marten. 'I find the way you cross-examine me really so uncouth. You really are a heartless human being.'

'Did you cover her up with a beer can?'

'No ...' Marten paused, as if knowing she couldn't deny the pictures we had all seen. 'It wasn't because we didn't care.'

'Is that a caring act, putting your dead baby in a plastic bag with sandwich wrappers and a beer can?'

'Of course it's not nice. Obviously we weren't going to keep her in a bag like that. We were trying to figure out what to do.'

Marten tried to explain that after Victoria died, they were in a state of shock.

Smith resumed his attack. It didn't last long. By the end of the day, Marten had collapsed in tears. She was at breaking point, she said, and couldn't go on.

. . .

When Marten arrived in court on 13 May, due to continue cross-examination, she stood in the dock. 'I'm not going to give evidence any more,' she said. 'I've made a decision.' Godfrey, Marten's barrister, turned his head in surprise. Marten wiped tears from her eyes. She had no fervour today, no imperious fury. It was as if she had realised that the relentless forward motion of the trial would continue whatever she did. The last power she had was a refusal to take part, and now that had been deployed, she sat curled over herself as if crushed.

For the previous three weeks, I realised, we had been in thrall to Marten, the centrifugal force around which the trial revolved. Now that she had relinquished her hold, it became Gordon's domain. Every day, he dragged a large sack of legal papers into the dock — a sack that became so heavy as the weeks went on that it took him longer and longer to come up to court from the cells.

At first, Lucraft appeared to develop an almost paternal working relationship with Gordon, as though he were coaching him in the law. The solicitor helped Gordon draft his questions and these were sent to Lucraft to check. But Gordon kept pressing for more time and resources. Lucraft made small allowances but Gordon was unhappy, and declared he was going to make an application 'about issues affecting the fairness of this trial'. Three days later, Lucraft read Gordon's complaints aloud to the court. He had not been given enough time or even a desk, he said: the process was unfair.

'These are serious allegations about my conduct,' said Lucraft. 'I will have to give this serious consideration.'

Gordon appeared to panic a little. It was just his point of view, he said. This was a serious case and he was representing himself.

'You have chosen to represent yourself,' Lucraft reminded him. Did he want a new barrister?

'I don't want a new barrister,' said Gordon. 'What I would like is materials. If I had the Criminal Justice Act ...'

At this, Lucraft could not contain himself. 'Do you want three years while you do a law degree?'

On 21 May, Lucraft suggested that, in the absence of barristers, he could ask Gordon some simple questions to prompt his evidence. Gordon would then be cross-examined by the prosecution. 'It would be nice to say my piece,' agreed Gordon.

For the rest of the day, Gordon spoke freely, retelling their whole story. He began with his childhood, growing up in England before moving to Florida. 'I come from a decent background,' he said. 'My mother was a nurse. She worked very hard and did well for herself. She was a very passionate woman, very empathetic, and always helping other people.'

As he talked through the events after Victoria's birth, he kept addressing the jury directly: *What you need to know; What I want to tell you; You need to know the truth.* Again, he emphasised his and Marten's state of mind. They were deranged, he said, an effect of having their children taken from them. 'We weren't normal,' he said. 'It's like a vacuum, a hole, an emptiness — you can never fill it.'

At the back of his mind, he said, he thought they would hand Victoria in to social services. He had no problem with the system. 'But it's not a perfect system,' he said. 'I don't want to stand in the Old Bailey with my wife, and with my baby passed. I have to explain myself criminally for the loss of the baby I loved.' Gordon's voice began to tremble with emotion. He swayed in the witness box, his arms gesturing into the air. 'I will never forget the pain, the feeling of picking my baby up.' By now, Gordon was crying. '*We* are the ones who have to live with what happened … You have to understand our perspective if you are judging us.'

Both Gordon and Marten made this point. You cannot understand someone, Marten liked to say, until you have walked a mile in their shoes. But to truly understand Gordon and Marten would require the kind of long rewinding the judge was so desperate to avoid — not only back to the removal of their previous children, or even to the beginning of their relationship, but to their childhoods. On one side there was English privilege and family acrimony; on the other, violent crime and years in American prisons. Both had grown up fighting authorities — a wealthy family and a criminal justice system — that they believed were working against them. The pattern was set separately and early. When they met it was as if they found common cause in each other: it was them against the world. The mix of their personalities was like nuclear fusion, unleashing a relentless, destructive energy.

At the end of Gordon's evidence, Little rose on behalf of the prosecution. Gordon's portrayal of himself as sympathetic had created a false impression of his character, he said. To counter this, the prosecution would like to bring his previous convictions before the jury: not just the American convictions of rape and battery, but his arrest for assaulting a police officer in a hospital in Wales in 2017 after Marten had given birth to their first child, and the reported domestic violence incident in 2019 in which Marten had fallen from a window. Marten had suffered a ruptured spleen and Gordon had not allowed paramedics to enter their property.

When the issue arose again the next morning, Marten yelled from the dock. 'It's not true! My husband never laid a finger on me!' Gordon said he would need the day to consider his response, and suggested the prosecution were distorting his words: he'd never claimed to be perfect. It wasn't fair, he said, the refrain sounding more childlike every time he repeated it. If he could take back what he'd said, he would. Lucraft reminded him that once something is said in court it cannot be unsaid. But Gordon persisted: he was without representation; he hadn't realised what he was doing.

'As I've pointed out,' said Lucraft, 'you have chosen to represent yourself. It was not forced upon you, that was your *choice*.'

'If I was aware that this was how self-representation was conducted,' said Gordon, 'I probably wouldn't have done it.'

When Gordon returned to the witness box on 23 May to be cross-examined by Little, he looked morose.

'That's it,' he said.

The court seemed to stop breathing.

'I will answer no questions,' said Gordon.

At times, a trial can move with devastating speed. Lucraft ruled that evidence from Gordon's American convictions and the arrest in Wales could be put before the jury. In response, Gordon tried to suggest that he didn't accept the convictions were real or valid, but he was rapidly outmanoeuvred. The prosecution dug up the relevant paperwork that proved his convictions, and Little announced that he was going to call one of the Welsh police officers who'd arrested Gordon in 2017 to give evidence. In the midst of all this, Gordon's solicitor resigned.

On 29 May, a police officer came into the witness box. Little led him through the details of Gordon's previous convictions by asking a series of questions, each answered with a simple 'yes'.

Did he break into the house of a next-door neighbour?

Before doing so had he placed a stocking over his face to conceal his identity?

Was he armed with a knife and hedge clippers?

Did he attempt to vaginally rape her?

Then did he orally rape her?

Did he perform other sexual assault offences?

Was that female held against her will for four and a half hours?

Gordon was then allowed to cross-examine the officer.

'Are you aware that the American police interviewed a 14-year-old child without parent or adult supervision?' he asked, referring to himself.

The officer said he wasn't aware of the circumstances of the case.

When Gordon suggested he had been mistreated and advised to plead guilty, Little tried to intervene. Gordon said he only had one more question.

'Do you know that the American police in the south are racists and prejudiced against people?'

'That is not a question this officer is going to answer,' said Lucraft.

· · ·

The defence closed its case at the end of May. Once, in a hearing for another case, I heard Lucraft joke that he might be running this trial for the rest of his life. But over three months of multiple near-collapses, he had somehow held its fragile structure together. In his directions to the jury, Lucraft told them to ignore the 'numerous delays and disruptions to the smooth running of this trial'. Nor should Gordon's previous convictions and the family court proceedings be seen as support for the prosecution case. If they wished, however, the jury could interpret Gordon and Marten's refusal to be cross-examined as the defendants having no answer to the prosecution case. But the jury could not convict either defendant because of their refusal.

Just after 2.15pm on Monday 14 July, the jury delivered their verdict. Unanimously, they found Marten and Gordon guilty of manslaughter, the most serious charge. Neither Gordon nor Marten stood to hear the verdict, but quietly shook their heads. Marten was heard saying, 'It's a scam.' After the jury left court, Gordon began offering his views, until Lucraft cut him off. Sentencing, he announced, would take place in September.

Whatever time Gordon and Marten will now serve in their respective prisons seems tangential to the real pain and damage of this case. A child was born and lived too briefly. On their eventual release, Gordon and Marten will return to lives which are now shattered and yet, while entwined with each other, bound to create further chaos. The law, with all its weight and logic, can impose order temporarily, but it does not have the power to save people from themselves.

23 July

'We have faced hunger before, but never like this'

MALAK A TANTESH AND EMMA GRAHAM-HARRISON

Mohammed's skeletal arms stick out of a romper with a grinning emoji-face and the slogan 'smiley boy', which in a Gaza hospital reads as a cruel joke. He spends much of the day crying from hunger, or gnawing at his own emaciated fingers.

At seven months old, he weighs barely 4 kilograms (9 pounds) and this is the second time he has been admitted for treatment. His face is gaunt, his limbs little more than bones covered in baggy skin, and his ribs protrude painfully from his chest.

'My biggest fear now is losing my grandson to malnutrition,' said his grandmother Faiza Abdul Rahman, who herself is constantly dizzy from lack of food. The previous day the only thing she ate was a single piece of pitta bread, which cost 15 shekels (£3).

'His siblings also suffer from severe hunger. On some days, they go to bed without a single bite to eat.'

Mohammed was born healthy but his mother was too malnourished to produce breast milk, and the family has only been able to get two cans of baby formula since.

The ward at the Patient's Friends Benevolent Society hospital is crowded with other skeletal children, some doubled up on the 12 beds. There are only two functioning paediatric teams left in Gaza City, and up to 200 children turn up daily seeking treatment.

Dr Musab Farwana spends his days trying, but often failing, to save them. Then he goes home to share meals that are too small with his own hungry sons and daughters.

The whole family are losing weight fast, because his salary buys almost nothing, and he doesn't want to risk the deadly race for supplies handed out by the Gaza Humanitarian Foundation after another medic, Dr Ramzi Hajaj, was killed trying to get food at one site.

Gaza has never been hungrier, despite several warnings about impending famine over the course of nearly two years of war. Over just three days this week public health officials recorded 43 deaths from hunger; there had been 68 in total before that.

Faiza Abdul Rahman, who has stayed in Gaza City throughout the war, said even the time of the most intense controls on food entering northern Gaza last year was not as bad. 'We faced hunger before, but never like this,' she said. 'This is the hardest phase we've ever endured.'

Testimony from local people and doctors, and data from the Israeli government, the Gaza Humanitarian Foundation and the UN and humanitarian organisations, shows food is running out.

Empty shelves are reflected in soaring prices, with flour selling for more than 30 times the market rate at the start of the year.

Even money or influential employers can no longer protect Palestinians. 'Humanitarian organisations are witnessing their own colleagues and partners waste away before their eyes,' more than 100 aid groups working in Gaza, including MSF, Save the Children and Oxfam, warned in a joint statement this week.

The journalists' union at AFP said on Monday that for the first time in the news agency's history it risks losing a colleague to starvation. On Wednesday the head of the World Health Organization, Tedros Adhanom Ghebreyesus, said a 'large proportion' of Gaza's population was starving. 'I don't know what you would call it other than mass starvation — and it's man-made,' he said.

For months Israel has choked off food shipments. The total amounts allowed in since the start of March are well below starvation rations for the 2.1 million population, and Palestinians are already weakened by the impact of prolonged food shortages and repeated displacement.

'For nearly two years, children here have suffered from famine. Even if some days they felt full, it's not just about being full, it's about receiving the nutrients the body needs. And those are completely absent,' said Farwana, the paediatrician.

Those years of malnourishment make them more vulnerable to other diseases, and their low immunity is compounded by the severe shortages of basic medical supplies, which Israel has also blocked from entry.

'Often, I feel devastated because there's something so simple the child needs to survive, and we just can't provide it,' he said. Three severely malnourished patients died in intensive care this week, one of them a girl who would have probably survived if doctors had been able to give her intravenous potassium, normally a basic medication, and now impossible to get hold of in Gaza.

'We tried to give her oral alternatives, but due to her malnutrition and resulting complications, she had poor absorption.

'These cases haunt me, they never leave my mind. This child could have gone back to her family and lived a normal life. But because one simple thing wasn't available she didn't survive.'

Israel imposed a total siege on Gaza from 2 March. When the prime minister, Benjamin Netanyahu, lifted it on 19 May he claimed the government was acting to prevent a 'starvation crisis', because some of the country's staunchest allies told him they would not tolerate images of famine.

In fact the Israeli government simply shifted course to draw out the starvation crisis, letting in only minimal quantities of aid so that Gaza's descent towards famine progressed a bit more slowly.

The Israeli government announced plans to channel all aid through a secretive US-backed organisation that runs four militarised distribution points.

Hundreds of people have been killed trying to get food handed out at sites Palestinians describe as 'death traps', which have handed out supplies that meet only a fraction of Gaza's needs.

By 22 July, GHF had been operating for 58 days but the food it had brought in would only have sustained the population of Gaza for less than a fortnight, even if it was distributed equally.

On Tuesday Umm Youssef al-Khalidi was preparing to try her luck at a GHF distribution centre for the first time. She had avoided them for months because her youngest child is two and her oldest 13 and her husband is paralysed and confined to a wheelchair.

'We have been silencing our hunger with water,' she said. 'My fear for my family is greater than my fear for myself. I fear something bad will happen to me, and I'll leave them without anyone to care for them.'

But her family went without food for four days last week, and when they broke the fast, eight of them had to share a bag of rice and two potatoes given to them by a passing stranger.

The children were excellent students before the war, who always won scholarships. Now they spend their days sitting on the edge of the street under a bombed mosque in al-Wehda neighbourhood in Gaza City, where the girls try to sell bracelets rather than just begging.

There is little demand for cheap jewellery in Gaza today, and although sometimes a passerby takes pity on the gang of skinny kids with dirty faces and tattered clothes, soaring prices means it buys little food.

'My children have become skeletal, skin and bone,' Khalidi said. 'Even the slightest effort makes them dizzy. They sit down again, asking for food, and I have nothing to give. I can't lie and say I'll bring them something when I know I won't be able to.'

So she had decided that in the grim calculus of risks for her family, the hope of getting a little food finally outweighed the risk of losing the adult who held their lives together.

Her husband's phone had been stolen earlier in the war, so they would have no way to communicate over the long hours that she would spend trekking to the GHF site, then racing to try to get food, and walking back. The family would just have to wait and hope.

'I have no one else to send,' she said. 'It's painful to watch them suffer, and their health gets worse every day they go without food.'

24 JULY

All rather complicated

BEN JENNINGS

27 July

One of the greatest heists in the history of English sport

JONATHAN LIEW

They thought it was all over. Quite a few times, in fact. Written off after their opening game against France; knocked to the canvas in their quarter-final against Sweden; behind with seconds remaining of their semi-final against Italy; a goal down against the world champions in the final. England have cheated death so many times in Switzerland this month as to have become basically uninsurable.

But these Lionesses are also escapologists. And on a breezy night in Basel it was once again the strains of 'Sweet Caroline' playing over the stadium sound system. Once again Leah Williamson holding aloft the European Championship trophy. Victory was secured on penalties against Spain, the final plot twist of what will surely be remembered as one of the most magnificent heists in the history of English sport.

So the three years of hurt are over. And in so doing Sarina Wiegman's side have secured what no other football team from these islands have managed to secure: a dynasty. An enduring record of excellence, a reputation for guts and grace under pressure that will sustain English football for generations to come. New stars in Hannah Hampton and Michelle Agyemang. And if victory three summers ago was a project blown to fruition by the happy winds of home advantage, this was a triumph earned in the teeth of a roaring gale.

Has there ever been a team so comfortable in adversity, so nonchalant in the face of certain disaster, so accustomed to a state of emergency? Even if at times their difficulties have been self-inflicted, there is also a richly stirring quality to the way England have calmly picked their way through every obstacle placed in their path. Whatever has been required — last-minute winners, desperate tactics, the nation of Sweden suddenly forgetting en masse how to take a penalty — somehow they have mustered it.

And so at a quarter to eight local time, Chloe Kelly of Arsenal stood over her final assignment. For Kelly, the scorer of the iconic winning goal at Wembley in 2022, in particular this has been a scarcely believable narrative arc: frozen out by her club Manchester City, dropped by Wiegman in February, and yet ending the season a Champions League winner with Arsenal. This summer she has been England's ace in the pack, coming off the bench against tired defences and totally changing the dynamics of the game.

Here, Kelly was introduced shortly before the end of a first half in which England were again sinking fast. Mariona Caldentey had scored the opening goal for Spain, the culmination of an exquisite and very Spanish move: almost a minute of patient passing, clever baiting and sneaky decoy runs, finished with a bullet header. This is the deadly delight of Spain in microcosm: the ability to bide their time, keep you guessing, keep you chasing, and of course keep the ball in the process.

How do you counter it? Two years ago, at the World Cup final in Sydney, England had no answers. But Arsenal's unlikely Champions League triumph over Barcelona in May had offered a template: patience and composure to keep the ball under pressure, restless aggression to win it back. For much of the first half, England had been the reverse: too frenetic in possession, too passive out of it. Lauren James, patently unfit, was replaced with Kelly, and immediately England had a more direct threat on the left flank. Which created space further back.

Keira Walsh had been tightly marked by the great Alexia Pute-llas all game, but when Putellas failed to follow her, Walsh had time to turn and find Georgia Stanway on the edge of midfield. Stanway found Kelly, and her cross was met by a quite remark-able header by Alessia Russo: off balance, leaping away from goal, a neck of wrought iron, a forehead like an anvil, a goal of pure training and pure technique and above all pure longing. It was 57 minutes and England were level.

Overall this was one of the best games of the tournament in terms of quality. There were great performances all over the field: from Williamson and Stanway and Russo and Walsh and the restored Jess Carter and Hampton in goal. Yet Spain, driven by the magnificent Aitana Bonmatí and Patri Guijarro in midfield, carried on creating: a tally of 22 shots to eight a measure of their attacking supremacy, a reminder of England's reliance on scrambling defence, blocks and saves, grapples and ricochets and occasionally blind luck. Salma Paralluelo's miss from two yards in extra time was the moment that will haunt Spain's players well into the early hours.

And so, with a kind of grim inevitability, to penalties. But without the foreboding that has stalked so many English teams of the past: under the leadership of Wiegman, England had never lost on penal-ties in three shootouts. The victory over Sweden last week — albeit one strongly tinged with farce — was still fresh in the memory. And here again, against a team convinced they should have won in regular time, England believed harder, stayed calmer, treated the shootout as an experience to be relished and not survived.

Beth Mead missed the opening penalty. Well, it wouldn't be 'proper England' without a little intrigue. Hampton, a goalkeeper enjoying a breakthrough tournament, saved from Caldentey and Bonmatí to give England the edge. Williamson put her penalty too close to Cata Coll. Paralluelo slammed hers wide. And so here we were again: Kelly with the ball, all alone in this great green pasture, every eye on her, just as she likes it.

Kelly had missed against Italy. Somehow she was never going to miss here. The penalty disappeared into the top corner, and somehow Kelly disappeared with it: into the great green beyond, swamped by white shirts and the good tidings of a grateful nation. And in these past three years women's football in England has catapulted itself into the mainstream. The players are cover stars; big stadiums sell out year on year; the long reactionary tail of cynicism and misogyny has been silenced.

And of course for all its adhesive, addictive qualities women's football is still not a perfect sport, still a place occasionally riven by tribalism and inequality, plagued by issues of representation and access. Still, anyone who was at Wembley three years ago for that first great awakening could be forgiven for wondering how that experience could ever be matched; how these players could ever summon the vivid adrenaline highs of that afternoon. As it turned out: it was so nice, they had to do it twice.

22 AUGUST

A victory for the women who spoke up — and for journalism

KATHARINE VINER

Sometimes you just need to pull on the thread.

That's how it started for two *Guardian* reporters in the spring of 2021, when they began to investigate claims about the behaviour of Noel Clarke, the prominent British actor and filmmaker.

Sirin Kale and Lucy Osborne spoke to many sources, including more than 20 women who shared their stories about working with Clarke. Their accusations covered all manner of misconduct: sexual harassment, unwanted touching and groping, sexually inappropriate behaviour, taking and sharing sexually explicit pictures and videos without consent, and bullying.

The allegations spanned a long period, from 2004 to 2019, and were the basis of a powerful series of *Guardian* articles and a podcast, which led to Clarke suing the *Guardian*.

The six-week trial took place in the high court in March and April, and the judgment came in today. Mrs Justice Steyn ruled that what the *Guardian* published was true, and that publishing it was in the public interest.

The judge praised our reporters' and editors' exhaustive approach to covering the story and noted the 'extensive efforts they made to investigate, test and corroborate the information they received, and not to publish allegations which they could not substantiate'.

It is an overwhelming victory for the women who spoke to us, for the *Guardian*, and for investigative journalism in Britain.

Almost every day over my decade as editor-in-chief of the *Guardian* I have had to take difficult decisions. In many ways, deciding to fight Noel Clarke's defamation claim was not one of them. I believed from the start this was a case we needed to see through to the end – primarily, of course, for the women who had spoken to us for our original investigation, and those who then came to the court to give testimony.

I remember when I was first told about the investigation: what struck me was the sheer scale of it all.

In cases where there are claims of sexual misconduct, even post the #MeToo movement, it is rare to find women who are prepared to speak to journalists. When you're talking about someone who is much more powerful than you are, and is a big name in the film and TV industry, it's a huge risk. Yet every time I received an update from the investigations team, the numbers of women had risen. Within days, we had more than a dozen sources.

By the time we had published our first investigation we had heard credible first-hand allegations from 22 women, and our superb reporters had done extensive work on corroboration. By the time we published our last article, we had spoken to more than 100 sources.

At trial we were able to rely on testimony from 26 different people, some of whom had travelled to the high court from abroad.

The many women who came to give testimony in court did not flinch, despite the often intimidating tactics used to try to deter them both before and during the trial. I attended court most days and found it very moving that so many of the women came forward and spoke so powerfully and with such commitment about some of the worst times of their lives. As the great British writer, actor and director Michaela Coel wrote about our sources: 'Speaking about these incidents takes a lot of strength because some call them "grey areas". They are, however, far from grey. These behaviours are unprofessional, violent, and can destroy a person's perception of themselves, their places in the world, and their career irreparably.'

One of those witnesses, Gina Powell, a former employee of Clarke's, was an important source in our reporting and a witness at the trial in March. Powell accused Clarke of sexually assaulting her and told the court that she was speaking up because she did not think he should be 'around young women in the film industry'. Her decision to speak out, like that of all of our witnesses, was incredibly brave. In addition to calling her an impressive, honest, compelling witness who did not overstate or exaggerate any of the matters she addressed, Mrs Justice Steyn said of her: 'Courage is not evinced by the absence of fear but by mastering it, and Ms Powell demonstrated admirable bravery and integrity.'

The *Guardian* stood by Gina and all these women, and the media as a whole will benefit from the bravery the women showed, thanks to a judgment that has fully vindicated their decision to come forward.

So this judgment is a victory for them.

It is also an important exoneration of the *Guardian* – our reporters, editors and lawyers. Investigative journalism is risky and expensive, and reporting that involves allegations of sexual misconduct is famously extremely challenging to publish.

There is the constant threat of litigation, which is unpleasant and time-consuming. There is the toll that it takes on the witnesses, who may have already suffered abuse, and who can often, understandably, feel they cannot put themselves through the trauma of a gruelling court case.

That's also something faced by our journalists. Six of us were cross-examined in the high court. One reporter was on the stand for three days. Another was the subject of extremely personalised questioning. Baseless allegations of a 'conspiracy' were levelled. All performed superbly, standing up for journalism in the public interest, standing up for the *Guardian*.

And then there is the threat of ruinous costs. At one point, and doubtless in an attempt to force us to settle the case on his terms before the trial, Noel Clarke tried to increase his damages claim to the eye-watering sum of £70m.

The *Guardian* is lucky to have the support of the Scott Trust behind us – our owners, who are committed to journalism in the public interest rather than pursuing commercial or political interests. They backed the journalism every step of the way.

Few defamation cases make it to trial precisely because of the financial and reputational jeopardy. But this was a case where I felt the *Guardian* needed to take a stand and trust in the women, our journalism and the court process.

It's a good day for the *Guardian*, for media in the public interest, and for women.

23 AUGUST

'They talk of trading people like when they were serfs'

DAN SABBAGH

In a branch of the Ukrainian coffee chain Lviv Croissants in the frontline city of Kramatorsk, there is a noticeboard where people leave coloured Post-it notes with simple hand-drawn messages. One just says 'Kramatorsk', with red hearts below and a yellow and blue semi-circular fan above, the colours of Ukraine.

Among those looking at the notes is Bohdan, a 26-year-old, who has been serving in the army for the past three years. The soldier, now in logistics, has chosen to spend his one day off in Kramatorsk with his dog Arnold to photograph for himself recent Russian bombing on a city where he was based for 18 months.

'I have a history with this place,' he says. 'It is part of my destiny and my puzzle.'

Kramatorsk is the core of the 30 per cent of Ukraine's Donetsk oblast that its military still holds in the face of a grinding Russian advance. This week, the region was the subject of what appears to have been a failed negotiation between Donald Trump and Vladimir Putin. The Russian president demanded all of Donetsk — which together with Luhansk oblast makes up the Donbas region — as part of a peace deal, a proposal that Trump seemed to have briefly endorsed even though Ukraine rejected it.

Russia's arguments change, but in Putin's eyes, Donetsk, traditionally a Russian-speaking industrial region in Ukraine's east, is culturally closer to Moscow than Kyiv. People who live there, however, have a very different view. They show no interest in seeing the land of Donetsk given up; it is their land after all.

A few minutes earlier, Bohdan had photographed the nearby site of a Russian bombing in the centre of the city on 31 July that had killed five, taking an image of a damaged tree in front of a ruined apartment block. His plan is to turn the image into a tattoo: 'The tree is symbolic; like Ukraine, it holds on despite the strike.'

It is not his first body art. On the soldier's left calf is a list of all Russian airstrikes that caused more than 15 civilian casualties anywhere in Ukraine. Bohdan had it done four months ago, while changing units. As the transition was taking place, he says, 'I was having a civilian life, mostly. It was so easy to forget what's going on.'

The frontline is about 12 miles away at the nearest point, but Kramatorsk remains relatively lively in the daytime August sun. Though the air raid alarm goes off regularly, that is for missiles passing over, locals say; when an attack on the city does come, they add ominously, there is no warning.

About a quarter of a million Ukrainian civilians live in Kramatorsk and the rest of Donetsk, about an eighth of pre-invasion levels. Many windows are boarded up, but the city is not significantly damaged. Some shops and cafes still open, such as Kateryna Seledtsova's Sweet Coffee House Bakery, which has an array of fruit cakes, eclairs and other creamy-looking offerings behind the counter.

The change in Kramatorsk's population — it has become increasingly male-dominated because of the arrival of soldiers into the area — means that Seledtsova has refined her menu. 'Men like simpler food,' she says, explaining that she had switched out French-style pastries for layered Napoleon cake or trubochki, waffle tubes filled with condensed milk. Whatever she bakes, she adds, sells out daily, such is the demand.

Giving away the rest of Donetsk strikes Seledtsova 'as idiocy. Men have been digging trenches here. All of those fortifications for nothing? I don't believe it will happen, it is just stupid.' The baker's life is here: Seledtsova is from Kramatorsk, the city also of her father and eight-year-old son, and the idea of being forced to move out is, she says, so hard to take seriously that it is best not thought about much.

Could there be a price worth paying, giving up land in Ukraine, including where she lives, in return perhaps for Nato membership? She just sees practical complications: 'There are already a lot of problems with evacuation. For example, it's impossible for us just to go somewhere and buy or rent an apartment elsewhere in Ukraine because we don't have the money.'

Relocation programmes, she says, are not attractive because the housing offered is not comparable. 'A lot of people who fled, as far as I know, are living in kindergartens. They don't even have money to buy things like proper medicines,' and she wonders how the Ukrainian state with its limited resources would be able to make a programme work.

What about staying under Russia? 'I would never work under those motherfuckers. Of course no, no,' and giggles at the strength of her feeling.

In Sloviansk, north of Kramatorsk, Valentyna and Yelena are with their grandsons aged five and six in the city's well-tended central park. The children play in small electric cars, but the *babusyas* (grandmothers) are frustrated. 'You are a journalist, you could make some efforts for peace, we need to shout out for peace,' says Valentyna. Pressed on whether they believed giving up land could be acceptable, all Valentyna will say is that 'we want the war to stop.'

If Ukraine is forced to give up Donetsk they would flee if they have to, Valentyna says, because 'the children have problems with their mental health. They are shaking during the nights.' In-person classes, lasting four hours a day, have been halted again as the security situation has deteriorated. 'We were in a playground and we saw a Shahed drone just above our heads, flying so low, three days ago — and there were 10, 12 children who were playing there, just watching.'

At Sloviansk market, local people sell surplus produce from their gardens, some of the best agricultural land in the world. A woman, also called Valentyna, offers grapes for 80 hryvnia (£1.44) a kilo. 'They are talking about trading people, like ancient times, when there was a lord and his serfs,' she says as she sells 2 kilos from the piles of red and white grapes on her table. 'We should keep going and fighting for our lands. These are Ukrainian lands; there are recognised borders.'

Donetsk province remains where the heaviest fighting is taking place along the long frontline, particularly around Pokrovsk, 35 miles south-west of Kramatorsk. Regional officials prove reluctant to give interviews, because of the political sensitivities of the moment, but Vadym Filashkin, the governor of Donestsk, reported on Thursday morning that three had been killed in Kostyantinivka, while on Friday settlements were attacked 26 times and 3,649 people were evacuated.

The consequences of the unceasing war can be seen in nearby Pavlohrad, to the west, in a neighbouring region. A refugee centre has been operating in the city for nearly a year, to receive people with nowhere to go. But as the Russian offensive has intensified, the number of refugees arriving has increased to '350 to

450 people a day for the past two weeks', according to Kateryna Makarova, the team leader on the site. It compares with 200 a day two months ago, and 100 during the winter.

Conditions at the site, a former cultural centre, are cramped. In an auditorium, beds are placed next to each other on the stage for those who cannot immediately be rehoused. An emergency dormitory shelter is being built in a tent to increase the overnight capacity from 100 to more than 200, though that is not obviously a solution when the weather turns. Another reception centre is being opened in the city of Dnipro, further west, Makarova adds.

News reports indicate Trump's peace efforts have gone nowhere. Few in and around Donetsk are surprised. Planning continues in Ukraine to deal with Russia's gradual advance, attacks that show no sign of halting. Netting is being erected along the safest supply route into Kramatorsk before it can be targeted by Russia's increasingly effective drone crews, though at the current rates of advance it will probably take years to conquer Donetsk, and at a cost of 30,000 Russian casualties a month.

Nevertheless, it is prudent to plan for the worst. 'We are trying to figure out the algorithm for how we should work when there will be more evacuations,' says Makarova. 'There are a large amount of people living in Kramatorsk, Sloviansk and other towns, and if there will be an evacuation there, there will be a huge amount of people coming. We need to understand how to act in that situation.'

. . .

Serhii and Nadiya, a couple who have been married 46 years, are sitting out in the early evening sun with their lives' possessions in a dozen or so plastic bags by them. They are not even from Donetsk, but Mezhova, 10 miles into Dnipropetrovsk oblast, victims of a metastasisation of the war that, for all Russia's stated interest in Donetsk, is spreading beyond its borders. Serhii admits 'we never thought the war would come to our village' until drone strikes began two months ago.

The couple are surprisingly calm, in the circumstances, though Serhii admits to taking some Valium to help, and are hoping to join one of their daughters, whenever a volunteer can drive them from the refugee centre. Tonight, though, they are staying at the refugee centre and Nadiya comes over to say goodbye as we leave.

'They [the Russians] are saying we're brothers, but if I would have such a brother, I would change my last name and my father's name,' Serhii says. 'I don't need this kind of brother.'

24 AUGUST

Flags as tokens of prejudice not pride: welcome to England 2025

JOHN HARRIS

It was a sun-soaked weekday in the West Country, and all I could think about was the flags. Around the sedate Wiltshire town of Devizes, they fluttered from trees and upstairs windows, with crude versions sprayed across roundabouts. In my adopted home town in Somerset, meanwhile, local desperadoes had vandalised a pedestrian crossing close to a school, which had sparked an online row, partly because they had jettisoned their paint cans down a nearby alley. 'Apart from the paint being dumped, I applaud them,' said one Facebook post. There was talk of more St George's crosses appearing at the car park near the GP surgery — and, in among scenes I usually associate with calm and quiet, a sudden and unsettling sense of mischief and menace.

Such is the impact of Operation Raise the Colours, a campaign which seems to have begun in the suburbs of Birmingham. Its origins apparently lie in a few flags being cleared from lampposts as the city council tried to install LED lighting. In the hands of online provocateurs, that was enough to confirm stories about woke local bureaucrats denying people their national identity. That narrative has quickly ballooned, with sometimes grimly comical consequences: the dependably restrained Reform UK MP Lee Anderson says that any elected official who supports removing British or English flags 'should be removed from office for betraying the very country they serve', while his party's council leader in Northamptonshire insists that for health and safety reasons 'we may need to take them down in the best interests of our residents'.

That very small subplot is probably the only halfway amusing part of the story: everything else is deadly serious. Despite claims that it is all about patriotism rather than prejudice, what has materialised up and down the country feels like an unauthorised version of what the Home Office used to call the hostile environment, as if football hooligans have taken control of road markings and street furniture. And the relevant mood music is not exactly subtle. On the campaign's Facebook page, there are enthusiastic looks ahead to September's 'free speech' rally fronted by the far-right figurehead Tommy Robinson, notices about looming protests outside hotels used to house asylum seekers and terse allusions to the usual conspiracy theories ('our masters have sold us to Islam ... the replacement has begun').

The anti-racist group Hope Not Hate points to known far-right activists who are involved. Picking through it all, one thought repeatedly hits home — that whatever this self-styled operation's apparently haphazard beginnings, it marks yet another instalment of a story that could not be more serious: the long march of a politics full of audacity and ambition, which is now reaching people and places that the left gets nowhere near.

The result is a self-evident political emergency. For proof, look at Reform UK's stubborn lead in the opinion polls, and the very real prospect of Nigel Farage becoming prime minister. Consider also the post-Brexit transformation of English Conservatism, and the fact that many Tories' hopes now lie with Robert Jenrick, the aspiring leader whose recent visit to a protest in Epping put him in close proximity to an infamous far-right activist, and who has loudly endorsed Operation Raise the Colours (Kemi Badenoch soon followed suit, in yet another example of who is really in charge of her party). But also bear in mind something much more frightening: the fact that what is afoot goes far deeper than the manoeuvrings of politicians and parties. It goes into the cultural spaces where people live their lives.

Some of this is all about the grim synergy between the right's use of disinformation and provocation, and how politics has changed in ways that most of its practitioners seem to barely understand. In the past, orthodox television and what we now call the legacy media ensured that people who supported the merchants of hard-right ideas were exposed to arguments against them. But the 21st century does not work like that: radicalisation happens in sealed-off online spaces that operate according to their own deranged logic, opening a path from unthinking first steps to full-blown conversion. One minute you might be spraying the road just for the likes; the next, you could be disappearing into a mob surrounding a mosque. From the outside, that is a very difficult cycle to break.

But that is not to say that no one should try. At the moment, the new right's bark is probably worse than its bite: once again, compared with all the talk of mass uprisings and social breakdown, this weekend's hotel protests were a thoroughly damp squib. But one of the most depressing aspects of this summer has been the sense of progressive forces so dumbfounded and confused by what is happening that they seem almost completely unable to respond, and a feeling that many people in positions of power now accept that ridiculous proposition that England is now the country Farage et al say it is. The Labour party, needless to say, either meekly echoes Farage's talking points or makes the laughable claim that people shouldn't support him or his party because of his views on the NHS. Even the trade unions, whose workplace reps and conveners presumably understand people's support for the new right as a matter of everyday experience, are bafflingly quiet.

And what of any fight on the terrain of popular culture? Older readers will recall a rightward cultural shift and the brief surge of the National Front in the late 1970s, which was met by the inspirational work of Rock Against Racism and the Anti-Nazi League, choking off the far right's appeal to the young. I can well remember the anxiety and alarm triggered by the surge in popularity of the fascist British National party, which happened twice: 15 or so years ago, when it was undone by dogged Labour campaigning and its own ineptitude, and circa 1994, when the election of a single BNP councillor in east London sparked a huge anti-racism concert, acres of coverage in the music press and the revival of Rock Against Racism's old spirit.

I know: that was a very long time ago, and comparing then with now risks ignoring how much popular culture has since been diluted and weakened. But there are still musicians with huge platforms and devoted fans, and organisations — such as Love Music Hate Racism — ready to play their part. The promi-nence of Palestine flags at this year's festivals proves that music's radical edges have not been completely blunted; even the most apolitical artists surely understand that what they do is a product of exactly the kind of cultural mixing and open attitudes that the new right wants to squash.

Something else keeps nagging at me. Up until a few years ago, we heard a lot of talk about progressive patriotism, a new vision of England that was truer to 21st-century reality, and the final wresting away of symbols of nationhood from people with the most malign and nasty ideas. It was right that we did: the fact that these conversations never really went anywhere might be one of the reasons we are in such a mess. The noise the new flag-wavers make is getting louder; there are increasingly brazen links between thugs and supposedly mainstream politicians that need to be called out. This is what defines the urgency and fear of this summer: as the Clash long ago sang in a peerless and prescient piece of music titled 'Clampdown', what are we going to do now?

Picture credits

Plate 1
top: Jim Watson/AFP via Getty Images
bottom: Ukrainian Presidential Press Service/Reuters

Plate 2
top: John Wessels/AFP via Getty Images
bottom: Fadel Itanil/UPI/REX/Shutterstock

Plate 3
top: AFP via Getty Images
bottom: Mohammed Saber/EPA

Plate 4
top: Clement Mahoudeau/AFP via Getty Images
bottom: Dimitar Dilkoff/AFP via Getty Images

Plate 5
top: Marko Đjurica/Reuters
bottom: Pedro Sarmento Costa/EPA

Plate 6
top: Brian Snyder/Reuters
bottom: Carl Court/Getty Images

Plate 7
top: Richard Sellers/APL/Sportsphoto
bottom: Ray Giubilo

Plate 8
top: Carly Earl/The Guardian
bottom: Luis Tato/AFP via Getty Images

Index